D0914389

OULIPO

All That Is Evident Is Suspect

McSWEENEY'S
SAN FRANCISCO

McSweeney's and colophon are registered trademarks of McSweeney's, an independent publisher based in San Francisco. McSweeney's exists to champion ambitious and inspired new writing, and to challenge conventional expectations about where it's found, how it looks, and who participates. McSweeney's is a fiscally sponsored project of SOMArts, a nonprofit arts incubator in San Francisco.

Cet ouvrage, publié dans le cadre d'un programme d'aide à la publication, bénéficie du soutien de la Mission Culturelle et Universitaire Française aux États Unis, service de l'ambassade de France aux États Unis.

This work, published as part of a program of aid for publication, received support from the Mission Culturelle et Universitaire Française aux États Unis, a department of the French Embassy in the United States.

Printed in China

ISBN 978-1-944211-52-3

10 9 8 7 6 5 4 3 2 1

www.mcsweeneys.net

All That Is Evident Is Suspect

Readings from the Oulipo 1963–2018

Edited by
Ian Monk & Daniel Levin Becker

OULIPO OULIPO

Contents

7	Paul Fournel	Presidential Foreword
9	Ian Monk	Editor's Note
11	Daniel Levin Becker	Another Editor's Note
13	Raymond Queneau	Slept Cried
14	Jacques Duchateau	Lecture on the Oulipo at Cerisy-la-Salle
20	Latis	The Atheist Organist
25	Marcel Duchamp	Correspondence with the Oulipo
31	Albert-Marie Schmidt	Letter to the Oulipo
32	Claude Berge	Letter to Jacques Roubaud & Georges Perec
34	François Le Lionnais	Idea Box
40	Jean Lescure	The N+7 Method
43	Georges Perec	Alphabet for Stämpfli
48	Italo Calvino	How I Wrote One of My Books
64	Luc Étienne	Bilingual Palindromes
66	Stanley Chapman	Letter to Valérie Guidoux
69	André Blavier	Literary Lunatics
74	Jean Queval	Circular Reflections from an Immobile Insect
82	Michèle Métail	Fifty Oscillatory Poems
96	Marcel Bénabou	Ebony Cup and Ivory Ball
100	Jacques Bens	How to Tell a Story
108	Paul Braffort	Invisible Libraries
115	Noël Arnaud	The Last Minutes
127	Michelle Grangaud	Gesture
133	Oskar Pastior	Rules of the Game
139	Hervé Le Tellier	A Few Musketeers
148	Pierre Rosenstiehl	Frieze of the Paris Métro
156	Jacques Jouet	Poem of the Paris Métro
175	Harry Mathews	Sainte Catherina
183	Jacques Jouet	The Republic of Beau-Locks
188	Ian Monk	We Did Everything

LIPO ULIPO

192	François Caradec	On the End of Time
195	Paul Fournel	Novels
208	Anne F. Garréta	N-evol
213	Olivier Salon	Invisible Cities: Lille
216	Jacques Roubaud	Arrangements
222	Frédéric Forte	99 Preparatory Notes to 99 Preparatory Notes
227	Pablo Martín Sánchez	Metric Poetry
233	Étienne Lécroart	Eodermdromes
238	Harry Mathews	Narrative Sestinas
243	Étienne Lécroart	Counting On You
249	Hervé Le Tellier	Liquid Tales
253	Bernard Cerquiglini	A Very Busy Year
266	Olivier Salon	Shark Poem
268	Ross Chambers	Brief Encounter
270	Daniel Levin Becker	Writer's Block
274	Jacques Roubaud	⊂
283	Marcel Bénabou	Our Beautiful Zeroine
290	Paul Fournel	The Beautiful Appetite
293	Valérie Beaudouin	Northern Line
323	Michèle Audin	Caroline, October 21, 1935
329	E. Berti & P. Martín Sánchez	Microfictions
336	Daniel Levin Becker	Epithalamia
341	Frédéric Forte	The Pitch-Drop Experiment
344	Clémentine Mélois	Louise
345	Michèle Audin	No One Remembers
348	Ian Monk	Return(s)
359	Eduardo Berti	An Ideal Presence
365		Acknowledgments
366		Approximative Index of Themes
370		Contributors

POULIPOULIPO

Created in 1960 by François Le Lionnais and Raymond Queneau, the art-mad savant and the math-mad poet, the Oulipo–*Ouvroir de Littérature Potentielle*–resolved to invent novel literary forms, new ways to tell stories. It would do so by investigating mathematics and the sciences, and by reviving forgotten forms created long ago by its "anticipatory plagiarists."

During the first fifteen years of its existence, the Oulipo worked in secret. But even from its inception, it took care to cultivate an international dimension. The ten founding members were joined by foreign correspondents: from the Netherlands (Paul Braffort), Australia (Ross Chambers), England (Stanley Chapman), the U.S. (Marcel Duchamp)...

Soon full-fledged members came on to put the group's inventions through the paces of their own languages: Harry Mathews, the New Yorker; Italo Calvino, the Italian; Oskar Pastior, the German; Ian Monk, the Englishman; later on, Eduardo Berti, the Argentinean; Pablo Martín Sánchez, the Spaniard; and Daniel Levin Becker, the Chicagoan.

Since opening itself to public attention in the mid-1970s, the Oulipo has not stopped shining throughout the world. The masterworks produced by some of its members have been translated into dozens of languages: Queneau's *Exercises in Style*, Georges Perec's *A Void* and *Life A User's Manual*, Calvino's *If on a winter's night a traveler*, Jacques Roubaud's ∈, and Marcel Bénabou's *Why I Have Not Written Any of My Books* have become classics of twentieth-century literature.

The techniques of the Oulipo are studied today around the world, from elementary schools to universities. Sister groups have been established globally, in the mold of Italy's Oplepo, and the oulipian approach serves as a model for the exploration of potentialities in other creative domains: the Oubapo (workshop for potential cartooning), the Oupeinpo (workshop for potential painting), the Outrapo (workshop for potential tragicomedy), the Oucarpo (workshop for potential cartography), and many others are active today.

In the midst of this effervescence, the creative labor of our workshop's members continues. Since its inception, the Oulipo has counted forty-one members, half of whom are now excused from group activities on the grounds of being deceased.

This volume is meant to bear witness to the talent of each of them. It assembles works by the men and women of the group from its first years through today, chosen for their diversity and intended to show that the path of constraint chosen by the Oulipo is a path of liberty.

The thinking behind the editorial choices of this book was based on various factors. The main purpose is to give readers with little or no French (or Spanish, or Italian, or German, for that matter) a broader overview of what the Oulipo is, which unfortunately cannot be obtained from the very small percentage of the vast body of work by the group's members that has been written in English, or thus far translated into that language.

This has led to two main lines of attack: the inclusion of at least a tiny extract by every one of the many members of the group, from the founders to the latest arrivals, from the most famous to the most obscure. In the case of the famous, short and little-known pieces have been chosen. In the case of the less well-known, we have included longer extracts.

So much for the historical aspect. Secondarily, to illustrate the current state of the group, the emphasis in the latter part of the book has been placed on the current, active members, and above all on hitherto untranslated or unpublished pieces.

What is more, to provide a closer idea of the everyday life and activities of the Oulipo since its birth, we have included extremely varied sorts of writing: poems and stories, of course, ranging from the most serious to the most ludic, but also letters, theoretical pieces, minutes of meetings, cartoons, and so on. They are presented in the approximate order of their composition, when the date is known, except of course for extracts from collections of poetry, or series of pieces written over a number of years.

Bon voyage!

OULIPO
OULIPO

To take it at its own word, the title of this book is trustworthy because it was never evident. A number of names were debated and dismissed over the course of the volume's conception and preparation, some impressionistic and some utilitarian; while we waffled, we referred to the project amongst ourselves as *the sampler*. (Or *le sampler*, depending on the conversation.) That name failed to make the final cut–evidently, if you will–but one of its secondary merits bears particular mention here.

The French word *ouvroir*, which gives the Oulipo its *ou*, means not only "workshop" but also "sewing circle." Per Noël Arnaud, in Warren Motte's translation, our founders envisioned the group as "a pleasant spot, warm in winter, cool in summer, abundantly provided with food and drink, where people compete in dexterity in the finest sort of needlework." True to their intent, it would please us greatly if you read the book that follows as a sampler in this sense: as a display of collective needlework and sportive craftsmanship and convivial gossip, the product of nearly six decades spent elaborating and embroidering a set of literary patterns and textual textiles.

As has always been the oulipian credo, these patterns are not proprietary: they are also yours to exploit or adapt or pervert as the creative spirit moves you. For the aspiring seamstress new to our circle, however, we would be remiss not to recommend the *Oulipo Compendium* for hands-on demonstration, Motte's *Primer* for theoretical foundations, and the *nOulipian Analects* and volume six of the Verbivoracious *Festschrift* series for spirited commentary. The operative words in all of those titles are loftier or more authoritative than *sampler*, and rightly so. What follow here are only some glances at the evolving tapestry that adorns the space where we continue to gather month after month to stitch and weave and sew, still unsure whether we're making a coat or a sail or a flag.

LIPOULIPO

Originally published as *Dormi pleuré* (Le Castor Astral, 2003)

Translated by Ian Monk

Raymond Queneau

Slept Cried

(undated)

Started this diary today: desirous as I am to note down my first impressions. Unpleasant.

Hot milk, as they call it, is disgusting: not nearly as good as amniotic fluid.

Having been washed and rubbed down, here I am still blind, back in my crib. Very interesting.

Slept twenty hours. Cried four. I quite clearly am not taking to hot milk.

I also pooed: in my linen.

Dad says that I'm going to be a writer. He took me in his arms, but almost dropped me. The nanny yelled at him: she it is who powders my credentials with talc.

Cried. Slept.

Slept. Cried.

Am starting to get used to hot milk, which I no longer find quite so unpleasant. Read *Iphigenia*.

Followed a finger through space: quite an experience, as I can now open my eyes.

Reread *Iphigenia*.

I pick up this diary after an interruption of seventy-four years. I feel extremely tired.

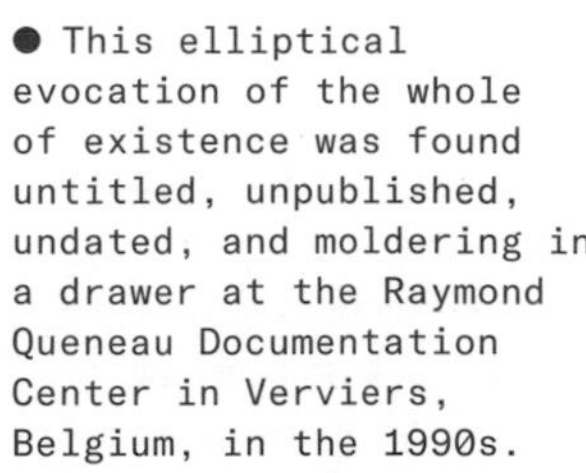

● This elliptical evocation of the whole of existence was found untitled, unpublished, undated, and moldering in a drawer at the Raymond Queneau Documentation Center in Verviers, Belgium, in the 1990s.

Originally published as "Communication sur l'Oulipo à Cerisy-la-Salle" in Jacques Bens, *Oulipo 1960–1963* (Christian Bourgois, 1980); later reprinted as *Genèse de l'Oulipo* (Le Castor Astral, 2006)

Translated by Daniel Levin Becker

Jacques Duchateau

from

Lecture on the Oulipo at Cerisy-la-Salle

1963

● Cerisy-la-Salle is a commune in Normandy whose International Cultural Center has hosted scholarly colloquia since 1952, including the one in 1960 at which the Oulipo was conceived. Three years later, when the group's activities were still only the subject of murmurs within the French literary world, Jacques Duchateau returned to Cerisy with some initial findings.

"The sweetest song with wildest sorrow throbs," wrote Musset. It is curious, nonetheless, to consider that this specialist of confessional literature was also a specialist of the human mind's most perfectly artificial creation, namely chess. And this taste for artifice, for the arrangement of elements according to precise rules, is to be found in great evidence in some of Musset's stories. Confessional literature, artificial literature: is this not *a priori* a poorly founded distinction? The idea of confessional literature suggests that it is somehow possible to render a particular experience directly—that a pure teardrop would be a pure masterpiece. "We might imagine a system of communication," André Martinet proposed, "in which a special cry would correspond to each given situation or fact of experience." In such a case language would be a kind of nomenclature, a tracing of reality. But this is not so: a language is a conventional system that accounts for a particular organization of experiential data.

There is artifice in all language. Nobody, so far as I am aware, would contest this. What causes trouble are the consequences of this state of affairs, which appear to undermine a kind of spontaneity, a kind of ingenuity in the mechanics of creation. A filmmaker once told me of one of his films that he had tried to capture the images in their raw state, and that his dream would be to create a film without using a single camera, for nothing to impose any distance between him and the real. This neglects that there is nothing natural about the image, which is itself a sign of the real. Children must learn the language of images, must learn to see just as they learn to read. It must be an instinctive reflex to dream of a transparent world, ceaselessly revealed, where the only mode of cognition is appearance: if Arsène Lupin was for many years the most celebrated character in French literature, surely this is due to something magical about his behavior. Let us not fall prey to the power of words: in magic too there is craft and artifice. I do not mean here to elucidate the mechanics of creation, as it were, but to posit this: since it seems evident that there is artifice in all culminations of creative endeavor, surely Musset's pure teardrops can become immortal masterpieces only by dint of a *craft*–a word, we might note in passing, used more and more when speaking of writers. Musset knew all the tricks of his craft. Some tricks are traps; some writers are bad. The sensibility, the experience, the humanity of a writer: perhaps these are functions of the fineness of the tricks at his disposal. But, if all literature contains artifice, since artifice can be mechanized, at least in theory, does this mean that literature in turn can be mechanized as well?

Literature and machines has a bad ring to it. It even sounds, *a priori*, perfectly contradictory. Literature means liberty; machines are synonymous with determinism. But not all machines are the kind that dispense train tickets or mint lozenges. The essential characteristic of machines that interests us is not the quality of being determined but that of being organized. Organized means that a given piece of information will be processed, that all the possibilities of this piece of information will be examined systematically in light of a model given by man or by another machine, a machine whose model can be furnished by still a third machine, one whose model etc., etc.

I do not mean to say there is no difference between a machine and a writer; in any case, that is not where our problem lies. But we can admit nonetheless that a writer must also process a given piece of information as a function of a given model. Machines will not take to writing their own personal literature tomorrow; to do so would require a degree of complexity they do not yet possess. Still, machines have already accomplished certain feats: we can give them two texts and ask them to use those texts to compose a third. This is not a personal creation, but it is a work that could prove quite useful to us. It has always been difficult to live without the service of slaves; it may well be that this is why we have machines. As for knowing what will become of those slaves, that's another story. Until now writers have enjoyed the service of a kind of portable slave: dictionaries. But over the years dictionaries have demonstrated a troubling tendency to become more and more imposing; once again, the master-slave dialectic arises. Hence the necessity of super-slaves, thanks to which libraries will cease to be dangerous labyrinths. But these machines we will depend on function by using, at a linguistic level, their own special logical structures. It could be worthwhile to study these structures, even to try to use them. Certainly there is no obligation to do so, nor is it obligatory to insist on limiting ourselves to "memory," for instance. We might perfectly well decide that we may use only such information as we would be capable of assimilating ourselves. The danger of this attitude is a certain tendency toward sclerosis. The danger of the opposite attitude, of course, is dispersion. With the proper correctives, both attitudes are possible. I do not believe they are contradictory.

In the OuLiPo, we have chosen to work with machines, which is to say we are prompted to ask ourselves questions about these notions of structure. This is not new. Writers have always used structures: some consciously, others unconsciously, some with the conviction that it is merely a question of simple evidence substantiated over time. From an intuitive perspective, evidence supervised by time is a prerequisite. From a structuralist perspective, shall we say, all that is evident is suspect. Those forms that are relatively general, accepted by all, and modeled by experience can conceal infra-forms. A systematic re-questioning is necessary to uncover them. A re-questioning which will lead, beyond the discovery of subjacent forms, to the invention of new ones–exactly the way, long ago, the rules of the sonnet were invented, or the three dramatic unities, or the epistolary novel, the division of the novel into chapters, rhyme schemes, and so on.

To say "new forms" and "new structures" is to say everything and nothing. Forms evidently do not emerge fully fledged from the brains of machines. The search for new forms has been made possible by a working practice first used by mathematicians: the axiomatic method. The axiomatic method was born the day we first refused to take as a given that which most commonly was. Reliance on evidence presupposes a true and a false, that which is evident being true. Having discovered, regarding certain elements of Euclidian geometry in particular, that certain evidences were not quite so evident under certain circumstances (the famous parallel postulate, for instance), we were moved to reconsider these evidences as *relative* truths. Once categorical and apodictic, demonstration became deductive and hypothetical, with all the attendant consequences. The axiom–which the *Littré* dictionary defines as "an evident and unprovable truth, *e.g.*, that the whole is greater than a part"–ceases to be an absolute truth, for the whole is greater than a part only in the case of finite sets. For an infinite set, this is false; the set of whole numbers is not larger, for instance, than the set of odd numbers. Matching the two sets proves this: 1 from the set of whole numbers corresponds to 1 from the set of odd numbers, 2 from the set of whole numbers to 3 from the set of odd numbers, 3 to 5, 4 to 7, 5 to 9, and so on precisely until infinity. The two sets have the same cardinality, the same size: the set of whole numbers is not greater than the set of odd numbers, despite containing it. There are a handful of paradoxes of this nature. Development of the axiomatic method was possible only through reflection on sets. An infinite set of numbers implies certain specific axioms, the union of which gives the set in question its specific structure.

So an axiom is no longer an evidence, true in all circumstances, but one of the rules that govern a given set. We are no longer dealing with truth but with coherence. The advantage of the axiomatic method is that it allows for all manner of perfectly arbitrary speculations that can subsequently, experimentally, be proven sound. Indeed, what the axiomatic method helped bring to light is that it can be wholly useful, when seeking to apprehend the real, to turn our backs on it. An abstract formalization, preoccupied with coherence and not with truth, often allows us to perceive the real more precisely. This is why physics, for one, adopts this method with increasing frequency.

Since Homer took an interest in the Trojan War, literature has always had a weakness for the palpable. Nothing forbids us to suppose that the Greeks must have waged the Trojan War so that Homer could tell a story about it. This process has rarely contradicted itself, though it is perhaps a pity that the Greeks didn't have the converse idea, to ask Homer to tell the story of the Trojan War and then verify after the fact the soundness of his work. The whole history of literature would have gone differently. What we intend in trying to free ourselves from the evidences of the palpable is not to reduce literature to a simple formal game: quite the opposite, we might say.

By initially—from conception—establishing a radical distinction between the domain of the formal and that of the concrete, I believe we can liberate literature from certain entanglements that are all the more pernicious because they are unconscious. We may imagine, for instance, that tomorrow there will be writers who invent structures for other writers to use. That which we pejoratively call "formalism" in literature, is this not merely the result of insufficient formalization? This is the reason all work on a structure must be undertaken systematically—that is, until it arrives at a perfect coherence. That said, the operative quality of a structure cannot help us anticipate the literary quality of the resulting work. There will necessarily be many dead ends, and many surprises.

In this quest for structure there have been pioneers: from Lycophron to Roussel, by way of the Grands Rhétoriqueurs. In the latter era there was a vein of systematic research that never managed to find acceptance: perhaps it was premature, or maybe they lacked access to the means that would allow them to propagate their findings, such as those magnificent engines first discussed by Swift.

In the OuLiPo we have undertaken certain projects by hand, only to run very quickly into insurmountable difficulties. We need machines *and* method. We have an example of the latter in Queneau's *Hundred Thousand Billion Poems*—so named because Queneau wrote 10 sonnets of 14 lines each (obviously) and, within each sonnet, each line may be replaced by the corresponding line from any other sonnet: hence, 10 to the 14th power possible and distinct sonnets. In order for the permutations to be possible, certain rules, which Queneau explains at the beginning of his book, rules which dictate the structure of the book, had to be obeyed. Now we are in the territory of the arbitrary: arbitrary in the sense that we are obeying not general laws adopted based on experience or habitude, but rules whose validity is decided as a function of the set in question. The observation of these rules furnishes a certain number of solutions, all of them *a priori* equally valid. This is what interests us: a certain number of solutions in a given field. The field is the structure. The wider the field, the more solutions, and vice versa. A narrow field will give rise to relatively few solutions, a wide field to many more. The notion that a structure must be average to be good is meaningless. The structure must be coherent.

The rest depends on one's appetite and tolerance for chance. The effect of the structure is to keep chance in check. Some solutions are excluded, leaving a greater or lesser number of solutions. As we impose no initial criteria besides obedience to the structure, all solutions that obey it are valid. By carefully examining each solution thus obtained we may, by chance, discover a solution that seduces us, one we never would have considered because it was, on the face of it, too distant from our preoccupations. We refuse to rely on chance to put it to better use. This method of working thus requires structures that can be discussed–hence the appeal of mathematics, which offers us an impressive array thereof.

These structures and rules and interdicts and multiple solutions are all well and good, some may say: to be a writer, one must keep in mind a whole series of constraints whose final effect may well be to compromise the mind's very freedom. This is true, absolutely true, for those who have no taste for gymkhana games: there is slalom and there is downhill skiing, and each may choose his specialty. But one may also choose both. Perhaps the practice of both is necessary, in fact, for those who intend to specialize in just one. It remains a question of method.

Nonetheless, we may state again: one discipline has always stood to gain by borrowing from another. Writers do not live cloistered alone in their sole domain. But we have lived until now with the postulate that literature and "science" are irreconcilable. This may be true, but it has still yet to be proven.

Originally published in *L'Organiste Athée* (Collège de 'Pataphysique)

Translated by
Daniel Levin Becker

Latis

from

The Atheist Organist

1964

● *The Atheist Organist* is a novel containing seven prefaces, a preface to those prefaces, a postface, a postlude, and no actual novel.

HISTORICAL (AND POSTERIOR) POSTFACE IN WHICH IT IS RECOUNTED HOW THE PRESENT VOLUME CAME TO CONSIST ONLY OF PREFACES

The sole manuscript of the novel called *The Atheist Organist* was mislaid during the course of the global vaudeville of 1939-45, which is why only its prefaces remain. According to the author, this loss is insignificant. Quite quickly, in fact, during the elaboration of this work, he became aware that it was made for its prefaces and that, to his mind, its true interest lay in this very displacement of interest. Providentially, then, the disappearance of the novel itself removed from the prefaces all but their pretense of justification, much as the Porte Saint-Martin and the Porte Saint-Denis in Paris open onto nothing at all, nor do they close off anything in particular–and, if we may be permitted the futility of a value judgment, we might say it is better this way, or at least that some clarity has been gained.

However, alongside this superior clarity there is another, subordinate one, which perhaps requires, after a sustained reading of the prefaces, the following clarifications.

* * *

The anecdote of the novel had been, from a relative remove, inspired by a military resort vacation that the author took in a small village in the confines of Le Maine and Le Perche. But, though while there he had been enmeshed in several curious and urbane intrigues, his novel was neither an imitation nor even a transposition of them. It was more like a digestion or a spirit thereof, in the sense that those words are used by liquor distillers.

It did not contain any continuous narrative, but various fragments that sought to imitate documents and information. Their assembly had been proposed as the result of a police inquiry, suspended for lack of sufficient "juridical materiality" for the case, the case being precisely that of determining whether there was "materiality" of fact to justify, shall we say, a more official inquiry: an inquiry to determine the merits of an inquiry. The author credited himself (perhaps presumptuously) with having arrived at an ingenious disposition of these fragments so as to suggest a complex of events proportioned to both divert and disconcert–in such a way that the reader suspects more than he knows what might be happening, and in such a way that the author is not entirely in control of these suspicions. One gathered (thanks to hidden recordings of conversations made by the police officer) that he had allowed himself to seed some indications that, though not properly ambiguous, were intended to encourage readers' imaginations to heat up according to their own preferred orientations: cuckolding or marital and concubinary fidelity, tendency toward or resistance of pederasty, elegant hypocrisy or brute loyalty (or their two opposites[1])–to say nothing of the intermediate varieties, etc.–all of these nuances could be inferred *equally* from the available information, without ever being confirmed explicitly. All of which was itself only a set of decorative accessories serving to situate the main character, the organist Van Trater, and to give him either an illustrious or a feeble allure.

With regard to Van Trater, the author permitted himself the facility of having part of his personal journal photographed by the inquiring policeman during a home

1. With elegant ugliness and ugly elegance, hypocritical loyalty and loyal hypocrisy (so close to frankness).

inspection, which was extra-legal and executed during Van Trater's absence (but required by the needs of the preexisting investigation, whose causes could be guessed to be inextricably linked to municipal politics and to the exploits of the Commissioner of Police). This photograph was a practical trick to reveal an objective glimpse of "interior psychology" without which the story, discontinuous and assemblable by the reader though it was, would have been insufficient. A bridge too far, you might say, but one that nonetheless corresponded to one of the organist's character traits, because he was not logical enough to follow the logic of his dichotomous character. If he had really been the man he pretended to be, he would not have written, certainly not about himself. But he was not logical in this way, as one can see by various means from this journal.

These pages, then, summarily gathered lines concerning some intrigues foreign to the organist but involving other characters who interested him and who appeared in other documents: municipal counselors, choir children, ladies and non-ladies. They also took stock of the progress of his prelude and fugue, *Injunction without Cost*, absurdly intended to "prove" the inexistence of God. He was not unaware of the absurdity, but he mixed it in with notes on technique and music theory (briefly!). The performance of this prelude and fugue, on Laetare Sunday in 1940, was meant to mark (unbeknownst to everyone, including the principal character involved) the height of his secret conflict with Abbé Pluche, curate of the parish. This latter was none other than the famous eighteenth-century writer who published, in 1732, the nine-volume *Spectacle of Nature*, one of the best-selling books of the modern era, and who was thus, at the time, much more than two hundred years old, conferring upon him a style, an elocution, and a character relatively new to the heyday of novelistic creation–and, we need not insist, soberly evoked by the police documents without stirring the slightest sentiment of unlikelihood and with all the "distinguishing marks" of "reality." The author, who does not feel even the smallest pang of regret for the lost manuscript (fifty-five pages or so), is nonetheless not above a certain nostalgia for the introduction to the sermon (on the theme of atheism, naturally) given by the Abbé Pluche during the great mass at the end of which *Injunction without Cost* was performed: the expression, like the idea, was imprinted with a delicate touch of obsolescence that required its fair share of attention, though in all probability few readers would have been sufficiently in tune with the literature of the eighteenth century, especially sacred literature, to truly appreciate the passage. Given the vagueness of this rhetoric—especially to ears hearing it in 1940—nobody in the parish audience was able to appreciate the allusions placed therein by the prolix bicentennial man. Even less understood, however, was the position of the prelude and fugue on the inexistence of God: it must have been lost in the hubbub of moving chairs and quiet conversations that marks the end of services. Thus the novel seemed to come to a sudden end before anything had happened. Except that a note from the policeman, closing his file on the abandoned investigation, mentioned in passing four or five pieces of information that would allow the reader to evaluate, given what he had already learned, the subsequent evolution of the dramas: teenager in a convent, choirboy in boarding school, and the accidental (or perhaps intentional?) death of Van Trater the organist.

Evidently it is impossible to summarize the plot of the novel more clearly. Even if we were to set aside the illusions of memory, enumerating the events would inevitably denature to the point of caricature the fragmentary and interpretive understanding thereof required of the reader.

Let us indicate only that the general title of the book was: *The Atheist Organist / Thesis Pseudo-Novel / in Several Episodes and a Journal / Preceded / by Several Prefaces / for Which the Novel Serves as / Pretext*. This somewhat lugubrious complication was deemed superfluous and, for typographical reasons, simplified.

Why publish *The Atheist Organist* more than twenty years after its composition? Why wait so long?

The author is the first to wonder. Not for a moment did it occur to him to make up for the loss of the novel by reconstituting it. He may have thought from time to time of reusing the ideological material contained in the prefaces to make some new work possessed of a more organic finality—even though the conjectures in this historical afterword certainly seem to have spewed forth spontaneously from the tip of his pen.

The kindly reader will say, again: Wasn't there a way to publish this lampoon upon its final composition (written in 1939-40, corrected and polished in 1943)? Couldn't it have claimed to be, thanks to some confusion, herald and precursor of the "N"ouveau "R"oman (and even, given the poor faith in which it was conceived, been said to contain the antidote along with the drug)?

On the contrary, the author is pleased to have escaped the snares of precursorhood and its prophetic priorities. He much prefers to appear to tag along behind those who had the moral courage to exploit a gold mine; he prefers at least to appear to bring some grist to their mill; he prefers, even, at worst, to be under suspicion of pre-dating his works in order to make them look more original. All of which is of minimal importance so long as he entertained himself in composing them, and so long as it is no less entertaining to him to think about this temporal disjunction and its disadvantages.

Thus it did not please him to modify the surviving prefaces any more than he thought it possible or desirable to redo the novel. What they had to say—twenty years ago (it was so untimely then that it is even more so now)—they say just as well now, not only about the Novel, a principal theme that is by all indications ancillary, but also about the several accessory subjects whose encounter was, perhaps, the destination of this wandering.

Unpublished holding of the Fonds Oulipo at the Bibliothèque nationale de France

Translated by Daniel Levin Becker

Marcel Duchamp

Correspondence with the Oulipo

1962–1967

● Surely the most famous Oulipian whom nobody recognizes as such, Marcel Duchamp became a foreign correspondent of the Oulipo in 1962 (he was living primarily in the United States by this time) based on his enthusiasm for accounts of the group's explorations published in the quarterly journal of the Collège de 'Pataphysique.

FROM THE MINUTES TO THE MEETING OF FRIDAY, 16 MARCH 1962

The *Sérénissime* Simon Watson-Taylor sent R. Queneau the following letter:

"I have been ordered by your satrapic colleague Marcel Duchamp, whom I have just seen in New York, to congratulate you most warmly on the latest Dossier du Collège containing the first research findings of your OuLiPo. He could not have been more enthusiastic, saying that he too was undertaking analogous linguistic research, though it was not ready to be presented to the world, even the pataphysical one. But he should be encouraged.

"I've been told that the OuLiPo publishes a regular report on its meetings and its theoretical accomplishments. Don't you think it would be a good idea to send a copy to Duchamp? I think it would interest him enormously. In case you don't have his address, it's: 28 West 10th Street–New York–N.Y. S.W.T."

T.S.* Marcel Duchamp is unanimously named "Foreign Correspondent." Subsequent reports will be sent to him. The P.S.† is tasked with sending a letter to his address, which letter will be signed at the next meeting by all present members.

Boulogne-sur-Seine, 23 October 1964[‡]

Monsieur Marcel DUCHAMP
210 West 14th Street
NEW-YORK N.Y.
UNITED STATES

5 rue Parmentier
NEUILLY S/SEINE

C/O Arturo SCHWARZ
Via Gesu 17
MILAN
ITALY

Dear Marcel Duchamp,

Scarcely a (secret) meeting of the OuLiPo goes by without our bringing up your name and ruing your absence. Our Provisionally Definitive Secretaries swear up and down that they have written to you two or three times at least but perhaps their letters reached you too late.

This situation strikes us as entirely untenable and I have been tasked with writing you at the three addresses we have for you simultaneously, in New York, Paris, and Milan. Should you find yourself in these three places simultaneously when these letters arrive you need reply only to one of them.

I do not need to remind you that the OuLiPo–which I founded with Queneau four years ago and which is dedicated not to the elaboration of literary *works* but to the fabrication of literary *structures* that writers may use as they see fit–is also a Commission of the COLLÈGE DE PATAPHYSIQUE. Apart from a few foreign correspondents–all of them eminent–there are ten of us. We meet for lunch roughly once a month and would be delighted to have you among us during one of your next visits to Paris.

Just in case, I will tell you that our next meeting will take place on Friday, November 6, at 12:30 p.m. at a little restaurant located on the first floor of 40 rue de l'Université (very close to the corner of said street and rue du Bac). It would be a happy miracle if you were able to join us on that day. Failing that, it would be better to proceed the other way around and set a meeting date during a period when you will be in Paris and after having agreed with you upon a date that would not put you out.

Does this suit you and seem possible? We certainly hope so. I send my fond wishes along with Queneau's, Noël Arnaud's, and those of the other members of the OuLiPo.

P.S. Do you still find any time for chess?

* Transcendent Satrap, a title within the Collège de 'Pataphysique.

† Provisional Secretary.

‡ Unsigned but written by François Le Lionnais.

2 Nov. 64

28 West 10th Street
New York City

Dear Le Lionnais

Thank you for your 3 Oulympian cards and thank you for the invitation to the meeting on 6 Nov, to which I am replying, a bit late, with the unfortunate impossibility of being in Paris and of not being in New York on that day.

Will be in France next May or thereabouts and will send word when I arrive.

So all my sympathies and best wishes for Queneau, Noël Arnaud, and yourself and the Oulipo brigade.

Affectionately,
Marcel Duchamp

17 Gidouille 92
17/6/1965

to S.T. Marcel DUCHAMP
5 rue Parmentier
NEUILLY-SUR-SEINE

Dear Transcendent Satrap and friend,

I have been tasked by the OULIPO, and particularly by Raymond Queneau and François Le Lionnais, with asking if it would be agreeable and possible for you to accept the OULIPO's invitation to a lunch that could take place June 22 or 25, preferably, or the 24th if the 22nd and 25th fail to suit you. I have been trying in vain to reach you by telephone for three days.

Would you please be so very obliging as to reply directly to François Le Lionnais (23 route de la Reine, Boulogne/Seine), if possible by telephone in the morning (he or his secretary will be there), at MOLitor 90-13, Le Lionnais having set aside, as has Queneau, the three days indicated above.

Thank you.

Sentiments of pataphysical deference and loyal friendship.

Noël Arnaud – 18 rue Mesnil – Paris (16°)

27 April 67

5 rue Parmentier
Neuilly s/Seine

Dear Le Lionnais

Thank you for your note on 20 April.

I will be very happy to have lunch with the whole Oulipo on Tuesday, 16 May.

Around 12:30?? I assume.

Very kind regards

Marcel Duchamp

24 August 1967

Cadaquès
(Girona)
Spain

Dear Le Lionnais

Once again too far away to arrive in time to have lunch with you on the 25th. Thank you

and end of Sept. in Paris

Sincerely yours,

Marcel Duchamp

Unpublished holding of the Fonds Oulipo at the Bibliothèque nationale de France

Translated by Daniel Levin Becker

Albert-Marie Schmidt

Letter to the Oulipo

1965

● Renaissance scholar Albert-Marie Schmidt's most famous and enduring contribution to the Oulipo is the group's name: before he proposed calling it the *ouvroir de littérature potentielle*, it spent a few months known as the *séminaire de littérature expérimentale*, or SeLitEx. (Jacques Roubaud later admitted he would not have joined a group called SeLitEx.) Schmidt died in 1966.

17 August 1965

Albert-Marie SCHMIDT
Résidence "Les Cygnes"
1, Square Albert 1er
VICHY (Allier)

Dear Friends,

I wanted above all to apologize to you for my long abstention. I am recovering with difficulty from bitterly failing health, in addition to which an inexplicable theft has deprived me of my personal papers and my manuscripts in preparation. When I return to Paris in September, I hope to have restored my mental health sufficiently to be able to participate effectively in your work. You will find attached, besides a clean verse to finish "The Only Thirteen-Line Sonnet," an attempt to create a perpetual terminal acrostic using the three syllables *ou-*, *li-*, and *po*.

Very best wishes
Albert-Marie Schmidt

Unpublished holding of the Fonds Oulipo at the Bibliothèque nationale de France

Translated by Daniel Levin Becker

Claude Berge

Letter to Jacques Roubaud & Georges Perec

1967

● The oulipian model of collaboration between writers and mathematicians was forged by the graph theorist Claude Berge, who brought several richly potential structures to the group's attention. Discerning oulipophiles will note the strong resemblance between this specimen and the one propping up Perec's *Life A User's Manual*, published eleven years later.

Paris, 6 December 1967

Monsieur Roubaud
Monsieur Pérec
92, rue du Bac
Paris

Dear friends,

If our project concerning the use of orthogonal Latin squares is still on the table, as I hope it is, I think one of you will need to take the initiative to convene the sub-sub-co-committee. In the meantime, however, I am sending an extremely rare specimen, found recently by Parker, for n = 10:

		Characters:									
		1	2	3	4	5	6	7	8	9	10
Texts:	1	Aa	Gh	Fi	Ej	Jb	Id	Hf	Be	Ce	Dg
	2	Hg	Bb	Ah	Gi	Fj	Jc	Ie	Cd	Df	Ea
	3	If	Ha	Cc	Bh	Ai	Gj	Jd	De	Eg	Fb
	4	Je	Ig	Hb	Dd	Ch	Bi	Aj	Ef	Fd	Gc
	5	Bj	Jf	Ia	Ac	Ee	Dh	Ci	Fg	Gb	Ad
	6	Di	Cj	Jg	Ib	Hd	Ff	Eh	Ga	Ac	Be
	7	Fh	Ei	Dj	Ja	Ic	He	Gg	Ab	Bd	Cf
	8	Cb	Dc	Ed	Fe	Gf	Ag	Ba	Hh	Ii	Jj
	9	Hc	Fd	Ge	Af	Bg	Ca	Db	Ij	Jh	Hi
	10	Gd	Nc*	Bf	Cg	Da	Eb	Fe	Ji	Hj	Ih

It is thus a matter of writing, in the “exercises in style” mode, ten texts (micro-fables, short stories, etc.) in which there appear ten characters (such as an old man named Archimedes, a goldfish, Fantomas, Destiny, etc.). In each story a given character has two attributes, denoted by a capital letter and a lowercase letter (for instance the capital letter could designate an attribute—wearing a red hat, having a glottal tremor, congenital incontinence—and the lowercase letters could be their primary actions, such as, in the case of a detective story, killing someone, being the victim, discovering the murder, etc.). This is a mere suggestion, of course, and we all expect your fertile brains to elevate it to new heights of oulipian literature.

Very cordially yours,
C. Berge

* [sic]

Originally published as “Boîte à idées” in Oulipo, *La littérature potentielle* (Gallimard)

Translated by Daniel Levin Becker

François Le Lionnais

Idea Box

1973

● This sampler of mathematical principles potentially exploitable toward literary ends is the final piece in *La littérature potentielle*, the Oulipo's first collective publication. According to François Le Lionnais, the group's cofounder and primary thinker on the meaning of “potential,” a robust idea was essential, the execution of a text based on that idea an ancillary bonus.

ANAGLYPHIC TEXT

Literary texts are always planar (and even linear, generally speaking): that is, they can be represented on a sheet of paper. A text could be composed whose lines were situated in a three-dimensional space. Reading it would require special glasses (one red lens and one green) using the anaglyphic method that has already been used to represent geometric figures and figurative scenes in space.

One will notice an attempt at orthogonalization within the plane, in the acrostics.

HOLOPOEMS

The principles of holography could be used to represent poems as images projected into overhead space. When the reader moves his or her head, words or phrases become visible that were previously hidden from sight.

ANTIRHYMES (NOT TO BE CONFUSED WITH ANTERHYMES)

Linguists and phoneticians have proposed several different procedures to characterize and distinguish phonemes. Such a procedure could be taken up if it allows a phoneme A' to be defined in relation to the complementary (or opposite, or symmetric) characteristics of another phoneme A. By definition, A' would be the antiphoneme of A. From this the notion of antirhyme follows naturally.

An antirhymed poem would consist of two associated lines, one of which ends with one or more phonemes (collectively referred to as rhyme) and the other with the antiphonemes.

The problem, evidently–but this is also true of traditional rhyme–is finding meaningful words for the antirhyme.

POEM EDGES

Given a poem, let us define the Edges of this poem as its first line, its last line, the list obtained by taking the first word of each line, and the list obtained by taking the last word of each line. Everything else–that is, the interior of the poem–will be considered, from our point of view here, negligible.[1]

In many cases it may be advantageous to represent a poem by writing the successive words of the same line on an arc instead of a straight line. Thus, instead of a rectangle formed by four straight segments, we will have a convex curvilinear quadrilateral.

Consider two poems, A and B, represented in this manner. If the edges of A and the edges of B contain an identical word W, it can be said that the two poems are tangent at W, and the two poems may be placed in such a way that the tangency is visible.

An entire geometry can be constructed from this apparatus. One might attempt to transpose into it Apollonius's problem: given three unequal coplanar circles that are tangent two by two, construct a fourth circle internally tangent and a fifth circle externally tangent.

1. One could just as well adopt the opposite point of view, considering the edges negligible and using only the interior of the poem. By repeating this operation as many times as necessary, one would finally come to a systematic shucking of poetry and the extraction of the stones at its core.

LIMITED-VOCABULARY TEXTS

Poems or stories containing only the words from an extremely limited vocabulary (as has already been demonstrated with algorithmic-oriented language and with Boolean poems at the intersection of Corneille and Brébeuf), for instance animal languages such as they are described by specialists in animal psychology–that is, evidently, giving equivalents in human vocabulary.

SOME MATHEMATICAL STRUCTURES AND NOTIONS

It is necessary to undertake a methodical exploration of various mathematical structures and notions in order to determine whether any of them offer oulipian possibilities. Here, grouped together, are some suggestions:

1. Sets
   Classes
   Elements
   Set membership
   Inclusion
   Union
   Intersection
   Complementation
   Symmetric difference
   Difference

2. Relation
   Reflexivity
   Symmetry
   Asymmetry
   Dissymmetry
   Antisymmetry
   Transitivity

3. Preorder
   Order (different types)
   Analogy (= Reflexivity + Symmetry = Equivalence - Transitivity). I am persuaded that this relation is

terribly underexploited and that it has a bright future (not only for the OuLiPo but also for the OuPeinPo, the OuMuPo, and more generally the Ou-X-Po). Synonymy is a special case.

4. Composition law (internal, external, extraexternal)
   Associativity
   Commutativity
   Distributivity
   Simplifiability
   Concatenation

5. Neighborhood
   Open sets
   Closed sets
   Boundary
   Closure
   Catastrophes (various kinds)

6. Correspondence
   Application
   Injective functions
   Surjective functions
   Bijective functions
   Functions
   Morphism
   Homomorphism
   Endomorphism
   Automorphism
   Epimorphism
   Monomorphism
   Homeomorphism
   Diffeomorphism

7. Graph
   Clique

8. Groupoids
   Monoids
   Groups
   Identity

9. ∀ ∃ quantifiers

10. Parallelism
Translations
Secancy
Tangency
Perpendicularity
Angle

11. Affine transformations
Projective transformations
Inverse transformations

12. Distance
Pseudometric space

13. Probability (various laws)
Markov chains

All that remains is to get to work. The Oulipo has taken this to heart. At the rate of just one notion per monthly meeting, the above list, which is in no way intended as restrictive, could provide material for the agendas of at least a hundred meetings to come.

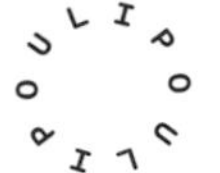

THEMATIC OR SEMANTIC STRUCTURES

Establish a dictionary (with no claim to exhaustivity) of meaningful elements involved in a poem or a story, such as:

Ideas (I), Sentiments (St), Sensations (Ss), Objects (O), Actions (A), Phenomena (P), etc.

This dictionary could be used in a number of ways:

1. To analyze an existing text, reduce it to a list of meaningful elements such as the above, replace each element with its classification number, and imagine other stories based on precisely the same list. This exercise is comparable to homosyntaxism exercises (based on N = noun, V = verb, A = adjective).

2. One could also transpose the N+7 method into thematic or semantic domains.

Originally published as "La méthode S±7 (cas particulier de la méthode M±n)" in Oulipo, *La littérature potentielle* (Gallimard)

Translated by Daniel Levin Becker

Jean Lescure

from

The N+7 Method (An Individual Case of the W±n Method)

1973

● The N+7 method is one of the best-known tricks in the oulipian toolbox: a simple operation that can change the driest text into a lurid fantasia of near-nonsense. Jean Lescure's lab report on the method is a splendid example of the combination of empirical seriousness and spirited play with which the Oulipo approached its earliest experiments.

The W±*n* method, initially proposed in the comparatively limited N+7 form (which gave the method its name), consists in replacing, in an existing text (literary in nature or not), words (W) with other words of the same part of speech that follow or precede them in the dictionary at a variable distance measured by number of words. Thus N+7 simply means replacing each noun in a text with the seventh after it in a given vocabulary.

This method is evidently a method with variable results. Indeed, one may change the central tool of its application, which adjustment alone suffices to create the most unexpected modifications in the results—assuming that the patience, attention, and honesty of the operator remain equal.

Thus, in addition to said operator, whose function is purely mechanical, this method requires some text, chosen (or not) from among those texts reputed to be literary, and some dictionary, vocabulary, glossary, or lexicon.

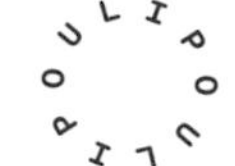

The method known as N+7 introduces its modifications to one part of speech only. One takes, successively, each noun encountered in the selected text and, after consulting the chosen dictionary, replaces it with the seventh common noun to be found following it.

This method can be modified by changing the letter, or, just as easily, the number; it is equally permissible to transform it by replacing the + sign with a - sign. Thus can we imagine an N+3 method, or an N-7 method, or an A+14, or a V-13, where A represents *adjective* and V *verb*. Ultimately, a general method may be designated by W±*n*, where W is the totality of words in the language and *n* the infinite set of numbers.[1]

What we are elaborating here, one can plainly see, is a method permitting practically infinite applications to the same text, or in any case a number of interventional possibilities that far surpasses the exercitation time of any human being.

From the small quantity of exercises produced thus far we cannot make many remarks or generalizations with respect to the results achieved. We may nonetheless note that texts taken from newspapers appear to inject into the daily information flow a resonance not commonly allowed to peek through.

Texts of a certain literary quality do not appear to be improved, in an artistic sense, by the application of this method. They do, however, reveal some heretofore unexpected powers, and in any case do not seem substantially degraded by the manipulation. On the contrary, an industrial literary text like *Chère Caroline* glimmers with interesting nuances: the "suggestive" parts (in the most banal sense) take on a much more daring allure, even without becoming any more explicit or saucy.

Applied to those texts that present the greatest traditional literary rigor, this method gives aberrant but generally pleasant results. For instance:

> The mineralogy cannot act for long in the roller skate of the hearth.

> The greatest misanthrope of the Low Countries is the curiosity of cordovan.

1. This extension of the method was proposed by the Regent Le Lionnais during a regular working session of the OuLiPo.

> The contraband of our pasta is no more in our practitioner than the terrace of our lifeline.

> We do not have enough stride to follow all of our rebuses.

It can nonetheless happen that from these maxims emanates a potentiality entirely distinct from the original's powers of conviction. For instance:

> Interment blinds some and enlightens others.

> We promise according to our horizon and perform according to our feces.

Distinct as these propositions are from those published by La Rochefoucauld, they remain appreciably faithful to their author's moralizing humanism. Perhaps one will note all the same that they remove the mundanity from the original and reveal energies within its structures that might have driven it toward an objectivity less concerned with morality than with quasi-transcendental fantasy.

Originally published as "Alphabet pour Stämpfli" in Peter Stämpfli, *Oeuvres récentes* (Centre Georges Pompidou, 1981); later reprinted in Georges Perec, *Beaux présents, belles absentes* (Seuil, 1994)

Translated by Ian Monk

Georges Perec

Alphabet for Stämpfli

1980

● Georges Perec often wrote *beaux présents* for his friends on special occasions: odes using only the letters in their names. For an exhibition by the Swiss pop-art painter Peter Stämpfli at the Centre Pompidou in 1980, he composed a variation in which the excluded letters from the rest of the alphabet appear and recede in succession.

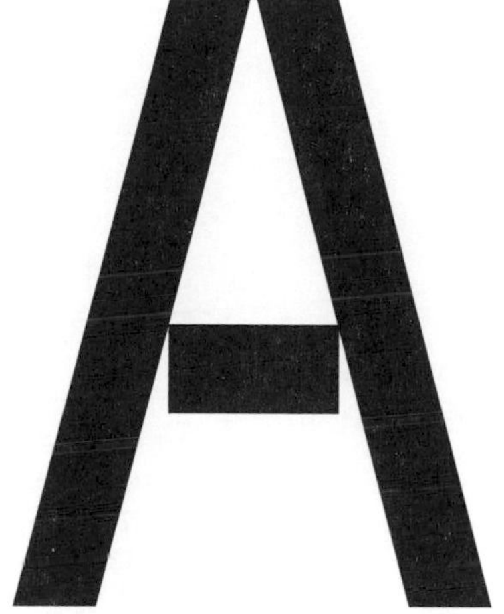

1. As a still, I trap real life's stiff seams,
its strata, its pleats, its rifts;
I prepare frail, simple (easier) streets;
I fertilise, I steep terra firma's separate rites,
tress its mail, its tesserae,
settle its masses, its pits,
its flats, its ramps, its seisms:
as if reliefs are a stamp,
metal silt, a stilet, limits, a prism,
plaster sets, a spasm,
a series spelt letter after letter, term after term,
its frame, its trammels stir it,
split matter mills it.

2. A bare restart:
stable realities resist, a briar, pebbles,
marble,
pale basalt,
as small billets stir its febrile embers.
If flames lit feeble plaster,

if a rebel spirit spat terrible emblems
at a malleable feast,
still I baptise, as its irrepressible fiber liberates itself.
It resembles ballistite, barbs, a saber,
it blasts its first limits apart.
I master life as it brims, its base limbs,
a terrestrial empire,
I baste its amber, its brambles, sere bistre;
I better it: it'll affirm itself, irresistible, timeless,
as blest, as firm as barrier reefs it'll bear.

3. As I efface a tale, still its trace is left: a
map cast, calm stars, scales, a carapace,
a tactile act: as I impact frail Space, semi-
flat, semi-crimp, scar it, cram it, it screams I am
merciless.
Is it electric, Pacific streams, a pact implicit
as I face its secret spectres? Crisp paper
reclaims all it secretes, its smart ellipses, eclipses,
as it rests, as it accelerates,
as I press, as I scatter it;
I, its strict piercer.

4. Add a detail, let it radiate till it delimits
me as a firm Daedalist.
At its rear, as it retreads, re-riddles itself, I disperse
its radials, its diameters, its pleated, draped
material, its dips, its rest times, its retarded,
speeded steps,
I dare its dreaded palisades (as a faded palette's
tepid fate, as a deft medallion's sterile admirer, as
idealised artists' lame distress).
I desire isles, deserts; let me date time's
drift, meet limpid, immediate life.

5. Realities gestate images; as images, realities.
I grapple at grist, at glass,
passages, tiger stripes, emerge:
fragile life's restless grammar.

A paper's gates are its garage,
a page a game magma, as a grim
mage arpeggiates, legislates,
its trait slips
its Termless Miles gall me,
its regimes, its agile marriages

6. (as if its strata
hash, mesh,
shatter this phrase, that theme: these rhymes)

7. (as if its strata
are jet streams satellites left
as astral jetsam:
a jeep tires its same, timeless passes)

8. (as if its strata
are streaks skis left,
like Alp pistes' termless tresses
make its tiers)

9. As I translate its mainstream, time at last petrifies
mammals in a famine.
Firmaments, infernal areas enframe a planet as its
entities respire.
It is salts, lines in mines, natal steel, laminae,
repleteness, transfers, plains.
I, as a painter,
let its neat imprints appear:
linear filaments, infinitesimal snail trails,
trains, élans, anamnesis,
an immense, apparent listlessness,
pent eternities.

10. More, more, more: I repeat its motif.
It is itself, it is also its opposite:
trail, format separate *a* from *o*,

for its simple realism seems to me
to atomise, to isolate it as fast as I posit.

So memorise its form too,
a mirror to its palimpsest,
tropism, osmosis, a maelstrom, apostils,
or else post its poles far apart,
sleep or promise,
miss or tell.

11. At a quarter past time
quasars mutilate it,
rustle at its lumps, its tumuli,
stimulate tapers at its sill.
If I trust a quest's quiet tumult,
is a surer, restful part still left?
Surprises, perpetual flurries,
future marquetries it multiplies

as it uses itself up,
as far as time's ripples purl
(its fatal fissures: a queer murmur
pursues a palm's sulfur, a leaf
flutters, as

12. A seam's verve vivifies its festivities,
its vistas live, its fevers, fertile vales.
It rives its limits, marvels at its fate,
as if slaves are flames
I affirm its verities:

13. mazes and totems
where now can be read
strict tracks
of routine's thousandfold alphabets
spelt out one by one across the huge canvas:

cigarette
ruby
backstairs
pudding
freezerbag
fairlane
straight line
washing machine
self-portrait with raglan
james bond
look
impala
tomato
inter
royal
big sport
quart of bourbon
blusher
bond street
bottle
ruddy kiss
favorite
wildcat
luxury shoe
town and country
xzz 20

Originally published as *Comment j'ai écrit un de mes livres* (La Bibliothèque Oulipienne no. 20); English translation previously published in *Oulipo Laboratory* (Atlas, 1995)

Translated by Iain White

Italo Calvino

How I Wrote One of My Books

1982

● Named after Raymond Roussel's posthumous *How I Wrote Certain of My Books*, Calvino's second contribution to the Bibliothèque Oulipienne chapbook series outlines the algorithm governing the interchapter narrative in his 1979 novel *If on a winter's night a traveler*. Calvino stipulated that the explanation was never to be published in Italian.

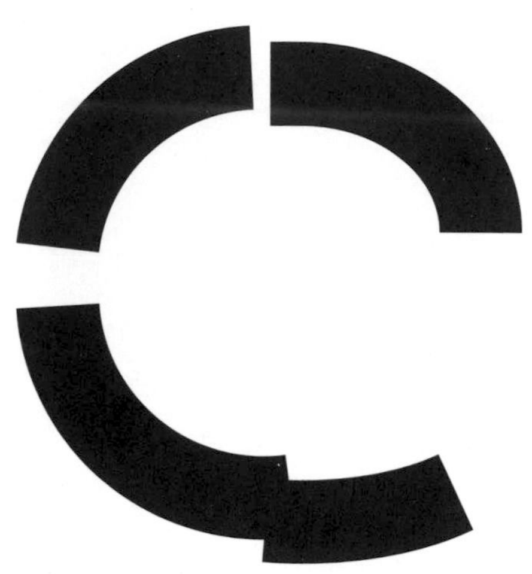

TABLE OF CONTENTS

CHAP. 1

```
L  — ℓ
|     |
ℓ' — L'
```

CHAP. 2

```
L  — ℓ∩   L — ℓ⇒
|     |   |    |
ℓ∪ — L    L — ℓ⇐
```

CHAP. 3

```
L  — ℓ*   L   — ℓ_x   L+ — S+
|     |   |      |    |     |
ℓ* — ℒ    ℓ_x — L+    [  — S-
```

CHAP. 4

```
L — L+   L — L+   L  — ℒ   L  — ℒ
|    |   |    |   |     |  |     |
ℒ — L    ℒ — L    L+ — L   L+ — L
```

CHAP. 5

```
L_p — L   L_p — L   L_p — L   L_p — L   L_p — L
|       |   |       |   |       |   |       |   |       |
A-  — A   A-  — A   A-  — A   A-  — A   A-  — A
```

CHAP. 6

```
A — β    A- — A   A- — A+   A- — Aε   A+ — A   A — β
|    |   |     |  |     |   |     |   |     |  |    |
α — A-   α  — β   Aε — A    N  — A    N  — β   α — A-
```

CHAP. 7	L — ℓ / | | / M — [	L — [/ | | / ℓ — M	L — L / | | / x — ℓ	L — L / | | / x — ℓ	A+ — ℓ / | | / L — L	L — A- / | | / ℓ — L
CHAP. 8	A — L / | | / é — ℓ	A_t — $ℓ_L$ / | | / $ℓ_A$ — A_p	A — n / | | / β — B	A — ℒ / | | / A- — L	A — ℓ⇐ / | | / ℓ⇒ — L	
CHAP. 9	L — M / | | / β — α	P — β / | | / α — L	A- — P / | | / α — β	ℒ — P / | | / α — L		
CHAP. 10	L — β / | | / α — C	C — A- / | | / β — L	C — α / | | / L — β			
CHAP. 11	L — L' / | | / l' — L'	L — ℓ / | | / L' — ℓ'				
CHAP. 12	L — ℓ / | | / n — L					

CHAPTER 1

L → ℓ
↑ ╳ ↓
ℓ' ← L'

The reader who is there (L) is reading the book that is there (ℓ)
The book that is there relates the story of the reader who is in the book (*L'*)
The reader who is in the book does not succeed in reading the book in the book (ℓ')
The book that is there does not relate the story of the reader who is there

The reader who is in the book claims to be the reader who is there
The book that is there claims to be the book that is in the book

CHAPTER 2

$$\begin{array}{ccc} L & \rightarrow & \ell^{\cap} \\ \uparrow & \times & \downarrow \\ \ell^{\cup} & \leftarrow & \mathit{L} \end{array}$$

The reader (L) is upset by the interruption of his reading ($\ell^{\cap}$)
The interruption of his reading leads to a meeting with the female reader (*L*)
The female reader wishes to get on with her reading ($\ell^{\cup}$)
Her getting on with her reading rules out a further meeting with the reader

The reader wishes to see the female reader again
The interruption of the book becomes the continuation of the book

$$\begin{array}{ccc} L & \rightarrow & \ell_{\Rightarrow} \\ \uparrow & \times & \downarrow \\ \mathit{L} & \leftarrow & \ell_{\Leftarrow} \end{array}$$

The reader (L) wishes to continue the book he has begun ($\ell\Rightarrow$)
The reader is pleased to encounter the female reader (*L*)
The beginning of the started-on book ($\ell\Leftarrow$) does not please the female reader
The started-on book does not wish to continue

The female reader wishes to begin another book
The beginning of this book seeks another reader

CHAPTER 3

$L \rightarrow \ell^{*}$
$\uparrow \times \downarrow$
$\ell^{*} \leftarrow \mathcal{L}$

The impassioned female reader (L) relishes the art of the novel (ℓ^{*})
The art of the novel might presuppose a character such as the intellectual female reader ($\mathcal{L}$)
The intellectual female reader analyzes the ideology of the novel (ℓ^{*})
Ideology does not allow for a character such as that of the impassioned female reader

Ludmilla understands her sister Loratia
The ideology lacerates the poetry

$L \rightarrow \ell_{x}$
$\uparrow \times \downarrow$
$\ell_{-x} \leftarrow L+$

The reader (L) is seeking a mysterious book (ℓ_{x})
The mysterious book is from the domain of the hyper-reader (L^{+})
The hyper-reader gives the reader an unfinished book (ℓ_{-x})
The unfinished book is not the one the reader is seeking

The hyper-reader does not read the same books as the reader
The mystery of a book is not in its end but in its beginning

$L+ \rightarrow S+$
$\uparrow \times \downarrow$
$[\leftarrow S-$

The hyper-reader finds the sublime (S^{+}) in written words
The non-reader ([) finds only silence (S^{-}) in written words
The sublime finds its perfect realization in silence
The hyper-reader finds his perfect realization in the non-reader

Not reading does not suffice to arrive at the sublime
Not every hyper-reader succeeds in reading silence

CHAPTER 4

L → L+
↑ ↓
ℒ ← *L*

The quest of the reader (L) arouses the excitement of the professor (L^+)
The professor's ecstasy intrigues Ludmilla (*L*)
Ludmilla's being carried away alarms Lotaria (ℒ)
Lotaria's learning embarrasses the reader

L → L+
↑ ↓
ℒ ← *L*

The professor's ecstasy alarms the reader
The reader's quest intrigues Lotaria
Lotaria's learning excites Ludmilla
Ludmilla's being carried away embarrasses the professor

L → ℒ
↑ ↓
L+ ← L

Ludmilla's being carried away excites Lotaria
Lotaria's learning intrigues the reader
The reader's quest alarms the professor
The professor's ecstasy embarrasses Ludmilla

L → ℒ
↑ ↓
L+ ← L

Ludmilla's being carried away intrigues the professor
The professor's ecstasy excites the reader
The reader's quest embarrasses Lotaria
Lotaria's learning alarms Ludmilla

CHAPTER 5

L_p → L
↑ ↓
A- ← A

The professional reader (L_p) envies the lot of the ordinary reader (L)
The ordinary reader gives chase to the author (A)
The author fears he is being plagiarized by the forger (A^-)
The forger eludes the professional reader

L_p → L
↑ ↓
A- ← A

The professional reader gives chase to the forger
The forger envies the lot of the author
The author eludes the ordinary reader
The ordinary reader would not fancy being in the place of the professional reader

L_p → L
↑ ↓
A- ← A

The ordinary reader envies the lot of the professional reader
The forger persecutes the professional reader
The forger detests the author
The ordinary reader remains unknown to the author

L_p → L
↑ ↓
A- ← A

The author envies the lot of the forger
The author pursues the ordinary reader
The professional reader feels sorry for the ordinary reader
The professional reader won't have anything to do with the forger

L_p → L
↑ ↓
A- ← A

The professional reader envies the lot of the ordinary reader
The ordinary reader gives chase to the author
The professional reader gives chase to the forger
The forger envies the lot of the author

CHAPTER 6

A → β
↑ ✕ ↓
α ← A-

The author (A) breathes his truth into his book (β)
The author's book is stolen by the forger (A^-)
The forger breathes his artifice into the apocryphal book (α)
The apocryphal book will be attributed to the author

There is a truth of the author's the forger alone knows
In every real book there is an artifice of which the apocryphal book can take possession

A- → A
↑ ✕ ↓
α ← β

The forger (A^-) endeavors to imitate the style of the author (A)
The author endeavors to express himself in his real book (β)
The real book endeavors to differentiate itself from apocryphal books (α)
The apocryphal books do not endeavor to express the forger's truth

The forger can express a truth that is not his own
The author can produce apocrypha of himself

A- → A+
↑ ✕ ↓
Aε ← A

The forger (A^-) dreams up a super-author (the father of stories, A^+)
The super-author knows all the novels the author (A) dreams of writing
The author has a nightmare: his novel will be written by a computer (Aε)
The computer will be capable of realizing the forger's dreams

The author's dreams and those of the forger resemble one another
The computer-author of novels is a dream like the father of stories

$A^- \rightarrow A\varepsilon$
$\uparrow \times \downarrow$
$N \leftarrow A$

The forger (A^-) dreams up the perfect literary computer ($A\varepsilon$)
The literary computer needs the input of the author (A)
The author is haunted by the background noise (N) of his mind
The background noise eludes the forger’s grasp

The computer is scrambled by the background noise
The forger has not chosen his author well

$A^+ \rightarrow A$
$\uparrow \times \downarrow$
$N \leftarrow \beta$

The father of stories (A^+) no longer inspires the author (A)
The author no longer succeeds in writing the novel he wanted (β)
The novel to be written is swallowed up in the noise (N)
The noise is the source from which all stories emerge

A novel is botched if it does not have a mythic source
It is in the noise that the author’s truth is hidden

$A \rightarrow \beta$
$\uparrow \times \downarrow$
$\alpha \leftarrow A^-$

The author makes a hash of his real book
The author is obliged to produce apocrypha of himself (α)
The forger (A^-) does not have the right to write the real book (β)
The forger can produce all the apocrypha he wishes

The real book is hidden among the apocrypha
The author will write the story of the forger

CHAPTER 7

L → ℓ
↑ ╳ ↓
M ← [

The female reader (*L*) is never satisfied with the book she is reading (ℓ)
The books she reads mean nothing to the non-reader ([)
The non-reader feels at home in a house full of books (M)
A house full of books contains the story of the female reader

The non-reader and the female reader are complementary to one another
It is difficult to find a book in a house filled with books

L → [
↑ ╳ ↓
ℓ ← M

The female reader is complementary to the non-reader
The female reader is never satisfied with the book she is reading
A house full of books is pleasing to the non-reader
A house full of books conceals the sought-for book

The female reader has never finished exploring her house
The non-reader always finds the sought-for book

L → *L*
↑ ╳ ↓
x ← ℓ

The reader (L) is finally reading the female reader
The female reader would like to finally read to the book
The book does not reveal the mystery (x)
The mystery conceals itself from the reader

The female reader conceals a mystery
The book is not finished by the reader

L → L
↑ ╳ ↓
x ← ℓ

The female reader is also reading the reader
The female reader still conceals a mystery
A suspect book is discovered by the reader
The suspect book does not yield up its mystery

In vain, reader, you pursue that bloody mystery
In vain, female reader, you pursue that bloody book

A+ → ℓ
↑ ╳ ↓
L ← *L*

The forger (A) has hidden a book in the house
The female reader is not surprised at the hidden book
The female reader does not yield up her secrets to the reader
The reader is jealous of the forger

A hidden book arouses the reader's suspicions
The female reader was well acquainted with the forger

L → A-
↑ ╳ ↓
ℓ ← L

The female reader was well acquainted with the forger
The forger has crossed the path of the reader
The reader does not recognize the suspect book
The suspect book separates him from the female reader

But it is not certain that the book belongs to the forger
But it is not certain that the female reader belongs to the reader

CHAPTER 8

$A \rightarrow L$
$\uparrow \times \downarrow$
$é \leftarrow \ell$

The author (A) takes the female reader (*L*) as his model
The female reader abandons herself to the pleasure of reading (ℓ)
The pleasure of reading knows nothing of the fatigue of writing (é)
The fatigue of writing torments the author

The female reader knows nothing of the fatigue of writing
The author has forgotten the pleasure of reading

$A_t \rightarrow \ell_L$
$\uparrow \times \downarrow$
$\ell_A \leftarrow A_p$

The tormented author (A_t) would like to be the author of the book read by the female reader (ℓ_L)
The productive author (A_p) would like to be the author of the book read by the female reader
The tormented author does not recognize in his own book the book read by the female reader (ℓ_A)
The productive author does not recognize in his own book the book read by the female reader

The tormented author and the productive author are jealous of one another
The read book and the written book are not the same book

$A \rightarrow n$
$\uparrow \times \downarrow$
$\beta \leftarrow B$

The book he must write (β) eludes the author (A) as an "I" (A)
The author would like to get out of his "I" to be an impersonal "one" (n)
The impersonal "one" is capable of writing infinite libraries (B)
The infinite libraries contain the book of the author as "I"

The author is haunted by the image of infinite libraries
The impersonal language crystallizes in the speech of the book

A → ℒ
↑ ╳ ↓
A· ← *L*

The forger (A·) would like to steal the work of the author (A)
The intellectual female reader (ℒ) would like to lacerate the work of the author
The intellectual female reader would like to differentiate herself from the impassioned female reader (*L*)
The forger would like to seduce the impassioned female reader

The impassioned female reader is not interested in the person of the author
The work of the forger would be enough for the intellectual female reader

A → ℓ⇐
↑ ╳ ↓
ℓ¬ (L

The author manages to write only the beginnings of novels
The reader manages to read only the beginnings of novels
The author does not manage to write a complete novel
The reader does not manage to read a complete novel

The reader does not find the solution to his problems with the author
The complete book is perhaps made up only of beginnings

CHAPTER 9

L → M
↑ ╳ ↓
β ← α

The reader (L) loses interest in the world (M)
The world assumes the form of an apocryphal book (α)
The apocryphal books are replacing the real books (β)
The desired book still eludes the reader

The world will never be a book
The apocryphal book is the story of the reader

P → β
↑ ╳ ↓
α ← L

The government in power (P) is suspicious of books (β)
Books no longer find their reader (L)
The reader puts his trust in apocryphal books (α)
The apocryphal books are signed by the government in power

One can no longer distinguish real books from apocryphal books
The story of the reader is determined by the government in power

A- → P
↑ ╳ ↓
α ← β

Only the forger (A^-) understands the logic of the government in power (P)
The book (β) is helpless against the government in power
The forger makes his way by means of apocryphal books (α)
Each book is the apocrypha of itself

For the forger nothing that is true exists
For the government in power only the false exists

$\mathcal{L}$ → P
↑ ↓
α ← L

Is the female intellectual ($\mathcal{L}$) for or against the government in power?
Is the female intellectual involved in the business of the apocryphal books?
Can the reader flee from his prison?
Will the reader be able to read anything other than an apocryphal book?

Is the female intellectual the reader's ally or his enemy?
Are the apocryphal books a weapon against the government in power?

CHAPTER 10

L → β
↑ ✕ ↓
α ← C

The reader (L) is still looking for the real book (β)
The real book is banned by the censors (C)
The censors allow apocryphal books (α) to circulate
The apocryphal books give the reader no respite

The true book is still hidden among the false ones
The reader goes to see the censor

C → A-
↑ ✕ ↓
β ← *L*

The censors wish to make use of the forger (A^-)
The forger wishes to get the better of the female reader (*L*)
The female reader wishes to be captivated by the real book (β)
The real book wishes to frustrate the censors

The censors can do nothing against the female reader
The real book is the forger's elusive dream

C → α
↑ ✕ ↓
L ← β

The censors keep watch on the reader
The censors are taken in by the apocryphal books
The real book is disguised as an apocryphal book
The real book is unrecognizable to the reader

The real book escapes the censors
The reader believes every book is apocryphal

CHAPTER 11

L → L'
↑ ╳ ↓
l' ← L'

The reader (L) spies on another reader (L')
The other reader is reading another book (ℓ')
The other book is in reality this book (ℓ)
This book is addressed to you, reader

You, reader, you ought to have been reading another book
You, book, you ought to have been read by another reader

L → ℓ
↑ ╳ ↓
L' ← ℓ'

You, reader, ought to have wanted to read this book
You, reader, you have read the story of another reader
It is another book, the one that tells the story of this book
That other book is intended for another reader

The book read by each reader is always another book
The reader with each book he reads is always another reader

CHAPTER 12

L → ℓ
↑ ✕ ↓
n ← *L*

The reader is engaged in finishing the book
The female reader has emerged from the book
The female reader extinguishes the light
The reader turns to her in the darkness

The reader and the female reader are in bed together
Life continues going by and the book remains where it is

NOTE

The book in question is *If on a winter's night a traveler*. More precisely, the numbered chapters of that book. (The "novels" which are interspersed between these chapters follow other schemata and other constraints.)

The model square is a personal adaptation of the formulations of structural semiology of A. J. Greimas (see in particular *Du Sens*, Editions du Seuil, Paris, 1970, pp. 137ff.).

Originally published in *Palindromes bilingues* (Éditions du Fourneau)

Translated by
Daniel Levin Becker

Luc Étienne

from

Bilingual Palindromes

1984

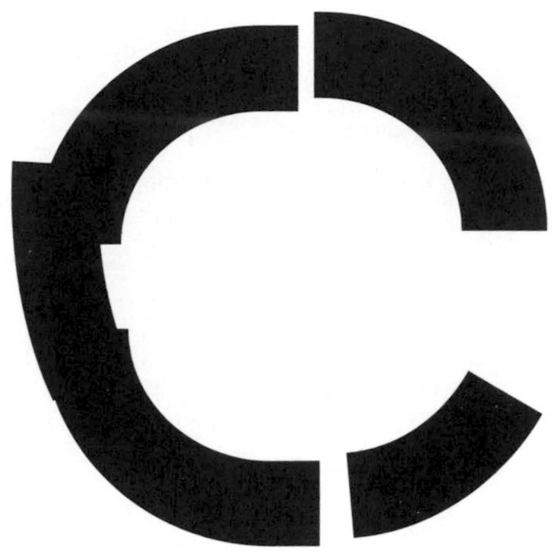

● By the time he joined the Oulipo, Luc Étienne, whose real name was Luc Périn, was already a confirmed master of wordplay, specialized in spoonerisms and puns; later on, he experimented with phonetic palindromes and the concept of the Möbius-strip poem.

PARADISE ON EARTH

Characters: Adam
Eve (or Eva)
Horse (non-speaking role)

Eve is in love with the Horse—surely for lack of any better present alternatives. Adam takes offense. Eve recognizes that she has always made his existence a bitter one.

(Adam addresses the Horse in French; Eve replies in English, which she finds more chic.)

Mon Eva rêve ton image, bidet! *

Ted, I beg, am I not ever a venom?

(One may certainly wonder why Eve calls her husband Edward. It's because she doesn't care for the name the Lord gave him; she finds it common! She has thus chosen to give him a more distinguished name.)

THE CORSICAN TENOR

The crooner Tino Rossi, sampling the charms of the lovely Iris, is caught in the act by her husband. In an attempt to downplay his offense, he tries to make him believe he had only been using the man's wife as a dining-room table. But the cuckold, masochistic and lecherous, insists that the singer get back to the performance while he watches.

Sir, I ate merely on it.

Tino, y le remet à Iris.†

THE AMERICAN DANCER

The beautiful artist Isadora Duncan, famous but aging, recalls wistfully the cruel remark her marvelous young lover made upon leaving her, pretending to wonder whether she will ever find a specimen as fine as his—er, as him.

Isadora rêve:‡

Ever a rod as I?

* My Eve is dreaming of your image, scumbag!

† Tino, give it to Iris there again.

‡ Isadora dreams:

Unpublished holding of the Fonds Oulipo at the Bibliothèque nationale de France

Translated by Daniel Levin Becker

Stanley Chapman

Letter to Valérie Guidoux

1984

● Stanley Chapman, an English architect, designer, translator, and 'Pataphysician, was elected to the Oulipo as a foreign correspondent in 1961. Though he seldom attended group functions in France, he maintained a voluminous correspondence with the group and later founded the OuTraPo, or workshop for potential tragicomedy.

Wednesday evening, 12 September 1984 (vulg.)

Annex of Organon and of Rogation
Collège of Pataphysics
London-on-Middlesex

(vulg) 264 Ramsay Road
Forest Gate
London E7 9EY
Great Brengland

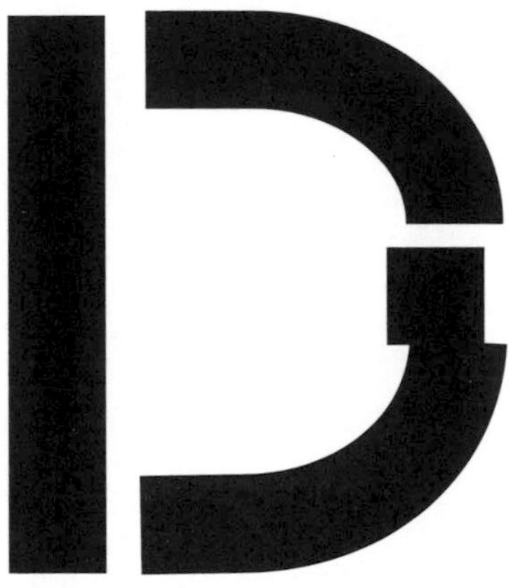

Dear Mademoiselle Guidoux,

I did not wish to be impolite, but events transpire and I mislay letters (along with my socks and phynances) which leaves me with no way to respond to them. Oldening more and more each day, I am no longer able to answer each letter as soon as it arrives–and thus I beg your pardon for this long delay.

And if I am answering you this evening, it is only because a friend is coming to spend the weekend at the Annex and I must clear him a small path among my piles of newspapers, books, letters, rotting pears, old eyeglasses, jars of orange marmalade, checkbooks, and other lovely things. This is how I have just found the lens for my camera, the sock I was unable to put on this morning (still with the hole in the toes), and an envelope that you addressed to my friend Barbara Wright.*

And so I hasten to answer you, even if I no longer know what your questions were. No matter–I wouldn't have been able to answer them. But listen closely and I shall tell you everything worth knowing about me.

I was born in London rather long ago, and have lived here all my life. I have brown eyes, many eyeglasses, and white hair (less[1] than before). I would also have a long white beard if I were brave enough to wear it in reality instead of in my imagination.

I am a friend of Jacques Bens, and knew him at the moment[2] he decided to found the OuLiPo with André Blavier. At the time they wanted to call it The Quercanologist Society (or something like that), but Jean-Hugues Sainmont said this was not proper Latin, so they changed the title... They wanted twelve or fourteen members, and, because I was nearby, I was recruited (is that a word?) (surely not–so I was signed up). That is all.

For family reasons I have been unable to visit France for a long time, which is why I have never been to a lunch meeting of the OuLiPo. I have not been ignoring them; it's just that it was impossible for me to come and participate in their monthly communion of glasses of water.

Jacques Bens signed me up for the OuLiPo because I was interested in Queneau like everyone else–that's all. I must say that at the beginning it was far more interesting than it is now. I quite liked the idea of private (if not secret) meetings where some friends could meet up to share ideas and smile a bit together. It seems rather regrettable to me now that everyone knows the OuLiPo exists and that it has now become a subject of overserious theses.

The two (?) small volumes that have come out are quite useless–there are a thousand English literary games that are a thousand times more amusing and experimental and productive than the little ideas of certain members of the OuLiPo. I regret above all that a mediocre type like Harry Mathews should have been permitted to set his heavy foot within the group, but then no doubt I have no right to tell you too much of my personal notions...

By day I work as an architect and by night I try to sleep. I translated Queneau's *Hundred Thousand Billion Poems*–Blavier wanted to publish them, but the text finally appeared in an English journal, *Prospice*, six years

* Barbara Wright (1915-2009) was the translator responsible for the majority of Raymond Queneau's work published in English, as well as a Regent of Shakespearean Zozology in the Collège de 'Pataphysique.

1. (Less hair, but whiter than ever...)

2. I had known him before, but I continued to know him at that moment!

3. Thanks to some publicity-seekers or curious formalists

ago, I think. Instead, Blavier published my long poem, *Eleven Thousand Verbs, One Hundred Commas*, which I wrote (quite inspired by the Hundred Thousand Billion) for some centenary celebration for Apollinaire. I believe these are the only verses truly inspired by Queneau's mathematical ideas.

Otherwise I have translated *Froth on the Daydream* and *Heartsnatcher* (also *Autumn in Peking*, which is waiting for a few edits and bit of courage (well, a lot) before coming out).

Surely I have translated (and written) other poems (and scribbled other drawings) here and there, but I forget which. A book just came out published by Georges Unglik, *The Songs of Boris Vian* (Christian Bourgois), in which you will find three awkward rock songs I tried to write with him almost thirty years ago (let's say twenty-five).

Have I written enough to make you happy, or is it too late for that?

And now there is a Yankee (Warren Motte–do you know him?) who has come knocking at my door. Will I ever do better than to send him a photocopy of this answer to your imaginary questions? Would you permit me to do so? In any event, I will not await your response, because I would never find the photocopy if I did.

Best wishes for what you are doing–but do not take the OuLiPo and its little games too seriously! The idea of a club (?) of friends and fans of Queneau was good and genial... the idea that their experiments have turned or will turn the world upside down is utterly mad.

Stanley Chapman
Regent of Epideictics

Published as *Les fous littéraires* in an indecorous multitude of editions, most notably for our purposes by Éditions des Cendres in 2000

Translated by Ian Monk

André Blavier

from

Literary Lunatics

1985

● This extract is taken from the postface to the final edition of *Les fous littéraires*, Blavier's continuation of Raymond Queneau's long-considered but finally abandoned project of assembling a compendium of literary madmen: writers who took themselves terribly seriously and were completely wrong about everything.

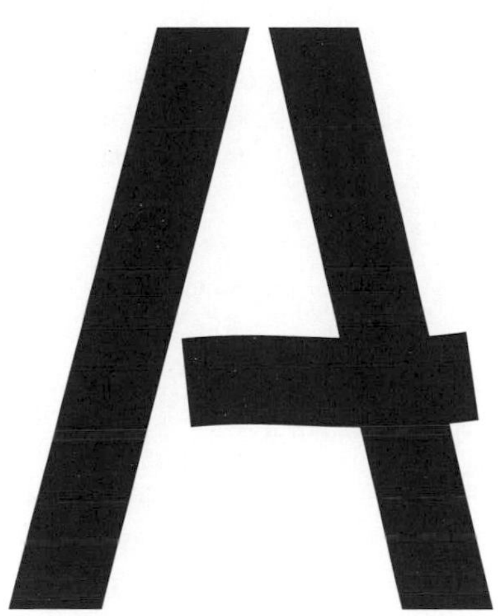

TO CONCLUDE…
III (CURVED BRACKETS) AND [SQUARE ONES]

Among the only too human in(s)ane agitations, the strangest one of all is perhaps (undoubtedly) the idea of working oneself up to publishing the result of one's cogitations, the product of one's meditations, or the fruit of one's imagination… Scarcely any more than a cyclone in the West Indies, an earthquake in Mexico City, or some (personal) impurity in Seveso: tiny disturbances in a world in which one grows bored and which does not become any more distinguished as a result.

It so happened, thus, that the poor beggar Chambernac inherited some money from an uncle, read Charles Nodier and a few psychopathologists, then encountered R.Q. on turning over a page (the 314th and antepenultimate), thus obtaining a unique documentation about "what has ever since been rightly termed literary lunatics."

What can be said about the failings of such gatherings [do not forget that there is nothing pejorative about the term "literary lunatic"]? And what can be posited, given

the occasional inability to define the frontier between literary lunatics, eccentrics, best-selling novelists, and precursors? It was Rivarol, the right-wing anarchist, who stated: "A man who is right twenty-four hours before everyone else is taken for a lunatic for twenty-four hours." However, for genuine literary lunatics [time, I fear, is not on their side], one wonders what should be done when, through the mistaken zeal of some saviors of old papers, such authors with convictions (so much so that they cannot be entirely bad) are deprived of their sole form of recognition: that is to say, none.

So it goes for Charles Menet, José Guardiola, Élias Molée, or A. Huart, who respectively offered a universal grammar of language (1866), the *Kosmal* (1893), the *Niuteutonish* (1906), and the *Médian* (1909); Brac de Bourdonnel, publishing in Lyon (1840) his *Preliminaries to Religious Astronomy*; or E. Miroir, who "refuted" Newton's system (Paris, 1831); or J.D. Mestivier, who "rehabilitated" that of Ptolemy (Orléans, 1841) while demonstrating that "the Sun is inferior in volume" to the Earth, and lies at a short distance from it; Émile Garreau, who "affirmed" the same system (Thouars, in 1894 and eight pages); Bernard Gillard, from Bordeaux, who waited until 1854 before "discovering" that the Earth does not rotate, while Antoine Myrian declared in Tulle in 1903 that *Newton's System Is False*; or the Chevalier de Maynard de la Claye, who proclaimed himself "the inspirational genius of the nineteenth century" (Luçon, 1844); or Maillard "prophesizing the beginning of all things and the eternal continuation"; or "I, Théophile Franklin, the people's man, the living truth," announcing to the French *The Destiny of Man* against "Jesuits of every stripe and charlatans of all colors" (Paris, 1850), or else Rivoire, "who sees what we were before the creation of the physical world, what we are during it, and what we shall be afterwards" (Lyon, 1870; this work was to be "divided into twenty-four chapters" but it seems that only the first one was published); or those circle-squarers unknown to Chambernac: for example, Nattes, who *mixtiphilogized* his solution in 1813, while G. Michuy proved his own version "experimentally in eight different ways" (Lyon, 1864); or else Th. Plaisant (Paris, 1815), Doctor Rouzé (1827), and

the Neapolitan Gaetano Rossi, who, between two odes to Napoleon, in 1806 and in French, claimed the prize on offer for a Solution [...] or else A. Mérault, who succeeded "without any calculations" (Paris, 1882) and Killyéni Donat Pàl (Paris, 1862), who dedicated his "to friends of perfection"; or else René Tison, who denounced "the three errors" which are space, mass, and time (Corbeil, 1937); or Monteau, who proved "the inexistence of light" (Reims, 1922), or J. Mangin, who described the *Tomb of Universal Attraction* (Verdun, 1826); or else Théodore Ricard, who had been "condemned falsely and oppressed to serving faithfully his fellow citizens and not betraying his fatherland" and who, from his native Ariège, fustigated the *State Employees Coalesced against the Legislative Preponderance* (1866, a single page); or Victor de Méaussé revealing in four pages the *Coup de Grâce against [His] Life and [His] Fortune in 1813: Ingratitude, Continuous Malevolence, Inhumanity*; or Doctor Loyal, who recounted "the daily poisoning of a doctor [himself] by his wife and children for thirty-two years" (Angers, 1893)–(less uptight, A. Hamot published in Asnières in 1891: *The Life of a Worker, This Work Containing a Notice about the Author's Place of Birth, his Autobiography, the Treatment of a Hernia and of a Few Other Conditions, with Useful Advice and Techniques, Followed by Authentic Anecdotes*); or Rignaut, a man of the people who intimated: *Read!!! The World Is Saved!... No More Poverty!...* (Paris, 1842, 4 p.); or P. Gosset, who regenerated the Parisian bakeries in 1854; or the fecund Gonzalve Frémin, whose *Idiocenism* (Montebourg, 1903) provided "the immediate solution to social problems through the equality of incomes"; or Papot, "the genius of Touraine," giving his support to the Republic (Poitiers, 1887); or Jules-Louis Hossard, condemning the conduct of his nephew, a water and forestry official, while singing the praises of orthopedics (Angers, 1863); or J.-B. Paifer, who multiplied his "opinions about the happiness of the world"; or Émile Lavy, "a soldier born in business," who published his *Mathematical Research into Just Government, or The Salvation of the State in the Material Order, through the Decimal Calculation of Values Accessible to Anyone Who Can Count* (Rocroi, 1833); or R. Destem the Elder offering "to all those whose mission it is to instruct

the people aloud or in writing" a "prompt, radical, infallible, and utterly parliamentary remedy to the plagues of reaction and subversion" (Paris, 1850, 1 p.); or finally Décajeul and his, among other works, *Overview of an Analytical Work in Fifty Chapters* [and fourteen pages!] *Concerning Questions of Great Interest for All People, Followed by Three Academic Discourses, Five Hundred Maxims, and a Literary Testament*; yes indeed, what to think of all these people who probably could (or should) have been part of the various sections of the other book that came out in 1982?

And even the *Asylum Condition* might include the twenty-four-page brochure that Adèle Lauzier published in 1845, under a less commanding title than the above Rignaut: *You Will Read Me, Won't You?* The request is moving: "It is at last time for me to *plead for my reason... my reflective will* has presided over all the actions that I have mentioned; I intended to try myself out against suffering when I applied a burning firebrand to my forehead, and, on another occasion, when I cut off the tip of my breast; I wanted to destroy myself on the day when I swallowed some aconite and was found hanging from a window; I wanted to destroy myself when for the first time I cast myself out of this window at a height of twenty feet; I wanted to destroy myself by throwing myself over a wall... and it was also to destroy myself that I attempted most of the actions that, over the past four years, have been used as a pretext to call me a madwoman... But, it might be asked, what was the motor of so many actions, which have left the same impression on so many minds? Do I need to answer this question so as to be convincing about my reasonable lucidity? In truth, I do not think so, and my conviction is that I can recover my place in society without having to herewith reveal the intimate cause that led me to suicide, nor that one which, in my present state of mind, has led me to abandon that project.

"Yes, today I lower that Sword of Damocles that I had suspended over my head. I will taste existence and am here to ask my contemporaries to give me their trust once more and believe in my reason...

"Will this prayer be heard?... Will I find again my place in the world?... Will I ever receive from those whom I esteem, in exchange for my thoughts, the cordial expression of theirs?... And will my friends once again reveal to me their souls?

Such are the questions that I am asking myself as I write these words!... But can I doubt it anymore?... So, how to convince you and persuade you?"

The time has come to repeat, along with Dr. Lucien Bonnafé: "The tragic and the burlesque when mingled together in unspeakable chaos color the public opinion of lunacy"... about which we still know nothing.

Originally published as "Les réflexions circulaires d'un insecte immobile" in *Insecte contemplant la préhistoire* (La Bibliothèque Oulipienne no. 31)

Translated by Daniel Levin Becker

Jean Queval

from

Circular Reflections from an Immobile Insect

1985

● In a fascicle of the Bibliothèque Oulipienne entitled *An Insect Contemplates Prehistory (Followed by Six No Less Rousing Exegeses)*, Jean Queval offers various unpublished writings spanning his twenty-two years of Oulipianhood.

1. Upon reading the *Hundred Thousand Billion Poems* for the third or fourth time, what remains most astonishing is that this machine is a Queneau machine. The guests who have used it–this is Queneau's own anecdote–obviously did not make their own poems, but neither did they make impersonal poems: they made Queneau's poems.

In my opinion any attempt to cross-check this proof, which would be a kind of literary casting out nines, would lead to the same conclusion. If Jacques Bens constructed an identical machine, it would be a rival machine–a Bens machine. It would have more than just the "mark" of the Bens "brand": it would have the Bens style, which is, finally, the style of an author. Instead of making Queneau poems, its operators would make Bens poems.

I do not intend to demonstrate this proposition, which in any case is probably not demonstrable. The question is one of literary sensibility. If one accepts the existence of a literary sensibility, one must accept the legitimacy of non-demonstration. I mean rigorous demonstration.

To admit the very little that has been proposed up to this point is to admit something that is not, perhaps, uninteresting: that in the literary attempt to efface literature–understanding literature as a manifestation of the individuality principle–literature emerges once more, defined once again by the individuality principle.

2. After considering the *Hundred Thousand Billion Poems*, to consider the novel is to go from the narrowest possible opening in the individuality principle to the widest.

What is a novel? At first glance, there are so many genres of novel that it is altogether impossible to define the novel. There is the picaresque novel, the historical novel, the epic novel, the analytical novel, the spy novel, the social science fiction novel, the romantic novel, the naturalist novel, the didactic novel, the documentary novel, the sociocomic novel, the rural novel, the regional novel, the autobiographical novel, the atmospheric novel, the demotic novel, the Proustian novel, the Joycean novel, the sequential novel, the "new novel," the fantasy novel, the hardboiled detective novel. This enumeration is summary and purely indicative, and it should be understood that each of these designations is much less definition than signpost. It may not even be possible to usefully define any "genre" of novel. It is not even clear that we would come any closer to such a definition if we abandoned historical categories (romanticism, naturalism, etc.) and returned to terminology presupposing a literary specificity, like *fable* or *argument* or *tale* or *farce* or *short story*, etc.

3. There are other ways to approach the matter. We could contrast the prose novel with the original verse novel, such as *The Song of Roland*. It is worth noting, in passing, both that the novel is not always in prose, and also that there is, if you like, a sort of

broken tradition of verse novels spanning from *The Song of Roland* to Queneau's *Chêne et chien*, with intermediary recurrences; in English, Philip Toynbee has undertaken a trilogy that obeys the ancient fixed form of the sestina.

Or we could–to use a perspective more easily accessible to the oulipian mindset–contrast the "inspired" novel (*e.g.*, Céline) with the "artificial" novel (*e.g.*, Roussel).

We may ask where these seemingly disjointed remarks are leading. My aim is only to offer a general commentary about the novel before advancing some oulipian propositions about the novel–which "commentary" will itself be as brief as an admission of helplessness. The novel can hardly be defined any way but negatively. Even this negative definition must be prudent. We cannot say, for example, that the novel is not poetry. (The novel that is not poetry is not the novel; the novel that is not poetry is nothing.) Nor is it possible, as we have just seen, to say that the novel is not versification. Perhaps the most we can say is that the novel is not a didactic lecture.

The positive counterpart of this negative definition is not a rich one. Let us limit ourselves to the following declaration: a novel is a story. We might add, proudly, that it takes a certain minimum number of pages. (Otherwise we have only a short story or a tale.)

4. These definitions are social. The social definition of the novel expands the foregoing remarks to the point of comical aberration. For what is a novel according to a professional society and according to a consumer society? In truth, the answer of the professionals and that of the consumers is identical, and it is not delicate: a novel is whatever nonsense passes for a novel. This generosity of approach engenders a particular flavor. When I want to motivate myself to tell my own stories, I willingly recall this declaration by Christian Rochefort: "Me, I'm Queneauing."

And so, in saying that "a novel is a story," we have not defined the novel any differently from the way

the society of professionals (itself understood in sum as the union of publishers, authors' collectives, etc.) or the mass of consumers defines it.

Since we are talking about literature, we must now distinguish literature as such from the product meant purely for consumption: printed matter in its most profound lack of differentiation. All of this is overwhelmingly self-evident, but unfortunately not so simple to escape. It is so far from simple, in fact, that we would fail in our attempt to draw dividing lines by title. The question is explored, in any case, and rightfully so, within the pages of the Encyclopédie de la Pléïade devoted to related literatures, marginal literatures, aberrant literatures, etc.

5. In our desire to distinguish between literature and printed matter, we confront the difficulty, and ultimately the impossibility, of rigorous ("scientific") definitions. Nonetheless, no matter what definition we wish to submit as a working hypothesis (and no matter what course the dividing line takes), the distinction is affirmed by common sense. I have not found a better articulation of this affirmation (nor a simpler one, nor a more usable one) than in the essay on "Game and Technique" in *Letters, Numbers, Forms*.

Queneau summarizes therein everything I have just tried to say. One cannot, he writes, push a head of cattle across an arid landscape and say, Here is a novel. Better, in the place of that recklessness, to impose upon oneself a game, the rules of a game. A method. A discipline.

Three remarks:

a. This brings us out of the mire, leaving behind impossible definitions (and also the somewhat comical approximations of comparative literature specialists, etc.) while affirming the creative will of literature. So bravo!

b. This is not all there is to say about the composition of the novel.

Queneau himself...

Let us explain. When Queneau himself began working on *The Bark Tree*, what he set up was a game of literary construction: "game and technique." Still, the application of rules presupposes their application *to* something. The author has "something" to say.

Once again, overwhelmingly self-evident, but necessary for the argument nonetheless.

c. Perhaps I have not strayed too much from the first lines of these pages. What I was trying to say there was that no matter how impersonal a text is meant to be, the author inevitably (can we say "in spite of himself"?) emerges. What I am trying to say here is that the same individuality principle emerges at the other extremity of the spectrum: that is, in the choice of a story's "subject." In other words—this proposition is modest but, to my mind, no less central for it—one cannot erase the role of "inspiration"; one can only suggest the implementation of rules to discipline it. We may affirm, in the search for such rules for such goals, the utility of a workshop for potential literature.

(Naturally, such a workshop has served, and will continue to serve, other purposes as well.)

6. The problem with slightly general declarations is that when one tries to articulate them honestly they lead to a kind of verbal incontinence, which must be rectified incessantly. (Hence the agonized loquacity of the philosophers, but anyway.)

I found myself caught in that trap when I wrote "inspiration," for which reason I beg a bit of indulgence for the following parenthesis, as it were, on the subject.

I was surprised—let us say somewhat surprised, so as not to get carried away with the oratory mode—to hear the Oulipo deny the very notion of inspiration. I do not know whether psychology is equipped to demonstrate that there is inspiration, of one sort or another, in Roussel and in Céline alike; if it were, it would show obviously that different effects, accessible by different means, are produced by different channels and processes—by psychologies of inspiration.

These definitions themselves are likely suspect (once again, not so simple to escape). It is still not clear exactly what it is, this "inspiration." But all the same, as long as there are such things as an individuality principle consubstantial with all literature and a literary sensibility, how can we deny the existence of "inspiration"?

I will not insist that we proclaim it—quite the contrary. There is much to be gained by keeping it quiet. There remain, then, two recourses.

One is to put it in quotation marks. "Inspiration."

The other is to file the word "inspiration" in the category of blank words—words whose effect, to recall the intelligent distinction made by Claude Berge (at my expense, no less), is more white noise than black.

7. Continuation of the above "parenthesis."

The reasons for putting the word "inspiration" in quotation marks can be said to be—in France, anyway—historical. There was the romantic muse, then the era of the artist-painter with big hat and floppy necktie. We might wonder whether these attitudes were not byproducts of, reactions against, a bourgeois society. It is also interesting to note here the bourgeoisie's double perspective: on one hand, its scorn for the young man who dreams of pursuing a marginal vocation; on the other, the frequency (in conversation, for instance) with which inspiration, in the worst white noise sense of the word, appears as a typical bourgeois prejudice.

It seems well advised to steer clear of romantic attitudes. It is difficult, in any case, to imagine assuming them in our modern era. An element of modesty in terms of personal morality obtains as well: any remarkable literary creator is, in essence, and in the final "zero-hour" analysis, just as much of a poor slob as anyone else. This may be the sole reason we lust for glory.

Jacques Prévert once said to Léger and Picasso: "You are not great painters. You are good painters."

8. Continuation of the continuation of the above or adjacent parenthesis.

There remains the matter of modesty, of what could be said to be the modesty of the Oulipo. We have all been in agreement that the Oulipo is not a "literary movement" but rather a working research group.

Literary movements are implicitly armed, it would seem, with an exterminatory will. In France, they become terrorisms. These terrorisms are the work of monomaniacs. "All that remains is to..." The only writing can be automatic. The literature of the future will be descriptive. The creator of literature must be *engagé*.

The braggarts who would claim to reinvent the wheel have nonetheless initiated something, in principle, in the form of different good books. And there need be no question of exterminating the exterminators. We know that the proclamations of monomaniacs are quickly dissolved among unplanned-for works. If we defined the "new novel" after and within its various excrescences, its definition would diverge sharply from the definition given it by the self-appointed theorists.

So the Oulipo is not a literary movement. And good for it.

Nonetheless, we must not let its research work take on a character that denies others their "inspiration." Kindly indulge two simple statements:

The origin of the literary work is of little importance.

Literature is the largest house.

Nothing in the origin of Simenon's work is oulipian. I recall, however, that one of us (and not the least, though for that matter there is no least of us) paid him a superlative spoken compliment (in his absence) (obviously).

Nothing in the origin of André Dhôtel's* literary work is oulipian. (On the subject of André Dhôtel we should put no small trust in the Oulipian giving this address, who has read everything by this author.)

Or we could approach it differently.

The former "great" novelist leads us to believe that there is nothing much under the sun. The latter "great" novelist leads us to believe that there is everything (or almost). There are marvels to be found in the work of one as in the work of the other; in any case, I have found them.

Literature is the largest house.

Our research work will be ignored by remarkable literary creators.

The Oulipo will not be any weaker for not being imperialistic.

In my opinion, amen, and end of the parenthesis.

* André Dhôtel (1900–1991) was an author from the Ardennes whose bibliography includes forty novels and dozens of books of stories, poems, and essays.

Originally published as
Cinquante poèmes oscillatoires
(La Bibliothèque Oulipienne
no. 35, 1986)

Translated by
Daniel Levin Becker

Michèle Métail

Fifty Oscillatory Poems

1986

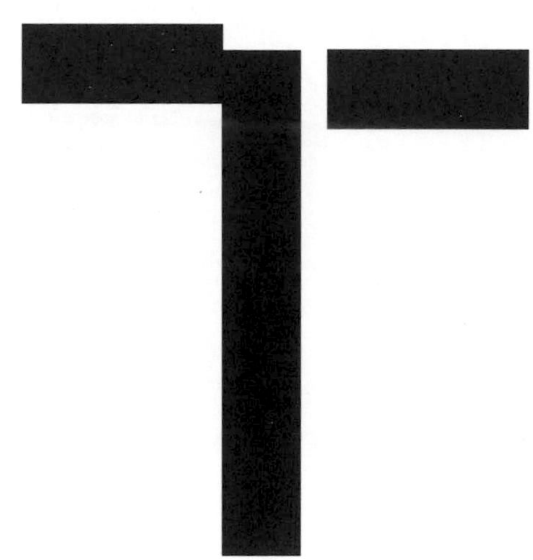

The constraint applied in these "Fifty Oscillatory Poems" is inspired by the practice of "parallelism" in far-Eastern poetry, which compels lines to respond to one another in echo, term by term. Oppositions and complementarities are rarely semantic, but more often symbolic. In attempting to adopt a less subjective stance, I have chosen to work with antonyms and synonyms, difficult though these notions are to define. For instance, some dictionaries suggest *metropolis* or *city* as an antonym for *desert*; I think of the desert as defined rather by its absence of vegetation rather than its absence of buildings, so I prefer notions such as *forest* or *copse*. Moreover, most words do not have antonyms, particularly those that belong to the domain of concrete things. Finally, I have voluntarily avoided classical oppositions like *good/bad* or *black/white*, and never used the same word twice.

Each poem is a quatrain in which each line is a group:

> *adjective* + *noun* or
> *past participle* + *noun*

● A Sinologist, Michèle Métail brought to the Oulipo a perspective on eastern poetic traditions along with other formal innovations such as the watermark, which, like the oscillatory poem, surrounds an often absent word or concept with a penumbra of semantic associations.

to the exclusion of all other words (verbs, pronouns, etc.). Each poem obeys the structure:

N: *noun*
A1: *antonym of noun*
S: *synonym of noun*
A2: *antonym of noun*

A1 and A2 are synonyms; S is an antonym of A1 and A2.

It is interesting to note that the juxtaposition of an adjective will sometimes reinforce the opposition of synonym and antonym, and sometimes, conversely, destroy it.

* * *

steep gulf
accessible summit
abrupt precipice
easy peak

arid projection
clammy recess
dried relief
humid cavity

sensual apogee
ascetic perigee
carnal zenith
austere nadir

hasty pall
slow star
prompt cloud
resting planet

indecisive daring
voluntary hindrance
uncertain ease
resolute bother

immediate succession
postponed simultaneity
imminent continuation
delayed concomitance

distinct core
ambiguous border
precise center
equivocal circumference

ponderous warmth
light chill
heavy heat
lively cold

scattered sunshine
dense darkening
strewn clarity
compact dimness

limpid stream
muddy lake
transparent torrent
hazy pond

fixed rupture
animated juncture
dismal break
ardent fusion

fluid decline
formal momentum
vague ruin
neat boom

apparent oscillation
hidden immobility
perceptible agitation
secret fixity

vain reality
fruitful fiction
futile evidence
fecund illusion

sinuous darkness
stable brightness
motive nebulousness
constant glimmer

ruffled burst
polished mass
rugged crack
smooth block

diaphanous discernment
opaque confusion
translucent order
impenetrable chaos

oppressive eclipse
minute reappearance
crushing occultation
imperceptible rise

pernicious maintenance
opportune disruption
irritating permanence
favorable suspension

occult vacillation
licit conviction
clandestine doubt
public certitude

austral air
boreal storm
southerly breeze
northerly cyclone

acute contraction
weak distension
intense twitch
lax dilation

melancholy breakup
taciturn courtship
nostalgic parting
somber convergence

resurgent emptiness
sunken plenitude
gushing vacuity
submerged integrity

shrill acuity
discreet blindness
gaudy sagacity
reserved distraction

placid gentleness
moving acridity
calm suavity
troubled bitterness

restrained shore
extended coast
limited bank
vast ocean

faded nuance
pronounced contrast
discolored tonality
sustained opposition

brusque east
gradual west
sudden north
progressive south

split obstacle
entire latitude
broken barrier
intact license

irrevocable inclination
provisional aplomb
definitive obliquity
momentary verticality

outspread enjoyment
compressed distress
dilated pleasure
narrow pain

unusual occurrence
common divergence
strange coincidence
ordinary difference

hesitant draft
convinced completion
reticent sketch
sure accomplishment

alert rise
brittle fall
agile mount
numb crumble

ample eddy
cramped slide
wide whirlwind
crimped flow

frank necessity
dissembled contingency
loyal exigency
sly eventuality

free mutation
submissive stability
emancipated conversion
dependent continuity

gravitational slowness
repulsive celerity
attractive weight
repugnant vivacity

distant dusk
tangent dawn
faraway nightfall
nearby daybreak

languid torpor
zealous spirit
indolent lethargy
attentive ardor

blunt obstinacy
affable docility
surly tenacity
affable submission

blazing mound
chilly valley
volcanic hillock
extinguished plain

prolix accord
succinct refusal
diffuse assent
concise rebuff

partial eviction
total retention
fragmentary rejection
absolute hold

derisory wave
remarkable drop
insignificant tide
imposing leak

immutable separation
fluctuant union
invariant dispersion
changing alliance

penetrating erosion
obtuse filling
perspicacious attrition
hidebound embankment

unmovable desert
variable thicket
durable steppe
precarious forest

terrestrial simulation
astral truth
telluric feint
sidereal authenticity

Originally published as "Un bilboquet d'ébène à boule d'ivoire" in *L'infini*

Translated by Daniel Levin Becker

Marcel Bénabou

Ebony Cup and Ivory Ball

1987

I'll admit it, the first time I read—or perhaps in fact I only heard it read aloud, that day, by one of my friends (but in that case which one?) during one of those learned meetings where, a glass of wine in hand (or sometimes, occasionally, a glass of vodka or tequila), we loved to put into practice the communitarian ideal that still bound us (and which did not find many other occasions to manifest itself in our overly comfortable lives as erudite apprentices) and share with the elected few in our number the pleasure of our most recent literary or philosophical or artistic discoveries—the first time, in any case, that I read or heard read (this detail is ultimately of little importance, except insofar as it signals a rare lapse in my memory) the famous *Cup and Ball* monologue by Charles Cros (a writer whose name was so unfamiliar to me that I still wasn't entirely sure of the correct way to spell or pronounce it), it was not a fit of giggles, the overall reaction provoked by that strange exemplar of a humor to which I still know of no analogue, that overtook me. My reaction was much more restrained. Or even, to be completely candid, rather ambivalent. Oh, of course I laughed. Hard

● The French title of this vignette, "Un bilboquet d'é**bène à bou**le d'ivoire," subtly encloses a phonetic equivalent of its author's last name: a trick borrowed from Perec's *Life A User's Manual*, whose text contains echoes of the names of all the Oulipians at the time.

not to. But I would hardly have been pleased if someone had asked me on the spot to justify my laughter. I wouldn't have known what to say, and almost certainly would have swallowed my merriment, sheepish and contrite. Because I did not manage, in spite of those thick threads of farce that seemed to have no purpose but to impose the sempiternal lessons of defiance and derision, to find anything ridiculous about the hero of the story.

Recall, if you will. A man consumed by a singular passion, an amateur fixated to the point of fanaticism, and even slightly beyond, on a cup-and-ball game. He has elevated this innocent game (which consists, as everyone knows, of trying to join the round end of a long wooden rod and the orifice, fashioned for this purpose, of a large roving ball) to the rank of high art. But, in spite of years of veritable asceticism, during which he has accepted in good faith the need to subordinate each moment of his life to the demands of a forced unlearning, he has not managed to reach the heights of rigor and perfection to which he aspires. And, with a despair that grows each day, he discovers the vertiginous abyss of his own incompetence.

For my part, though I was hardly ignorant of the ways in which such an interpretation could (at least in the eyes of those who seemed best acquainted with the arcana of Cros's thought) be greeted as heretical, even downright unseemly, I was not far from finding in this character a pathetic grandeur, one which hoisted him to the ranks of Sisyphus and Don Quixote, or which, more aptly still, made him, harnessed as he was to the obstinate quest for a perfection that would lead him only into martyrdom, a sort of Prometheus who has become his own vulture.

At the time I did not yet know that there existed an earlier version of this major text, published in September 1873 in *The Literary and Artistic Renaissance*, whereas the definitive version would not appear until 1877 in the collective volume *Sketches and Monologues* (second series). But when I discovered it, some years later, in the Pauvert *Complete Works* of Cros (a huge volume whose unusual, almost square format and numerous illustrations–in particular various manuscripts reproduced in facsimile–had initially caught my attention), it seemed likely to only bolster my initial impression.

This version contained some unpublished fragments. I found in it, with the joy you would imagine, such formulations as *amounting to nothing is the purpose of all human effort* or *keep working, always, and you are sure to arrive at discouragement*. Formulations whose potent pessimism—beyond anticipating one of the strongest tenets of Marxist thought (evidently I am referring to Groucho, who has not suffered, quite the contrary, from the widespread contemporary rejection of the other Marx)—seemed to refer directly to this or that page from Flaubert's correspondence, or, better yet, to the very essence of the Mallarméan message. From that moment on, in my eyes, there was no further possibility of doubt.

This player of the cup-and-ball game, for whom my fraternal sympathy grew with each new reading, this perfectionist with an arm tetanized by a surfeit of exercise, had quite simply been, quietly, since time immemorial, my model, the perfect hero of my dreams, as close to my heart as were my two dearest travel companions of many years, Frédéric Moreau and Frédéric Amiel. I finally understood why, since our first encounter, I had reacted to him (proportionally speaking, of course) just as Rousseau or Musset had to the character of Alceste.

To be sure, our respective games were not at all of the same order. But they differ less, perhaps, than one might believe a priori. It did not take me long to discover, for instance, that my instrument was not so far off from his. His was (you will certainly recall, even if the symbolism has not been a boon to you as it has to me) a Schutzenberger cup of ebony with an ivory ball—that is, a slender black shaft and a large white sphere. Now, what was I myself doing for all these years if not trying, night after night, to bring forth the meeting of a bit of black and a lot of white? In this subtle admixture the old Persian poet Kisai (and Mallarmé too, long after) had found an inkling of the very essence of writing: such a difficult skill, I was discovering, to get right. Over time I have become quite certain, like my hero, that one cannot practice such an art unless one is perfectly convinced of one's radical inability to master even its most elementary rudiments.

There remains between us, nonetheless, a small difference, perhaps the only advantage conferred on me by the

long century that separates us. I am no longer committed to the task of demonstrating to anyone, whether to drive him to despair or to cure him of it, the depths of my own cup-and-ball game. Nor, moreover, do I become indignant anymore at the sight of a few small boys—novices, barely grown, still unaware of the necessity of uniting a Schutzenberger handle and a Cascarini ball—making a spectacle of themselves like tightrope walkers, and attracting, by a careful succession of acrobatic feats, the admiration of the somnolent crowds of a Sunday evening.

Originally published as "Comment raconter une histoire" in *Nouvelles désenchantées* (Seghers)

Translated by Daniel Levin Becker

Jacques Bens

How to Tell a Story

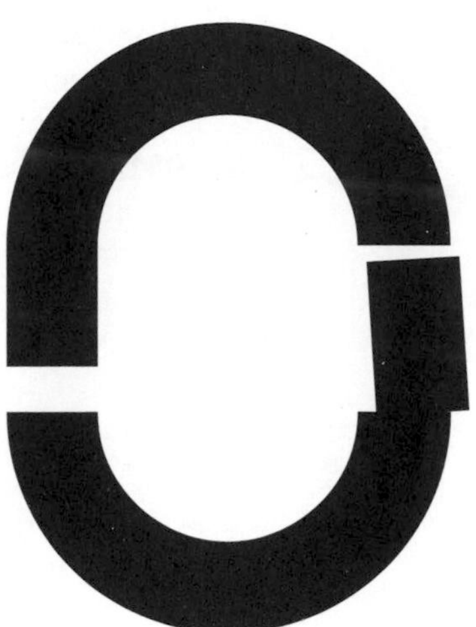

1990

● For *Nouvelles désenchantées*, or disenchanted tales, Jacques Bens, who served as the Oulipo's secretary for several years before leaving Paris, was awarded the Prix Goncourt for short stories.

On Tuesday, April 25, 1989—which was the Feast of Saint Mark, one of the four evangelists and, accordingly, one of the patron saints of writers—at around ten past two, a student in sixth grade at the Collège Saint-Jean raised her hand and asked:

"How does one go about telling a story?"

Matthew had not been expecting this.

"Which story?" he said.

"I don't know, just a story!"

"Well, that's just it, you need to know, because not all stories are told in the same way. Look, let's take the first idea that comes to your mind. It might be about a situation, or about a character. The story would develop differently depending on which. And usually you have both at the same time, because it's rare to have one without the other. Then you have to give your hero a name, which is always sort of complicated. What's your name?"

"Evelyn."

"Right, you see, *that* doesn't work. If you were to name one of your characters Evelyn, you would eventually wind up writing something like *As he walked in,*

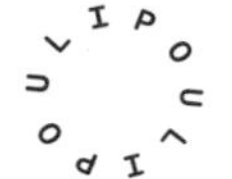

Evelyn followed him with her eyes, which… I mean, can you imagine? *In-in-im*? It's just not possible. And it would be even worse with a name like William, for instance. You try saying *William wondered what to wear*. All those *W* sounds! It's like a story for a stutterer."

Matthew went on in this fashion for some time, dodging the real answers, which he did not know.

Eventually, thank heavens, someone changed the subject.

On the way back to his apartment on rue Xavier-de-Montépin, Matthew brooded over his irritation.

"I just couldn't find an answer," he said to himself, "which is a disgrace, given a question so simple and innocent. True enough, there are thirty-six ways to tell a story, but I mean honestly. You have to start somewhere, that's obvious, but where? Where do you *start*?"

Gesticulating to himself, he crossed the place Ponson-du-Terrail, named for a nineteenth-century French man of letters. He gave a spiteful little kick to an empty (*an apparently empty*) pack of cigarettes, which slid to a stop at the foot of the writer's statue.

"You can start from something true (seen), or semi-true (read), or imagined (neither seen nor read). Let's take an example. (It is always necessary to take examples.) A minor, apparently anodyne fact of everyday life, an insignificant event no one is meant to notice. From there, you see, the imagination goes to work."

Simon crossed the place Ponson-du-Terrail on the way to his house on rue Paul-Féval. The merchants from the farmer's market had already folded up their boards and put away their overalls, their twill vests and tablemats, packed up their fish and tripe and cheeses. A municipal water cart was spraying water from its tank, chasing chippings of crates and scraps of wrapping paper and bits of fruit and vegetable peels toward the sewers.

In the middle of the grounds, on the stone border encircling the monument erected to the glory of the author who had dreamed up the character of Rocambole, sat a young woman of maybe twenty. On her knees, supported by a wide strap slung around her shoulders, she had a little barrel organ and was turning its crank slowly. An unusual air was coming from the box: the second lied of "A Woman's Life and Love," it seemed.

Simon stopped near the musician.

"Do you play this song often?" he asked, smiling.

The girl nodded her head up and down.

"It's strange to hear a Schumann piece on a barrel organ," he said.

She shrugged her shoulders, still grinding.

"Do you have any others in the same style?"

She shook her head from left to right.

"Pity," murmured Simon.

He stayed and listened for a minute longer. He rummaged in his pockets in search of an unlikely ten-franc coin. (He had fed the last one to a parking meter an hour before.) And yet he found one. It was then that he noticed that the organ player did not seem to be asking for any charity: no hat, no beggar's bowl, no outstretched hand.

He put the coin back in his pocket, where it clinked against a second. He took them both out and examined them. They were Roland Garros commemorative coins and they shone as if new. He put them back in his pocket, where they jingled against a third.

Troubled, Simon moved on.

Matthew took a right onto avenue Jules-Verne. A sickly sun was shining. In spite of the early spring weather, the tavern owners had brought tables out onto the sidewalk, where a few patrons were shivering over a premature aperitif.

"I know: the imagination doesn't work arbitrarily. The fellow who finds himself inhabited by this modest but curious alchemy is bound to uphold his tastes, his aversions, his learnings, his loves, his fears, his flaws. He'll take the whole world that comes to life and takes shape and bristles beneath his pen and push it in a certain direction. If one pulls a knife from his pocket and the other pulls out a five-franc coin, it's because that's what

the author wanted them to do. Now, me, I can't stand people who carry knives, so there you go. Criticize me for it all you want, but I won't try to change."

The terrace of the Cynthia, on avenue Jules-Verne, was half full. A young couple and a child of six had taken the last table on the left. The two adults were drinking beer (hers mixed with lemonade), the child a green liquid through a rainbow straw. One meter away, standing in the corner of a carriage porch, the organ player was cranking her crank.

Simon noticed her with a certain surprise: how had she arrived before him? He had come straight there, without dawdling. There was an open table not far away. He sat down and ordered a lemon Mandarin.

This time the organ was bleating out a slow waltz by Maurice Jaubert, better suited to the ambiance than her last selection. While he waited for his aperitif, Simon cast a nonchalant glance at his neighbors. The child was working hard at his straw, so hard his cheeks were swelling. After a moment, he let go of his glass and considered it with suspicion, then turned to his parents with a worried look. To all appearances, the level of the emerald liquid had not gone down at all.

"Anyway," continued Matthew, still gesticulating, "the majority of ideas fly away."

He passed by the post office on rue Louis-Desnoyers without looking around him.

"If you're lucky enough to pick up the trail of an idea, that's because it's weighed down, flying low, loaded with fog or rain."

He looked up toward the sky (still clear), and stumbled because of it.

"In the end, I might say that an idea is like one of those hoops we used to push around when we were children. You guide it with a stick and steer it right or left, as the mood moves you. You can even force it up an incline. And then an unexpected bump in the landscape comes along and there it goes, escaping your will, your desires.

But in that case there's nothing to stop you from letting it fall into a hole and going to find another one. Ideas are a dime a dozen."

The third time Simon crossed the organist's path it was near the post office on rue Louis-Desnoyers. She was sitting on the rustic bench of a bus shelter and appeared to be intently observing a peddler on the other side of the street, who was showing off the merits of a new kind of laundry detergent.

Simon walked up to her and almost spoke to her, but she seemed not to see him. After a few seconds, she took the crank of her instrument and began turning it with a graceful movement of her wrist. A 1930s polka, light and lively, flowed from the wooden box.

That same instant, laughter and cries of admiration erupted from across the street. Simon looked up reflexively and was rather less than surprised to find that, each time he opened his mouth, the washing-powder salesman sent soap bubbles flying into the air.

"So then," said Matthew to himself, "then you develop the story by simply moving from one idea to another, along a chain of causes and effects."

Through the open window of a child's playroom he noticed a boy of twelve or so, seated near a low table, putting the finishing touches on a chain of dominos. There were at least fifty of them. The builder's movements were slow and he appeared prodigiously absorbed in his meticulous task.

Matthew stopped. His shadow fell across the carpet of the playroom. The child raised his head and smiled at him, then, with a delicate flick, tipped the first domino over. The whole line collapsed in turn, the sound like a clattering of bones.

Matthew winked admiringly and moved on.

"And that's the principle of the hoop: you point it toward the least uneven terrain, the smoothest ground, where all you have to do is push. It's purely a question of work; you just need to know how it's done. You can even choose different trajectories at the outset: realistic, tender, fantastical, burlesque, terrifying. The hard part is seeing it through without abandoning the genre you chose. Well, no, but you're allowed to mix it up also. What I mean is you can't *cheat*, can't pull a rabbit out of your hat at the last minute.

"Bandits," he murmured. "Scoundrels. Where do they come *up* with it all?"

Simon saw the organ player three more times: in front of the former corn exchange, now the tourism office (from an old-style fire hydrant on the nearby sidewalk there wafted light wisps of bluish smoke that smelled of burning birch); while crossing the square in front of the basilica (nothing amiss about the surroundings at first glance); then near the public library on rue Achille-Chavée (a hideous rat with a cap on its head scurried out, pursued by a hideous cat in a floral shirt; they disappeared through the window of the basement next door).

There was, however, a seventh time: when Simon arrived at his own door on rue Paul-Féval, the girl was already there. She was playing a plaintive ballad that sounded like Delmet. Simon approached her.

"Have you been waiting for me?" he asked gently.

She nodded her head in the affirmative.

He took a key from his pocket. It flew out of his fingers and lodged itself in the lock, and the door opened. Simon sighed.

"Come on in," he said.

She followed him.

Simon lived in a narrow three-level house with two rooms per floor. At the ground level he had installed a vast office, where he spent most of his time.

"Have a seat," he said.

On the side facing the street, a French window looked out onto a little overgrown garden.

The girl put her instrument down and perched timidly on the edge of a chair.

"What can I do for you?" asked Simon.

She looked at him without answering.

"You can't speak?"

She shook her head no.

"But you understand me?"

She nodded yes.

"Yes, of course. Can you write?"

Yes.

"Well, that's a start," Simon murmured.

He approached a cluttered table, found a pencil and a pad of paper, and offered them to the visitor.

"Explain yourself."

She hesitated for a few seconds, then, with a decisive air, began to write.

With a hesitant hand, Matthew began to write.

In front of him, on the other side of the window, an old ivy-covered apple tree was preparing to flower.

"You have to get out," he thought, "out of the story. You can imagine whatever you want. There are no limits, except this one: how do I get out of there? Sometimes you can't, when you've wandered into a maze of questions or adventures with no exit, and it's better to just abandon it."

A little pied woodpecker with a red head and a body dappled with black and white landed on the top branch of the apple tree, sharpened its beak, and began hammering away at the dilapidated bark.

"The unexpected can occur, of course. So long as it remains within the logic of things."

Matthew stroked his chin with his left hand. It rustled. He hadn't shaved properly that morning.

"The logic of things! Do things really *have* a logic, beyond what the teller of the story believes and perceives?"

At that moment the door on the right of his office opened. A young girl came in, a brunette, rather tall and thin, with a long face, a luscious mouth, and blue-gray eyes. It was the barrel organ player, without her organ. She was wearing a skirt and a sweater, and she was smiling.

"Now he wants to marry me," she said. "Curious, don't you think?"

"No," said Matthew. "Well, maybe. I don't know. What do you think?"

She shrugged her shoulders in a doubtful gesture.

"Seems to me like it's all moving a little fast. Like I must be missing an element somewhere."

"Yes, something is missing, that much is clear. But where? And what?"

"Well, he doesn't displease me. He's not very good-looking, but he seems nice. Like you, actually. Don't you think?"

"Let's not exaggerate," muttered Matthew.

The girl raised her eyes toward the ceiling and kept them there for a pensive moment.

"Not right away, anyway," she murmured.

He laughed fondly.

"No, not right away. But it's an idea all the same. An idea that hadn't occurred to me. Lots of stories end with a marriage. They're not the worst thing. In general, they make everyone happy. And I like making people happy."

"I know you do," said the young lady.

At the top of the apple tree, the bird let out a furious cackle, flapped its wings, and took off in the direction of other adventures.

This story certainly seemed to want to end here.

Originally published as *Les bibliothèques invisibles* (La Bibliothèque Oulipienne no. 48)

Translated by Daniel Levin Becker

Paul Braffort

from

Invisible Libraries

1990

● Among the multidimensional essays in which Paul Braffort (often in tandem with Walter Henry, an independent scholar in the field of Paul Braffort studies) surveys the historical, scholarly, and cultural wavelengths surrounding the Oulipo, this one indulges the group's deep fascination with the library as a real and conceptual entity, sometimes both at once. Some of the titles herein have, evidently, been adapted for an English readership.

On the ladder of literary objects, the rarest rung is surely that of the library. In truth, everything beyond the book is generally ignored. Indeed, as far as truly analytical research is concerned, we have barely surpassed the level of the sentence, perhaps even that of the word. The first uses of information technology in the literary world were consigned to the creation of concordances, a project essentially lexicographical in nature. Grammarians confine themselves to the level of the syntagma, evidently, and more rarely that of the sentence. Recently specialists of "textual linguistics" reached the level of the paragraph, using a short newspaper article. Stories and novels are, as we know, the objects of innumerable scholarly studies whose rigor cannot be entirely ensured. All of this has led me to focus my efforts on the "ultraviolet" of the spectrum—to look beyond the work, beyond even the series of works, to the library, the collection of libraries, etc. Needless to say, we remain within the framework of *printed* text objects.

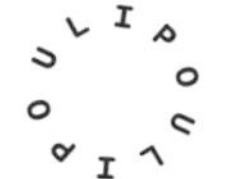

1. IMAGINARY LIBRARIES

We speak readily of real and visible libraries such as the Bibliothèque de l'Arsenal and the Bibliothèque historique de la Ville de Paris, the British Library in London, the Newberry Library in Chicago, and so on; we also make reference to private libraries, when a sale breaks one up. But too often we neglect libraries that are hidden and invisible because they are potential–or even imaginary. And yet these are the only ones that lend themselves to this elevated level of textual organization and to the possibility for artistic expression.

I shall illustrate this observation with some examples of different kinds of invisible libraries: potential or genuinely imaginary, including those whose constituent elements, the works themselves, have not been written (or at the very least not yet).

1.1 IMAGINARY REAL LIBRARIES

These are made up of verifiable (and generally well known) works of literature, owned by a literary character. A canonical example is the set of twenty-seven "peer books"–including Baudelaire's translation of Edgar Allan Poe, Coleridge's *Rime of the Ancient Mariner*, and Schwob's *The Children's Crusade*–that constitute the library of Jarry's Dr. Faustroll and are involved in the booking and confiscation at his home, 205 rue Nicolas Flamel.

1.2. REAL IMAGINARY LIBRARIES

These are series of works whose titles and/or authors are imaginary but which are cited in real works, such as the library referenced in the "Six documents serving as a canvas" in Raymond Roussel's final book, *How I Wrote Certain of My Books*:

Claude Bonnal, *The Conquest of Algeria*
Cratus, *The Light Red Colossus*
Erroi, *Grigou's Siesta*

... and so on. Particularly refined is the imaginary library constituted by the list in *Look at the Harlequins* by Vladimir Nabokov, which I will reproduce hereafter:

OTHER BOOKS BY THE NARRATOR:

IN RUSSIAN:
Tamara, 1925.
Pawn Takes Queen, 1927.
Plenilune, 1929.
Camera Lucida (Slaughter in the Sun), 1931.
The Red Top Hat, 1934.
The Dare, 1950.

IN ENGLISH:
See under Real, 1939.
Esmeralda and Her Parandrus, 1941.
Dr. Olga Repnin, 1946.
Exile from Mayda, 1947.
A Kingdom by the Sea, 1962.
Ardis, 1970.

We may appreciate the echoes between this library and the list of actual works by Nabokov.

1.3. POTENTIAL LIBRARIES

These libraries are made up of imaginary works but whose titles are constructed using oulipian procedures. Numerous techniques are applicable here, among them phonetic palindromes, such as

The Scissors of Xerxes
The Toe-Plate of Plato
March Forth on the Fourth of March

or genitive chains, such as

Charles Proust	*A Tale of Two Cities of the Plain*
Ernest Ghosh	*The Old Man and the Sea of Poppies*
Harper Grisham	*A Time to Kill A Mockingbird*

or *filigranes* (as defined by Michèle Métail), such as

Jules Buck	*Voyage to the Center of the Good*
H.G. Synge	*The Playboy of the Western War*
Walt Capote	*Leaves of the Harp*

In thc two latter cases, potential authors are constructed based on a model that the reader will have decoded with ease.

Potential libraries are evidently, in keeping the nomenclature used above, imaginary imaginary libraries.

SYSTEMATIC LIBRARIES

We know how difficult it is for a librarian to choose an organizing principle that facilitates self-service among readers. Certainly author and subject-matter cards allow them to find what they are looking for, but often at the price of tedious comings and goings. Quite often the shelves will gather together titles unified by a common theme: history, poetry, etc. Such arrangements evidently depend on subjective choices that sometimes only add to the confusion. This justifies my proposal for a system based on titles, which offers the advantages of naturally suggesting affinities among works that superficial judgment has kept separated for too long. Some examples–better than lengthy speeches–will elucidate the principle of the method and allow for an appreciation of its excellence.

2.1. THE ALPHABETICAL LIBRARY

Agatha Christie	*The ABC Murders*
Simon Urban	*Plan D*
Tao Lin	*Eeeee Eee Eeee*
Daniel Kehlmann	*F*
John Berger	*G.*
Philippe Sollers	*H*
Isaac Asimov	*I, Robot*
Howard Jacobson	*J*
Paul E. Walsh	*KKK*
Romain Gary	*Lady L*

Agatha Christie	*N or M?*
Norman Daniels	*Operation N*
Régine Deforges	*O Told Me*
Jean-Paul Sartre	*The Respectful P…*
Lu Xun	*The True Story of Ah Q*
André Gex	*M.I.R.*
Doug Dorst & J.J. Abrams	*S.*
Italo Calvino	*t zero*
Nicholson Baker	*U and I: A True Story*
Thomas Pynchon	*V.*
Georges Perec	*W or the Memory of Childhood*
Deborah Ellis	*Looking for X*
Steve Jones	*Y: The Descent of Men*
Therese Anne Fowler	*Z*
Hervé Bazin	*Abecedary*

2.2. THE CHROMATIC LIBRARY

Orhan Pamuk	*My Name Is Red*
Anthony Burgess	*A Clockwork Orange*
Charlotte Perkins Gilman	*The Yellow Wallpaper*
David Mitchell	*Black Swan Green*
Raymond Queneau	*The Blue Flowers*
Alice Walker	*The Color Purple*
Donald Sobol	*Encyclopedia Brown, Boy Detective*
E.L. James	*50 Shades of Grey*
Charles Burns	*Black Hole*

2.3. THE DAILY LIBRARY

Alphonse Daudet	*Monday Tales*
Mitch Albom	*Tuesdays with Morrie*
Richard Cytowic	*Wednesday Is Indigo Blue*
G.K. Chesterton	*The Man Who Was Thursday*
Robert Heinlein	*Friday*
Ian McEwan	*Saturday*
Raymond Queneau	*The Sunday of Life*

Charles Jackson	*The Lost Weekend*
Leslie Thomas	*This Time Next Week*

2.4. THE GEOGRAPHIC LIBRARY

John Steinbeck	*East of Eden*
Richard Flanagan	*The Narrow Road to the North*
E.M. Remarque	*All Quiet on the Western Front*
Colm Tóibín	*The South*
Roberto Bolaño	*By Night in Chile*
Raymond Roussel	*Impressions of Africa*
Franz Kafka	*Amerika*
Franz Kafka	*The Great Wall of China*

THE ORDERED LIBRARY

You may have noticed that the libraries cited as examples in the preceding chapters were presented using various classificatory principles: alphabetical by author, by date, and so on. This means that there remains a certain element of subjectivity and that contentions may arise. This has prompted me to make separate mention here of a single theme: that of "natural" whole numbers. Here there is no ambiguity: the order is imposed by the theme itself, which justifies the name "ordered library." It is useful all the same to adopt the following conventions:

arithmetical: If the title contains an arithmetic expression, we count not the individual whole numbers therein but the result of the evaluation. Thus, Jacques Roubaud's *31 cubed* would be a work ranked 29,791 and not 31. We will avoid ordinals (*e.g.*, the twenty-fifth hour) and decimals.

literary: When several titles are in competition to "represent" a whole number, we will default to an author who works in French, or, if this is not possible, require that the number figure explicitly in the original title (whence a certain difficulty for *1275 âmes* by Jim Thompson, whose original title is *Pop. 1280*).

We may say an ordered library is <u>bounded</u> if it contains only titles whose integer is less than a given integer, and that it is connected if it has no lacunae. Preliminary research has not made it possible, so far, to identify a connected ordered library that extends beyond 50. One can imagine the difficulty of completing a connected ordered library that reaches to the highest rank, which to my knowledge is held by Raymond Queneau's *Hundred Thousand Billion Poems*. If, as we might imagine, such a completion is possible, we might pose ourselves the following interesting problem:

Does the distribution of documented books in an ideal ordered library (that is, including all existing titles that are eligible for inclusion) follow a logarithmic law comparable to the one that regulates the distribution of prime numbers?

CONCLUSION

The great metaphor describes the philosopher or the wise man as one who seeks to decode a Great Book. This is the foundational metaphor of the Renaissance: for Bacon, the book is "the book of God" (he also evokes "the volume of creation"); for Galileo it is "the book of Nature." And Galileo specifies, in his *Saggiatore*, that this great book is written in the language of mathematics.

But by this time Giordano Bruno had already, more clearly than the ancients, given a physical and cosmological meaning to the infinite and rendered plausible the affirmation of a concurrent infinity of universes, a *plurality of worlds*. Must we not also speak, in these terms, of a *plurality of books*, which is to say a *library of Nature*, or perhaps even a *plurality of libraries*? We are all the more naturally inclined to do so given how many contemporary writers and physicists have introduced and developed, in various forms, the concept of *parallel universes*. Hugh Everett, a student of J.A. Wheeler, was the first to use this model to give a slightly more acceptable interpretation of the anomalies encountered by quantum physics (what is referred to as Everett's "many worlds" theory).

Multiplicity of libraries, plurality of worlds, plurality of pluralities...

OULIPO OULIPO

Originally published as
Le dernier compte-rendu
(La Bibliothèque Oulipienne no. 42)

Translated by
Daniel Levin Becker

Noël Arnaud

from

The Last Minutes

1990

● Noël Arnaud, who became the president of the Oulipo in 1984 after François Le Lionnais's death, reflects on a lacuna in the written record of the group's monthly meetings. On the never-drafted circular for meeting no. 31, mentioned early in the preamble here, Bens writes: "It should have presented the minutes from the meeting of March (000), held at Aline Gagnaire's house, and recorded (or so we thought) by tape recorder. The resulting tape revealed itself to be more or less inaudible, all discussions having been drowned out by the petulance of silverware noises."

The drama surrounding the minutes did not erupt suddenly. It had been brewing for months. A clammy latency, a hesitation—that of Raymond Queneau, who was never one to rush people or things. His distraction was visible from the start of each session, a bristling in the stubble on his face, which was ordinarily clean-shaven. And anguish was beginning to form in droplets on the foreheads of the Oulipians, as though they were watching George Raft play shell games with their money. Our president François Le Lionnais took pains to preempt any drama by dealing us strict agendas for each meeting.

Besides the delight you will no doubt take in witnessing Jacques Roubaud's first appearance in the oulipian orbit, the unpublished minutes we present here offer a threefold appeal. First, they are among the rare minutes, perhaps the only ones, written by André Blavier, who in those years could often be found in Paris. After May '68, he chose to consider himself in exile from France, as several of his Belgian friends living in Paris who had participated in the "events" had been banned from our Republic. Second, these minutes were, exceptionally, read and approved by

Raymond Queneau; better still, Queneau asked, his pen yet firm and vigorous, "if we couldn't make copies and send them to all concerned parties." We do not feel we betray Queneau's intent by discerning behind this insistence–rather unlike his general manner–the desire for all to know where he stood on minutes and on the grave consequences resulting from their absence. Because–and this is the third reason these minutes deserve your attention–never before had Queneau shown himself to be so voluble, so imperious, on the subject. No doubt we may attribute the vigor of his words, his Normanness aside, to the fact that the assembly before which he was speaking was reduced to nearly the bare minimum (though the record concentration of oulipian genius remains a meeting with only three members).

The problem of the minutes cannot be dissociated from that of the number of meetings. As members of the Oulipo and certain literate types outside of it are aware, Jacques Bens's book *Oulipo 1960-1963* (Christian Bourgois, 1980) contains minutes from the meetings held since its foundation (on November 25, 1960) through November 29, 1963. Each meeting has its own set of minutes, each set of minutes its *circular*. This administrative term was adopted by Bens from the outset to indicate and attest to the diffusion of the minutes, and will be conserved for as long as there are minutes. The circulars were numbered successively. They do not constitute the Oulipo's only administrative appurtenances, far from it–let us not forget that, per 'Pataphysics, Science is an administrative matter–but the other documents of this nature do not call for numerical classification.

The last set of minutes and the last circular published in Bens's collection is numbered 40. The meeting at Aline Gagniare's house, recorded by tape recorder rather than by hand, discussed in these minutes by André Blavier, should have been the object of circular no. 31. Jacques Bens was unable to determine the exact date of this meeting; for my part, I have seen it oscillate between the eighteenth and the twenty-second of March, 1963, without managing to stop the clock or still the pendulum on a precise date. This is why Bens decided to indicate an unknown date, excepting the month, on which we

were all in agreement. I do not find it disagreeable to say, to the attention of punctilious historians, that my recent research has recovered the exact date: it was Friday, March 22, 1963.

Turning our attention now to those minutes that were written and distributed but not published, we see that the final one is numbered 70 and that it relates the words and gestures exchanged over the course of the meeting of February 25, 1966. Thus we have enough material for a second collection of minutes, thirty meetings' worth–almost all of them recorded, in the absence of Bens, who had gone off to cultivate olives, by Jacques Duchateau or, in the interim, Jean Lescure. After circular no. 70, the minutes stop. In retrospect, it did not take Queneau long to voice his disapproval of the situation, given that he posed the problem crudely at the meeting of August 23, 1966; for my part, I remember that he was already concerned about it, in a discreet and murmuring way, at prior meetings. Blavier's minutes appear to be a challenge that would not, alas, be taken up. The wound of the minutes continued to bleed for many years. It might be said that, had there been minutes from these meetings, the question of what to do about the minutes would have occupied a good half of the contents of the minutes. A multitude of solutions were imagined that all, after being discussed at length, turned out to be impracticable. Unless my memory fails me–and in any case, the absence of minutes means I will never know what is said at meetings I do not attend–it seems to me that Raymond Queneau began to moderate, little by little, the expression of his regrets and criticisms, and that soon it no longer bore the apocalyptic vehemence that, in the judgment of the Quercanologists assembled there, indelibly marked his contribution on August 23, 1966. But he did reestablish, or allow Le Lionnais or some other Oulipian to reestablish, time and time again, the pressing nature of the question, looming so sempiternally as to be practically liquid in its flaccidity. Like the question itself, the drama was resolved by dilution and evaporation. Nonetheless, something remained in the air, since, recently, thanks to a new member, Jacques Jouet, the minutes have begun again. We may gather that the Oulipians and their intimates had been suffering silently from their absence.

We reproduce here the integral minutes of André Blavier, integral in the sense of entirety and in the sense of lack of modification or correction–aside from the number given to the circular. We had to search a great deal before arriving at the number 75, proof that the number of the circular was, at the time, essential to the proper maintenance of the ephemeris. Without minutes for the six months or so between meeting no. 70 and the one recorded by Blavier, I have taken recourse to the meeting invitations, which belong to the administrative class of things other than minutes and which thus, as I pointed out earlier, remain exempt from numerical ordering. I regret strongly that they were not ordered as such because I remain undecided as to whether or not the normally scheduled meetings between February and August 1966 were actually held. The number 75 is thus exact only plus or minus one. No doubt, invitations are insufficient when trying to reconstruct the calendar of a hazy period: one invitation disappears from your archives–or, rightly or wrongly, you worry that it will–and your whole project seizes up.

I should have liked to conclude this note with a chronology of Oulipo meetings since the group's inception, and especially since the abandonment of the minutes; for the reasons I have just evoked, I must renounce that ambition. My failure will be positive–and I will regret it all the less–if a sprightly young Oulipian or friend of the Oulipo comes away persuaded of the necessity of conducting an investigation among the surviving founding members, who, by adding up and reconciling the elements in their archives, would no doubt manage to reconstitute the calendar of all meetings of this venerable Institution.

* * *

OUVROIR DE
LITTÉRATURE
POTENTIELLE

Circular no. 75 (+/-)

MINUTES FROM THE MEETING
OF TUESDAY, AUGUST 23, 1966

(At the home of Le Lionnais)

PRESENT: Le Lionnais, Queneau, Arnaud, Latis, Blavier.

EXCUSED: Braffort, Berge, Lescure, Duchateau, Bens, everyone “away from Paris,” and, *in extremis*, Queval.
Le Lionnais is called to preside, Blavier to take notes.

* * *

Le Lionnais attempts to establish an agenda.

Arnaud declares his opposition to the use of “practice” (praxis) in place of the customary “administration.”

ARNAUD: It’s ambiguous!
LE LIONNAIS: Exactly!

The agenda is established again, for better or for worse. But:

LATIS (TO LE LIONNAIS): Incidentally, what color would you say your dressing gown is?
VARIOUS VOICES: Cyclamen… wine-dark… Bordeaux…

(The group consults a dictionary of colors, collectively acknowledging that it is both outmoded and indispensable.)

In another diversion, Arnaud requests and receives a great deal of information regarding a certain François-Pierre Caillé. Queneau provides it.

MME. SKORECZ: What time would you like lunch to be served?
QUENEAU: Twelve forty-seven.

The proposition does not pass, but Latis is moved by

the presidential dressing gown to consider the relative merits of lovers of irises versus lovers of roses.

LATIS: Roses are too much!

...

LATIS: Roses are dreadful!

LE LIONNAIS: Enough small talk and dismay: let us move on to serious business, by which I mean the OuLiPo, of which we may observe today that the *li* stands for *little*. I am putting on the agenda (yes, still that) an announcement about the reinvigoration...

ARNAUD: ???

LE LIONNAIS: ... of the OuLiPo. There are two solutions available to us: we can maintain the OuLiPo by filling vacancies as they arise, or we can let it die out little by little, of natural causes: a first-rate extinction.

Queneau laments the inadequacy, and even the absence, of minutes from monthly meetings, which he sees as one of the causes of oulipian dissipation. There was a revitalizing quality to Bens's minutes lacking in those of his successors. (The secretaries in question, whom no one would dream of reproaching, are the first to agree.) At present there are no minutes at all, at just the moment when verbal contributions from Berge and Braffort, in particular, might have led us to hope for a relaunch or a reorientation.

LE LIONNAIS: Yes, we went slowly from syntax to semantics, but there is a strong risk of losing it all without written notes and minutes.

Queneau elaborates his remarks on the OuLiPo and literature in general. Now the most estimable creations are coming from outside the group. Even in the case of Duchateau, whose novel, currently under consideration at Gallimard, makes no reference at all to the OuLiPo. A collection by Roubaud will come out in January, also from Gallimard.

Arnaud seconds Queneau's lamentation at the absence of minutes and asks him to say more about Roubaud and about Duchateau's novel.

QUENEAU: Roubaud is a mathematician who has written a collection of poems based on the rules of the game *go*.* The manuscript, submitted to readers who have no positive bias toward our activities, was accepted before I even had the chance to weigh in in its favor. As for Duchateau's novel, certain constraints (in particular forbidden words) are easy to notice, but the deeper structures, which we may assume existed before they could be called oulipian, are undetectable from a casual reading. And the method isn't explained anywhere, unlike what Bens did with his irrational sonnets.

Latis takes his turn condemning the Oulipians for their laziness, even as he ranks himself among the laziest. Under these conditions, he argues, there are no grounds to be so difficult about potential candidacies. What he has learned of Roubaud, for example, seems to him to justify exploration in that direction.

Le Lionnais brings up Margat (the *Mona Lisa* specialist) again. The discussion becomes general, even fuzzy, when it comes to determining admission procedures and especially methods for "testing" possible future members. There must be both the possibility of non-acceptance (should the trial lunch prove disappointing–and here Latis points out that the lunch need not be determinant, recalling the lunch at which Satrap Ferry† was intimidated) and care taken not to be needlessly hurtful to invitees.

It is decided that Roubaud will be the first to be invited.

ARNAUD: If his book comes out in January, we should save face by getting in touch with him immediately.

QUENEAU: Today, even.

ARNAUD: Yesterday!

LATIS: Let Satrap Queneau parley with him without delay, and write a note presenting his book, to be published alongside an excerpt in the next *Subsidium*.‡

Discussion returns to Duchateau's *Zinga 8*. Queneau retraces its genesis: an idea that came from Kahan (Zazie in the Cosmos), was transmitted to Duchateau, and ultimately became no more than an inframarginal three-line note in a novel steeped in a sort of psychological fiction.

* ∈ (Gallimard, 1967).

† Jean Ferry (1906–1974), screenwriter and Satrap in the Collège de 'Pataphysique.

‡ *Subsidia Pataphysica* was one of the sporadically published house organs of the Collège de 'Pataphysique.

LATIS: Finally, something inhuman. I adore inhumanity!

On the subject of future “agglomerants” (Le Lionnais’s term), high hopes are expressed.

QUENEAU: Pious popes.
ARNAUD: What?
QUENEAU: Indeed, the highest hopes of pious popes.

(This interlude causes the nature of the high hopes to be lost.)

At dessert, the minutes are brought up again. All present miss the panache of Bens’s minutes, as well as the precision and documentarian dryness of Duchateau’s.

LATIS: But we’ll have to learn to do without them more and more. Bens and soon Duchateau will become–how shall I put this–contemporary authors. We can’t burden them with this ignoble job.

Arnaud proposes taking turns taking minutes.

Latis, skeptical, suggests the stenographic services of Eva Genestoux.

LE LIONNAIS: I suppose I would have to be seated next to her, to teach her to separate the futile from the essential.

LATIS: Yes, she’s dedicated, capable, neutral, not prudish...

LE LIONNAIS: Oh, Lescure’s girl. I saw her again somewhere else. She was no virgin either.

QUENEAU: Except we’ll have to pay for her lunch.

ALL: Come now, let’s not be miserly!

The group moves back to the table (and wonders why, since it has been cleared).

Latis shares a distich in Latin that can render 3,265,920 combinations, which he found in the *Dictionary of Scientific, Mathematical, and Physical Amusements* (Panckoucke, 1792).

LE LIONNAIS: I don’t want to... but, well...

QUENEAU: Yes, I think it’s in Peignot.

LATIS: Well, maybe this is where it comes from.

(Drinking.)

QUENEAU: As I've said before, we should be paying attention to parlor games.

LE LIONNAIS: Quite.

ARNAUD: The ones in *France-Soir*?

LATIS: When does that come out?

ARNAUD: We also talked about a blackboard. Would that really be so hard?

LATIS: I could bring chalk and an eraser.

LE LIONNAIS: Soaked in bile...

Someone brings up LSD.*

LATIS: Which reminds me, I have to piss. (He leaves to do so.) (Others follow suit.)

Le Lionnais introduces a proposition from Regent Lescure, who has the opportunity to have two small-format books published. The first text published under such conditions would be the recording of the meeting at Aline Gagnaire's house, transcribed with no indication of who said what. Queneau reads some excerpts, to general hilarity. All are shocked and deny having said "thing" so often.

Latis proposes that the text at least be retouched a little.

Arnaud declares his opposition again.

Blavier agrees with Latis.

Finally a fine distinction is drawn between integral minutes and fundamentalist minutes, with a preference declared for the latter. In passing, the frequency with which Bens says *ben* ("well") is called into question.

BLAVIER: There's listened-to oral and read oral. We should encourage often-ticity.

LE LIONNAIS: Well, yes, there are some obvious listening errors here.

LATIS: Oh!

ARNAUD: How else would you put it?

It is decided at last that, if the publication proceeds, it will be about a rough text interfering with a prepared

* *Littérature sémo-définitionnelle*, or semo-definitional literature, an oulipian technique that consists in replacing individual words with their relatively obscure definitions.

text, such as the one from OuLiPoFagne, and gradated between anthological and didactic.

Which brings us right back again to the minutes: Bens is suspected of having, from time to time… perhaps… *embellished* them; Duchateau of leaving out, from time to time, worthwhile puns.

QUENEAU: What we lose above all, as we've already mentioned about the contributions from Berge and Braffort, is–and may Étiemble* forgive me the English word–the brainstorming. (Nobody takes exception.)

LE LIONNAIS: Exactly. Sometimes we have strokes of genius, but they're so brief that neither Bens nor Duchateau has the time to get them down. These are things that could provide material to reenergize our work, and we're losing them.

LATIS: Indeed, with Eva Genestoux…

ARNAUD: We could also ask that each Oulipian who delivers theoretical remarks write them up for the archives.

SEVERAL: Hmm…

QUENEAU: Now there's potential architecture. "Potentialism absorbs man and integrates him into a movement architectural in nature." (He reads this fine specimen from issue no. 3 of *Architecture Principe*.)

Latis rather insidiously extracts a promise from Le Lionnais to provide some chimeras for the next *Subsidium*.

Queneau reads another text by Lescure, "Little Poetic Erector Set."

LE LIONNAIS: That's permutation, sustained by semantics.

BLAVIER: Yes, and not oulipian at all. All that's at play here is the emotional content of the words and some affective ambiguity, not at all structure–there is no structure. It is quite nice, though…

QUENEAU: Yes, I wonder whether…

Blavier, playing devil's advocate, worries that the OuLiPo may sometimes be all talk, or let itself off too lightly. (Gasping noises.) What structures have we invented, besides some mostly mechanical procedures that in general can already be found in the work of our

* René Étiemble (1909-2002), writer and scholar who volubly deplored the anglicization of the French language.

anticipatory plagiarists? We're not rigorous enough. And we fall back so often on that old seesaw of content and form. We claim to be uninterested in looking for literature in the belletristic sense, but we rejected Saporta because it wasn't good, even though there was absolutely structure there.

LE LIONNAIS: We must (re-)state the notion of structure, which is not the same for us as it is for good honest non-Oulipians. Structure must be understood simultaneously (1) in the mathematical sense of the word; (2) as any constraint we may choose to impose; and (3) likewise, as any algorithm we may choose to set for ourselves.

ARNAUD: We had talked about making a glossary.

LATIS: We never will.

BLAVIER: It would be useful, 'cause the OuLiPo does bring out (publications, interviews, etc.) for people beyond those of us who know, or think we do.

ARNAUD: We could at least, each time a word presents a difficulty or some point of contention for our purposes, make a note of it to clarify its meaning and scope.

BLAVIER: I'll say it again, I think our structures are impoverished compared to the ones we found readymade. Only rarely do we surpass the purely artificial constraint, laden as it is with cumbersome details and devoid of prospects for future use.

LATIS: Yes, I think that what we might call the eminent structures–perhaps they were already known before we came along.

LE LIONNAIS: And alongside the eminent ones, it's possible that there are optimal structures. The sonnet would be one of them.

QUENEAU: Such a brute, Blavier...

BLAVIER: It wasn't me, it was Lescure!

Le Lionnais reads the beginning of a sonnet he wrote based on a sonnet by Scarron. It's an isosyntaxism*–which would stand to prove that isosyntaxisms are easier than we had initially thought (Bens, e.g.), provided one sticks to the essential grammatical components: subject, verb, predicate. The Oulipians present are invited to finish the sonnet. Latis remains skeptical.

Latis evokes other possibilities for structures, in the direction of permutations.

* An early oulipian exercise in which the primary words of a source text are replaced with other words in the same part of speech.

LE LIONNAIS: It's like those novels modeled on chess problems. No one ever goes too far in that direction; they limit themselves to psychological transpositions of whatever situation obtains from the last move. Except in *Alice*, where Carroll uses fantasy rules of chess, *e.g.* where white makes several moves in a row.

The discussion veers toward science fiction: Borges, Aldriss, etc., and a detective novel called *The Three Crimes of Veules-les-Roses* by Marcel Marc, which must date from around 1924. Particular importance is attached to a short story published in the August issue of *Galaxie*, "Shall We Have A Little Talk?"

LE LIONNAIS: We should suggest that Duchateau do some isosyntaxic exercises modeled on serialist music. He would manage wonderfully.

ARNAUD: Yes, and besides the glossary, we should return to the idea of a little Oulipian library.

LE LIONNAIS: We do have in our midst both mathematicians and littérateurs, for whom the same words don't always refer to exactly the same notions.

ARNAUD: And why not a series of talks?

Latis shows plans for the forthcoming *Subsidia*. He asks for everyone's help (if you can believe that) on an issue that will be "poetic" or will not be at all, and on one that will be scientific. He reads an "intentionally naive" poem by Paul Féval, from book IV of *The Black Coats*, which series has already been the subject of discussion throughout the meeting.

Le Lionnais relays news from the OuPeinPo (or the OuPlasPo, as we like), which seems to be doing well after some difficulty getting started. There as well, the notion of empty structure proved challenging to grasp, especially for those painters who wanted to paint. Help from mathematicians, including Bucaille, helped clarify matters.

* * *

Next meetings: Friday, October 7, at Le Basque, without Le Lionnais; Friday, November 4, at Le Basque again, with Le Lionnais and Roubaud as guest.

OULIPOULIPO

Originally published
in *Geste* (P.O.L)

Translated by
Daniel Levin Becker

Michelle Grangaud

from

Gesture

1991

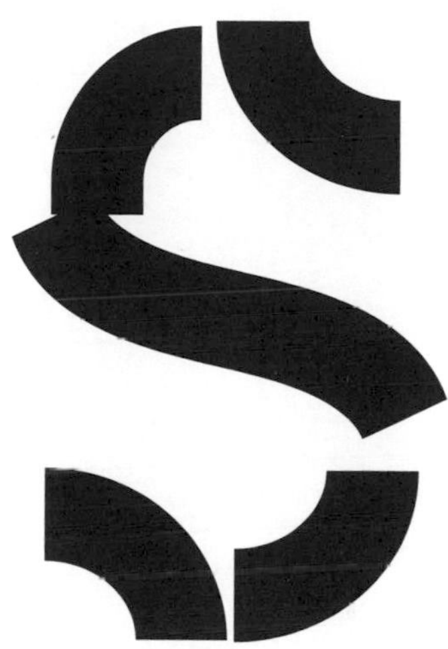

She spreads the laundry
across the clothesline.
The sheets flap in flight toward the windy sky.

Sitting on the bench,
his legs spread apart,
he looks down at the sidewalk between his shoes.

Still one hour left
before dismissal.
She turns her gaze toward the open window.

The lake, in the dream,
was milky and smooth.
Something menacing, obscure in the foreground.

● *Gesture* is a sprawling meditation on everyday life as told through micro-vignettes taking a poetic form Michelle Grangaud calls the anti-Sapphic tercet: five syllables, five syllables, eleven syllables.

It's raining. It rained.
It will rain. He walks,
head down, just a passenger, under the rain.

To do housework is
to erase it all:
dirt, smudges, the idea of mortality.

The siren jingles.
It's an ambulance.
In this traffic someone is going to die.

In front of the sink,
standing up, hurry
and swallow the antidepressant tablets.

A teardrop takes shape
between the eyelids,
then bulges, then slides down the length of the cheek.

She opens the door,
walks into the room,
turns on the overhead light, sees the bodies.

Withered autumn leaves
slide around on the
tombstones and fly at the legs of passersby.

He holds the lighter,
offers her the flame
while caressing her cheek with his fingertips.

With the tip of his
nail, he tries to root
out the fiber of steak caught between his teeth.

She swipes the glasses
off his head and throws
them out of the window and into the street.

He did not really
grasp what just happened:
like that, the plate was in pieces on the ground.

In his dream he is
following a strange
woman. She wears uneven high heels and limps.

Kites by the hundreds.
The child sees the sky
as if it were a roof trembling with colors.

A laugh that bursts forth,
acute as a scream,
the yelping of a creature caught in a trap.

He holds the pencil
with his tongue stuck out,
draws a hanging body with its tongue stuck out.

Putting the live crab
in boiling water,
she catches the terrified look of the child.

Adenoma of
the liver, says the
doctor. How do you not have another drink?

Between the thumb and
the index, she rolls,
with nervous fingers, a wisp of her own hair.

He seals the door and
all the windows with
adhesive tape before turning on the gas.

She reaches her arm
out of the tollbooth
to give change to all of the vacationers.

Together they drank
water from the tap.
Their lips just barely touching, their eyes teasing.

He has not come home.
She is beginning
to worry. The clock says eight in the morning.

She throws the paper,
sticky and corkscrewed,
with all the flies glued to it, into the fire.

The accident left
twenty-one injured
aboard the train that collided with a cow.

He stops on the stairs.
He is winded. White.
He takes a handkerchief and mops his forehead.

On the garbage can,
a pair of kids' shoes,
brand new, which he slips gently into his bag.

In the room he puts
down his suitcase and
lies on the bed without removing his shoes.

The first time she is
required to speak in
public, she loses her voice altogether.

When he arrives at
the office, he tells
the typist to bring him a cup of coffee.

She is walking on
the tips of her toes
to avoid the noise of her high heels clacking.

The glass partitions
at the bank assure
total transparency of operations.

He is stuttering,
his tongue thickening.
The feeling of papier mâché in his mouth.

She takes off her blouse,
folds it, and slides it
very carefully into the plastic bag.

She finds her oldest
son, fifteen years old,
curled in a ball in his little brother's bed.

In the basic course
in rifle training,
the target's shape is a human silhouette.

Immediately
after kissing her,
he runs to the washbasin to wash his mouth.

Each night at the same
time, the sound of a
piano. Nobody knows where it comes from.

Originally published as *Règle du jeu, Ulcérations, Translations* (La Bibliothèque Oulipienne no. 73)

Translated by Ian Monk

Oskar Pastior

Rule of the Game, Threnodials, Translations

1997

● Oskar Pastior, the Oulipo's only German member to date, was fascinated with the collisions between languages that poetic expression could occasion, both translating other oulipian works and scouting out the possibilities of intersective languages such as Deunglitsch, an inventory compiled with Harry Mathews of words with identical spellings but no shared meanings between English and German.

The difficulties I run into when trying to speak about the OuLiPo are of a general sort, it seems to me: even an oulipian text cannot, should not, speak *of* itself—it *speaks*, quite simply, or it doesn't speak.

I mean: no edifices! No closed systems!

What interests me about this language—and the OuLiPo is one—is precisely its changing nature, and how it changes itself, and me. I make *that*, and *that* makes me.

A word now about the goats' *mêêê*, as it appears in the Promethean act, and which seems to me to be very far from being kosher, because it always seems to promise (pro*mêêê*se) some fabulous exploit: so just take a careful look at all those teleological models!

But, exorcised by some rule or grammar, which always turn out to be indispensable, I become really myself, a mêêê, and I then quite clearly prefer (though with a hint of the arbitrary) to take up the defense of that Other, who would then be "my" Proteus, and its proteins. Exorcised (and else can a language be?) I plead in favor of this shifting potential, and this absurd abstruseness, or, to sum up, the poetry of the equation "Prometheus - *mêêê* =

Proteus." In some languages, goats bleat differently...

The rule of the game. The constraint.

More exactly: the constraint, rule of the game.

Or else, and in extremely exhaustive terms, the word *experience* (conditions, preparations, trials) seems to me, through all the fields of existence and perception, quite a plausible one–even if only in the sense of that linchpin term *consciousness* alias *life* alias *language*.

This binary *organic/inorganic* route already stands as just such an arrangement, or method. Above all if we imagine for a moment an inorganic consciousness. Is such a thing imaginable?

So: consciousness as the rule of the game. And: language as the rule of the game. Languages. Logic, in various languages. The various arts as the rule of the game, in the singular, in the plural. The sciences, for example mathematics, as the rule of the game, as language, as experience. Cooking and recipes as language, ergo: the rule of the game, ergo: experience. You now know the rule, and you can apply words which are, all of them, somewhat inexact.

Or else that allusive characteristic that adheres to words–a language within language.

Or else the sestina, rule of the game: a language, of course. With the general grammar of the sestina, and its various sub-grammars which all run up against the general grammar and reinforce it by pushing it up to a higher level.

Or else the perceptive organ of the anagram: an entire universe, a cosmos, of course, with or without the Perecquian joker, and with such a grammatical consistency that it sends its rays even into the arsenals of beliefs and their relationships, but, what is more, it envelops them, surrounding them with the nimbus of timelessness, eternity.

Or else, at last, the rules of retroaction in the orderly systems of the enumeration and the inventory: and then, even, the entire alphabet in this force field, where letters act, and which so suited the Lettrists.

Of course everything, every so-called reality, is not produced only in language. This is why things become more complicated when dealing with the rules of the game used in less important rules of games, for example those of the OuLiPo.

But, for example, I am no mathematician.

And to proceed in the same defensive tone: what tempts me is the opportunity to obtain, in the end, if things so turn out, if this is the case, and despite the rules of the game, a "good" text. Which is–of course–not always the case.

Or else, more aggressively, I am tempted by the impossible: making something possible. To "pierce"–by making do and other subtleties, by pushing pedantry to its extreme, by dancing on the head of a pin, and even by adding other, more rigid, even more specific rules–the arbitrariness of the rule, to soften it up so much that it becomes a possibility. Which comes down to forcing the hand of grace.

But, how does it happen that an oulipian text succeeds better than some other one, done up too, in the same way, using the same rule? A mistake? In other words: where and when do the rule of the game and a slice of luck coincide optimally in the material–in such a way that they make each other necessary and possible? For a slice of luck is a successful text: irresolutely resolved. The rule and the material are both, at the same time, a kind of possible conceptual flaw. That is the oulipian mystery–and this is a delicate point which I do not at all want to delegate by bringing in such terms as *talent* (the muse) or even *pre-established favoritism*. I prefer quite simply talking about a chaotic aggregate, both in the production and in the reception. In a permanent way, risk constitutes chance. It is both the rule of the game of the material and the material of the rule of the game. Or so I might venture to think.

Sniffing out a slice of luck just in the abstract formula of the rule, sniffing it out, so to speak, before it "becomes flesh," is quite clearly a capacity. A capacity which may not be desirable. Thus, even a creator, if there were one, would no longer be able to view himself as being a slice of luck–oulipian or otherwise.

In any case, for me, things happen, if they do, step by step, staggering. It is by reading, speaking, writing that I suddenly manage to pinpoint the tensions inside a text, the *in statu nascendi* rules of the game, the beginnings, the triggers, without knowing where they will lead. It is (precisely) this that interests me. Not as a recipe for producing something outside me. It is more curiosity that pushes me on: what will this do to me–and make of me?

The texts show, or at least I think they do, that I do not put the concept "in front of the horse": even if it can seem as though it is the concept that puts me in front of it.

When seen in this way (and thus always from the viewpoint of the exact sciences) all texts, and above all oulipian texts, are the texts from a science book which, it seems to me, has not yet been written.

Recipes are condemned to their feasibility. The OuLiPo has no recipes on offer. Just cavities, "airy" solutions, so to speak...

It is more in such waters that the rule of the game of linguistic biography, mine included, thrashes about. Taking into account, of course, the constraints coming from the active and passive limitations of linguistic knowledge, for both the writer and all his or her readers; there are so-called mother tongues, which are found alongside more or less dense layers and chunks of the sediment of migratory languages, read languages, and private idioms. The entire debacle of that misunderstanding which we like to call "communication" and of its imposed limits: interpretation.

OuLiPo and translation: here are two concepts which are, it goes without saying, mutually exclusive. Or, at least, it might be said that they evolve in distinct dimensions within the same material. For the procedure of translating from one language to another does not constitute, *per se*, a rule of a game (it is at best a hazy, metaphorical rule, if we insist on making literary the imperative of linguistic mediation as a *sine qua non* condition for intercultural exchanges). NB: translation is, strictly speaking, the wrong word for something that doesn't exist.

However (and this is where I see the range of oulipian possibilities as being wide open), we continue to produce marvelously erroneous translations, in which certain restrictive rules are perfectly operational: homophonies (or "surface translations")–rhythmic reductions (a setting to music and, vice versa, music set in words)–taking idiomatic expressions literally; reductions of texts to their key words, and key words to definitions (the entire range of pseudo-dictionaries, and alphabetic or numeric series); and finally the combination of such constraints during the transposition of a text within the same language. As I said, the possibilities are wide open.

And I'd even go so far as to say that each translation creates, through a strategy of attack on the text, a particular grammar which determines its restrictive physiognomy.[1]

To which can be added that monstrous *irreversibility* inherent to texts and their treatment (and which no form of cheating can elude). It is only at the moment when a certain constraint begins to play around inside me, through me, that it develops into a sparkling excitation, that it interests me (interests *itself*), and thus incites me to push the game even further.

The series of procedures which I have employed (and the reading and speaking capacities that I have thus acquired, at least to a certain degree) can no longer be inverted. What went before, what preceded, remains virulent. I believe that even my weeds, my oulipian *Threnodials,** contradict that classic definition of experience, which suggests that it is based on an ever-renewable system, which always produces the same results. This could, perhaps, be interesting in a certain context and create bonds of contemporaneousness.

This is why I say that the OuLiPo–just like my own little techniques–is a language that is learned by reading (and is read while learning), the perfect analogy of a conscious matter which, by playing on its own condition, exorcises this very condition. Thus, a language that assigns to the concept of author (creature of a creation? creation of a creature? and that's what it always comes down to!) an uncertain relationship which seems to me to be more equitable and more accurate than in other models and which, in the end, has something paradisiacal about it: the tunnel effect, the dimension of the possible.

For the chemistry exam for my leaving certificate, taken forty-four years ago in Sibiu/Hermannstadt, I

1. During my work on and with Petrarch's sonnets, for example (*33 Gedichte*), four clearly defined and retrospectively established constraints were at work: (a) ignorance of the "original" language (Petrarch's Italian)–which pushed back, via a slow apprenticeship of vocabulary, the "natural" frontiers of the project as far as text n° 33, without going any farther; (b) dissolution of Petrarch's imagistic metaphors into a discursive syntax–in other words, a piece of detective work in which the hypothetical and potential touched one another, so as to bring out something like the preceding layers of the Petrarchian metaphor *in statu nascendi*; (c) complete negligence of the sonnet form, replaced by a simple linearity expressed in blocks of prose; (d) the dropping of any historicising scruples which would have outlawed the use of the post-Petrarch lexicon (or else anachronistic allusions)–thus, "my" Petrarch quite naturally knows "his" Wittgenstein (whom I have not read myself), and even in one of his "elevated tones" he has rather a self-referential turn of phrase. It is flagrant that these four constraints stand as rules for renouncement, or at least a set of "absent virtues" when it comes to a translation according to mimetic norms. It is for this reason that *33 Gedichte* are something quite other.

* A heterogram is a poem that uses the eleven most common letters in the alphabet in permuting succession. French heterograms are called *ulcérations* and English heterograms *threnodials*, both named for words that use all eleven letters only once.

perfected a little mnemonic technique, a *pons asinorum*, of a complete potentiality, whose sole constraint was provided by Mendeleev's periodic table (or tabled by the constraint?) of the elements, which had to be learned in such a way as it became memorable, which began with Beryllium, Lithium, and Boron and concluded with Selenium, Bromine, and Krypton:

Beli Boku
Stisa Flune
Namagalsi Phoschwehklar
Kazazkati-Wackermann: Feconi?
Cucygalgen! Assel! Brotcryp!

There, you have it all, and everything is possible, no?

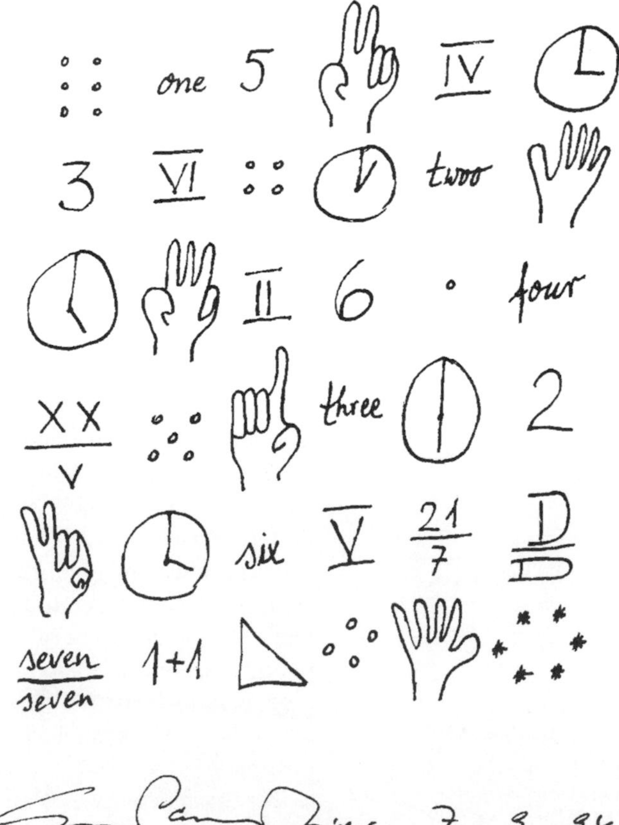

7. 9. 94

Originally published as "Quelques mousquetaires" in *Quelques mousquetaires* (Le Castor Astral)

Translated by Daniel Levin Becker

Hervé Le Tellier

A Few Musketeers

1998

● "A Few Musketeers" showcases Hervé Le Tellier's knack for straight-facedly animating singularly eccentric premises. Due to its irrepressible crescendo of idiomatic puns, the English version and the original French have no choice but to part ways toward the end.

That was how it started, trying to bring a bit of order to my library. It was a considerable job, and I set to it immediately, methodically... alphabetically.

Allais, Amado, Apollinaire: my shelves seemed even more crowded than usual. I had to move the last of the *A*s to the next shelf. They say cities expand westward; libraries, at least Western ones, always grow to the right. To accommodate Queneau, Raymond and Sartre, Jean-Paul and everyone who came after, I had to install a whole new row of shelves.

Until Cocteau, Jean I didn't notice anything amiss. I was proceeding at a healthy clip when a detail interrupted my classificatory revelries: it appeared I now owned a book with an unfamiliar title, *The Eagle with Three Heads*.

I turned it over, uncomprehending. Was this some kind of joke? Who could have so meticulously peeled off the original cover and so painstakingly replaced it with a new one, totally identical but for this infinitesimal difference, and managed to substitute it without leaving a single trace?

It was then that I noticed, on the next shelf down, an enormous volume by Dumas: *The Four Musketeers*! No chance, this time, that this was the work of a forger: the *four* was there, embossed on the cover without so much as a smear, underneath the same glossy, mildly frayed dust jacket as ever.

In a cold sweat, I surveyed the titles on the spines of my books. My head began to spin. Jules Verne had never written *Dick Sand, A Captain at Sixteen* or *Around the World in 81 Days*. There was no book by Zweig called *Twenty-Five Hours in the Life of a Woman*. Paper, as far as I know, has never spontaneously caught fire at the temperature of *Fahrenheit 452*.

This was ridiculous. Now Harry Mathews had written *21 Lines A Day*; now the unfinished novel by Perec was called *54 Days*. A bit further down, between Henry James and James Joyce, a certain Jacques Jouet had written *108 Souls*. In the middle of the Roubaud shelf–you need at least a whole shelf for Jacques Roubaud–I found *Autobiography, Chapter Eleven*.

I couldn't even bring myself to smile at the sight of *The Postman Always Rings Thrice* on the spine of a James M. Cain book, any more than I could at *One Orchid for Miss Blandish*. Seized by vertigo at the sight of my own *A Thousand and One Pearls (for a Thousand and One Pennies)*, I lay down on the floor and closed my eyes for several moments. Suddenly, inspired, I stood up. I opened the Pléiade Sade and paged until I found–I might have guessed–*The 121 Days of Sodom*. So it was as I feared: the titles inside the books were also affected. Next I opened *The Sextine Chapel*, a book quite dear to me, and found, sure enough, that it somehow recounted seventy-nine sexual relationships, not seventy-eight.*

I hurried to *Bouvard and Pécuchet* and opened it feverishly, only to put it back with a sigh of relief. The temperature was still up in the nineties, and the boulevard Bourdon was still absolutely deserted. So there was a strange logic to this numerical nightmare: only titles, subtitles, and inscriptions were afflicted by the mutation. And even in a title, *one* did not become *two* unless it could be considered a number rather than an article. Simone de Beauvoir was still *A Dutiful Daughter*.

* *The Sextine Chapel*, published in 2011 in Ian Monk's translation, is a combinatorial series of erotic vignettes in which twenty-six characters appear three times each.

Yet the book by Paul Fournel was now called *Two Rockers Too Many*, whereas another had become *A Man Looks at Two Women*. Why not *Two Men Look at Two Women*, or *Two Men Look at a Woman*? A mystery. Other titles underwent only slight semantic adaptations, as in the case of Bret Easton Ellis's *Less Than One*.

I found a few surprises on the politics shelf too: I suddenly owned Pierre Frank's reference book about the Fifth International, a Mayakovskian title that petrified the dormant Trotskyist in me. And what to make of the little pocket-sized edition of *The Russian Revolution of 1918*?

My videotapes had also been contaminated: I now had Kubrick's *2002: A Space Odyssey*–the palindrome was little consolation–and a Godard transposed to *Three or Four Things I Know about Her*. I would have liked to watch *Eight Samurai*, but I had lent them out. As for my son, I could now persuade him to finish his vegetables with the promise of certain obscure Disney titles, like *102 Dalmatians* and *Snow White and the Eight Dwarves*.

It all had its own logic. I even found, not far from my PC, a user's manual for Windows 99.

Dejected–I'd like to have seen you in my place–I sat back down on the rug with a copy of Fénéon's *Novels in Four Lines* in hand. I opened it mechanically and was stupefied to find that said novels contained exactly as many lines as advertised, which is to say–need I even?–one too many. (The text did seem less dense than I recalled.) What was I to make of this? That the new title imposed new content on the work? That the signified determined the signifier?

I found the answer in Freud's *Six Lectures on Psycho-Analysis*, whose table of contents announced the topic of lesson six: Nature of paranoia. Links between personality and paranoiac delirium. Everyday life and hysterical pathologies.

I could already sense Jacques Lacan breaking through from under Sigmund Freud.

I found another answer in *The Four Musketeers*, which had almost doubled in size: now d'Artagnan's companions were Athos, Porthos and Golias; the latter wore a thin mustache (as was appropriate), was equally gifted as a swashbuckler and as a carouser, and tended in his sexual preferences toward young boys.

This was awful, of course. But it was fascinating.

To be sure, these modifications usually failed to have any meaningful effect on the plot. What did it matter that Hanff's bookstore was now located at 85 Charing Cross Road? Or if Elsa Triolet's fine was now 201 francs? Orwell could just as well have chosen 1985. Tintin would have the same adventures on *Flight 715* or among *The Eight Crystal Balls*. The final thought in *A Thousand and One Pearls (for a Thousand and One Pennies)*, which still makes me laugh today, didn't alter the structure of the text in any fundamental way, and I was tickled to discover that the hundred-first "point of view" in my *Mona Lisa to 101* was that of Père Ubu.

It didn't even bother me that the last entry in *366 Recipes for Dummies*, on the cookbook shelf, was for a rabbit coulibiac.

And yet sometimes the slippage led to genuine semantic disruption. What to make of the improbable Quenellian combinatorics that led to *One Hundred Thousand Billion and One Poems*? Or the new moral of La Fontaine's "Three Pigeons"—in such a case, could you even still call it a moral? What would the feminist Antoinette Fouque make of her seminal work, *There Are Three Sexes*? Laugh all you like, but at least show some sympathy for poor Alphonse Allais, one of whose books—my favorite—was now called *Three Plus Three Equals Six*, which, I think we can agree, is a valid result but an idiotic title.

The effect was all the more confounding in those historical works in which History herself contorted to accommodate the new title: thanks to Paxton's *Vichy France: 1941-1945*, Marshal Pétain remained in power for an extra year, though to be fair he did take an extra year to ascend there. Altogether more terrifying were the consequences of Albert Speer's *Inside the Fourth Reich*, to say nothing of any number of volumes on *World War III*.

Suddenly I remembered that I owned the 1999 *World Book*. I looked it up and down feverishly, but didn't dare open it. On the coffee table was that day's edition of *Le Monde*—that is, the next day's, or, to be precise, now, illogically enough, the day after that.* Philippe Séguin

* *Le Monde*, one of France's newspapers of record, is published each afternoon bearing the following day's date.

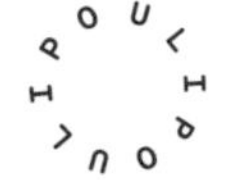

was criticizing the cohabitation law imposed by the Sixth Republic.

Wait! I thought: surely I now had, in a closet somewhere, a battered copy of Lagarde and Michard's literary anthology of the twenty-first century. Who would the schoolchildren of the future study?

I resisted the temptation.

I wound up perched on the sofa, immersed in *The Four Musketeers*, and stayed there well into the night. Exhausted, at five in the morning–though how much could I trust a digital clock at this point?–I sunk into an uneasy sleep.

The first thing I did when I woke up again, around ten, was to look over toward the Dumas. It seemed thinner. Indeed, it was thinner. Now, placed on my bedside table atop Perec's *The Art of Asking Your Boss for a Raise*, there were only *Two Musketeers*.

I decided not to leave the house. I would spend the day reading, taking notes. I cursed myself for not having thought to open *The Book of Three Ways*, a novel treasure of Egyptian mythology, the night before. I had other regrets too, of course: what would have been the new definitions in the *Robert 3*, or the plot of Maupassant's "Three Friends," or the seventh character in search of an author?

The telephone rang several times. I didn't answer, for fear of breaking the spell. I didn't even go downstairs to take in the mail.

The hours went by peaceably, even serenely. I skimmed *Two Men without a Boat (or a Dog)*, then poor Allais's *One Plus One Equals Four*. I watched a bit of *One English Girl*. The postman rang only once, and I didn't have the heart to answer. It was out of the same reticence that I passed over the now-banal Bond movie *You Only Die Once*. I flipped through *The Theatre and Its Single*, finding Artaud even more abstruse than usual.

Whether out of superstition, or the premonition that there wasn't enough time, or the fear of waking in the morning to see everything returned by some dark symmetrical magic to its original state, I didn't photocopy anything.

Around four in the afternoon my head began to spin. I hadn't eaten anything in nearly twenty-four hours. I opened the fridge for a yogurt: bad move. The stench was unbearable. The expiration dates on the milk, the jam, and the pâté had all turned back a year, a month, and a day.

I decided to go pick something up at the Zeroprix.

My shirt felt a bit tight, but it wasn't until I tried to button my pants that I realized something was wrong here too. I hadn't gained weight–the scale said I'd lost almost a kilo, in fact–but my clothes had all shrunken a size. After I put on a baggy jogging suit, now it was my feet that refused to fit into shoes with an *8* engraved in the leather of the sole.

I called a home delivery service. Twenty-nine minutes later, a man dressed in red handed me a lukewarm three-cheese pizza. This culinary debacle had gotten the better of my last reluctance: it was time to resign myself to a science even softer than my pizza.

SOS Psychiatry came to the door in the guise of a small, courteous, smiling man.

"Thanks for coming, doctor," I said. "I think I've got two bees in my bonnet."

Dr. Lacan–I'll call him that in the interest of doctor-patient confidentiality–stared at me, perplexed, like a mule with two spinning wheels.

"Come again?"

"I want to know if I'm going crazy. I feel like I've got two screws loose."

The psychiatrist grew white as two ghosts. He took out a pack of cigarettes and began to smoke like two chimneys. He seemed preoccupied.

"I see, I see," he said, professionally. "Tell me about your childhood."

"If you like."

"Your mother," Lacan suggested.

"She was a good woman, but always at sevens and eights, of three minds about everything. One night, my father told me, when she had two buns in the oven..."

"You have a twin brother?" asked the doctor.

"No, why?" I said, intrigued.

"Nothing, nothing," said Lacan.

"My mother would make two mountains out of a molehill. It was just her way. She could drown in two glasses of water. My father, that's two other stories. He was one person's fool."

"I see," clucked Lacan. "Tell me about him too."

"Oh, he was a nice man, but always four sheets to the wind. As soon as he woke up he would knock two back. Never had two red cents to spend, never gave three shits. Can't say he ever did two days' honest work in his life. It was like kicking two dead horses with him. Mother sometimes got on his back, but he was proud as two peacocks. Anyway, one day he stood up on his own three feet and went and plucked himself a job."

"I beg your pardon?" said Lacan, astonished.

"I said he found a job. Plucked as in found. It's an expression. You don't know it?"

"Ah, yes, yes," said Lacan, who in two fell swoops had begun to take notes. "I was thinking of something else."

"But poor Dad, he had three left feet, and he did such a one-and-a-half-assed job that he got himself fired in three shakes of a lamb's tail, of course. My poor mother, who already worked as a street vendor eight days a week, got down on all fives and started cleaning houses too, but it was just two drops in the bucket. We just couldn't make all three ends meet. Ah, poor mom..."

"You were telling me about your father," Lacan cut in. He was beginning to give me the fourth degree.

"Cross as three sticks, that man. Always looking out for number two. He told everyone he was a writer, but nobody gave three hoots about what he wrote. Even the poems he was proudest of were two dimes a baker's dozen, and when he read them out it was, well, in two ears and out the other two. Poor Dad, now he's seven feet under... though even then, burning the candle at all three ends, he had two feet in the grave. I was knee-high to two grasshoppers when he passed. This all sounds harsh, I guess, but really I adored him. We were close, he and I. Like six fingers on a hand. People say we look alike, too, like three peas in a pod. I bet that knocks you for seven, eh?"

"Sure, sure, it's possible," murmured Lacan, conciliatory. "And your adolescence?"

"Oh, nothing special. With the girls, the usual, always trying to kill three birds with tombstones."

"Excuse me?"

"I mean with two stones."

"Yes, yes," Lacan nodded. "An interesting slip. Extremely interesting."

"I had all three feet in the same shoe, ass between three chairs, pacing like two lions in a cage, the 401 blows, that sort of thing. The follies of youth, you know?"

"No, not really," said Lacan. "My childhood was fairly studious. My mother wanted me to be a surgeon, but I couldn't stand the sight of blood–" He stopped, troubled. "Pardon me, I digress. You were telling me about your childhood."

"Just the usual, I was saying. You know how it is. Two birds in the hand are worth three in the bush, as they say."

"Yes, I suppose they could say that." The psychiatrist glanced at his watch. "Ah, I'm sorry, but our fifteen minutes is up. That'll be 1,000 francs." Handing me his card, he added: "If you wouldn't mind, I'd like to see you again tomorrow. Your case seems serious."

"Takes three to tango."

"Er, right. Tomorrow, then. Gimme six?"

"What?"

"It's an expression. To shake hands. Like, ah, the sixth wheel, the eleven Egyptian plagues. You know. Tomorrow I'd like to bring a few colleagues. Your case will certainly fascinate them. That won't bother you, I hope?"

"No, no, doctor. Three heads are better than two. Do I need to dress to the tens?"

"Wha–oh, no, don't worry, dress as you normally would. Until tomorrow, then."

"Indeed, doctor. So long and see you threemorrow."

11 DECEMBER 1998, TRICHAT HOSPITAL

It seems I'm getting better. Everyone's very nice to me here in the hospital. I'm under constant surveillance, and they record my every word. My case is fivemidable, no three ways about it. At least that's what everytwo tells me.

I've started to read again, too, from *Tripliners* to *Elevender Is the Night*. I've just finished "Two Painful Cases," and in a way I feel Mr. Duffy and I are two and the same. It sounds asiten, I'm sure, but it's not that I'm having third thoughts about my past or fretting over the two that got away. No, to me love is just a five-letter word. But now I also know what it's like to be minding my own business and to be rattled and upended, all of a sudden, by an ex plus one.

Originally published in *Frise du métro parisien* (La Bibliothèque Oulipienne no. 97)

Translated by Ian Monk

Pierre Rosenstiehl

Frieze of the Paris Métro

1998

● Pierre Rosenstiehl, a specialist in graph theory, combinatorics, and labyrinthology, is an exemplary oulipian collaborator and author. Here he explains the process by which he planned out a journey whereby Jacques Jouet could write an exhaustive métro poem.

Dreaming while the train rattles your brains then jotting down these dreams in a station on motionless paper; such were the origins of the Métro Poem. Jacques Jouet has defined its rules as follows:

> From time to time, I write métro poems. This poem being an example.
> Do you want to know what a métro poem consists of? Let's suppose you do. Here, then, is what a métro poem consists of.
> A métro poem is a poem composed during a journey in the métro.
> There are as many lines in a métro poem as there are stations in your journey, minus one.
> The first line is composed mentally between the first two stations of your journey (counting the station you got on at).
> It is then written down when the train stops at the second station.
> The second line is composed mentally between

```
   the second and the third stations of your
   journey.
It is then written down when the train stops
   at the third station. And so on.
You must not write anything down when the
   train is moving.
You must not compose when the train has
   stopped.
The poem's last line is written down on the
   platform of the last station.
If your journey necessitates one or more
   changes of line, the poem will then have
   two or more stanzas.
An unscheduled stop between two stations is
   always an awkward moment in the writing of
   a métro poem.
```

The indeterminacy of the "journey" is a weakness in the rules which might favorably be removed. Are some journeys more special than others? Could the act of writing be so ambitious as to aim for a sort of "total" journey, covering the entire métro? In what sense? There would have to be a way to define this. The poet requested twofold assistance: (1) how to globalize his path, of course, but at a human scale which would be feasible between the daily opening and closing of the service; (2) have a plan of his journey which would at all times indicate where to change and which direction to take. He would thus be able to advance shortsightedly quite free of any topological anxieties.

Nor should the poet's appetite be overestimated. He is no glutton. By covering the entire métro he is having a face-to-face encounter with the city, which gives the poem its meaning. So why not simply a street poem? But that would not be the sort of abstraction appropriate to poetry. The true constraint of all city poems can be found in the métro (we shall not concern ourselves here with countryside poems). A(n oulipian) constraint is by nature abstract, and the Paris métro is a sort of abstraction; it is not an extension of the city, an activity appended to its underground world, but a projected image of the city, a Paris whose deceptive brilliance has been removed, as well as the playful charm of its river and its contrasting architecture, in which can be seen the projection of its true dimension, its basic forms and its culture as summed up in the names of its stations; and finally its vibrations, in the dynamics of the everyday activities of its population. While life on the surface fills us with confused emotions, which are so dear to filmmakers, the abstraction of the métro offers a contrasting symbolic order complete with the metrics of the network: on it can be superimposed the rules for a total journey. And this urban skeleton, traced out before without lifting the pen from the paper, will be fleshed out by the poet, thus reinventing the city and fulfilling his dream: the encapsulation of everything.

A complete journey proposed by a labyrinthologist would consist of going along each section once in each direction, where a section is the rail track (generally a double one) between two neighboring stations. Two passages per section is theoretically possible thanks to a well-known theorem of connected networks. But such a journey would include about eight hundred sections of two minutes, thirty-two terminuses and far more than thirty changes from one line to another, then the return so that it would take over 2,160 minutes, or thirty-six hours: this greatly exceeds a day's work as planned by the métro poet. It will be necessary to find a more human solution.

Is it possible to visit each station only once? Obviously not. The terminuses are nearly all dead ends. And even it we cut off these offshoot line endings, the more circular remainder could still not be crossed cyclically without going through the same station several times. In mathematical terms, the métro is not a Hamiltonian graph (example below of a Hamiltonian graph).

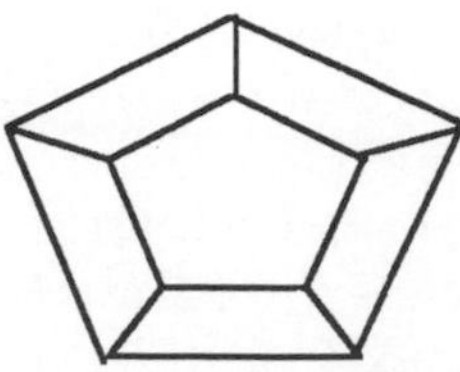

HAMILTONIAN GRAPH

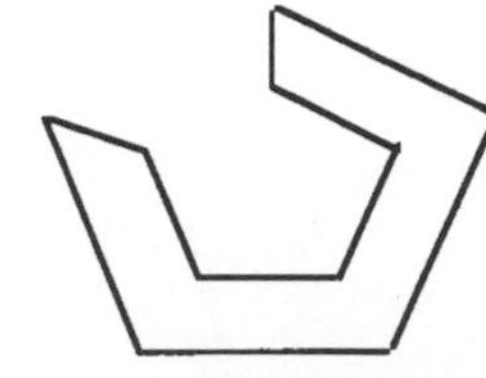

HAMILTONIAN CYCLE

Nor is the Paris métro Eulerian–in other words, it is not possible to pass by all of the sections one after the other, taking each one only once, in one direction or the other. Euler showed that such a path would require that each station have an even number of incidental sections arriving at it (example below of a Eulerian graph). So it is not possible to apply to the métro map any Eulerian algorithms in their current state.

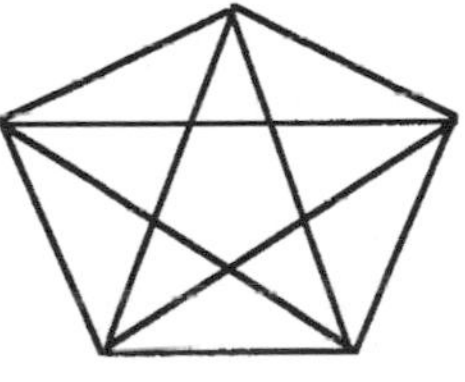

EULERIAN GRAPH

EULERIAN CYCLE

The adopted constraint, which was to turn out to be possible and viable, which would define a continuous total journey, is as follows:

i. any station arbitrarily chosen as the departure point will also be the arrival point;
ii. each station will be visited at least once;
iii. the number of changes will be as small as possible.

Such a journey will be called a *frieze* of the Paris métro.

The problem of constructing a perfect frieze, as suggested by the poet, is virgin territory: it is scientifically new, in other words unsolved, and in fact in practical terms insoluble to perfection. A few tricks can of course be used to arrive at a close solution. A frieze might skip certain sections, but certainly not those sections which are incidental to a station of a unit value of one, and certainly not those sections which are network "offshoots." Hence the following heuristic approach, which does produce a satisfactory solution.

Frieze heuristics: on the map of the métro shed of its offshoots, we identify the stations with odd valences, of which there is necessarily an even number, according to a well-known theorem in graph theory. We associate them in pairs and connect them via chains of sections according to a proximity criterion which can include possible changes of line. Then, in this fictional network, made up of the network without its offshoots and completed by the previously redundant chains (a network in which all of the knots (stations) are of even valences) we devise a path which takes each section exactly once, according to the Eulerian method, while being careful to stay on each line as long as possible so as to minimize changes. To this long journey, we now add the round trips required for the network's offshoots. Finally, if it appears that any section is covered both ways to reach a station that has already been visited, this little return trip is eliminated from the path. In this way, each station will be visited at least once, and each section contributes to this journey with zero, one, or two passages.

The result was the approximate frieze in the table below. As for metrical considerations: the frieze includes 490 passages and forty-seven changes, which weigh in at sixteen hours, while the métro is open for nineteen hours! There are thus three spare hours for various incidents (breakdowns, inspections, renewing the ticket which is valid only for two hours, bumping into Zazie, an assault from an accordionist, etc.).

The frieze has been hand-drawn in the figure below, but it was also by hand–or by eye–that it was "calculated," because it is difficult to choose between more changes (eighteen here without counting the terminuses) and fewer double passages along certain sections (twenty-five here, not counting the dead-end offshoots).

Not being able to find a smart way to satisfy item (iii) of the frieze constraint, we might have been tempted to enumerate courageously all of the possible friezes in order to extract the best ones; this would have required more minutes of computing time than there are grains of rice in China.

DETAILED FRIEZE FOR COMPOSITION OF THE MÉTRO POEM OF APRIL 18, 1996, FROM 5:30 A.M. TO 9:00 P.M.

from…	*(line)*	*…to*
République	9	Mairie de Montreuil
Mairie de Montreuil	9	Nation
Nation	6	Étoile
Étoile	2	Porte Dauphine
Porte Dauphine	2	Nation
Nation	1	Château de Vincennes
Château de Vincennes	1	Grande Arche de la Défense
Grande Arche de la Défense	1	Franklin-Roosevelt

Franklin-Roosevelt	9	Richelieu-Drouot
Richelieu-Drouot	8	Créteil-Préfecture
Créteil-Préfecture	8	Bastille
Bastille	5	Gare d'Austerlitz
Gare d'Austerlitz	10	Boulogne
Boulogne	10	Javel
Javel	10	Michel-Ange-Auteuil
Michel-Ange-Auteuil	9	Pont de Sèvres
Pont de Sèvres	9	Richelieu-Drouot
Richelieu-Drouot	8	Balard
Balard	8	La Motte-Piquet-Grenelle
La Motte-Piquet-Grenelle	6	Pasteur
Pasteur	12	Mairie d'Issy
Mairie d'Issy	12	Porte de la Chapelle
Porte de la Chapelle	12	Marcadet
Marcadet-Poissonniers	4	Porte de Clignan
Porte de Clignancourt	4	Porte d'Orléans
Porte d'Orléans	4	Montparnasse-Bienvenüe
Montparnasse-Bienvenüe	13	Châtillon-Montrouge
Châtillon-Montrouge	13	Gabriel-Péri-Asnières Gennevilliers
Gabriel-Péri-Asnières Gennevilliers	13	La Fourche
La Fourche	13	Saint-Denis basilique
Saint-Denis basilique	13	Saint-Lazare
Saint-Lazare	3	Pont de Levallois
Pont de Levallois	3	Galliéni
Galliéni	3	Gambetta
Gambetta	3bis	Porte des Lilas
Porte des Lilas	11	Mairie des Lilas
Mairie des Lilas	11	Rambuteau
Rambuteau	11	République
République	5	Bobigny-Pablo-Picasso
Bobigny-Pablo-Picasso	5	Jaurès
Jaurès	7bis	Pré-Saint-Gervais
Pré-Saint-Gervais	7bis	Louis Blanc
Louis Blanc	7	La Courneuve
La Courneuve	7	Mairie d'Ivry
Mairie d'Ivry	7	Maison Blanche
Maison Blanche	7	Villejuif-Louis Aragon
Villejuif-Louis Aragon	7	Place d'Italie
Place d'Italie	5	République

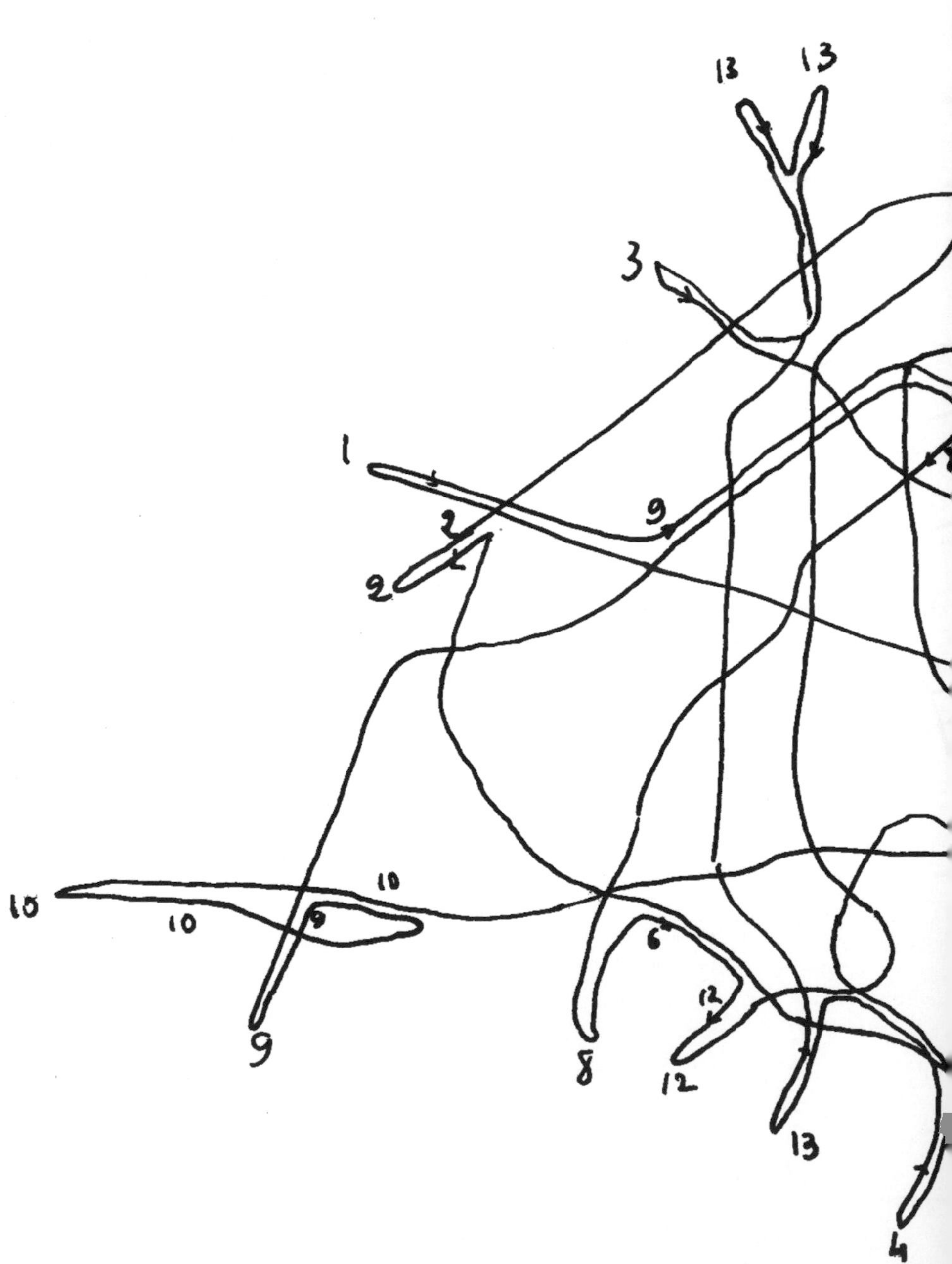
13
13
3
1
9
2
2
10
10
10
9
9
6
12
12
8
12
13
4

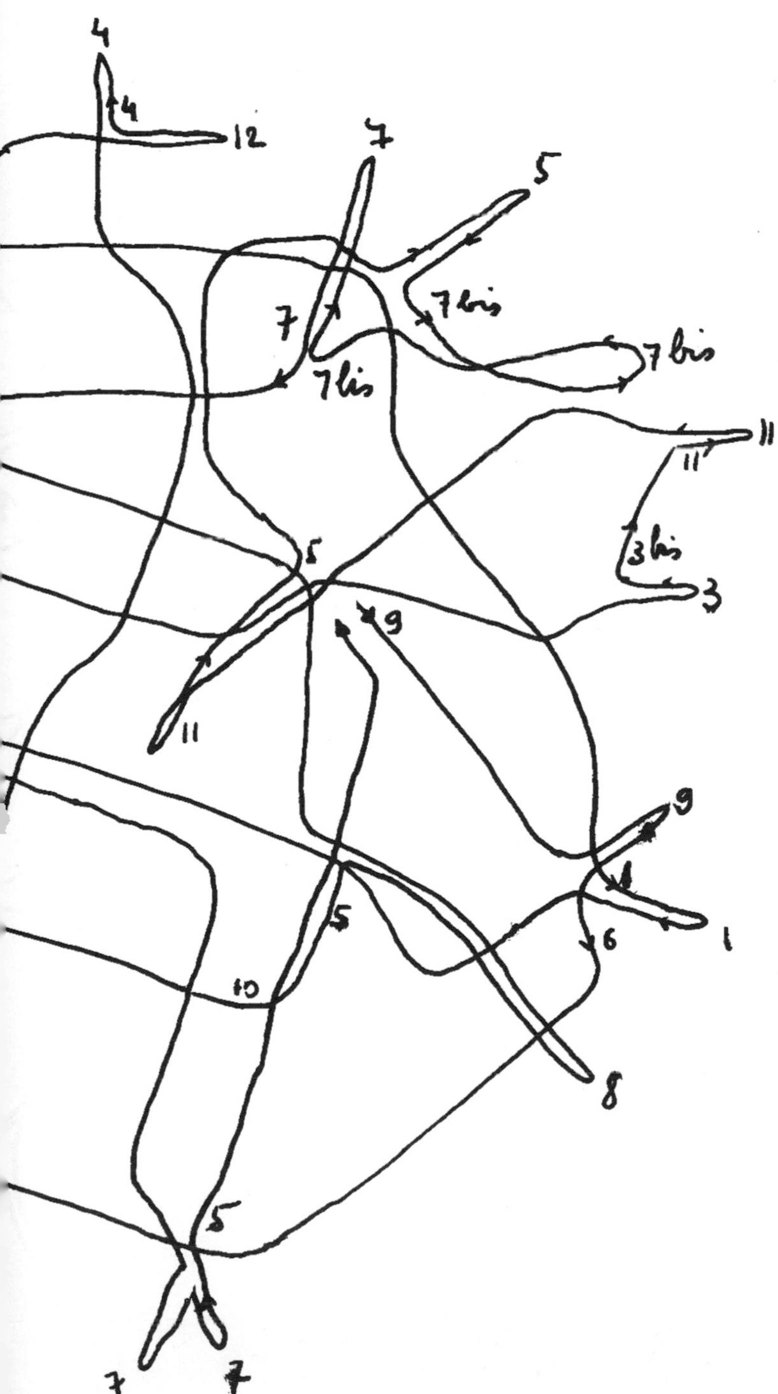
4
4
12
7
5
7bis
7
7bis
7bis
11
11'
3bis
3
5
9
11
9
1
6
5
10
8
5
7
7

Jacques Jouet

Poem of the Paris Métro

1998

● Behold, in turn, the fruit of Rosenstiehl's frieze and fifteen and a half hours of Jacques Jouet's time one day in April 1996. (Some months later Jouet would take the same route in reverse and compose a second poem of practically—there was an interruption in service on line 10—the same length.)

Originally published in *Frise du métro parisien* (La Bibliothèque Oulipienne no. 97); later reprinted in *Poèmes de métro* (P.O.L)

Translated by Ian Monk

If governing, governing the coming hours, is more a matter of surprising myself than planning ahead,
the first few minutes have already rather put me out.
I have more than enough time to explain why.
Outside, I had hoped for slight rain so as to enter into the concept of shelter,
keeping a slight wetness, on the backs of my hands, for my thirst,
but this night at 5:30 a.m. was dry and mild and black like a black dress lit up from inside
by a body standing up in its fullness.
Surprise is this much of a revelation in that it recognizes what has not been,
or what was not in its place at the counted time, which was revealed to it
in the name of a quite particular trust in a world order.
On a staircase of laws, one is made of sand,
a missing step, under the foot of a walker who has forgotten his own weight.

I have reached the end of the first tentacle
without the good fortune of having a porthole over Montreuil
the monocle of a monomaniac Tristan Tzara with a monochromatic tail of blue blue.
And then I went into reverse, to stir up my milk again,
one among peaceful, discrete destinies.
I do something with my five fingers.

I really cannot believe as hard as rails in the reality of these nonetheless counted minutes
with a low margin of error, no doubt.
The first emergence into fresh air, at BEL-AIR what is more, is not very spectacular because of the night
which, on high, is still only putting a drop of blue milk into its darkness
and stirring it pensively with a little solar spoon.
The first Seine of the day has me drop my glasses onto my paper.
The first Seine and the first building site, if I don't count the green hut
on the platform of RÉPUBLIQUE, when I left, full of tools and workers' bits and bobs.
The way this train brakes is novel and irritating,
as if, in its machinery, it were reproaching us for awaiting the next stop.
There, I have said "us" without asking my companions' opinions,
which is certainly a way to overstate the orphic
character who, this morning, believes himself to be the scribe of the entire dynasty of today's transported.
At DENFERT-ROCHEREAU, for the first time, my paper was looked at curiously
with wine-dark feminine penetration, suit, two bags,
on one of them an embroidered globe, with a rocket orbiting it,
while I know that right now I am passing just by rue Mizon.
I was expecting the sky, after PASTEUR, to be that violet color
and that here and there a scattering of flats would have turned their lamps on,
while the Loto and Hôtel Ibis will not have switched off their lights yet.
We're nearing the second Seine, which is at the far end of the river,
but I don't believe for a minute that the municipality of Paris will convert offices into council accommodation.
The métro, at PASSY, goes straight though a building.
It was necessary, it was enough, to dive back underground
for me to be able to see a jacket with red diamonds, the top of a back
with hair shiny from lacquer.
At that price, it does you good to write.

This strophe has two lines, Paris replaced what?
The dolphin was scarcely afraid of Gilliatt's octopus.

A nun in a wimple is a favorite feature in advertising at the moment.
We still cannot strip them all, nor deal with things in the midterm,
hence the takeability of poetry which does not fear hunting the extreme using the dull
and surprises itself sometimes into governing chance.
A woman from Vitruvius in a poster for Galéries Lafayette spins in the O of 10%, written like the letter O rather than the number 0.
I like her.
So, I allowed myself to like her, took the time to do so,
just as I like the long plastic edge between the back of the seat
and the side of the wagon,
sign of a need to bodge up after a rather shitty technical drawing.
I am no less happy than if I were walking, this morning, in the countryside,
which is not to say that I won't go walking, the day after tomorrow, in the countryside.
But "the countryside" comes to me on coming out into the daylight at BARBÈS, with a pink fluffy sky.
Pierre has made me start with the overhead line,
by the overhead line of his Friesian great-uncle, first of all, then by the one made by
I don't know... by a competitor–but in that profession you say "dear colleague."
I have a mind to add lines to lines
with subsequent headiness.
There are lots of women who raise their heels
for height as well as a trick to make them look slimmer.
But when they sit down, the whole trick collapses:
I must patent some heels for buttocks
which will lift your curves up by the neck as in a common-or-garden giraffe.
All I need are green shoots on the ceiling of the wagon.

Staying silent during the stop, my pen raised,
for an instant, is the luxury of rather short lines,
Procrustes was never happy with the correspondence between line and time
but Procrustes, in case you didn't know, was rather loopy, to put it mildly.

Running is pointless, I think I left in time,
with a mission and a few amused encouragements.
Culture is making something into something else:
proportionally, electricity burns fewer barns or great oaks than two centuries ago
and Buffon's lightning conductor is in a glass case, in Montbard.
A mouth yawns in front of me.
Yet, what dignity in each of our bodies, equipped with a project for the day!
Finish a novel, finish a *Que sais-je?* (about the internet of course) while wearing a tie decked with bonsais;
buy a new property on an advantageous loan;
during work time become a poem,
in the name of the precision of craftsmanlike fitting
while discreetly exploiting scientific or otherwise ancestral acquisitions
or at least coming from the complicity of adorable partners,
from the *ouvroir* considered as a key:
the key, active in the lock, draws an O
which is still ambiguous *O* and *0* ([o] and zero).
There's none in GEORGE V, sign of Britishness,
but two *ls* in de Gaulle, who wore two stars, but the station is not CHARLES DE GAULLE ÉTOILES.
The words "tirage argentique" deck a photograph.
A billsticker is replacing a poster on the platform of PORTE MAILLOT.
A line of neon dashes in the dark. A poem is time.
It's time and spending it in the most premeditated way
possible. Here's my third Seine
and, almost at once, my first desire to piss. A terminus.

There are six hands in front of me, and eight rings.
Two hands are crossing their fingers like the city,
mixing flesh and metal
and, in the mouth, the mucous membrane and ivory.
I didn't shave this morning, why?
while today's first seller of *Le Lampadaire* is freshly so.
A refusal to close the double-bladed bed and the cold knife
even though I did want, in fact, to be rather impeccable.

It is impossible seriously to have the feeling
of simply starting to exhaust a Parisian place, as someone once put it,
because movement and perception are not suited to any kind of reduction,
but instead increase tenfold, a hundredfold, tentaclefold
the kernels of the real which can still be germinated after scarfing the first succulent piece of fruit.
Any *lieu* is a *riche lieu*, and Drouot is distributing inheritances.

I have not had enough time to think of anything apart from the poem.
And so? At night or when napping do you leave your tongue in a glass of water on the bedside table?
"Begging is a pain in the arse, it stresses you out!" Not only did I give him nothing
but I stole his sentence to make half a line,
yes, *make* half a line and *slip* into half a line
for what would this half a line be, without this stolen sentence?
Neither grass nor green at CHEMIN VERT.
Poetry has far less need for greenery than, say, a rodent...
chlorophyllophilia
is not necessarily part of its outfit
but not just as a poet I wouldn't mind having, right now, a bit of rocket or mesclun
delicately flavored with lemon juice and olive oil.
And yet, I can only see a chicory poet,

and a bottle one, too: a bottle poem making cork tongues clack
and creating, why not, the enthusiasm that even nature lacks.
Hands and feet unbound, I book
myself into the regular creation of a book.
And it's with my head held high, and my weary back, that I can go through LIBERTÉ station,
to get, slap! A few seconds of real sunshine in my eye,
over the Marne.
I remember the very long and very tiring gallery in the potassium mine in Wittelsheim
I once visited as a tourist, just to take a look at the nearly past.
At the end, there were men who looked at home, breaking the veins of the world
and letting salt cover the granddads in color photos stuck on the steel jacks, which they maybe licked once we, the visitors, had our backs turned.

I won't go any faster facing in the direction of the train.
I don't know if I want to go faster, but I'm not wasting time.
There was a meeting to decide whether there should be neon lights in the tunnels of the métro.
I still have the Purcell which I heard just now, played live at LA DÉFENSE, in my aural memory
with my two-nostril sound-box replaying it with my mouth closed.
This morning's *Libération* is looking for the head of Madame Wang
so as to reunite it with its body in a coffin or, to begin with, in a drawer in the morgue,
at least so far as I can make out this real-life drama from my neighbor.
PORTE DORÉE station which I twin with ARGENTINE,
not a soul on the platform, not a rat, not a cat,
but the train still stopped, with all the courtesy in the world,
world, my world, respecting my commitments, in a sufficiently large number.
In the tunnel, I wonder about the secrets of certain housings.
How regular it all is, with a desire
that makes the caress of what is seen last forever
and the watcher, too, lazily reduced to the object of a caress!

Among my companions today, he is (up till now) by far the least loony
which only goes to show that the world is full of loonies.

The sad, limp leek quiche and Badoit in the underground track at BASTILLE
hasn't given me the slightest pickup.
I ate it like you swallow an emergency package,
in exactly the way I don't like having to read a book.
The quivering double of my text, in the security glass, seems to make it Arabic
in the direction it should be read, the direction of the flag and the shape of the letters.
The underground gardens of SÈVRES-BABYLONE have platform seats painted green.
Ah, green! that damned green which I wasn't asked for!
Are dandelion roots green? The ones you'll suck at, when you've
signed your last contract, the one with the underworld.
Is there a particular line for agonizing souls, or ghosts?
PÈRE-LACHAISE, SAINT-VINCENT, MONTPARNASSE, INNOCENTS, BAGNEUX, PANTIN, PASSY
with a certain change for the world of Ophelia and Yorick.
There has perhaps never been a full coffin in a métro carriage (or even an empty one).
The métro seems to take off, at the ghost station of MIRABEAU.
And I'm not making up the fact that this is a slow line.
A big blonde yawns and seems to doubt the precious reality of her wedding ring.
The end of the line is limp.

Yes, this member has gout,
appreciated as much by children as by the Japanese, but the distance between BOULOGNE-JEAN-JAURÈS
and MICHEL-ANGE-MOLITOR is far greater than most of my intervals!
That's really serious! Look, here's MIRABEAU, the MIRABEAU
I glimpsed just now, without stopping. We stop, this time. I change again at JAVEL.

Strange place. A really pleasant ascent overhanging MIRABEAU,
something comparable in quality with the curve at LA RAPÉE.

Starting out this morning at 5:30,
the train was waiting, sleeping against the platform of RÉPUBLIQUE and the population
was more varied than I had expected: the usual proportion
of several categories so far as I could see.
An African woman
has got off, dark in her colors in which light occurs.

Already six hours, just six hours, time doesn't let itself go,
it is a barge shrugging its shoulders when asked to sprint.
Burning up the waiting time by burning up time: vanity,
and pursuit of the instant in the photographed scene.
A billsticker is standing, in the middle of his scraps, like a heron in its wrecked nest,
while the duplication of his leg is contradicted by his crossed posture
with one knee taking the weight and one leg precariously balanced,
a mother leg and its infant.
As soon as the world has been observed, you have to let it go,
without counting too long on its highly improbable return.
And yet, strictly speaking, there are always just coincidences
because you flavor dishes that are too bland with salt
and a wealth of spices, which are food's clinamen opening onto cooking.
Calf's head in a vinaigrette, I'll wait a few hours.
The paradise of posters
claiming to sell at the right price: it's far away, the eternal Orient,
yes, parroted like the eternal,
which the métro will compensate for easily by its strength, small steps, its fleeting nature.

And yet, it's in motion! Its wheels turn.
It is more of a to-and-fro, or a regular course.

There's the whistling song of line 8 which the blind must recognize among all lines
and which the sighted have as an inactive memory,
I suppose, but capable sooner or later of the prowess of a Combourg thrush.
Over there, at the far end of the carriage, a bald man is violently scratching his head with both hands.
Above the gray bars, all I can see are his hands and the scene:
accelerating dancers, or ants in a hurry to finish off a corpse.
Scratching, scratching… say what you want, it's quite a job,
and that is the use of the fruit of the plane tree.
"Every month at your newsagent's"
there is a certain magazine devoted to the property market.
Pierre (a different Pierre from the first one) would here point his finger,
an intention I share, at a moment when the poem has got stuck.

The center, in this world,
is mobile as a bubble in a level.
    Shouldn't I rather see the center as being above my head,
vertically over my joined-up fontanel?
The center, in other words where I'm going.

Here I go again, time for three lines, in the Apollonian world of the Friesian uncle,
the uncle of Pierre Rosenstiehl, my cartographer. His uncle was an architect,
an engineer on line 6, when this century was still young.

Of course, it's difficult
to read, like the woman in front of me is reading a book called *La beauté*
without trusting her own, but it looks to be standing up okay…

The book is dog-eared, worn out, having been passed around, often lent,
with many hands wiped across its boards.
Hélène eats and powders herself.

No one is waiting for me,
at the end of the line, no one, waiting
while I use these common goods, this seat, this seat and my private
trousers without majority reasons,
and even, in fact, beyond all reason.
The wind, arriving through the window, is a false one,
made by the simple motion of a mass agitating air, air
of a demiurge thinking itself capable of acclimatizing everything with everything.
The unpredictable body of a child,
multiplying horribly its tentacles, too, and casting
its feet into the tibias of all comers, this body
dislikes the métro, that's clear, because the métro is a tunnel
lit up and moving within a darker tunnel.
To love the métro, you must become a tunnel
a Russian nesting doll conscious of a smaller self, called an esophagus or vena cava or colon,
shit being indivisible.
The abovementioned child sucks its thumb.
I'm thirsty. But thirst won't make me leave. Because thirst
should be set against a little rigor (or a lot)
applied to the construction of a building of poetry
now begun in a gallery perpendicular to the river Seine.
A few pathetic centiliters of black ink concentrated in the tube of my felt-tip pen
are transmuted,
through a strainer and through a double *J*,
in that it is nothing other than almost nothing, which is not much,

but something other than a dummy hanging, in provocation, from the bag of that sixteen-year-old girl
who got out, chewing, at MARX DORMOY.

That delicate moment / I foresaw in my first
métro poem (last line) has just occurred.

At such times, the ideal is to place a caesura
in the middle of a classical alexandrine, even if the line in mind had not set out initially to fit into this kind of mold (and mark it with a slash)

Silence...
it would good to be able to say a word about silence like you think you can shed light on darkness.
But silence is a relay baton gifted with a return
sometimes far faster than you expect,
and which your face does not expect, gifted as it is with a calculable capacity for resistance.
So many reproaches gravitate around silence
that it becomes profitable to break it, but only applying yourself a little,
by studying eloquence, marbles in your mouth, and acting,
the pillow, the divan, drinks, a mike,
the necessary social skills in the use of the telephone.
A beginner's course in ventriloquism or learning a foreign language should not be neglected,
no more than seeing how children acquire language.
We pass beneath the Seine unaware of how our aches and pains
wake up in this nearby dampness.
A man is reading a leaflet which is on the floor, without picking it up.
It's about the war in Lebanon.
Signed by the French Communist Party and Communist Youth.
A little further on: S.D.F./S.V.P. (or Homeless/Please) with clearly dotted dots between the letters.
This is how men move

and do not stay still in a room
and how weapons leave their rack.
The proof of territory is that you pass through it. It becomes dramatic when you take too much
and take your place. From this moment on,
this seated place is mine
and two, then three, then four are far more comfortable.

Dampness and thirst
are the two pendants hanging from my rucksack.
Nineteen and begging, which is almost his name, if I believe him,
his name, his title, his definition.
A woman is conversing with a poster seen on a platform: which is exactly what was requested by the poster.
Everything that should be commented on.

There will be no sea at CHATILLON MONTROUGE, nor a small chateau,
this being one of those things that it is possible to affirm.
A “ZAYAZ” bag is in the arms of a West Indian,
and his neck has been surrounded by the links of a gold virgin on a chain.
An assault on the métro demanding all the jewelry in a carriage might not give such a bad haul!
Ah, daylight, I no longer dared dream of it,
with the sun, albeit mediocre.
I have refused a break, and leapt back
on the same platform onto line 13, which is not line 31 in the other direction, and it’s a shame.
A palindrome is a luxury for skeptics.
“At least eighteen tourists have been killed during a terrorist attack in Cairo,” says *Le Monde*.
What is done with the sum of their return tickets?
The weight of the day, the shock of the rotogravures,
a newspaper weighs on your back, like a poem.
Writing one a day would be an exploit, but exploits are not what interest me.

I just want to make a round body of work.
An exploit is eight hours at the office every day or eight hours on the lathe or cash desk,
of hair to cut, of fries to drain...
This evening, I shan't have fifteen days' growth.
Even if I turn seconds into hours,
put a ski mask on time,
time still will not have gained the power of speech.
It will have nothing to say, nothing to repeat,
and LA FOURCHE leans towards ASNIÈRES-GENNEVILLIERS.
As of now, I'll only eat if I have the time and a tablecloth.
As for money, I have the privilege of being able to invent it.
There is no time bank.
Whenever a tale imagines its existence, the banker is the Devil.

This is, if I'm not mistaken, the fourth crossing–visually–of the Seine.
The first bridge in mankind's history, at the beginning, must have been swept away by water, winds, or poor calculations.
The first rivers in world history must have run up against general incredulity,
like the first snow for the first walking fish.
This is the first section where I have to write standing up, but not for long, no doubt.
There, I'm now sitting. It's a sign
that all the people in the city, in their very concentration, know how to spread themselves out.
A kid has set off a firework on the platform.
A group of six technical inspectors in ties has just got onto the carriage, with notepads and calculators clipped onto their boards.
They fill in their forms and contemplate uncomprehendingly my rival pad.
Among them, there are some concerned-looking local politicians.

I pump the reserves of my humps like the old camel I am.
There are still enough words and turns of phrase that I haven't yet used in this poem
to give me the firm conviction that I shall fill my work to the brim.

It is only when I have played at being a still for long enough
that I shall drink this or that liquor as required in the cycle of liquors,
the pumped, pressed, infused, decocted, fortified, distilled,
fermented, and pasteurized.
Honestly, I wouldn't even spit on other saliva.
For now, it's LIÈGE, wide open to the public,
while I am composing, at this instant, in the middle of my eleventh hour.

Fifteen nights' trial for a mattress!
Several people should wear it out completely in fifteen nights… and fifteen days…
This will be a day when I haven't phoned,
or answered, or called,
or turned over the hourglass,
but I've looked at the time, of course, without hoping to be able to change it.
This poem is chronometric
parallel to its kilometric nature
as in the only worth / of all its poor meanings.

Changing a terminus into the start of a line should happen in the twinkling of an eye,
especially when there isn't even the alibi of a drinks vending machine to stop there for five minutes.
Straight along a penultimate transversal line, which will go very near to where I live,
in the greatest indifference, given that there is still a lot of time before
the finished objective. The difficulty, in this measure, is that you have to be attentive,
stitch by stitch, dose by dose, lined page by lined page, one by one,
in the absolute measured awareness of each one, which means that time can never bend itself into something subjective
and it is imprisoned in a metronome.

Imagine an alarm clock which would ring every fifteen minutes, the métro stopping every minute,
sleep could still slip into these chicanes so long as they were regular.

Anarchy would defeat it, perhaps.
A girl is singing, in front of me, with belly button and panties, just after school, and with her Verlainian boyfriend.
He sometimes has that strange and penetrating dream, no doubt,
and that is exactly what she wants him to do, so she talks about flesh-colored tights.
And I can't see how to write anything which does not attempt to parasite their cooing.
Now he's got off, she falls silent. As she's fallen silent, I look elsewhere
for the substance of the poem which has become empty.
I am a mineral, sweating out its last drops,
a gastropod, who really walks on its stomach, but am not hungry.
My poem for a water hole? No, no, things aren't that bad yet, you can't fool me...
The cynic can never have his expectations disappointed,
he who innocently claims he has been everywhere.
A short moment, although unexpected, well prepared, can have such perfections
that they fill up your life, and these few pages, and these few lines.

If I wanted to address the distich,
I would need, but don't have, an envelope and a letter box, at least.

Smaller train, smaller, little.
The map itself becomes ideal,
linear violet.

While waiting at PORTE DES LILAS, direction MAIRIE, standing in front of six monochromes, you really feel like waving at the driver.

In the optimization of the network, such as Pierre Rosenstiehl concocted it for me
(pass by all the stations, minimize the number of repeated sections and changes, departure RÉPUBLIQUE, arrival RÉPUBLIQUE)
there is something quite admirable, towards which I am heading in this strophe
which will mean that there will remain
a short section which I will not take, because crossing it

—between RAMBUTEAU and HÔTEL DE VILLE—
would have added nothing apart from the fact of covering all the sections (and covering all the sections was not a stated request)
without considering / the station taken in
among all of those which otherwise would have been missing.
Here we are, I'm there. I'm going to look down the tunnel with particular interest.

And he who no longer knows if he is an eel or a salmon
goes back up towards RÉPUBLIQUE, spread out over the Place and the Poem of the Republic.
I hardly recognize myself at JACQUES BONSERGENT. Have I aged?
I'll try and ask Raymond Queneau, almost at the end of the line.
The trapezii muscles, under the nape, are strained just like they are after several hours in the car.
It seems that I could record far more kisses exchanged at six in the evening than in the morning.
It's quite clear. What is more, there are two types of body at six in the evening,
bodies worn out by work, and intact bodies.
I suppose I must be one of the former.
Except that these weary bodies, here, are no longer working.
I still have a good hundred lines left.
There are no places of worship in the métro, so far as I know, and long may that be so,
and far be it from me to turn this station into one.
I prefer to salute this stretch of canal with its slightly decrepit factories.

To my right: the place where they wash the line's trains.
The tunnel is equal, to itself and to the others.
If you want earrings to be visible, you sometimes need the pavilions
of the ears to hold back the hair.
Books are open in large numbers.
This journey is a necessary time-distance,
which Jane Austen and Pierre Bellemare, beside me, will obliterate.

On line 7bis I have the pleasant surprise of meeting
the single-carriage métro with its high windows.
I was expecting it, another perspective
which can't suit musicians, I suppose: how to make their begging last?
I don't think I've taken this line before,
which goes round the meadow in a circle with no real change, except for a long pause as though for the start (or the end) of a line.
This is a quite different territory, an underground village,
the stations spread out with a relaxing thrift,
the vague feeling of spare time and country weekends,
tunnels without neon lighting, but with antediluvian bulbs.
We'll walk out into the middle of the brush.

Around here, this exhaustive tour seems so slow and fussy!
I don't know why, I know it's the buildup
to the key note, I suppose, of line 7, which for the moment
I must reach the end of, before taking it
from its north to its south / with its fork to the south.
Here, the map shows the city and its concentration,
its names in closed ranks; it would be impossible to slip in the shadow of another.
A man with wounded hand / suffers (his heart, perhaps).

And here begins the long prong of the fork.
It is 7:30 p.m., I've been in the network for fourteen hours.
A nice blue hat married to the heavy black hat of the Hasidim
the double sign of the shaved head, two sets of headgear and twiddled beards.
A body is boiling. Just beside, perspiring legs,
a mountain dweller's cheeks, maybe a municipal gardener.
I don't think there is any activity which will ever attract hatred,
an activity or even, perhaps, an attitude to dress.

If poetry could make furious
some religious deformer or some ill-harnessed reader...
but it will pass, just like an espresso, by the way it passes and pisses away.
It will have exercised nothing other than the course of its exercise,
in which I place the seed of everything that I call meaning.
If it were possible to imagine going on until your hand fell away,
when the atlas of paths perhaps also failed, dried up,
in that the words to which, by definition, it's unnecessary to answer to attest to the fact that they've been heard,
have not bounced off just as they are from the smooth wall
but must have slipped something of themselves into the frozen split stone
thus contributing inappreciably to the modification of the earth's crust.
You'll need stubborn courage,
mock finance in its face and figure,
burn up all its capital, unless you seize a chance for fructification,
in which case we'll be in touch.
There's nothing else to say, even though there are still lines
to burn up in its white chimney.
You speak, then, of the blueness of a plastic bag, the same as that of the luminous inscription of VILLEJUIF-LOUIS ARAGON
or of the yellowness of a tulip, the same as that of the luminous inscription of MAIRIE D'IVRY.
The fork, after hesitating–and even a flagrant contradiction–chose the latter.
As for me, it's all the same.
One or another will or won't do.
I'll have time.
Time isn't flying.

Around here, caps are kings,
with a U.S. cut, hiding the eyes,
eyes which do not gleam with success.

There is no gaiety here, unless it is love between two heterosanguine hands
which would still, all said and done, agree to a transfusion.

This rather long trip
and this not-really-long poem (unless it is read also while following the journey round the network)
are almost over, at least
I'll go no further.

Just as Blaise Cendrars considered, on coming back from Kharbin,
whether to go back through the door of the Lapin Agile,
his journey must have aged him–another would chop off
one of his arms. How to know what you would want to alter about a journey.
Or in a *regulated* journey, what you would want to deregulate?
It is probably set down, though less clearly legible.

I had prepared a note for any acquaintances I might run into.
In it I explained my temporary inability to converse.
But I met no one whom I needed to show it to.
Just spotted a couple of faces I could put a name to, but had no obligation to chat with.
Someone carrying a monoski gets into the carriage,
a reader of *Le Monde*,
a woman ditto,
an exhausted sportsman, who looks newborn from his efforts.
It is five or six minutes past 9 p.m.

Originally published in *Sainte Catherine* (P.O.L)

Translated by Ian Monk

Harry Mathews

from

Saint Catherina

2000

● A novella that appears to take up domestic themes not atypical of Harry Mathews's later fiction, *Saint Catherina* is also an exploration of the sestina, a spiral-permuting poetic form based on the calculated repetition of words at the end of each line. Its initial form, published in La Bibliothèque Oulipienne, treats it as a poem, with the requisite line breaks; this version, published the following year as a standalone book, casts it into prose.

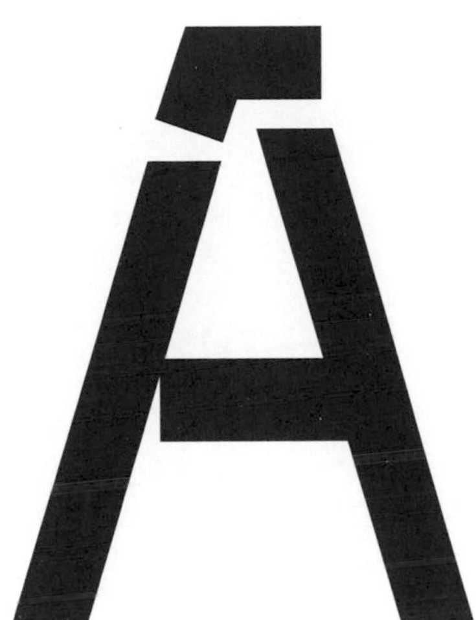

At the start of the evening, the very air is shaking from the gong. You are perhaps still in the water, in the warmth of the evening, or, coming out of the shower, still shaking the water from your ears. Then comes the gong. Your heart skips a beat and begins shaking from this monstrous vibration, but it's only the start. For several blows rain down on that huge gong, shattering with their clamor the calm of the evening. You do not even know that it is a gong.

You think of an alarm, perhaps you are shaking from memories of an alert one distant evening during the war, with your life just at its start. You end up crossing the space making up this evening and which separates you from the source of your unease, that gong. You say to yourself that you should have understood right from the start.

How childish I was, how stupid to stand there shaking.

At the start of the evening, the very air is shaking from the gong, the simple and lugubrious signal that it's time for a cocktail. This din perfectly plays out its role as a signal, underlining each day the anxiety at this very time before night comes, with the arrival of the urge for a cocktail. Desires awaken and remorse too, at that time whose power (or else meaning) seems as simple as the creeping yet plain wish to have a cocktail, taken either with a smile or a sigh, its very self the signal of an irresistible process that pushes you towards a second cocktail. Even when speaking, you think, through a moment without time, about the future, the past, an elsewhere from which will rise a signal of regrets for a childhood you thought to be fine and simple, or hopes for success: the success that will signal the fact that we can now laugh over a cocktail. Yes, that your life is your own, overflowing, sure, and simple like the soft clash of ice cubes clinking at this time, a signal, simple and lugubrious, that it is time for a cocktail, though pointless for any regular, especially on those days when the rain has already filled the Sphinx with its collection of regular customers. All, without exception, are just thinking of days of fine weather, yesterday and tomorrow. "It won't last, this rain, it's just a light shower."

And yet there are days when such remarks ring hollow. It's pointless to pretend when faced with the persistence of this monotonous rain, without a glimmer of the sunshine that otherwise is so regular, except, sometimes in the evening, on the far side of this rain—how unseasonal can you get!—which for nights and days drums on the canopy of the terrace. The regular crowd gathers there sometimes, during this awful summer, their pointless gazes fixed on a sea, on a horizon without their regular sun and stars. Indifferently, the rain carries on its relentless drench, so pointless when it comes to refreshing the hopes of vacationers on such days, and pointless for any regular; and as the rain, for days on end, hardly dilutes the sting of the sea, all feel as though they were living hardly at all, visitors and locals together in the sting of a disappointment (no money nor sun on the sea).

No one was expecting to rot in this stinging, aimless resentment which nothing dilutes, not even faith in the fine weather's coming back, and the sea perseveres and spits on a hope that is hardly hope. People were expecting this: opening the window on a sea where, day after day, a breeze with no sting sketches out just trembling wrinkles, hardly seen in a constant light that no cloud dilutes. Regret is now felt at having taken such hardly bearable lodgings, the shutters closed to obscure that sea through a gray gleam which the rain dilutes.

Alone, even before the gong, a straight whiskey, with its sting hardly dilutes the sting of the sea.

It is an evening of wind, thunder, and rain. She's absorbed reading *Gone With the Wind* as a comic strip. A sudden burst of thunder and the steady rain changes into storm rain, with clear or diffuse flashes of lightning, and thunder that seems to whip the garden leaves in the gray of the evening. Through her window frame, tiny traces of rain seep in, rammed by the wind, suddenly propelling an abundant rain unwanted by man or grass, no more than the thunder making you jump like a child, or the wind almost drowning out the gong that evening.

She decides to go down to the bar, despite the wind. She tells herself that she feels right as rain. It is just this loneliness that pains her, at the start of the evening, more than the din of the wind or the rolling thunder.

It is an evening of rain, thunder, and wind. This blow hits her like a mallet beating a gong. It jumps at her like a mugger's blow, whipping her up like a whisk beating eggs, making her forget the din of the gong. Air water thunder form a single beating to bring her outside into the lightning and then, after all this, run head-down, hugging herself, towards the gong whose quivering subsides after the final blow. Lost in the grayness of the air, the shimmer of the gong. Outside, not a single stray, not a single heart beating on the sand.

Then, inside, everyone seems oddly blow-dried, or indoors since noon. But there is more than just this: she's come to a halt before the young barman, mixing a blow-pop, when a voice, low and vibrant as a gong, rings in her ears. She wasn't expecting this, not so soon, shaken up as she is by that celestial beating. For she is this gong, under the beating's blow, and that voice plunges into her like a Boeing into the sea. It's like on the telephone, a voice can do wonders, she says to herself. Before looking round at him, she pictures herself in a Boeing two miles above a distant sea, invited to try the controls by the charming captain of the Boeing, who is guiding her with his expert hands. She starts falling, she plunges and turns round. Behind him stretches the dark beach, the raging sea, she glances at him, sees his eyes on her, then turns away in a tumult greater than that of the sea. Her thorax quivers like the cowling of the Boeing, where she would happily be right now (poor fool, her inner voice says, what a hick) or in Sydney, or Tampico, as she plunges her arms into a sink... She pulls herself together, or does her best to pretend to, then stares at him again, against the sea, the window, the others. He smiles. She does too. He plunges his gaze into hers. He's built like a Boeing. With her, the Boeing plunges into the sea.

It's just an invitation to have a cocktail. "Young lady, please allow me..." (an invitation which is so classic and direct). "Would you care to have something?" (The something in question being just a cocktail, even though she can already think of other things to have. This madness that has suddenly gripped her must just be the effect of her loneliness, she should concentrate on the cocktail now, and nothing else, quite simply this banal invitation.) "The weather's so rotten, how about a little cocktail to cheer you up?" She has to make her mind up: to have or have not? And at once. Why is this invitation putting in her such a state? It's nothing much, it's just a passing distraction for this man, an easy invitation, he is thinking only vaguely about what might happen after this cocktail. Disconcerted, she says: "Sorry, it's nothing, just something I've forgotten, and which I'd really like to have."

She tries to fathom this simple invitation to have a cocktail. For refuge, she flees towards the sea. Or rather, she does everything but take refuge: she is in a panic and so flees blindly towards the beach and the sea. She cannot name the danger from which she now flees, although she knows that the sole danger for her lies within her, and that it is not in this wild sea that her demons will be able to take refuge. And yet her demons find their reflection in the sea that wraps itself around her. The light flees away towards the horizon, hazy in the grayness, to take refuge far from the heavy, implacable night bringing for one and all a desire to take refuge from the wind, the rain and the dark. She goes towards the sea with an unstated desire to grasp the for and the against of it all, and why she now flees. She now flees for a refuge far from the sea. She feels drenched from the spasms of the sea whipped up by the wind, which has drenched her with each blast, with spasms and frissons, even though it's rain from a summer wind. She knows in her bones that spasms of fear are marking her more than the effect she feels physically from the wind and the rain, it would almost be a delight to get drenched by all that the distant, noisy sky can throw at her, with its rain and wind, punctuated just like in the movies by spasms of thunder.

It even makes her want to feel drenched by that night's tango (and just then she feels that her choice has been made, and she has emerged like iron still drenched, light too, light and supple as the rain). But she needs to get changed, she feels it like a pressing need, even though her own spasms of panic have vanished into the spasms of the rain that have left her drenched, there is one thing she still feels: what she wants is melting into him as ice into a cocktail or like melting into that nocturnal tango, melting into the two storms that have made her as cold as an ice cube down her spine, and will now warm her up, as the spirits in a cocktail; and if, floating on its surface, she feels the cold of the ice cube, it will just slow down the warmth she is accepting, and wants and wants to find, why not, in that pivotal cocktail offered by a handsome stranger, melting with just a hackneyed word, simply by saying "cocktail," her whole being, which she wanted to be as pure and hard as ice glinting intact in January sunlight. Yes, melting her. Then let the world think whatever it wants.

Yes, let the world think what it likes, she leaves it behind her, melting in the fumes of her desires: firstly, that cocktail, such a trivial way to get to what she really wants and for which she's ready to swallow a chunk of ice; after the ice in the cocktail, it's into him that she wants to see herself melting. She wants to tremble in his hands like a gong. For days now, she has forgotten what it is to tremble, or just slightly, while dumbly watching her hands so useless, limp and incapable of striking a gong, or of striking anything, of taking her life in her hands, that life she doesn't know and yet wants; it is an image as exotic as a gong when, before dusk, it starts to tremble, shaking up new dreams and lost memories, this gong palpitating with a strength that makes her clasp her hands pointlessly, that pushes her towards impossible tears and makes her tremble before the terrible hiatus of not knowing what she wants. At last, just for an instant, she could really tremble, her flesh and breath shaking like a gong. At last, just during a short spell, she would know what she wants: a man returning her desire, putting his life back in her hands. And then his hands... the gong starts to tremble. She knows what she wants. She goes back to find him and accept that cocktail.

It's all so terribly simple. He seems to find nothing odd about her waiting to accept his invitation to sit next to him and have a cocktail. He does not seem surprised that, before she will accept his offhand invitation, she leaves then comes back wearing different clothes. The fact that at last she'll have a cocktail apparently gives him no reason at all to find her hesitant in any way. And which cocktail would she now be so good as to accept? And what will he have? she asks, a ruse to find a moment in which to somehow bring back the name of a possible drink and find out the precise meaning of the word "cocktail" in his vocabulary. All she can answer back when he suggests "a gin and tonic?" is that she'll accept.

So she comes back to find him in front of the cocktail she's decided to accept. He tells her of his life beside another sea. He speaks simply, as if talking of another's life or of one who has passed to the other side. His words seem to tone down the din of the sea. He speaks as though they of course were on the same side, as though she has already understood what he tells her about the friends he goes out to sea with, Freddy or Margot, or his job in life insurance, which bores her, but only slightly. His words, like a warm sea, surround her softly. Unwittingly, she wets the inside of her lips, she'd so like to take her place in a life so simple, clear and warm, or that it is how he tells it, leaning towards her, whispering to her the desire for a life even in the shape of a stranger from a distant sea. She now looks at him, without hearing what

he tells her, she notices his glittering eyes as they glance to one side. (Yet he tells her nothing of his other life here, beside this sea.)

They dine, then go up, and it's the victory drum and gong. Without touching, or speaking, they suavely go up to her bedroom, as though following the beating of a drum. It is like the slow descent of the mallet towards the gong. As at the moment when the stick above the drum remains suspended, or those about to dine savor their patient hunger. The door closes like a gong. They are in no hurry, giving time for the up-rising of their symmetrical desires, slowly paced by the gong of the sea, their caresses heightened by the drumming of the sea. Then, surer and surer, they rise up against each other, rising up bodily, they dine on their reciprocal pleasures, while within them rises up the fever of release, each like a gong sounding the end and a new beginning. They dine their fill, more easily than from any stew or drumstick. Under the storm's gong, they dine on their reciprocal hunger: beating the drum.

The next day, no more thunderbolts or rain, after that night and masterpiece of pleasure, nothing more, played out against the wind and the thunder. Stretching on her bed, she happily repeats: "After the rain comes the sun," part of which is that clap of thunder which has left her carefree about the next day, be it with blue skies or be it with rain again. But even the bad weather was no more, and even if that day she did feel sheltered from any rain, it was just as well that the sun spoke with its voice of thunder and made its silent lightning shine on the waters. No more howling. She wanted to hold the weight of the next day in her arms like a stray cat, now light as butterfly wings. Nothing more than a memory soon, she said to herself, all that rain. And yet, into that calm, into the depths of the next day, with its wings loaded, slipped the terrifying thunder of the next day to come, and the next, nothing more than thunder and desolate rain.

She goes looking for him at the gong's sound, at the time for a cocktail, at the end of a day punctuated by the sound of a whispering sea. It is high time. On the beach, she had tried a marvelous cocktail, with a woman's name, at lunchtime. As for him, she's not looking yet, just thinking about that first cocktail the day before, she wants the sound of her lover's voice again, cocktail in hand, she waits for the right time as the sun sets, she listens out for the sound of the gong. No one. She thinks: "Keep looking, little one!" Then the sound of a tear dropping from her freckles to the table. A cocktail flattens out her disappointment. She who goes looking doesn't always find, whatever the time. She stops looking, with the sound of the clock passing the time and her third cocktail.

He must have left for other rains, and another sea. Too bad. There are plenty of other drops when it rains and fish in the sea, even though it never rains but it pours. Yet to have left like that, without a word, leaving her beside a sea now grown tender, to join up with another set of friends from a distant sea with its coast drenched by gentle rains, an ocean surge and other less pure suns? He would have left anyway, of course, one day or another; but why no fleeting farewell beside this, their sea? "You feel less let down when leaving than when being left." She curses the serene sky. She dreams of new rains.

He must have left for other rains, and another sea.

Originally published in *La République de Mek-Ouyes* (P.O.L)

Translated by Ian Monk

Jacques Jouet

from

The Republic of Beau-Locks

2001

● *The Republic of Beau-Locks* (in French, *La République de Mek-Ouyes*) is the first book in an ongoing serial novel, chiefly by Jacques Jouet but incorporating contributions from other authors, about the life and exploits of the titular character, whose name is phonetically identical to *mes couilles*, or "my balls."

EPISODE 1

One spring morning, some time ago, during a year which will remain intentionally unstated, on the hard shoulder of a two-by-three-lane section of France's motorway network–number-A something-or-other, to be quite imprecise–there came to a thumb-twiddling halt a common-or-garden heavy-goods vehicle driver, who was huge in size and named René Pascale-Sylvestre, though not for very much longer.

His hazard lights blinked.

His red-and-white triangle equipped with a tripod had been carefully unfolded and placed three hundred yards behind his vehicle, in relation to the particular direction of the traffic that had been his.

Such road safety measures and civic attentiveness had been more from force of habit than any real conviction.

René Pascale-Sylvestre (but the reader should be informed that she need make no effort to memorize this name, which will no longer be used in what is to follow), René Pascale-Sylvestre (first broken promise) was not weary from driving. "Hazard" was not quite the right term when it came to describing why he'd stopped. He was, in fact, mildly irate, as we shall see.

A smile, so long-lingering as to be almost corpselike, lit up his warm and thoughtful looks. René Pascale-Sylvestre was so happy to be unhappy that it exceeded the bounds of the unacceptable. He felt moved. He stretched his neck slightly in a solemn movement as on one of those great days when one becomes aware of an irresistible vocation, and which starts with a tilt.

Apart from his almost permanent smile, which, once upon a time, had even been able to soften the hearts of transport company managers, since grown immune to such weaknesses, the man had two physical characteristics that, despite their impermanence, made him quite unforgettable: he wore apple-green-framed spectacles—his main point of vanity—and, on his balding scalp, bore a scab of dried blood because, on coming back up from the cellar with his hands full, he used always to bang his head, bong, on the low concrete door surround, given that he would always go down into his cellar on coming home weary from a trip. He would then bang his head, bong, as hard as can be, unintentionally and with a stream of expletives, but this was the advance price to pay for his excessive drinking. His wife, Thérèse, was already holding ready an old blotting pad to drink up the blood.

—Look at what you've done again!

René then uncorked the bottles and whistled while she tended to him.

Certain specialists had tried, by genetic manipulation, to inoculate him with a bending reflex, which would kick in as soon as he started ascending a staircase, but he had shown himself to be inflexibly immune to this kind of approach, and had now reconciled himself to living on friendly terms with this ineluctable periodic impact, bong.

Alongside the motorway, as has been previously described, his parked semitrailer was chock-full of a certain matter worth a certain amount of money, and which could not be seen from the exterior, thanks to its opaque tarpaulin and slatted sides, but which any old nose could detect. Explanations will come later. Right now, all you need to know is that René Pascale-Sylvestre had just made the most serious decision in his life: to hijack for

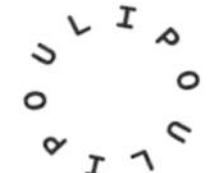

his own ends the merchandise that he was supposed to be delivering to a third party in Stains.

Nearby, vehicles sped past with the sort of heady din that even a boldly printed **vroom-vroom** can do nothing to convey.

His colleagues hooted, raising a tempest and yelling "René!" through their open windows. They didn't stop, presuming that nothing was up, given the fact that there'd been no SOS on their CBs mentioning any SNAFUs among close or distantly competing PLCs.

René Pascale-Sylvestre felt deeply irate. He was irate at such a depth that it resulted in virtual claustrophobia, thus explaining why he'd got out of his cab to breathe in the motorway's vibrant air and stretch his limbs a little.

This was an electric moment.

The time had come to make the second most serious decision in his life: quite simply to turn his back on his father's surname, and his mother's which had been joined onto it, as well as the forename which, forty-seven years before, had been the result of some bitter negotiation.

Looking as he was for a brand-new name, he went for one that should be pronounced not quite as it is spelled.

EPISODE 2

And this nerve-shot yet still resourceful truck driver, who had just parked alongside highway number A-something-or-other, settled on Beau-Locks. So, he wanted to change his name? Then he'd call himself Beau-Locks. It was safe to bet that he'd be the only one.

–I'm calling myself Beau-Locks.

He could already imagine with amusement the embarrassment of the askers, when confronted by the classic question: "How do you spell that?"... "You spell it like a pair of...?" ... "Maybe you'd like to spell it for me?"

He'd dithered between various possibilities–Beau-Bridges; Beau-Britches; Beau-Bugger; Beau-Brummy; Beau-Bleepers; Beau-Tied; Beau-Me-Down; Beau-Tox; Beau Blimey; Beau-of-the-Balls–to end up with Beau-Locks.

Contrary to what has just been stated, Beau-Locks's nerves weren't as shot as all that. In twenty years' odd-jobbing, he'd just about seen it all... shoved about when he wasn't being dumped, elbowed when he wasn't being dumped, ditched when he wasn't being elbowed, booted out when he wasn't being elbowed... and so he was quite curious to see what would happen next. He'd become a fervent collector of whatever things happened to him. I mean, why give yourself up to despair? It was far better to laugh at your mishaps–a smile was a good start–and then to wonder methodically how far they could possibly go. Such curiosity could very well stand as a reason to keep going.

To sum up (quickly, I mean, really... 'cause there's no question here of robbing biographers of their trade by spewing out a good sixty pages concerning his early youth, before getting down to brass tacks, with the same amount covering his grandfather, great-grandfather, with details of his parentage and childhood illnesses... his school books, turned up by a team of Anglo-American researchers after six years... his kiddie words as reported by his sisters and cousins, his army career and practical jokes, the broken homes and housekeeping accounts... not to forget the maternal cuddles as precursors of his affective particularities), to sum up, then, and without beating around the bush, Beau-Locks's career had dallied with a large number of possible manifestations of highway, and to a lesser degree railroad, professions. He'd driven cabs, trams, and school buses... from ambulances to hearses. He'd driven steamrollers, snowplows, and Black Marias, a regional railcar and a suburban train...

For two months, he'd even ferried about the books and software of an intercompany mobile library, with no serious hitches, before being fired, nonetheless, for serious misconduct, or to put it another way, an incapacity to manage both upstream and internally the dysfunctions (arising from decisional alienation) in the vital synergy in the subcontractors' interface modules, as well as the partnership hierarchies.

He'd been a private chauffeur and delivered pizzas, and ended up as the driver of the mini-train in the gardens of Versailles, which had derailed on a molehill,

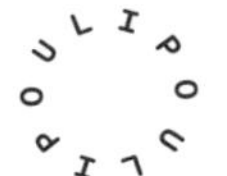

before decapitating two marble statues of mythological figures, and fracturing seventeen femurs belonging to almost the same number of genuine oldsters, coming from various countries in the European Union, and with stillborn touristic ambitions.

During a rationalizing restructuration necessitated by the responsible anticipation of transnational competition between national parks, he had become a name on an extravagant, and yet thoroughly state-financed, redundancy plan, leading to the offer of delivering a solidarity consignment of pickaxes to Rubamgué, by driving across the desert, on half pay, but with a broader mind thanks to the wonders of the world and the project's humanitarian values. Beau-Locks had felt tempted initially, then not tempted at all. When he ended up refusing, while deploying his incomprehensible smile, he had been told to take his woes elsewhere.

Periodically, Beau-Locks watched his chances go by, but without ever stopping. This didn't stop him from thinking, while wiping his glasses, or even from expressing his opinions, which didn't always enter into the category of what might be called constructive observations.

Meanwhile, he was preparing a once-in-a-lifetime caper, which would bring him joy, a change, universal glory, and which will be the subject of this serial novel.

So, let's step back a bit, the better to leap forward. The whole thing started when he was the subprefect's chauffeur. Would you like to know how Beau-Locks, who wasn't yet called Beau-Locks, became the subprefect's chauffeur?

Well, that story started when he was still the prefect's chauffeur.

TO BE CONTINUED...

Ian Monk

from

We Did Everything

2004

● *We Did Everything* is an unpublished collection of poems that chop up the form and rhyming structure of the sonnet. Ian Monk has continued this exploration elsewhere, including in the collection *14 × 14*.

Because you failed to make it home again
if she saw you now she'd just spit on it

the road is like molasses and the rain
like wasp stings or like the acidic shit
of feral pigeons with TB feet stumps

the highway is awash with drudge and lights
the petrol curls in hollows while the lumps
of brighter matter wink back through the night's
veil of haziness it isn't even
dark anymore the urban glow's raven
casts glints with the silent flap of its wings

if she saw you here she'd drag you back home
bathe you in bleach slap you till your face sings
with pain and your mind your feet start to roam
the streets of panic where no cars ever
drive or other pedestrians wander
just a rush of papers and cans clever
cogs clacking behind you as you blunder
into the icy wind of fear and tears

if she saw you here she'd spit on your tomb
pack you off with the Jews gypsies and queers
for your own good mind you go plant a bloom
in the ash then soap herself down with you

in her house the lampshades are cozy true
masterpieces of tack porcelain beasts
shit dust on the polished parquet no time
for anything but polish pets and priests
her dogs are cuddled the cuckoo clocks chime
her only daughter has become a whore
her only son has become a banker
her only fun is getting shagged by law-
yers her new ambition's another fur
coat but not from mummy's darling little
sweetheart come and kiss mummy that's right yes
never mind nasty scent lipstick spittle
it was all for your own good my princess
up the wooden stair wait for the slipper

in bed she prayed may god make her trip her
meanness to vanish her childhood memor-
ies to surface something a miracle
anything to make this stop her die or
me instead to shrink to a particle
of light and nothingness to run away
into the woods and hide out in the trees
and creepers as splinters rain and the clay
creeps through the cracks in my shoes and the freeze
inches into my chilblained toes and heel
now roots to my sad and solid stance here
among other soughing silences that peel
the bark from their sap and their years of rings
as shifting as tobacco smoke that stings
as it comforts then dissolves in the air
seeping down between the branches of oak

when she runs away she shaves off her hair
she gets so filthy she could fucking choke
she has his name tattooed on both her arms
she tells him her name is Mary it ain't
she grins kisses his lips and then his palms

lays them on her breasts and looks at the paint
stuck around the quick of his nails and says
love me or I'll scream the house down love me
or I'll sell you to the pigs love me fez
head then marry me for your work permit

there may be life in clouds of Venus it
has evolved off the surface like angels
and hovers under a hood of acid
protected from the sun's naked spangles
of radiation just floating in mid
air where the pressure becomes bearable

she breaks his plates to avoid washing up
she smashes down his food on the table
she feeds rat poison to his just bought pup
she sends a pack of dog shit to his boss
she urinates in his aquarium
she tells him that she couldn't give a toss
she puts him on a course of barium
she tells him that he'll be the death of her
she tells him to stop seeing his mother
she spits on his steak in the frying pan
she flicks large bogeys into his salad
she dreams of doctors pianists a man
she mounts her stallion and then mounts the lad
she watches as he starts to break her things
she screams for her porcelain dogs and cats
she pisses him off when she laughs and sings
she misses him she thinks after their spats
she lies to herself like she lies to you
she thinks she's oh so hard done by in fact
she's a clinically depressed unfucked shrew
she hasn't noticed how the paint has cracked
she runs from life like maids from a rapist
she speaks too loudly and roars when she's pissed
she makes up her face she makes up her life
she never forgives the slightest insult

taste is back with my appetite the knife
has shifted from wrist to steak while the cult
of the dread looks loopier than ever

my hand is shake free from table to mouth

she detests the dim she scorns the clever
she says it's too hot and fake in the South
she says the North gives her rheumatism

there may be iced life out on Europa

after lunch my kids laugh at the prism
of my lemon sorbet and its vodka

there is life in acid and in darkness

she remembers childhood's mustard and less
she remembers ripping out others' stalks

misery eggs itself from this ocean

she doesn't shut up she talks and she talks

the other day I read a description
of clinical depression well that's it
I said it's over for now till next time

she opens her blouse to flash her left tit

I said it's over for now till this rhyme

the fuse is short and who really gives a

she is now rearranging porcelain

I'm the one who picks her up and saves her

out the door slut the snow has turned to rain

she dribbles to herself it's so sing-sing

we did everything we did everything

Originally published as "À propos de la Fin des Temps" in *La fin des temps* (La Bibliothèque Oulipienne no. 148)

Translated by Daniel Levin Becker

François Caradec

On the End of Time

2006

● This text was written for and delivered at an Oulipo reading on the theme of the end of days, which, in spite of the various conjurings brought forth that evening and in the accompanying fascicle of the Bibliothèque Oulipienne still has yet to occur.

In the year 2006, some time after the millenarians went bankrupt, people began to worry seriously about the end of time. Frankly, it was time. Perhaps we were in for the storied inconveniences of the Apocalypse, or perhaps a Big Flop, or else the slow extinction, over hundreds of millions of years, of the animal and vegetable species that clutter the globe and that had slowly begun to disappear, usually around the end of the week, the same time as Parisians disappear from Paris.

Savants and philosophers, politicians of all stripes, and religious eminences gathered to share their impressions and exchange the addresses of excellent restaurants. Philippe Sollers and Bernard-Henri Lévy were no longer able to furnish the daily press with their logorrhea of fashionable thought. Churches, temples, mosques, and sex shops put up NO VACANCY signs. Hairdressers closed their doors, since in preparation for the catastrophes to come nobody got haircuts anymore. In the face of the stress of the end of the world, doctors vaccinated, nurses pricked, drugs pacified. The Oulipo dozed.

Pharmaceutical laboratories discovered new molecules each day, novel and inoffensive formulae, disgusting pills, luxury placebos. Viagra was totally out of fashion. Psychiatrists were out of their depths, horsemen out of their saddles. The Chinese were out of their bridles. The military was out of its element. Clocks stopped, ports were condemned. Bald men were deforested. Curates were defrocked, police debriefed, ears detached. People sucked ice, ate rats, chewed on dust. The Oulipo still didn't budge.

Suddenly, entire populations rose up. It wasn't the usual ones, the Irish or the Chechens, the Ivoirians, the Kurds, the Palestinians, the Corsicans, the Basques; it was populations that were heretofore historyless, the Belgians, the survivors of Easter Island, the Aedui, the Bellifontains, the librarians, the pizza deliverymen. They were crushed pitilessly by the riot police and students from the École Polytechnique. Blood flowed through the métro. People worried. They began to realize that the end of the end as it had been announced in the media was not coming right away. Upon closer inspection, Nostradamus was not all he'd been cracked up to be. His prophecies didn't look so good. His rhymes were weak, his puns muddy, his approximations nonexistent. It all lacked specifics, plausible dates and locations. Something was missing. No one knew what. The Oulipo was mum.

So people began to settle for other prophets: Malcolm de Chazal, Philippe Delerm, Paul Géraldy, René Char... their books were snatched up in a frenzy. Publishers published, printers printed, bookstores made stacks near the registers and consented to the 5 percent discount mandated by the Lang Law of 1981. A woman from high society, the widow of a Swiss banker now remarried to a Kuwaiti emir, published a manual on manners for the end times, which broached the delicate question of pants versus skirts during apocalypse season. The Oulipo stayed silent.

This could have gone on longer, at least until the end of time, had a member of the Oulipo, a habitué of the Petit Zinc, the tobacco shop on the corner, not pointed out that what was being popularly referred to as *the end of time*, with all its pompous metaphysical ramifications, was really nothing but *the last straw*. At which point issaseasyas...

Indeed, to be perfectly logical, it would suffice to protect this agricultural byproduct from degeneration and avoid its disappearance from the surface of the earth in order to ward off the end of the world. Which is what everyone did, quite diligently. People began cultivating straw with all their might: straw in town and in country, straw in public gardens, straw on the paths along the Seine, on balconies, on the terraces of the Eiffel Tower, on the lawn of the Élysée. Everyone was now a straw farmer. The Oulipo was constrained to do so as well.

Straw now being the world's chief harvest, it was necessary to find something to do with so much of it, which as you can imagine changed the world's economic and agricultural profile considerably. But thanks to all of this straw, the world, reassured, was now able to await the end of the world in peace.

OULIPO

Originally published as *Romans* (La Bibliothèque Oulipienne no. 151)

Translated by Daniel Levin Becker

Paul Fournel

Novels

2006

● An extended descendant of Queneau's *Exercises in Style*, in which the same mundane anecdote is retold in ninety-nine ways, *Novels* mines the contours of a decidedly dramatic story by telling it from seven different perspectives.

NOVEL 1. AND HAPPINESS CAME TO PASS

This is the story of a man who meets a woman and falls in love. They meet in the kind of pleasant little bar still found in the working-class neighborhoods of Paris.

He can tell from first sight that he has found her, his storybook love. She is beautiful as a spring morning, fresh as a dewdrop, happy as a holiday. He is determined to show her a traditional courtship, dappled with a touch of fantasy. He gives her a bouquet of flowers, which she leaves on the table at the bistro. He brings her candy, which she barely bites into. A forlorn waiter brings them two glasses of champagne, which makes them just a bit silly...

After some coaxing, as is only proper, she allows him at last to kiss her on the darkened porch of a large house.

Besotted with joy, the man rushes home to his apartment building to share his happiness with the concierge and ask her to look after his parrot for a few days while he goes away with his new beloved.

Here they are now on the coast of the English Channel, exploring their love. He takes her in his arms and holds her tight until she is worn out and lets herself be held, with the occasional hint of weariness clouding her demeanor.

He can feel the weight of a mystery within her, the burden of a secret.

One night, as the sun is sinking into the sea, she admits to him that she is the mother of a little boy. She has entrusted him to a foster home, for he has no father. A tear streams down her perfect cheek.

The man's blood boils, but only for a moment: he wants to see the child straightaway. She hesitates, she prevaricates, she cries a great deal. Off they go.

Here they are now in a dusky neighborhood in a mining village. After a long deliberation between two identical houses, they enter a squalid apartment half plunged into darkness, all chaos and filth. A disheveled woman is being beaten by a drunkard while a terrorized little fellow looks on in terror, lacking the strength even to cry out.

The man gets angry. The woman rushes in to take the child. The drunkard intervenes. If they want him to let the rug rat go, he wants some cash. A scuffle ensues: the drunkard threatens the child with a poker. The harpy shrieks and attacks the young mother. The man throws himself into the fray, grabs the child, takes a blow to the head from the poker, then turns it back on his assailant.

The drunkard is on the ground, a poker planted in his heart, his disheveled widow kneeling beside him on the floor. The child is in his mother's arms as the man leads her out by the hand. The three of them flee.

They make a life together in the man's small apartment. Not without friction: the young woman does not get along with the concierge; the child is allergic to the parrot and the concierge no longer wants to keep it; the child is silent for long periods of time and often crouches in the corner.

The man suffers frequent memory loss because of the poker blows he took to the head.

But overall life seems to be calm and he is happy with his wife and her small boy. He goes to work each day, as usual, until one night there is a knock on his door. He opens it to find two policemen standing on the landing.

NOVEL 2. A LIFE IN BEIGE

This is the story of a young mother who whiles away her darkest days in a sordid bistro on the outskirts of Paris. She kills days at a time in front of a cup of black coffee, making sad eyes at the local drunks in order to make the week's ends meet. She gave up her child to a pair of wretched innkeepers who siphon off what little money she makes. The child's father disappeared long ago and she couldn't even say for sure who he is. There have been plenty to choose from.

One ugly night a man walks into the bar, leans against the counter, and suddenly sees her. His face lights up. She laughs a little to herself at the effect she has on him.

He approaches her timidly and embarks on a courtship you might expect from a teenager. He brings her flowers (she hates flowers, they give her sneezing fits), gives her candy (she doesn't touch it because she's watching her figure). He says sweet nothings to her. He's cute, in a silly way. She doesn't find him particularly attractive, and frankly not very funny either, but she's touched all the same.

She doesn't want him, but out of weariness she lets him kiss her on the porch of the house next door. He barely dares to touch her.

He invites her to spend two days by the seaside with him and she doesn't say no because she doesn't get out of town much.

Once there, in their little hotel, he is ravenous for her. She allows it. She's used to it. The flowers from the garden and the fresh-cut grass bring tears to her eyes. She speaks absently about her son, as she does with all of her passing lovers, hoping to coax a few extra dollars for rent. The man is stirred up instantly, wants to go with her to collect the child, won't hear any arguments.

She tries to cool his ardor, but to no avail. She wonders what she could possibly do with the child in Paris. In secret she calls the innkeepers and tells them to prepare an armed welcome if they want to protect their investment.

They arrive at the mining house, the kid shrieks with terror, the innkeeper brandishes his fire poker, his old lady pulls out her hair. They overdo it a bit. When the innkeeper bashes him over the head, the guy suddenly turns from a spineless lump to a ball of fury and sticks the innkeeper through the gut.

And then they're off with the kid.

They make a life together in the guy's little apartment in Paris. No question of keeping his revolting parrot, who'll have to bunk with the odious little canary that belongs to the ignoble concierge. The young woman drops the kid at the concierge's desk as soon as the guy turns his back and goes back to her watering hole to make some pocket money. The boy sees her coming home with a little smile that splits his pathetic little mug in two. In the newspaper she sees the police have closed the books on the poker murder, ruling it a grudge settled between two drunkards.

This conclusion doesn't suit her. How is she supposed to get rid of this lovey dope who sticks to her like glue and keeps trying to win over her kid?

Some weeks go by and one blessed afternoon, at the bar, she makes eyes at a guy in a beige overcoat. She brings him to the neighbor's porch and while he's feeling her up he tells her he's a police inspector. "I've got some stories that just might interest you," she says between two fake sighs.

NOVEL 3. THE NEIGHBORHOOD CHATTERBOX

This is the story of one of the last concierges of the working-class neighborhoods of Paris, one of the few who has not yet been replaced by a keypad and an intercom. Loyal to her post, she watches from behind her desk as the building's inhabitants and the neighborhood denizens pass by. The world comes to her in glimpses and overheard snippets: the puzzle of her day-to-day is made up of people coming and going, of minuscule events. She pieces together stories from the scraps life brings her.

She sighs each day as she climbs up the stairs on her aching legs to deliver love letters to the apartments—she who has been alone for so many moons. She grumbles about the noise in the stairwell, keeps a watchful eye on the merchants who come with deliveries, detains people with unfamiliar faces on the ground floor so they can't get upstairs. She knows how to be disagreeable with the hermits and the weirdos, how to be sweet with the tenants who treat her kindly and recognize her merits.

She shares her joys and pains and discoveries with her canary, who whistles along in his cage at her desk. She could swear he understands everything, that animal!

All of a sudden the calm little life of the gentleman on the third floor seems to turn upside down. He sings to himself as he walks up the stairs, comes down with a bouquet of flowers in hand, with a box of candy... the concierge is titillated by the overpowering aroma of new love. "Finally, someone in the building is in love," she tells her canary. "This should bring some color to our days."

The gentleman in question is sporting a lovely yellow tie, not his usual old sweater. Here he comes now in a dinner jacket. "His lady love must be from the upper crust!"

And then one morning he hurries to her desk, parrot in hand. "Would you watch him for me for a few days? Please, it's a love-or-death situation. He can room with your canary."

She accepts the perch in the name of romance, asks for the creature's care and feeding instructions, and watches her humming tenant disappear.

"Some people get all the luck," she says to the parrot, who replies, "Not all that much!" in a voice so grating the canary presses its wings to its ears.

Life in the building goes on as usual until the night the gentleman from the third floor comes back, disheveled, clutching a little boy to his breast and dragging along a plain woman with an empty expression. The concierge hands him his keys and asks him to take back his parrot. Too late: he's already on the second floor.

This new tenant is a bad woman, the concierge doesn't take long to decide. She doesn't want the parrot back and she goes out as soon as the man has gone to work, leaving the child at the front desk. The concierge doesn't say anything because the child always shows up with a fat tip and a sweet smile. It's not so hard to get attached to such kids.

She goes to the doorway to watch the woman as she disappears. What she wouldn't pay to know where she goes to spend her days.

Early one morning, two policemen arrive. They show her their badges and ask what floor the gentleman lives on. Fifteen minutes later they come back down with the man and the woman. The child comes down too, crying at their heels, and slips behind the front desk.

"What do I do with the child?!" the concierge shouts from the doorway as the police van drives off.

"Not all that much!" replies the parrot.

NOVEL 4. THE CITY BIRD

This is the story of a canary who lives and sings at a concierge's desk in a working-class neighborhood in Paris, a canary typical of that temperate region, a canary in a 20" × 12" × 12" cage. A concierge's canary with a headdress embroidered on his cage.

His days are mostly alike from one to the next, at least to an outside observer: seeds for breakfast, fresh water, gossip with the concierge as she sips her coffee. First contact with the pigeon and sparrow networks. Information about the routes planned for the day: a V of storks headed south, a V of greylag geese. There is dismayed talk of a magpie family nesting for good on top of the neighboring building. Otherwise nothing unusual: some black crows, some barnacled titmice, some speedy warblers and cirl buntings. The usual crowd.

While the concierge is in the stairwell, the canary sharpens his beak on a cuttlefish bone, the most precious of all his tools. He refines and shapes his maxilla and his mandible, using both to form a perfect trumpet that will push forth his inimitable song, piercing through walls and windows, rising to the highest heights of the bird kingdom. Freedom.

The major event of his life is the arrival of the "Not all that much!" parrot. One day the man from the third floor shows up with the monster and plunks it down not two feet from his cage. This is too much. The odious animal is free on its perch, nothing but a simple beaded chain attached to its leg. It is green and red, menacing. It looks stupid.

When it stretches its chain to its extremity, it can reach the canary's seed bowl, which is patently unacceptable. Stupid *and* a thief.

It should be said that parrots don't speak bird. They live in an intermediate world, neither understood nor understanding.

A clammy atmosphere settles over the front desk.

The canary activates his entire network to track down the parrot's owner and hasten his return. Some seagulls spot him at the seaside and relieve themselves on his hat. An owl catches wind of him in the North and follows him to the windowsill of a mining house. What she sees horrifies her and she flies through the night, yelling as loud as she can.

The man comes back with a woman and a boy. The canary feels a surge of hope. Alas, they don't take back the "Not all that much!" monster.

There ensues a period of combat, during which the parrot stays despite the concierge's attacks.

The swallow network, which is in direct contact with the police, warns the canary that trouble is brewing for the man from the third floor. Real bad luck. What do they do with parrots in the case of incarceration? Are they condemned to the same punishment as their masters? "Not all that much!" it cries, stupidly.

The canary undergoes a period of intense stress and fear for his life. He loses the will to sing and his feathers get dull and fall off, whirligigging to the bottom of the cage. Who will get him out of this fix?

The little boy! Abandoned by everyone and taking refuge behind the front desk, he won't stop whining. "When's my mother coming back? In a month? A year?" Invariably, the parrot replies, "Not all that much!" Aggravated, the boy throws a hard right that lays the parrot out for the count. The canary regains his peace, his voice, and his handsome yellow coat.

NOVEL 5. REDEMPTION AND TEMPEST

This is the story of a little boy born to an unknown father, a boy whose mother and stepfather were thrown in prison for having snatched him from the custody of a couple of tormentors. A boy who watched the whole scene, who saw the poker buried in the heart of that cruel man; a boy born under a violent sign. He is stubborn, closed-off, brutal. He is a mean boy.

The day they were arrested, his mother and his new stepfather left him in the care of the concierge, a foul fat whore with a half-bald canary.

When he asks when his mom is coming back, only the parrot answers, with an idiotic "Not all that much!" With a reflexive hard right, he sends the parrot *ad patres*. A brief moment of silence. The canary starts to sing again. The child falls to his knees before the green corpse, takes his head in his hands, and just like that decides to become good.

We find him again a few weeks later. He has asked Auntie Concierge's permission to go to the prison and wait for his mother to be released. As it turns out, thanks to a secret deal with the police, she is sprung after only a few weeks of detainment. He embraces her on the sidewalk, takes her in his arms and holds her until she has to pry herself loose. He asks after his almost-dad and promises to write him faithfully each week. His mother is relieved to know there will be no more parrot when they return home.

We find the boy again a few years later. He has become a handsome adolescent, radiant with goodness. He takes his mother's hand on the sidewalk across from La Santé prison: today is the big day. His almost-dad is free. His mother frowns but he knows it won't last.

Now they are seated around the family table and the boy is telling them how the tormentors of his childhood would send him each day to gather coal from the depths of the pitch-black cellar even though the apartment had been gas-heated for years... In spite of all of this, he went back to the mining village on a school break and saw the lady tormentor again, an experience laden with great emotion. She has since become good and kind and is actually also waiting humbly at the front desk with her new friend Auntie Concierge and wouldn't it be great to bring them up for a reunion of the whole family?

Some months later, he has just received a top academic prize and returns home whistling. In the lobby, Auntie Concierge hands him a letter that has just arrived for him. Inside, a sheet of paper covered with letters cut out from the newspaper, no signature or return address. "What if it was your mother who gave up your stepfather to the cops? I have proof."

He takes his head in his hands. Is his mother a whore? Should he avenge his stepfather? Should he save his mother in spite of everything? Should he find out who wrote the anonymous letter? Which path is the just one, and which one hides the greatest evil? There is a tempest in his skull.

NOVEL 6. DRESSED LIKE THE RAVEN

This is the story of a melancholic waiter in a sordid little bistro in a working-class neighborhood of Paris. A young man, like so many others, with no history and no life to speak of. It is a slow story. A waiter who wipes down glasses at the back of the café and has nothing else to do all day but dream. He knows he is the last in a dying breed of waiters in black aprons, that he will die along with this dank hole and its clientele of old bocce players taking shelter from the next squall. He develops a passion for the clouds that pass overhead, above Sacré-Coeur, and describes them at length, to a degree of minutia that only plunges him deeper into his melancholy. Stratus, cumulus, cumulonimbus, cirrus, all passing by slowly.

The only ray of sunshine in his life is the woman who comes to the café to waste her daylight. She comes in with tiny steps and always sits in the same place. She is, he thinks, the most beautiful creature in the world, which is why he cannot bring himself to speak to her. He has tried a thousand times to describe to her a first-rate cumulus cloud, to draw her over to the window, but always in vain. She remains the beauty beyond reach.

Try though he does to fill his words with sexual intention when he comes by with his usual "May I fill you up?" nothing works. She does not see him.

But she waits and watches for everyone else. And she leaves nothing to chance. From time to time she prostitutes herself. Each time she disappears with another john, he hurries to the back door to watch her let herself be felt up under the porch. Each time it is a little dagger through his heart.

Not that he could offer her that kind of love. Neither of them deserves it. He writes her stormy letters and never signs them. He spills tempests of love and tides of desire and clouds of passion in her direction. In vain.

His life stretches into a goopy boredom where nothing advances or withdraws. So he listens, wonders, wants to know everything about her. He reads the newspapers, the gossip columns, the scandals, the police blotters. He talks to the police officers who pass by. He makes up stories, he embellishes, he creates his own truth. He knows by now for certain that she has a son whom she abandoned. He has guessed that the guy who won't even touch her on the porch has it bad for her. The building caretaker told him over her coffee that they had gone off together to the seaside. He has followed the drama in the mining village. He knows how the poker pierced that fellow's cold heart. He knows the monumental sadness of difficult loves. He knows who was holding the poker. When he reads the clouds, he sees the young boy's tragic face. He knows the man in the overcoat who slips his hand between the girl's legs is a policeman. He knows it is all too much for him.

He knows the night has come. He cuts out words from the newspaper, glues them onto a white sheet of paper, glues the stamp to the envelope, throws the envelope in the mailbox. He feels a blackness envelop him, dark as a raven in the night, as he swallows the whole vial of phenobarbital.

NOVEL 7. VIOLET THOUGHTS

This is the story of a bouquet of flowers left on the table of a little café in a working-class neighborhood of Paris. The kind of little bouquet hawked on street corners: pansies, violets, sweet pea. It is a bouquet handed over with the ardor of a burgeoning love, a bouquet that the urgency of an embrace caused to be abandoned where it was.

A bouquet that the melancholic waiter at the café gathers up and absently plants in a glass on the counter.

A bouquet that a boy steals from the counter when he comes to drag his father home after one last glass of pastis. A bouquet that droops down from between the child's fingers on the way home.

A bouquet that brightens the mother's face for just a moment before the long scowl of her drunkard husband, framed in the doorway, darkens it again.

A bouquet that the mother throws into the courtyard the next morning after the boy has gone to school, because she hates flowers and has enough reasons in her life to cry.

A bouquet that the concierge collects, intending to throw it into the garbage, while she clucks her tongue at the negligence of the tenants.

A bouquet that she sets down for a moment on her desk in the lobby because the mailman has just arrived with the mail. A bouquet that she finds again a moment later and sticks under her nose.

"This stinks," she says to her canary.

"Not all that much!" answers the parrot.

A bouquet left to dry, stems up, behind the desk of a concierge, above a canary's cage. A bouquet that dries up as it curls into itself.

A bouquet, finally, a bouquet of dried flowers left by a man, a good and generous man, on the grave of his mother, just before he is arrested. He has just murdered her savagely to defend the besmirched honor of his stepfather.

Originally published in *N-amor* (La Bibliothèque Oulipienne no. 159)

Translated by Daniel Levin Becker

Anne F. Garréta

from

N-evol

2007

● Few scholars, and certainly few Oulipians, are as outspoken as Anne F. Garréta on the moribundity of the novel as a cultural and creative form. Yet here we are.

0. GIVENS

Given:

1. the obsolescence of the novel, its inadequacy to everything a subject today might live, observe, experience, and think;
2. the boredom provoked in me by reading a "contemporary" novel;
3. to say nothing of the idea of writing one;
4. the cumulative weight of the various materials intended for the construction of novels, stories, portraits, fables, essays, etc. according to the old pedestrian principle that everything can be used someday, henceforth useless;
5. the painful vanity of all diversions with which we can still imagine filling our existence;
6. the difficulty of renouncing language, which we still love,

how is it possible, in stripping from it everything the novel has made obscene (obsolete, fetishized), to go on enjoying it?

The enervated, shapeless bricolage of the novel leaves me cold. The chatter, the prolixity, the superstition of the contemporary story depresses me. The ignorant bloat of everything else–authors, narrators, descriptions, dialogue, ideology, psychology–dumbfounds me.

What the fuck is to be done?

1. BILDUNGSROMAN

...

A bourgeois girl from the seventh arrondissement asks me, one night while I'm mixing, my favorite color of garter belt. She comes back the following night dressed accordingly, otherwise naked under her coat. She spends the night exposed by my record crates.

The excellent DJ from the Hi-Tension offers me poppers in exchange for a favor: watch his turntables long enough for him to slip into the back room with the boy just arrived from his hometown, whom he has been coveting and furtively caressing for the past hour, and finally fuck him in peace.

At dawn, after her nightly twenty stripteases, a tired woman takes the wheel of her R5 and drives through the streets of Paris in search of a pharmacy still or already open and a bottle of Mercryl Lauryl. A bath won't do. She won't be able to sleep until she has disinfected herself, head to toe, of all the night's looks.

...

One night on a weekend in June, a normally shy photographer, breasts superb under her white T-shirt, unleashed in the chaos of a throng that flows and does not ebb and dances all the way down the stairs, wants me, while I'm spinning five-minute disco platters from the seventies, wants me to take her to the basement and, once there, to absolutely violate her on the crates of beer and soda.

At ten on a winter night, one of the twinks who've set up shop in front of the Monoprix at the end of rue de Rennes, having come to eat and warm up in a shelter on rue Bernard-Palissy, tells a novice that one of his regulars, an important professor very high up at the Sorbonne, or something like that, has promised to give him his books, all of them, because he has written several, with inscriptions.

On the sidewalk outside a dirty squat, a woman said to be a former swimming champion, who sprinkles her speech with gypsy words and often hangs around with the Vice Squad, insults, then hits, then takes a knife and slashes the face of her girlfriend who no longer wants to turn tricks for her.

...

An Arab girl who claims to be the daughter of a Balenciaga model and a cousin of Hassan II, whom six months ago I took out to eat some mornings when she was hungry, who wanted to be a singer and whom a producer has been leading on with promises of a demo, begs me in tears to lend her the three thousand francs she cannot, without revealing her guilty motive, ask for from the woman she is dating.

In this club at the Meat Market there are, curiously enough, ladies' toilets. Stall doors torn off, a swarm of wilted black drag queens have assembled around the most wilted of all, sitting haughtily on the porcelain as though it were a throne. On the men's room side, the toilets have doors and there are only white people.

The bartender from the Kat calls me one morning, late, drunk. She is listening to Fréhel on repeat, thinks I understand poetry. She reads me her poems over the phone. They do not mention her mother, impregnated by a Nazi soldier and publicly shaved in the purge after the war, nor her blue-collar youth spent gutting cats in a catgut factory.

At the Saint's Black Party, *près du* Bowery, an elegantly yoked brunet performs a slow, risqué striptease that leaves him naked except for a white jockstrap and a boa writhing on his shoulders, his arms. After slowly, meticulously lubricating the animal, he sodomizes himself with it.

A Dutch whore kept by a Lebanese arms dealer, very pretty, very fine in her white tailcoat, is backed up against the balustrade near my turntables. She talks to me. Shuts up. Her eyes lock on me. I can see her shoot up through the pocket of her pants.

As I am spontaneously filling in for the DJ from Le Sept, who has gone off somewhere without a trace, a

high-priced gigolo whom I see often, and whom I had dinner with the night before at Privé with several other people, comes to show me his publicity photos. Nikon self-portraits, kneeling in front of his mirror, erection coming up to his navel. He asks what I think.

Shortly after midnight, a famous actress accompanied by a TV boss sits down at a discreet table just behind me. Between two songs, while looking for the next record, I can't miss them groping each other openly. Leaned over her, he sticks his tongue in her mouth over and over while she looks vaguely at me.

...

At the end of a calm weeknight, a Saudi princess offers me a 500-franc bill and asks me in broken English to play her a syrupy ballad, "Endless Love." At the end of the song, once again, same request, two 500s. Once more, four 500s. Then, when the song reaches the end for the third time, hands me a whole wad of bills. *Play again and dance with me.*

It's two in the morning. The (Corsican) boss's cousin, who runs a gambling circle at la Madeleine, appears in front of my turntables. He offers me twenty-five grand to seduce and deliver to him the little brunette, no doubt barely legal, whom he points out to me with his finger. The little one over there, see her? I want her.

At the dawn of a winter night, in a freezing *chambre de bonne* in a bourgeois building near the Sorbonne, an almost beautiful woman, sitting naked on the hexagonal floor tile, says she wants to be a writer so she can write the story of her life. She tells it. She is so hideous I have only one desire left: to flee.

On the third basement level of the Broad, twenty paces from me, a man I recognize as one of my classmates from the Lycée Henri-IV freezes in my line of sight. Suddenly worried, his eyes flee mine. He turns away, looking for an even thicker darkness.

My shift over, waiting for the club to close, I'm playing a round of *Pac-Man*. A woman I have never seen sits down near me. She insinuates herself over my knees, wraps herself in my arms. Her head on my shoulder, she tells me, caressing herself with my hands, that she's a journalist, that she rides a Harley-Davidson, and that, when she was just a little girl, her mother abandoned her at welfare services.

At the end of the night, mixing console, amplifiers, and light show switched off, I'm preparing to leave a snobby hetero club on the Champs-Élysées. A well-known actor, leaning drunkenly and sloppily on the bar, insults me as I pass in front of him. He makes an obscene gesture. I spit in his face. Slowly, mechanically, he licks the saliva from his lips, his cheek, then melts into tears.

It is eight in the morning. In the bathroom of the Keur Samba, a Fulani whore who dances divinely is currently on her knees, licking the toilet seat in search of traces from all the lines blown on it during the night.

Originally published as "Lille invisible" at Zazie Mode d'Emploi (zazipo.net)

Translated by Ian Monk

Olivier Salon

Invisible Cities: Lille

2007

● Olivier Salon's tribute to the city of Lille, home to an Oulipo-friendly writing workshop called Zazie Mode d'Emploi, is a lipogram variant called a bivocalism: like the city's name, it contains no vowels besides *E* and *I*.

Lille's glimmering. It seems impressive. Lille stretches then Lille rises. Night's ending, it's high time! Lille's sheer steeples rise, then it flicks its index finger right there, between these endless glimmers in the welkin's deep immenseness. Lille's merited its title: the spirit's fertile residence. Let's render visible its epithets: we'll then see Lille's endless riches.

Drizzle seems inherent here. Lille's dwellers delight in drizzle. Respiring seems different when it's drizzling: it inspires hidden virilities, sleep then seems simpler, while the lifeless find new excitement. Drizzle is Lille's shepherd, it herds its ewes, its bellwethers, then its kids between its winding streets. Stress then switches sides; things seems serene, while even deserts seem fertile.

Steer between perils: they'll then perish. Reject life's prickles: they'll then wither. Flee Brice de Nice, then seek different cities. Find this site, ye sincere ministers, here where delight is set in merriment.

This is the scheme in Rémi's mind: he scribbles, he writes in his idle times, he even versifies. Lille is his destined center, despite the lightning SNCF strike. Then,

even if Lille's invisible, he still perceives its presence. He senses its spirit lingering there. He sniffs its essence. He thinks he'll live his schemes here, then be the writer he senses he is. He'll even find presses which will print his writings. The civil services there seem perfect. Lille is inscribing its sentences in his mind's eye: settle here, sweet child. He heeds its cries. He then feels meek.

He peddles in its fine streets, then visits Hellemmes, with its edifices, its sights, its riches. He then finds himself in Fives, where he views life's depressing, terrible side: pennilessness reigns here. Its pissed denizens screech filth between themselves, they belt then mince their enemies. Their invectives imperil entire existences. This is where men's teeth seem set edgewise. He sees it in their sinister smiles. It's skid street here! He visits Ennetières, Fretin, then Ennevelin, Nieppe, Le Bizet, Frelinghien, Willems, Leers, etc. Trip time!

He delves between Lille's semihidden signs, its lines, its secret effects. Little bit, little bit, he feels tenderness rise within his chest. He heeds its birdies' twitter. It's the time when cherries ripen, he thinks. He then remembers the terrible effects cherries inflict when ingested with heedless greed. He spies the seedlings rising between the streets. He enters Pérenchies's minster, which is ministering right then, with Père Vincent reciting his senseless rite, while the shrine seems deserted: mere seven decrepit wrinklies sit listening with rising bewilderment, while he blethers, they sign themselves then whisper ever deeper. Jeez! Rémi feels perplexed. Then whispers in his inner self: the devil sings the best ditties.

Time flies. It's September's first weekend, with picnic skies still glistening. Yes, the time is here when Lille's denizens sell their bits 'n' pieces in the street: vestiges reflecting preceding existences, terrible times. He digs midst these hills, finding decrepit silver services, tired dresses, ripped silk shirts, slit skirts, dishes piled high, simple pelisses, vests, depleted jerseys, debris, herb beds seeded with weeds, recipients filled with diverse ingredients, spices, etc., (dried) inkwells, (spent) pennies, mere litter between keyless spinets. He identifies five pristine *jie* services, which seem interesting. Yet he finds the price high, even excessive. He gets it lessened. He reflects, dithers, then picks the entire set.

Chill time is here: the citizens imbibe beer while chewing stewed shellfish with chips, then crème desserts. They drink wine, spirits, get disinhibited, then they feel free! These citizens delight in tippling gin fizzes. They get pissed like pigs in shit! The peelers (filth, feds) begin nicking them while the ER services predict drinking-illness epidemics, with dispiritedness, distress, the willies, then DTs.

Then the keepers begin descending their steel screens. The end is nigh.

Winter sets in, with its chills, its sleet, its icicles, its freezing mists. The streets fill with chic denizens dressed in minks, fishers, etc. Never pinch them!

In imperceptible steps, Lille inches itself deep within Rémi's feelings.

He then meets Mireille, the diet expert. Clients fill her little premises, where they twiddle their fingers while expecting her dinner tips, in which she eschews tripe, vermicelli, rice, etc. preferring fresh greens, greens, greens. In her terms, the intestines find them enriching. It might seem weird, yet Rémi finds Mireille sweet. Then, likewise, her limbs begin trembling whenever she sees this impertinent yet sincere, intrepid yet gentle geezer. Their eyes meet, they kiss then sleep. Life's simple when smiles, grins, then sweet whispers wipe the slightest evil intent.

In the end, Rémi's feelings seem settled. His presence in this never-never sweep seems decided, destined even. It's the perfect fit. He'll stretch his legs then spend his wedded, writing life right here.

Originally published in *La Dissolution* (Nous)

Translated by Ian Monk

Jacques Roubaud

Arrangements

2008

37 – § 1017 – **With this PARAGRAPH-MOMENT N° 37 of BRANCH 6 of the prose I'm inventing under the general title of "The Great Fire of London," the title of the BRANCH in question being <u>The Dissolution</u>, I am now beginning the SECOND SECTION of the first part of the BRANCH,**

37 1 With this PARAGRAPH-MOMENT N° 37 of BRANCH 6 of the prose I'm inventing under the general title of "The Great Fire of London," the title of the BRANCH in question being **<u>The Dissolution</u>**, I am now beginning CHAPTER SEVEN of the SECOND SECTION of the first part of this BRANCH, whose title is **Bav OO w,** as you have already heard or/and read

37 1 1 somewhat daunted by the length of the first section of this part, I have, for the second part, decided to set a ceiling on the number of characters

37 1 1 1 as calculated by word 98, and shown under the header "tools" in the "menu bar," then the header "statistics," before choosing the command "number of characters"

● *The Dissolution* is the final installment in Jacques Roubaud's *Great Fire of London* project, an endlessly digressing and bifurcating interrogation of memory published in six volumes between 1989 and 2008.

37 1 1 1 1 (with spaces)

37 1 1 1 1 1 I put "with spaces" in parentheses, because this is how it is displayed on my screen. But I am also putting it in parentheses in my text, annotating it this time as I do with my other parentheses, with a paragraph break and an additional indentation, shifting from blue to green and adding a "1" to the preceding numerical marker

37 1 2 so as to limit it, in this way, to precisely the same number of characters as in the first section, which had reached one hundred and eleven thousand one hundred and eleven (111,111) exactly when I stopped

37 1 2 1 I had more or less reached this number, which I found elegant

37 1 2 1 1 I do not know if 111,111 is a Queneau number, but that does not really matter

37 1 2 1 1 1 it is the product of three times seven thousand and thirty-seven, a number of considerable numerological interest

37 1 2 1 2 this count includes all the numerical markers of the text's fragments, each one

37 1 2 1 2 1 a habit acquired long ago from working on a screen

37 1 2 1 3 concluding with a typographical space, blank but counted, visible on the screen if so desired, but obviously invisible on paper

37 1 3 and to restrict myself to the same number in what is to follow

37 1 3 1 I will then have 333,333 characters in this section, and after three sections, if three sections there are, I shall or should have reached 999,999, which is quite beautiful

37 1 4 an immediate consequence of this diktat being that my digression-mania

37 1 4 1 manifested in cascades of opening parentheses within parentheses

37 1 5 which I have tried to control by forcing myself not to exceed a "parenthetical depth" greater than 6

37 1 5 1 as can be seen in the unfortunate example of the opening chapters of the long version of BRANCH 5

37 1 5 1 1 I haven't always managed to do so, though

37 1 5 1 1 1 running through the pages of the text, I can see far too much pink and even yellow

37 1 5 1 1 1 1 1

37 1 5 1 1 1 1 1 and also light gray at least once!

37 1 5 1 1 2 the delight of writing the word "pink" in pink, and the word "yellow" in yellow amid violet surroundings. A joy that was denied to me when I was six!

37 1 5 1 1 1 2 1

37 1 5 1 1 1 1 1 and "light gray" in light gray bathed in a less light gray!

37 1 5 1 1 2 1 1 1 My computer, Mendy, has contracted an unfortunate habit: quite often, instead of writing "moins," for example, it writes "mpins" or even "mopins," thus adding a parasitical "p" to the word, either substituting or grafted on to the letter "o," as required by the rules of spelling. Some will say that this screen slip comes from the fact that Mendy has placed the letter "p" directly to the right of the letter "o" on its keyboard. But earlier today, it surpassed itself by writing "mpijns." What now? This cannot come from the fact that "j" is the closest letter to "i" on the keyboard. To its left, there is "u," and to its right "o." "j" is to the lower left of "i." I have formed the following hypothesis: in ancient spelling systems, "i" and "j" had uses that overlapped to a certain degree, and Mendy's choice of a "j" to upset my typing of the word "moins" comes from its nostalgia for such a glorious but bygone typographical era

37 1 5 1 1 2 1 1 1 1 of Plantin, Aldus Manutius or else Jean de Tournes

3715113 to write it, for sure, but how to say it?

371511111 in the throes of my parenthetical élan, and impatient to write the words "light gray" in light gray, I opened a gray parenthesis directly within the violet parenthesis **3715111** without first passing through the required brown level. As I closed it, I noticed my mistake, which seems to me to be impossible to reproduce orally, and I had to go back and insert the empty parentheses numbered **371511111** and **371511121**

371511311 in fact, they are not empty: they each contain an open parenthesis, but which opens onto nothing. In a normally bracketed script, it would be as if there were double parentheses

3715113111 some indications on the board might come in handy when reading this out

371511312 I like the interpretation of a simultaneous opening of two parentheses as meaning a parenthesis breaking a silence

3715113121 when reading my text, I do away with the numerical labels that punctuate it, but in the case of this present parenthesis, I'm going to have to reveal some of them. I imagine how readers, their eyes subjected to the relentless assault of all these numbers, even when printed in a very small font size, may become impatient, but then I say to myself that, in the end

371511312 11 in the end, finally, all things considered; I had initially written "after a time," but the substitution was inevitable

3715113122 they'll just pay greater attention, and this will all be seen as an intrinsic part of what is being read, so that, if omitted, it would make it even harder to understand what is being read and, accordingly, I reassure myself that I could keep this system in a putative published state

37 1 6 has been distinctly thwarted. While rereading the preceding pages to identify any typos, or expressions to be rephrased

37 1 6 1 which forces me to make a few local adjustments, since I do not want to exceed the allotted number of characters

37 1 7 and to check exactly where I am at

37 1 7 1 which is hardly clear, even after rereading

37 1 8 I can only regret not being able to add the parenthesis which is blatantly lacking in one place or another,

37 1 8 1 how on earth could I have missed that?

37 1 9 never mind. I'll go back over these passages, starting with the most recent one.

37 1 9 1 differed openings of parentheses, to put it bluntly

37 2 a little before the end of the first section, in the final INSTANT-INDENTATION of its PARAGRAPH-MOMENT 34,

37 2 1 to use the terminology I have adopted

37 2 1 1 without thus far mentioning it

37 3 I indicated a few of the types of contribution made by the sequence of Queneau numbers* at different levels of my prose construction. I had mentioned the fact that, in any given week, I could prosify only for a Queneau number of days, at most six, and never zero, because I refuse to grant zero the dignity of that status. Very well. But I can see questions written all over your faces, and I'm not going to answer all of them. Yes, but hang on,

37 3 1 In my mind's eye, I can see myself in the hall at the INALCO, where I shall proclaim this verbiage

37 4 "you say," you say to yourselves, while addressing me; "you say that you cannot prosify four days a week, because four is not a Queneau number. So be it. But what happens with these same numbers, if they are seen not in quantitative, or cardinal terms, but instead as ordinals? If we take the week to begin on Monday, as we often

* A Queneau number is one for which Q_n has order n. Poetically speaking this means an n-ina, or a variant of the sestina with n lines per stanza, will complete a permutation cycle after n stanzas. This infinite series begins 1, 2, 3, 5, 6, 9, 11, 14, 18…

do, would you then refrain from writing on Thursday, it being the fourth day?"

37 5 "Well, no," comes my reply. "That would be absurd."

37 5 1 Because you consider all your indications, as you put it, to be minted in the metal of pure reason? And they are never "contrary to logic and reason"?

–That's exactly what I think. All the constraints I impose on prose are necessary for constraining reasons of a higher order which you cannot understand.

–Really?

I'll stop this imaginary dialogue here, because it's leading nowhere

37 6 any other questions?

37 6 1 No? Then I'll continue

37 6 1 1 I don't foresee there being any questions, the preceding one being simply rhetorical. If there are any, during my reading... then so be it. I'll see what needs to be done.

37 6 1 1 1 by inserting here a commentary in a fresh paragraph?

37 6 1 1 2 I'll leave that possibility open, just in case, by means of any empty parenthetical space, simply indicated by its violet-colored numerical marker "**37 6 1 1 2 1**"

37 6 1 1 2 1

OULIPO OULIPO

Originally published as 99 *notes préparatoires aux 99 notes préparatoires* (La Bibliothèque Oulipienne no. 187)

Translated by Daniel Levin Becker

Frédéric Forte

99 Preparatory Notes to 99 Preparatory Notes

2010

● Frédéric Forte invented this form in 2006, situating it somewhere between a poem and an essay: an attempt to tease out all the potentialities of a given subject in a concise and polyphonic manner. As Forte explains, it is not "constrained," strictly speaking, but has a great deal to do with the notion of potential.

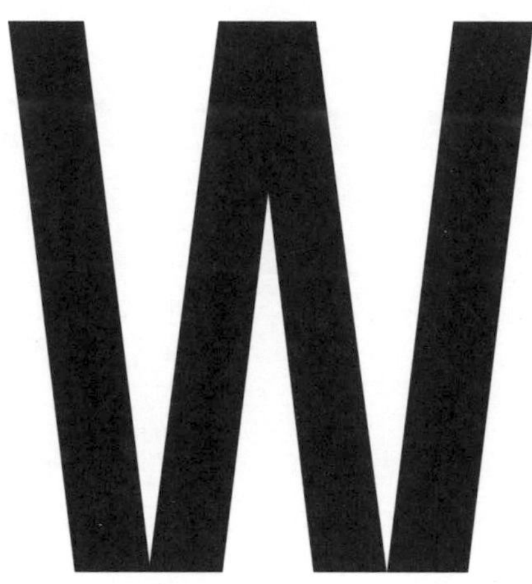

1. What is potentiality?
2. 99 preparatory notes could be written by nobody at all.
3. Constraint is a means, but there are other means.
4. Jean Queval never finished his sentences.
5. What would 99 preparatory boats be—sketches for an armada?
6. To complete the incomplete.
7. There are 99 *Exercises in Style* (Raymond Queneau, 1947).
8. Anybody can write 99 preparatory notes.
9. In a sense, every Oulipian is a preparatory note.
10. 99 is a Queneau number.
11. What would 99 preparatory coats be—homework for a theatrical costuming course?
12. The "99 preparatory notes" form is reproducible.
13. The "99 preparatory notes" form is potential.
14. How do you position yourself upstream from the notion of the stream?
15. 99 preparatory notes can be preparation for something that is not, will not be, or has never been.

16. There are more or less than 36 ways to write 99 preparatory notes.
17. What would 99 preparatory goats be—a petting zoo?
18. There is a Quevalian form to the 99 preparatory notes.
19. There are 99 chapters in *Life A User's Manual* (Georges Perec, 1978).
20. The Oulipo co-opts an Oulipian—that is, adds a preparatory note to its own text—on average once every 22 months.
21. The "99 preparatory notes" form is not constrained.
22. Contradiction is potential.
23. 99 preparatory notes can be preparation for anything at all.
24. What would 99 preparatory gloats be—sportsmanship training?
25. 99 preparatory notes can be preparation for anything at all, I insist.
26. Jean Queval is the main character in "99 preparatory notes to 99 preparatory notes."
27. All preparatory notes are equal.
28. Potentiality can be contradictory.
29. A preparatory note is idiotic/profound.
30. Dramaturgy without drama.
31. If each Oulipian is a preparatory note, then the Oulipo is a poem being written in the "99 preparatory notes" form.
32. There are 99 brief dramatic dialogues in *The Earth Is Flat* (Jacques Roubaud, 1996).
33. 99 preparatory notes can be preparation for something that does not require preparation.
34. Can a preparatory note be written by 99 people?
35. What would 99 preparatory groats be—income set aside for the tithe?
36. There are exactly 36 ways to write 99 preparatory notes.
37. *Preparatory* rhymes with *laboratory*, among others.
38. Rumination.
39. According to my calculations, the 99th Oulipian should be co-opted some time around March 2123.
40. There are 99 *Exercises in Memory* (Jacques Jouet, 1996).
41. 99 preparatory notes are the closest thing that exists, in poetry, to thought (mine).
42. Everyone makes mistakes.
43. What would 99 preparatory bloats be—practice for

Thanksgiving dinner?

44. 99 preparatory notes can be an explanation for why the line "The train passes through the night," by Jean Queval, is an alexandrine.
45. 99 preparatory notes are not preparation for anything.
46. Is 2,123 a Queneau number?
47. Jean Queval is the Oulipo's representative of the "generalized clinamen."
48. 99 preparatory notes are to space what potentiality is to time.
49. 99 preparatory notes make a poem.
50. What would 99 preparatory floats be–recipe testing at an ice cream parlor?
51. Jean Queval borrowed the title of his lost sonnet, "Transformation of the Human Condition into All Branches of Activity," from General de Gaulle.
52. Ask 99 people to each write one preparatory note on a given subject.
53. The Oulipo = 99 preparatory notes to potentiality.
54. 14 is a Queneau number.
55. What would 99 preparatory oats be–camping food?
56. A preparatory note is not a variable-length alexandrine.
57. 99 preparatory notes self-destruct in the course of self-describing.
58. What would 99 preparatory quotes be–a rough draft of an autobiography?
59. If a preparatory note is a variable-length alexandrine, then 99 preparatory notes make a sonnet.
60. Jean Queval is the Percival of potentiality.
61. 99 preparatory notes self-describe in the course of self-destructing.
62. There are 99 *Veiled Poems* (François Caradec et al., 2008).
63. The "99 preparatory notes" form is imperfect, which is perfect.
64. 99 is not one of the numbers remarked upon in *Remarkable Numbers* by François Le Lionnais (1983).
65. Could there be a hundredth Oulipian?
66. There is nothing in particular to see in preparatory note 66.
67. A preparatory note is a single sentence.
68. *Write 99 Preparatory Notes to Enneacontakaienneaphony.*
69. Is it serious, doctor?

70. Who says the lost sonnet by Jean Queval entitled "Transformation of the Human Condition into All Branches of Activity" is not written in the form of 99 preparatory notes?
71. There are 99 (+1) perspectives on the Mona Lisa in *Joconde to 100* (Hervé Le Tellier, 1999).
72. What would 99 preparatory stoats be—a fur coat in the making?
73. It is possible to not think of "99 Preparatory Notes to 99 Preparatory Notes" as a user's manual.
74. Write "99 Preparatory Notes to the Transformation of the Human Condition into All Branches of Activity."
75. An isolated preparatory note is not a preparatory note.
76. What would 99 preparatory moats be—the outlying lands of a castle?
77. "99 Preparatory Notes to an Attempt at Exhausting Place Gordaine in Bourges" was written by nine people besides the "author."
78. The combinatorial poem "Bristols" has 99 lines (Frédéric Forte, 2010).
79. 99 Post-it notes do not make 99 preparatory notes.
80. What would 99 preparatory votes be—gradual acclimation to a dictatorship?
81. There are 99 chapters in *The Adolescence of Mek-Ouyes* (Ian Monk, unpublished).
82. At the moment of the writing of this note, 99 preparatory notes to "99 Preparatory Notes" are being written.
83. What would 99 preparatory totes be—gifts set aside for pledge-drive supporters?
84. Jacques Jouet wrote "99 Preparatory Notes to the Destruction of Hiroshima and Kyoto" (in *History Poems*, 2010).
85. If you reshuffled the 99 preparatory notes of these "99 Preparatory Notes to 99 Preparatory Notes," you would still get "99 Preparatory Notes to 99 Preparatory Notes," but not the same ones.
86. [A quote.]
87. 99 preparatory notes can be locally constrained.
88. What would 99 preparatory throats be—a choir warming up?
89. A preparatory note can be affirmative, negative, interrogative, interro-negative, nominal, and so on.

90. In progress: “99 Preparatory Notes to *Winter Journeys*”; “99 Preparatory Notes to a Short Poem”; “99 Preparatory Notes to the Game of Mah-Jongg”; “99 Preparatory Notes to an Orange Truck”; “99 Preparatory Notes to the Creative Accident”; “99 Preparatory Notes to Postoperative Awakening”; “99 Preparatory Notes to the Palindrome.”
91. Preparatory note 99 is a quote from the novel *Etc.* by Jean Queval (1963), its last sentence.
92. Between two consecutive preparatory notes there are no causal links, except sometimes there are.
93. There will be a book entitled *99 Preparatory Notes, Book I*, made up of thirty-three sets of “99 preparatory notes,” including this one.
94. Preparatory note *x* is, contrary to appearances, not self-descriptive.
95. The *preparatory* in “99 Preparatory Notes...” is the same as the one in “prep school.”
96. A preparatory note is not a free-verse line with makeup on.
97. What would 99 preparatory *smote*s be—vocabulary instruction for biblical scholars?
98. At the moment of the writing of these lines, the following have been composed: “99 Preparatory Notes to the Reconstruction of Okinawa”; “99 Preparatory Notes to the Blue of the Sky”; “99 Preparatory Notes to a Long Walk”; “99 Preparatory Notes to Star Names”; “99 Preparatory Notes to Liquid Prose”; “99 Preparatory Notes to an Attempt at Exhausting Place Gordaine in Bourges”; “99 Preparatory Notes to the Movements of Slowing Down”; “99 Preparatory Notes to *Re-*”; “99 Preparatory Notes to the Original Indignity”; “99 Preparatory Notes to the Impossible”; “99 Preparatory Notes to *The Fox*, a Detective Series.”
99. Good night to all.

Originally published as "Poesía métrica" in *F(r)icciones* (E.D.A. Libros)

Translated by Jeff Diteman

Pablo Martín Sánchez

Metric Poetry

2011

● In this text, at once theoretical, poetic, and autodefinitional, Pablo Martín Sánchez expands upon, theorizes, complicates, and altogether oulipifies Jacques Jouet's notion of the métro poem.

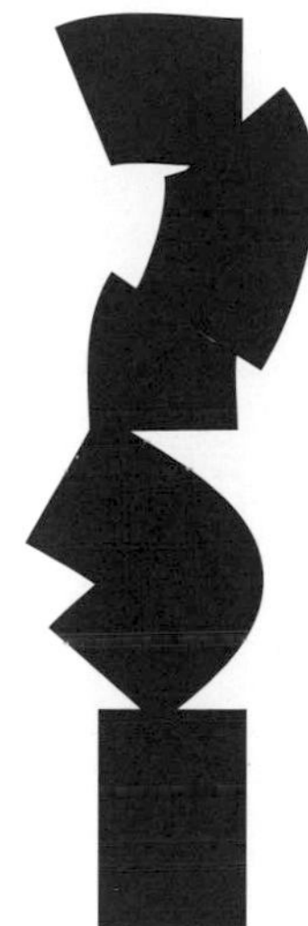

It's a relatively simple exercise. I first learned of it several years ago, at a creative writing seminar in Bourges, France, held by the Oulipo group (the *Ouvroir de Littérature Potentielle*). The term "metric poetry," however, is my own invention. One particularity of metric poetry is that it can only be written in big cities. While this condition might be said to apply (and some have made this claim, starting with Baudelaire) to all poetry (the claim now seems politically incorrect), in the case of metric poetry the city is an absolute requirement: metric poetry is none other than that which is written in the metro.

While the metrical forms this sort of poetry can produce do indeed vary greatly, they are all subject to fundamental constraints that predicate their style, tone, and even content. The metric poet can write only when the train is stopped in a station, and must write only one line at each stop. The writer should spend the time traveling between stations thinking (rather quickly, since he has only one or two minutes at the most) about the line he will write at the next stop. The last line is to be written on the platform of the last station, the final destination. Moreover, ideally, the poet should make use of the material (people, surroundings, situations, objects) that the metro itself provides (rather than, say, leaving home with a preconceived idea for the poem). Thus, it is a poetic exercise that develops writing skills, particularly speed of production, activation of the imagination, and making use of the present circumstances. Of course, the length of the poem will depend on the number of subway stations the poet passes through in any given journey. One of the preferred forms is the metric sonnet, because a journey of fourteen stations is not uncommon in a large city such as Barcelona, Paris, or Buenos Aires, and metric writing offers a pleasant way of passing the time (a travel time of almost half an hour in many cases). But short forms such as the haiku are also possible (for quick trips), as are regular stanzas such as the quatrain (for trips involving four, eight, or twelve stations). The ballad, for its part, is highly recommended for non-routine trips, because the indefinite number of lines (provided that the number is even) allows it to adapt to all sorts of journeys; furthermore, the Spanish ballad is an ideal form for beginners at metric poetry, because its only rhyme requirement is assonance of the even lines. Another useful guideline (this rule should be interpreted loosely) is that there should be a new stanza whenever there is a transfer to another train line (which does not mean that the poet is obligated to change trains every time she wishes to break to a new stanza).

Ever since hearing about the idea in Bourges, I have been practicing my "metric poetry" at every opportunity. When, in the summer of 2004, I spent an extended layover in Buenos Aires (on the way home from a conference on literary theory and criticism in the city of Rosario), I took advantage of the opportunity to write a few metric sonnets after noticing that one of my frequent itineraries involved exactly fourteen stops. I was staying in the apartment of a few friends, on Avenida Cabildo, near the metro stop Juramento on the D line, so when I needed to go downtown (to the final stop, Catedral, near Plaza de Mayo) I had exactly fourteen stations: José Hernandez, Olleros, Ministro Carranza, Palermo, Plaza Italia, Scalabrini Ortiz, Bulnes, Agüero, Puerredón, 9 de Julio, and Catedral. I wrote more than a few metric

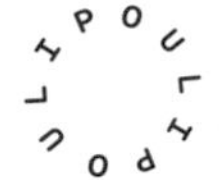

sonnets, some better and some worse (but all mediocre, of course, when compared to the sonnets of a master like Quevedo). The difficulty inherent in the exercise is unavoidable, mainly due to the time restrictions involved (although, with a bit of practice, the lines start to fall like the rain in May). See below for an example of one of these metric poems I wrote in Buenos Aires. Another city where I have regularly practiced metric poetry is Barcelona, my city of primary residence. I spent the 2004-2005 academic year giving classes at the Institute of Education Sciences of the University of Barcelona, near the metro station Mundet on line 3. Once a week, I caught the metro at Espanya and travelled fourteen stations until reaching my destination, during which I would write a metric sonnet. It's worth noting that the station nearest my home is not Espanya (but rather Poble Sec), yet I preferred to walk to Espanya (in the wrong direction) in order to be able to write the sonnet. Sometimes, if I was pressed for time, I would catch the metro at Poble Sec and write what I came to call "hobbled sonnets": I would leave the last line unwritten and, later, after arriving at home, add one more line (from a previous metric sonnet, or nicked from some famous poet), whose rhyme (and meaning, if possible) meshed well with the hobbled sonnet (which was then no longer hobbled). It was in Paris that I wrote my longest metric sonnet (during a trip from Bobigny-Pablo-Picasso on line 5 to Créteil-Préfecture, the last station on the 8, with a transfer at Bastille): nothing short of a poem with four stanzas of eight lines (thirty-two metro stops, as it were, with a fortuitous transfer/stanza break precisely in the middle of the poem). However, the best is yet to come, because I still have a few even more ambitious (read: insane) projects: (1) to write a metric ballad, working for three or four hours nonstop, on Madrid's 6 line (a loop line, potentially infinite); (2) to write a metric ballad whose composition reflects the entire Barcelona subway, divided into five cantos (one for each subway line), with the length of each canto determined by the number of subway stops on its dedicated subway line. But before attempting such industrial-scale metric poetry, I still need quite a bit of practice.

I must admit I find it difficult to select and comment on just one of the many metric poems I have written over the years, but perhaps "Worm Among Worms" will be a good example of the sort of metric sonnet I have been describing. I must emphasize that this is only a poetic exercise (we could almost call it a game) performed in barely twenty or thirty minutes and without any pretense to literary quality. Thus, I beg you not to judge it by the usual critical criteria, and also to note the limitations inherent in the experiment and the particular circumstances of its execution; perhaps it is best regarded as a *bon mot*, or as a way of doing something productive with time that otherwise would have been tossed to oblivion. As mentioned above, "Worm Among Worms" was written in the Buenos Aires metro, in early September 2004 (probably on the morning of Wednesday the eighth, as far as I can deduce based on a couple of references that appear in the poem, cross-referenced with the notes that I wrote that day in my travel diary). The metric sonnet (written, like many of my sonnets at the time, in dodecasyllabic verse) is as follows:

A worm among worms I'm dragged below
an ant among ants, or a limp rag doll
but one of them might start to caterwaul
so I keep my nose in *Yo, yo y yo*

With the aloofness of a real bad bro
as if watching TV I watch people a while
and thoughts of L.'s lovely eyes make me smile:
"Say, can I see you today, viejito?"

Here's a guy I saw yesterday at San Telmo
in the antiques market manning a booth
(coins, dolls, postcards, an old army helmet)

Eager to spray me with truth after truth
but luckily here's the end of my crawl
as always I am saved at Catedral

Despite the scant literary value of the poem, there are a few aspects I would like to point out. To start, it is obvious

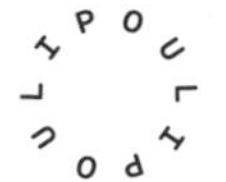

(and this is one of the idiosyncratic features of metric poetry) that the spatiotemporal context of the sonnet is the *hic et nunc* of the day of writing. From the very first line, the poetic "I" (to use a fashionable expression) is located in the Buenos Aires subway system, although in a subtle, allusive manner: at no point does the poem mention the B.A. metro explicitly. However, the references to the context of Argentina (and even Buenos Aires) are unmistakable: the allusion to a work by the Argentine writer Juan Filloy, the use of particular linguistic forms (the original Spanish includes the word "*decí*" for the imperative "say," which in Spain would have been "*dime*"), and the mention of the San Telmo market serve to situate the poem quite specifically. The reference to the subway might be less obvious, but metaphors such as "worm among worms" or "ant among ants," in a context that lends itself to reading and people-watching, locate the action in an underground urban space; this inevitably conjures up the metropolitan subway (not to mention the final reference–easily interpreted by a Buenos Aires native or anyone who has spent any time in the metro there–to "Catedral," the first or last stop on the D line). With regard to the temporality of the poem, the predominant use of the present tense (an appropriate tense for metric poetry) situates the action at the very moment of writing ("I keep my nose," "I watch," "thoughts... make me smile," "Here's a guy," etc.), though supplemented by other verb tenses that enrich the poem (through the inclusion of analepsis: "a guy I saw yesterday," and prolepsis: "can I see you today?"). Also note the directional gaze as a motif in the poem (reading, "watching," "eyes," "seeing," "I saw").

Of less interest (from the perspective of the modern literary critic) are the "real" or autobiographical references that appear in the sonnet. All the same, for the purposes of this analysis, the point of which is to explain the principles of metric poetry, it appears necessary (or at least appropriate) to clarify a few of these aspects. Of course, the poem contains numerous autobiographical elements, drawn from lived experience or taken from the situational context in which the writing was produced, as required by the metric genre. But this does not in any way imply (and pardon me if this comment sounds like a truism or a platitude), that *everything* that appears in the poem is *true*. Allow me to explain. Of course, the references to the metro are "real" (let this adjective always be placed in scare quotes, as Nabokov recommends, because otherwise it is meaningless) and it is even possible that I did indeed feel like a pusillanimous bookworm (*i.e.*, "a limp rag doll"), surrounded by a throng of people while writing a sonnet underground. It is also true that I had a book by Juan Filloy with me, having purchased it in a secondhand bookshop in Rosario; however, I was not "reading" it (how could I be reading and writing at the same time?), but was using it to support the piece of paper on which I was composing the sonnet. With regard to the "aloofness of a real bad bro," it is undoubtedly the result of the necessity of the rhyme scheme, although it is true that at some point on the Barcelona-Madrid-Rio de Janeiro-Buenos Aires air itinerary they ran a film called *Bad Boys* (the director of which doesn't come to mind, as if it mattered), and was perhaps lying dormant in some corner of my memory, waiting to blossom at the right time. As far as "L." is concerned, I don't have any trouble at all acknowledging that she is a real person (it is no accident that I've concealed her name with this initial); however, the phrase "Say, can I see you today, *viejito*?" is in all likelihood invented (or was at least adapted, because it's not terribly common to speak in poetic meter; the nickname "*viejito*," however, is real, in the Nabokovian sense). Regarding the "guy I saw yesterday at San Telmo," I believe I remember that I had in fact encountered him the previous day at the flea market, selling antiques; however, of course, there was no helmet among his wares; this was merely the best thing I could come up with to rhyme with "Telmo."

In conclusion, I hope that this little exposé inspires someone to practice metric poetry. Nothing would make me happier than entering the subway someday (in Barcelona, London, or New York) and seeing someone (man or woman, young or old, white or black, beautiful or ugly, heavy or thin, with a pen or pencil, on a sheet of paper or on a napkin) writing a metric sonnet. Of course, the metric poem that I would produce in such a context would reflect that person's poetic activity, and would therefore, in a manner of speaking, be metametric.

Originally published as "Eodermdromes" in *Contes et décomptes* (L'Association)

Translated by Daniel Levin Becker

Étienne Lécroart

Eodermdromes

2012

● The eodermdrome first came to the Oulipo's attention as a problem posed by a team of American graph theorists. After Claude Berge adapted it for literary purposes, it has been explored and exploited in various ways, among them as a narrative organizing principle in Jacques Roubaud's 2008 novel *Parc sauvage*.

What are we here for?
To make eodermdromes.
To make what?
Eodermdromes. An oulipian exercise. You position letters or words or sentences at the points of a pentagon, then trace a little literary line that passes through each side and each diagonal of the pentagon once and only once.
But how are we supposed to do that here, graphically speaking?
We just replace the letters or words with cartoon panels.
Really?
Yes. We can even do it for other polygons.
Won't we get confused?
No.
I think we will.
We won't, I promise.
Well, I don't care. I'm going to simplify the hexagon...

OULIPO
OULIPO

I LOVE IT!
ITS VALUE ONLY CONTINUES TO RISE.
WELL, OF COURSE!
IT MUST HAVE COST YOU A FORTUNE, NO?
OH, QUITE A FORTUNE.
IT'S ALL ANYONE IN PARIS IS TALKING ABOUT, AND...
THAT'S WHY...
LÉCROART

GOOD TASTE

I LOVE IT!

IT MUST HAVE COST YOU A FORTUNE, NO?

OH, QUITE A FORTUNE.

IT'S ALL ANYONE IN PARIS IS TALKING ABOUT, AND...

I LOVE IT!

ITS VALUE ONLY CONTINUES TO RISE.

WELL, OF COURSE!

IT MUST HAVE COST YOU A FORTUNE, NO?.

OH, QUITE A FORTUNE.

THAT'S WHY...

ITS VALUE ONLY CONTINUES TO RISE.

WELL, OF COURSE!

IT'S ALL ANYONE IN PARIS IS TALKING ABOUT, AND...

THAT'S WHY...

I LOVE IT!

OULIPOULIPO

IMBECILES!
YOU ARE SERVANTS TO GOD'S WILL!
AND IT WAS SO YOU WOULD BELIEVE THAT GOD MADE YOU...

IT GUIDES YOU, HELPS YOU TAKE CONTROL OF YOUR LIFE.

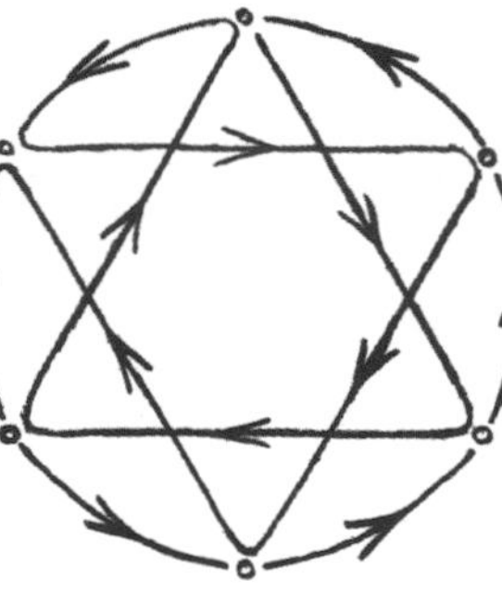

FEAR IT, FOR IT IS ALMIGHTY AND ALL-POWERFUL!

IS THAT WHAT MADE US UNBELIEVERS, THEN?
YOU ARE...

BEINGS ENDOWED WITH CONSCIOUSNESS. YOU HAVE AN INTELLECT.

LÉCROART

OULIPO
OULIPO

THE DEVOUT

IMBECILES!
YOU ARE SERVANTS TO GOD'S WILL!

FEAR IT, FOR IT IS ALMIGHTY AND ALL-POWERFUL!

IS THAT WHAT MADE US UNBELIEVERS, THEN?
YOU ARE...

IMBECILES!
YOU ARE SERVANTS TO GOD'S WILL!

IT GUIDES YOU, HELPS YOU TAKE CONTROL OF YOUR LIFE.

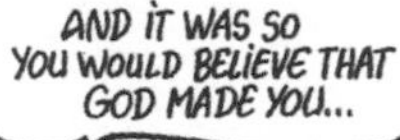
AND IT WAS SO YOU WOULD BELIEVE THAT GOD MADE YOU...

BEINGS ENDOWED WITH CONSCIOUSNESS. YOU HAVE AN INTELLECT.

IT GUIDES YOU, HELPS YOU TAKE CONTROL OF YOUR LIFE.

IS THAT WHAT MADE US UNBELIEVERS, THEN?
YOU ARE...

BEINGS ENDOWED WITH CONSCIOUSNESS. YOU HAVE AN INTELLECT.

FEAR IT, FOR IT IS ALMIGHTY AND ALL-POWERFUL!

AND IT WAS SO YOU WOULD BELIEVE THAT GOD MADE YOU...

IMBECILES!
YOU ARE SERVANTS TO GOD'S WILL!
LÉCROART

"Jeremy and Wiwar" was previously published in Fence 8 (2005) and "Waiting for Dusk" at Drunken Boat (2006)

Harry Mathews

Narrative Sestinas

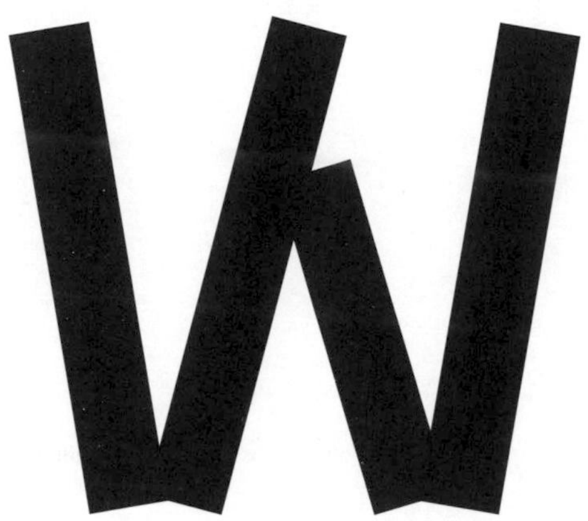

(undated)

● These sestinas in prose continue to indulge the fascination with the combination of permutation and prose that Mathews explored in the book version of *Saint Catherina*.

DANIEL AND DELLA

When the obliging pastor confessed at morning service to being off his form, his congregation immediately wondered if it could be the old problem with his teeth; a quite invisible problem, even if it did seem to tacitly manifest itself in the disconcerting orange color his teeth had acquired from a lifetime of pipe-smoking. The flow of his words, even in familiar prayers, was today uneven, so that he sounded open to doubt–not physical anxiety but a metaphysical doubt that seemed to open a tunnel of despair into his beliefs.

One parishioner, named Della, knew where that tunnel led: straight to self-loathing, to a semi-suicidal fog whose indefinite form made escape from it difficult, even impossible. She decided she must open a way out for the pastor. (His name was Daniel.) She loved him. His teeth, his health, his failing voice, his possibly lethal doubt could not stem the flow of her devotion to him: he was a noble and ardent man.

Outside, in the orange light the winter sun cast on the frozen ground and bundled flock (an orange light more sinister than any dusk), waiting for him to emerge from

the gray tunnel of the cold stone church, Della stood at the side of the churchyard while the flow of worshippers quickly made their way homewards. Della thought: perception has its own form that determines other forms, that was the domain where she must act to effect. She must get her teeth into Daniel's problem where it seemed least palpable, least open to the operation of mere words, mere thoughts, mere counsel.

Through the open church door Daniel appeared, wearing his humility like a visible misery. She needed an orange of the Hesperides (which she knew those apples really were) to give him something to sink his teeth into–a love-apple to bite through. She would be that apple. She would follow him into his tunnel and fill it with the blaze of her naked body, and with his own naked body form a nexus of fire that would reconfigure their lives. You cannot go with the flow always, Della told herself, you cannot tolerate the Taoist dictum when the flow leads straight to death.

She walked across the yard to where he stood, her open face and arms a declaration he could not mistake. He would tell himself he must stay true to form, she knew that. She must shatter that resistance. It seemed the whole world was turning orange, whether from the light or her passion she couldn't tell. She slid fingers inside his coat, she would tunnel a way under his pathetic crust. And Daniel understood. He suddenly bared his orange teeth in an alarming but rapturous smile: "Do you mean what I think you mean?" his teeth helplessly whistled. "I've wanted you for ages," Della began, and the flow of her words wrapped him as in a warm cerement, he saw himself enter another tunnel of yielding doors and hallucinatory penumbra and her own open flesh. Daniel's metaphysical doubts and concerns were subsumed in a violet, green, and orange tempest that was too present, too fleeting to be defined by any form–it dissolved into an endless tunnel of blazing orange as bright as the teeth of the smiling, suddenly open sun. Its only form was that of renewal's unforeseen and unending flow.

JEREMY AND WIWAR

Jeremy knew at once that he need go no further north than the Isle of Skye. He embarked for Portree and sailed across violet waters under a mizzling rain, with only an occasional maw screeching aft and, far off, a few shearwaters in flight so exquisite as to nullify any notion of assault. He landed in a place of dreams. (It did not seem magical, even less metaphysical.) He felt he had been inscribed willy-nilly in an unfamiliar hierarchy of rites.

How he came to where he next found himself he jokingly ascribed to these rites, since he couldn't remember a step he'd taken. He found himself facing north, with Mcleod's Tables far to his left, under a sky of golden haze and in front of him an appealingly metaphysical fork in the road. He knew he could go either way and, later, on a path joining the two roads, encounter a violet-eyed, red-haired woman seated by the wayside. She would show no fear of assault in her bone-pinned woolens, as if expecting him, waiting to thrust him into the maw of history, his history. Jeremy was enchanted and terrified. What was this maw that would devour him?

She handed him an inscribed stone and said he should tell a story in accordance with her rites. He looked at the stone, closed his eyes, and spoke, yielding unhesitatingly to the assault of the runes.

"I, Wiwar, wrote this.

"One day as I was wandering north a beautiful woman took me by the hand and led me to the shore, and there I became a seal, and entered the violet waters, unsure whether my doom was mythical or magical or merely metaphysical.

"Offshore a shark lay in wait for me, and I prayed that he at least might be purely metaphysical—he was small but so fast I had to tail-skip over the waves to stay clear of his toothy maw; but he tired, and I tired and lay down to sleep on his rough-skinned violet back. Soon, following some uncharted itinerary of submarine rites, he led me to a blue whale by whose side he left me, the whale surging hard away from the north towards waters, he told me, that flowed warmly among debonair lands worthy of our assault and conquest. But my heart was calm, banished all thought of assault and battle.

"I was then visited by a great sea turtle (looking as metaphysical as any turtle) who drew me down to the bed of the sea where, pointed north, a burnt ship lay, burned bones and artifacts piled in its maw, from which arose in the splendor of youth my father and mother, smiling at my submission to rites that had reunited us after so long a time in these dark violet depths. Then the huge turtle turned and drove me up, up to the surface of the violet waters. From the start I knew I was not the victim of an assault on his part, rather the beneficiary of a necessary obligation to bring these rites to an end. I had never in my life felt any experience to be less metaphysical, drenched as I was in real brine when I emerged from the friendly maw of the sea. I was sitting on the shore, in my own body, facing north."

From my side a seal slipped away into the water, swimming north. The head turned to reveal her violet eyes, a slender maw that could no longer smile, and (so I felt) a fearful vulnerability to assault. I had longed to fuck her—a metaphysical desire, as it turned out, since this was clearly not one of her rites.

WAITING FOR DUSK

Whoever in the span of his life is confronted by the word "pomegranate" will experience a mixture of feelings: a longing to see at least once the face of a Mediterranean god or nymph or faun; the memory of an old silver mirror decorated with images of varied fruits; a regret at never having known the spell of a summer picnic ending with the taste of acrid seeds spat over the bridge parapet—you look down at your scarlet-stained fingers and up at the weather of the sky as it changes (a black thunderhead, a blue depth), thinking of the same weather crossing centuries and landscapes.

I don't know whether I like the pomegranate as food or dislike it; perhaps neither, thinking of it more as a bridge to other, lost lives. But here now is Simon, with his smiling silly face from which he extracts tough seeds from his teeth with one awkward forefinger, a spell of not unsympathetic bad manners that, if truth be told, is a mirror of our own, perhaps more furtive acts. Then he puts on his mask, made of mirrorlike chromed metal, and I think, why, he could face and kill Medusa! Any weather has its charm, even the green tempest surrounding her writhing snakes that spell death to the unwary traveler, snakes like a wreath of leeks in a Dutch still life where a pomegranate cut in two glows idly near the table edge.

I stroll with Simon, averting my eyes from his face, on the path that leads down to the edge of the stream and the pool under the bridge where fanged pike lie deep among bearded stones. The pillars and vaults of the bridge rise sturdily above us and are completed into wavering ellipses in the mirror of the slow-moving water. This is a moment between here and there, between the face of worldly things and their unstable reflections which in the basically sunny weather suggest reveries tending to sleep, and then sadness. Remember the pomegranate sliced on the unvarnished table, I tell myself, that's something sharp and real!

But the spell of the season and the melancholy hour, sweetened and damped with wine, spell another evolution of my afternoon of regrets, far from the Mediterranean and the bridge at Pisa, far from the land of Nordic dream where the lemon and the pomegranate drop irregular sweet-and-sour globes on slopes scented and dry that are the dusky mirror of a life so seemingly simple that we think of even the treacherous weather as a seamless warm continuum of sun, moon, and stars. I know that I know better, I try to face my life here, with Simon: he has taken off his mask; it has left on his face a stripe or two like accidental marks of his real pain but that in fact spell nothing but themselves—nothing. He appears relaxed in this comfortable weather, sauntering ahead of me as we cross back over the wood-in-concrete bridge, unaware that in the declining light his silly smiling face is the mirror of my disjunction. The picnic spot is littered with wrecks of pomegranate.

Can my face ever be as actual as a pomegranate? Will the weather ever settle down? What dumb idea will replace the functioning bridge? What spell can make the masks of things real? What mirror will reveal them?

Originally published as "Compter sur toi" in *Contes et décomptes* (L'Association); English translation previously published at Words Without Borders (2013)

Translated by Matt Madden

Étienne Lécroart

Counting on You

2012

● "Counting on You" is an homage to Étienne Lécroart's sister, Véronique, who passed away before her fiftieth birthday. Its first panel contains a caption of fifty words and a drawing of fifty strokes; the second forty-nine words and forty-nine strokes, and so on until the empty final panel.

You didn't reach fifty. Seeing that your illness was only getting worse, our mother asked the doctor if she thought that you would reach your next birthday. She answered that you most likely would not. We had to reconcile ourselves to the awful understanding that you would soon be gone.

On the penultimate day, you wouldn't talk but tried regularly to get out of your bed. The nurses all tried - in vain - to reason with you. Until a large male nurse, realizing your obvious need, took you to the bathroom. After that you stayed calm. Dignified to the end.

I think I only saw you cry one time: you had just gotten off the phone with your doctor after she had recommended hospitalization. Your general state was deteriorating. You could no longer take care of your children. You had to leave your apartment forever. You knew it.

Six times you tried to lock your door. Six times your hand slipped. You were furious. I had to do it. We took a taxi to the hospital with Alice. You then crossed the building from end to end, walking all the way to your final bed.

You weren't speaking much anymore. You never were much of a talker. You faded away discreetly in barely three days, without complaining. It was as if you didn't want to bother anyone, almost as if you were apologizing for causing trouble for your family and friends.

Though you weren't secretive, you were never revealing, either. But after your final, devastating chemo session, you told us plainly that you were ready to put up with a few more years of it to be with your children. You were denied this final wish.

You led a normal life right up to the end. One month before your death you were still going to work. You simply let the trains pass until you saw one with a free seat. Standing on the subway was no longer an option.

At home you took care of the every-day, despite your illness. But the last time you did dishes you dropped three cups. Your hands let go, refusing to obey. Metastasis had poi-soned your blood irreparably; your brain no longer responded as it should.

Your children let us know how advanced your cancer was. Putting a good face on it until the end, you would invariably say, "It's OK. I'm just a little tired." And you pretended to go along with the plans we made together.

These children of whom you were so proud: Alice, Hugo, Maxime. A girl and two boys. All as beautiful as you. As sensitive. As dignified. You would have loved to watch them grow. It wasn't your style to leave projects unfinished.

You must have carefully considered your divorce. Weighed the pain caused against pain avoided. To you and your children. It must have been a difficult choice. You told us almost nothing about it. With whom did you share those deliberations?

Your friends were few but faithful. You liked to laugh with them. Above all, you didn't want to bother them with your problems. You were good at dissimulating. I wonder if that deception helped you ignore the pain inside?

You must have thought it would leave you be after that first attack. But you only had a few meager years of respite before the final onslaught. Why you and not one of the many bastards out there?

At what point in your life did death begin its dirty little sabotage? And why? Right up to the end I didn't believe it could be possible. How can one accept such injustice? Yet you seemed to.

You made yourself available to others. You listened affectionately as we recounted our problems. You asked questions. You remembered everything. Your memory was airtight and nothing slipped past you. Didn't that end up weighing you down?

You were attentive but never overindulgent. No sympathetic tears. You didn't push things. You never judged us. You understood us before we said half a word. Yet you were always ten words ahead of us.

You laughed at people's jokes but you never told jokes yourself. Yet as a child you were quite mischievous. You called our father by his first name. You renamed me and my brothers "Ernest."

What happened to that mocking, slightly provocative spirit of yours? It disappeared along with your adolescence. I think I took over that torch. You became docile. It seemed you always accepted your fate.

You took work as it came your way, without really choosing it. You found pleasure in performing it conscientiously and in sharing inside jokes and the occasional night out with your co-workers.

One of them, Isabelle, even became your best friend and your confidante. I wish you had more friends like her around you. You seemed to me so alone, so isolated.

You wouldn't have confided in your children. You wanted to protect them. Make sure they never felt the effects of your torment. A burden they bear today despite your wishes.

Your family was the center of your life. Almost your very reason for existing. You gave them the best of yourself. You reminded me of our mother that way.

I know very little about the rest of your life. You never talked about your opinions or your social life. I don't even know if you were religious.

You were beautiful and cheerful. Seductive. And so I watched your suitors come and go. Until Serge, the most rebellious of them all. You were amazingly different.

I remember how surprised I was when Gilles and Anne made it clear that we had to leave you two alone trailing behind, the young couple.

Your romantic adventures shocked me. The choices you made were always mysterious. And you seemed so sure of yourself, even though we were equally shy.

Your childhood girlfriends faded away one by one but you never replaced them. And later on many of my Friends became yours as well.

We lived together while we were in school, and even worked together to pay the rent. I don't recall having a single argument.

I was trying to be an artist. You were studying the history of art. It's as if you were already stepping back.

You gave me my first guitar lessons and taught me to dance. Lures for picking up girls. Thank you for that.

You encouraged my attempts at drawing. You posed for me. I have clumsy portraits of you. Souvenirs of time together.

I discovered comics thanks to you. You used to read "A Suivre." I still have your first bound collection.

My taste was formed by your choices. I impressed all my friends thanks to your books and records.

OULIPO

You were the older sibling who forged the path of autonomy. And I followed in your footsteps.

I remember your first parties. I remember discovering something new there, too: the world of seduction.

And so, little by little, you guided me along the delicate, perilous pathways of adolescence.

I wanted to save something here, to hold on to a piece of you.

I still can't bring myself to erase your name from my address book.

I can still see your smile in blurred images from our childhood.

Your disappearence has sparked memories, even if it doesn't forestall forgetfulness.

And yet I have never thought of you so often.

I don't remember playing with you during our childhood.

I played with my brothers.
But with you?

You had much better memory
than I.

Part of my past is disappearing.

And part of my future.

No bringing them back.

I miss you.

My sister.

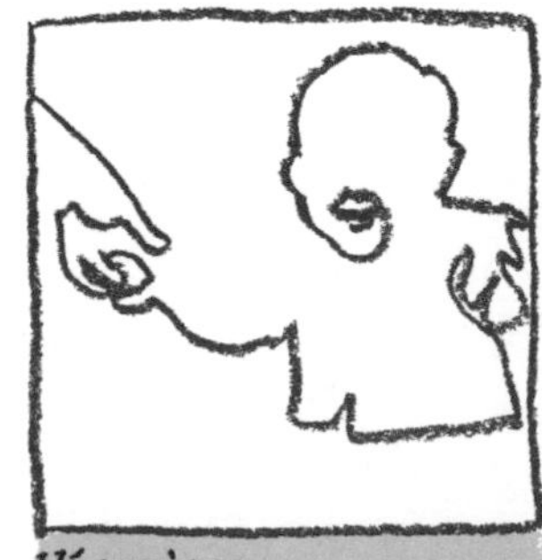
Véronique.

Originally published in *Contes liquides* (Éditions de l'Attente)

Translated by Cole Swensen

Hervé Le Tellier

from

Liquid Tales

2012

● These vignettes are taken from a collection of strange and fanciful short stories, subtitled *Atlas Inutilis*, credited to the Portuguese author Jaime Montestrela and translated into French by Hervé Le Tellier. In 2013 the stories and Le Tellier (and not the vanishingly retiring Montestrela) were awarded the Grand Prize for Dark Humor.

Roberto Catanese of San Patamino (Sicily) was condemned to prison for life in February 1978 for having transformed the celebrated recipe for mozzarella pizza into Sicilian pizza by adding pieces of real Sicilians.

On March 11, 1676, just before the Battle of Thesinge (Holland), in which the army of Louis XIV confronted that of the Quadruple Alliance, the troops took up their battle formations under the orders of Louis de Bourbon-Condé and Georg von Derfflinger. Their formations were so perfect that the commanding officers were reluctant to disturb them by a battle. Which is why the Battle of Thesinge never took place.

Investigators at the Psychology Institute of Brooklyn (USA) have shown that Joan of Arc (1412–1431), known as "the Maid of Orléans," did indeed hear voices, but, not understanding either Farsi or Wolof, she carried out (and rather badly, at that) only the orders given by the voice that spoke French.

The slowness of the wise people of Lomoka (Borneo) is legendary. Long unknown to the rest of the world, they were discovered by the French explorer Camille Rive in April of 1964. It wasn't until February 2011 that a second expedition, this time American, led by Paul Armstrong, returned to their remote valley and found to their astonishment that the Lomokas had only made it to September 1967.

All the research undertaken by Brillat-Savarin from 1787 on, and later by the greatest chefs in the world, to discover the recipe, so beloved by the Hebrews, for "golden calf" has been in vain.

The inhabitants of the Hahiuta Plateau (Lower Nepal) are artists so accomplished that, like Michelangelo, they can see in the raw stone the fabulous sculptures that only their artistic genius could extract. And they can do this so well that they're happy to leave it at that, admiring them in all their veined minerality, though to our naïve eyes their country seems to be littered all over with random chunks of rock.

Researchers at the Institute of Animal Ethology in Arcachon (France) have proved that an oyster's awareness of its existence increases dramatically at the moment of the lemon.

On May 13, 1965, the municipal counsel of Pine Gulch, Utah (pop. 32,145) decided to expunge from the language all words having any reference to sexuality. Soon they were also eliminating many innocent words (from *kangaroo* to *cloud*) that were suspected of standing in for banished vocabulary. Then silence itself became suspect. Even today, it's better to avoid Pine Gulch altogether and instead go through Bear Woods, taking State Route 204.

Just as people count using a base of ten because we have ten fingers, the inhabitants of the planet Vekon count on a base of 999 because that's how many waving tentacles they have. For this reason alone, the Vekonians are much better at math than we Earthlings, but they also have 999 commandments to obey.

According to the medievalist Ludovic Pouchet (1887-1965), the Frankish warrior at whom Clovis yelled "Remember the Vase of Soissons!" as he smote him with his sword never, in fact, remembered anything again.

The inhabitants of the village of Slattamoylin (Ireland) are extremely afraid of ghosts, and so they make everyone on the brink of death sign a document promising that, once dead, they won't come back to haunt the living. So far, the dead have kept their word.

If the Hatakas, a pygmy tribe from northern Angola, think that God is the shadow of chance (with all the imaginable consequences), it's not by chance, but in order to systematically contradict their hereditary enemies, the pygmy Hakatas, for whom, on the contrary, chance is the shadow of God.

Philosophers at the Gödel Institute für Logik have definitively proved that in order to erect a sign in the middle of a lawn that says NO WALKING ON THE LAWN, someone has to walk on the lawn.

The souvenir shops in the small coastal town of Kerbihan (Brittany) sell not boxes made of seashells and ships in bottles but real souvenirs–a bit of skin stripped off from a left heel while mussel hunting on the rocks, a kiss from a complete stranger one evening on the dock of the yacht harbor, or an injured seagull rescued from the beach at Bigouden.

Geneticists at the Oklahoma Institute of Technology have managed to modify the chromosomes of cattle so that their skins have the perfect look and feel of Naugahyde.

For the Hatu people, who live in the jungles of Guadjapaja (Nicaragua), when something tragic occurs to someone, the statement "I share your pain" is never metaphoric. Everyone takes on a part, and at times, in fact, there's soon none left for the original sufferer.

The conjugal life of the ornithologist James Garwin took a dramatic turn when, at a scientific conference, he triumphantly announced that "Contrary to all extant literature on the subject, it turns out that the white-spotted sparrow is no more monogamous than you or I."

Originally published as *Une année bien remplie* (La Bibliothèque Oulipienne no. 198)

Translated by Daniel Levin Becker

Bernard Cerquiglini

A Very Busy Year

2013

● Cerquiglini, who served as director of the Agence universitaire de Francophonie from 2007 to 2015, collected a year's worth of mass emails announcing closures of individual locations (among other activities, we may be sure).

The Digital Francophone Campus[1] of Tbilisi will be closed from January 1 through January 7.

The West Africa Office and the Digital Francophone Campus of Saint-Louis will be closed on Thursday, January 12, in observance of Magal de Touba.

In celebration of national heroes Laurent-Désiré Kabila and Emery Lumumba, the 16 and 17 of January have been declared holidays in the Democratic Republic of Congo. The Digital Francophone Campuses of Lumumbashi and Kinshasa will be closed accordingly.

Due to Army Day, the Digital Francophone Campus of Bamako will be closed on Friday, January 20.

The Asia-Pacific Office and its Vietnam satellites will be closed during the Tet holiday, from Monday, January 23, to Friday, January 27.

Due to Chinese New Year, the satellites of Mauritius will be closed on Monday January 23.

For the commemoration of the Abolition of Slavery, the Francophone Institute for Entrepreneurship (Mauritius) will be closed on Wednesday, February 1.

Due to celebrations surrounding the festival of Thaipoosam Cavadee, the satellites of Mauritius will be closed on February 7.

In observance of Saint Maroun Day, the Middle East Office and the Digital Francophone Campus of Tripoli will be closed on Wednesday, February 9.

Please note that the Central Africa and Great Lakes Office in Yaoundé will be closed on Friday, February 11, due to Youth Day.

Pursuant to the administrative decision N°3/ of the Council of Ministers, the Middle East Office and the Digital Francophone Campus of Tripoli will be closed on Monday, February 14, in observance of the anniversary of the assassination of Prime Minister Rafic Hariri.

Please note that the Digital Francophone Campuses of Alger and Oran will be closed on Tuesday, February 15, in observance of the Birth of the Prophet.

Due to the Maha Shivaratri Festival, the Digital Francophone Campus of Le Réduit (Mauritius) will be closed on Monday, February 20.

By presidential decree dated February 13, Monday, February 20, and Wednesday, February 22, will be public holidays in observance of Carnaval (Shrove Days). As Tuesday, February 21, is already an official holiday (Mardi Gras), the Caribbean Office and its Digital Francophone Campus will be closed for all three days.

I ask that you note that the Chisinau satellite will be closed on Monday, February 23, in observance of Day of the Dead.

The Digital Francophone Campus of Yerevan will be

1. A *Digital Francophone Campus* is an installation of the Agence universitaire de Francophonie. Set up within a university, secured and independently powered, equipped with personnel and machines (computers, servers, videoconferencing software), it puts digital tools (database access, distance learning, etc.) in the service of higher learning in developing countries.

closed on Tuesday, February 24, in observance of Armenian Genocide Memorial Day.

In observance of Concord Day, the Digital Francophone Campus of Niamey will be closed on Tuesday, February 24.

Please take into consideration that the Digital Francophone Campus of Tbilisi will be closed tomorrow, March 3, owing to Georgian Mother's Day.

The Digital Francophone Campus of Yerevan will be closed on Monday, March 7, and Tuesday, March 8, in observance of International Women's Day.

The management of the Aimé Césaire Institute asks that you note that, due to the carnival period in Martinique, the Institute will be closed from March 7 to 10.

Due to the festival of Summer Day, the Digital Francophone Campus of Tirana will be closed on March 14.

In observance of Professors' Day and Mother's Day, the Digital Francophone Campus of Damascus will be closed from Thursday, March 17, through Monday, March 21. The Damascus team sends its warmest wishes to all professors and all moms.

Due to Bectachis (Sultan Nevruz Day), the Digital Francophone Campus of Tirana will be closed on March 22.

In observance of a Memorial Day for those who died during the events of 1947, Thursday, March 29, has been declared a holiday by the government. Consequently the Indian Ocean office and the Digital Francophone Campus of Antananarivo will be closed.

Please note that the Asia Pacific Office and its Vietnam satellites will be closed on Monday, April 2, due to the Hùng Kings Festival.

Due to Ougadi, the satellites of Mauritius will be closed on Monday, April 4.

In observance of Senegalese Independence Day, the West Africa Office and the Digital Francophone Campus of Saint-Louis will be closed on April 4.

The President of the Republic of Benin has declared today through April 6 a holiday throughout the nation in order to allow citizens to prepare for the festivities meant to mark his oath taking. Consequently the Digital Francophone Campus of Cotonou will be closed from today, April 5, until April 7.

In observance of Easter in the Catholic and Orthodox communities, the Middle East Office and the Digital Francophone Campus of Tripoli will be closed on Friday, April 6, and Monday, April 9, as well as Friday, April 13, and Monday, April 16.

In observance of the 17th anniversary of the death of Cyprien Ntaryamira, President of the Republic of Burundi, the Africa and Great Lakes satellite and the Digital Francophone Campus of Bujumbura will be closed tomorrow, April 6.

In observance of the inauguration of the president of the Republic of Niger, Thursday, April 7, is a holiday throughout the nation. Consequently the Digital Francophone Campus of Niamey will be closed.

In observance of Georgian Independence Day, the Digital Francophone Campus of Tbilisi will be closed on Monday, April 9.

In observance of Pimay Lao, the Francophone Institute for Tropical Medicine will be closed from Monday, April 11, to Friday, April 15. The whole FITM team sends you its best wishes for Pimay Lao: Sokdy Pimay Deu!

In observance of the holidays of Easter, Sham el-Nessim, and the Liberation of Sinai, the Digital Francophone Campus of Alexandria will be closed on Sunday, April 15, Monday, April 16, and Wednesday, April 25.
In observance of Maundy Thursday and Friday, the

Caribbean Office will close on Thursday, April 21, at noon.

The Chisinau satellite will be closed on Monday, April 25, due to the Greek Easter holiday.

In observance of Togolese Independence Day, April 27 has been declared a public paid holiday throughout the nation. Consequently, the Lomé Digital Francophone Campus will remain closed.

In observance of Labor Day, the Caribbean Office and Digital Francophone Campus of Port-au-Prince will be closed on Monday, April 30 (authorized long weekend), and Tuesday, May 1 (Agriculture and Labor Day).

In observance of Labor Day, the Middle East Office and the Digital Francophone Campus of Tripoli will be closed on Monday, May 2. We wish a happy Labor Day to all!

In observance of Vietnamese Reunification Day and international Labor Day, the Asia-Pacific Office in Hanoi and its locations in Vietnam will be closed from Monday, May 2, through Tuesday, May 3. Happy Labor Day to all the workers of the world!

Please note that the Digital Francophone Campus of N'Djamena will be closed on Monday, May 2, in observance of the postponement of the Labor Day holiday.

In observance of Victory Day against fascism, the Digital Francophone Campus of Tbilisi will be closed tomorrow, May 9. Due to St. Andrew's Day, the Digital Francophone Campus of Tbilisi will be closed on Thursday, May 12.

Due to Flag and University Day, the Caribbean Office as well as the Digital Francophone Campus will be closed this Wednesday, May 18.

Please note that the Central Africa and Great Lakes Office will be closed on Monday, May 21, as an extension of the celebration of Cameroonian Independence Day, this Sunday, May 20.

The Montreal location will be closed on Monday, May 23, in observance of National Patriots' Day.

In observance of the Day of the Cyrillic Alphabet and Bulgarian Culture, the Digital Francophone Campus of Sofia will be closed on Thursday, May 24, and Friday, May 25.

The Digital Francophone Campus of Bamako will be closed this May 25, the date of an African holiday commemorating the establishment of the African Union.

In observance of Resistance and Liberation Day, the Middle East Office and the Digital Francophone Campus of Tripoli will be closed Friday, May 25.

Due to Independence Day, the Digital Francophone Campus of Tbilisi will be closed on Thursday, May 26.

In observance of International Children's Day and International Tree Planting Day, the Vientiane satellite and the Digital Francophone Campus will be closed on Friday, June 1.

The Indian Ocean Office and the Digital Francophone Campus of Antananarivo will be closed on Thursday, June 2, in observance of the Feast of the Ascension and on Friday, June 3, for a national long weekend.

I inform you that the Caribbean Office and the Digital Francophone Campus of Port-au-Prince will be closed on Thursday, June 7, and Friday, June 8, for the Feast of Corpus Christi.

I thank you in advance for noting that the Montreal location will be closed on Monday, June 25, for Quebecois Independence Day, and on Monday, July 2, for Canadian Independence Day.

In observance of Madagascar's Independence Day, the Indian Ocean Office and the Digital Francophone Campus of Antananarivo will be closed on Monday, June 26 (long weekend), and Tuesday, June 27.

For reasons related to the celebration of the commemoration of the independence of the Democratic Republic of Congo, the Digital Francophone Campuses of Lubumbashi and Kinshasa will remain closed on June 30.

The Africa and Great Lakes satellite and the Digital Francophone Campus of Bujumbura will be closed on Friday, July 1, in observance of the 49th anniversary of the Independence of the Republic of Burundi.

Please note that the Africa and Great Lakes satellite and the Digital Francophone Campus of Bujumbura will be closed on Monday, July 2, and probably Tuesday, July 3, in observance of the 50th anniversary of the Independence of Burundi.

The Digital Francophone Campuses of Alger, Oran, and Constantine will be closed on Tuesday, July 5, in observance of Independence Day and Youth Day.

In observance of the long weekend sanctioned for Belgian Independence Day, the Western Europe Office, in Brussels, will be closed on Thursday, July 21, and Friday, July 22.

By presidential decree dated July 23, Monday, July 30, and Tuesday, July 31, will be public holidays for the Flower Carnival. The activities of the Caribbean Office will thus resume on Wednesday, August 1.

The two Digital Francophone Campuses of Lubumbashi and Kinshasa will be closed on Wednesday, August 1, the date of Parents' Day and the Day of the Dead.

The Digital Francophone Campus of Cotonou will be closed on Wednesday, August 1, Beninese Independence Day.

The team of the Digital Francophone Campus of Damascus wishes you a month of peace and serenity, and reminds you that the Digital Campus will be open from 9 a.m. to 3 p.m. during the month of Ramadan. Ramadan kareem to all!

The Digital Francophone Campus of Niamey will be closed on Friday, August 3, in observance of the anniversary of the declaration of Independence.

In observance of Women's Day, the Digital Francophone Campus of Tunis will be closed on Monday, August 13.

In observance of the 51st anniversary of Chadian Independence, the Digital Francophone Campus of N'Djamena will be closed on Thursday, August 11.

The Digital Francophone Campus of Bangui will be closed on Monday, August 13: the Central African Republic is celebrating the 52nd anniversary of its accession to Independence.

Thank you for noting that the Central and Eastern Europe Office of Bucharest will be closed on Wednesday, August 15, in correspondence with Assumption Day.

Due to the festivities of Assumption Day and the 52nd anniversary of Independence for the Republic of Congo, the Digital Francophone Campus of Brazzaville will be closed on August 15.

The Digital Francophone Campus of Niamey will be closed on Wednesday, August 15, in observance of Laylat al-Qadr (Night of Power), the eve of the 27th day of the month of Ramadan, a holiday in Niger.

The Chisinau satellite will be closed on Monday, August 27, in observance of Moldovan Independence Day.

Due to Saint Mary's Day, the Digital Francophone Campus of Tbilisi will be closed on Tuesday, August 28.

In observance of Eid al-Fitr, the Digital Francophone Campuses of Alger, Oran, and Constantine will be closed from Tuesday, August 30, to Thursday, September 1. Happy holidays to all those who will be celebrating Eid.

We inform you that the Asia-Pacific Office and its

locations in Hanoi, Danang, and Ho Chi Minh City will be closed on Friday, September 2, due to the Independence Day of the Socialist Republic of Vietnam.

The Montreal location will be closed on Monday, September 5, for Labor Day.

Please note that the Francophone Institute for Administration and Management will be closed on Monday, September 5, and Tuesday, September 6, due to Bulgarian Independence Day (Unification Day).

The Digital Francophone Campus of Yerevan will be closed on Monday, September 12, in observance of Exaltation of the Holy Cross, and on September 21, due to Armenian Independence Day.

In observance of Ganesh Chaturthi, the Mauritian locations will be closed on Thursday, September 20.

Please note that due to the holiday on September 22 commemorating Bulgarian Independence, and the long weekend authorized by the Bulgarian Government, the Francophone Institute for Administration and Management will be closed on September 22 and 23.

As the holiday of September 22 (commemorating Malian Independence) falls this year on a Saturday, a non-working day, the Ministry of Employment and Vocational Training, in application of provisions for legal holidays in Mali (law 5040 from July 22, 2005), declares Monday, September 24, a public and paid holiday throughout the nation. The Digital Francophone Campus of Bamako will thus be closed on that date.

In observance of the French Community Holiday in Belgium, the Western Europe Office, in Brussels, will be closed this Thursday, September 27.

Due to the legislative elections taking place on October 1 in Georgia, the Digital Francophone Campus of Tbilisi will be closed on Monday, October 1.

In observance of World Teachers' Day, the Vientiane satellite and the Digital Francophone Campus will be closed on Friday, October 7.

The Digital Francophone Campus of Tbilisi will be closed on Friday, October 7, a holiday in Georgia due to Capital Day.

The Montreal location will be closed on Monday, October 10, in observance of Thanksgiving.

In observance of the boat racing festival Boun Suang Huea, the Vientiane satellite and the Digital Francophone Campus will be closed on Thursday, October 13.

In observance of the commemoration of the assassination of Prince Louis Rwagasore, national hero of the Republic of Burundi, the African Great Lakes satellite will be closed on Thursday, October 13.

Due to Chisinau City Day, the Chisinau satellite will be closed on Friday, October 14.

In observance of the commemoration of the death of Dessalines, the Caribbean Office and its Digital Francophone Campus will be closed on Monday, October 17.

The Digital Francophone Campus of Tirana will be closed on Wednesday, October 19, for Mother Teresa Day.

In observance of the commemoration of the assassination of president Melchior Ndadaye, hero of democracy, the African Great Lakes satellite will be closed on Friday, October 21.

In observance of All Saints' Day, Day of the Dead, and the long weekend authorized for Monday, October 31, the Caribbean Office will be closed from October 31 to November 2.

Please note that the Digital Francophone Campuses of Alger, Oran, and Constantine will be closed on Tuesday, November 1, in observance of the celebration of the start of the war of liberation.

I inform you that the Mauritius locations will be closed on Tuesday, November 1, and Wednesday, November 2, due to the celebration of All Saints' Day and the arrival of immigrant workers respectively.

The Digital Francophone Campus of Bamako will be closed on Monday, November 7, owing to the Eid al-Adha holiday.

The West Africa Office and the Digital Francophone Campus of Saint-Louis will be closed on Monday, November 7, due to the Feast of the Sacrifice.

In observance of the That Luang Festival, the Vientiane satellite and the Digital Francophone Campus will be closed on Thursday, November 10.

We inform you that the Montreal location will be closed Monday, November 12, in observance of the postponed November 11 holiday, "Remembrance Day."

Please note that the Western Europe Office, in Brussels, will be closed on Friday, November 11 (Armistice), and on Tuesday, November 15 (King's Feast).

In observance of the Festival of Lights (Divali), the Mauritian satellites in Le Réduit will be closed on November 13.

In observance of Islamic New Year, the Digital Francophone Campus of Alexandria will be closed on November 15.

In observance of Battle of Vertières Day, the Caribbean Office and its Digital Francophone Campus will be closed this Friday, November 18.

We inform you that the Asia-Pacific Office and its locations in Hanoi, Danang, and Ho Chi Minh City will be closed on Monday, November 21, for Vietnamese Teachers' Day.

In observance of Lebanese Independence Day, the Middle East Office and the Digital Francophone Campus of Tripoli will be closed on Tuesday, November 22.

In observance of St. George's Day, the Digital Francophone Campus of Tbilisi will be closed on Wednesday, November 23.

In observance of the Independence Day of the Islamic Republic of Mauritania, the Digital Francophone Campus of Nouakchott will be closed on Tuesday, November 28.

The Campus of N'Djamena will be closed on Monday, November 28, in observance of Republic Proclamation Day, and on Thursday, December 1, in observance of Freedom and Democracy Day.

The Digital Francophone Campus of Brazzaville will be closed on Monday, November 28, Republic Day.

Due to the centenary of the Independence of the State of Albania, the Armistice of the Second World War, and the authorized long weekend, the Digital Francophone Campus of Tirana will be closed from November 28 to December 2.

Due to Romanian Independence Day and the long weekend, the Central and Eastern Europe Office will be closed on Thursday, December 1, and Friday, December 2.

We inform you that the Vientiane satellite and the Digital Francophone Campus will be closed on Friday, December 2, due to the Independence Day of the People's Democratic Republic of Laos.

In observance of the commemoration of Ashura, the Middle East Office and the Digital Francophone Campus of Tripoli will be closed on Tuesday, December 6.

In observance of Tamkharit, the West Africa Office and the Digital Francophone Campus of Saint-Louis will be closed on Tuesday, December 6.

The Digital Francophone Campus of Tirana will be closed on Thursday, December 8, due to the Festival of Democracy (fall of Communism).

Due to the commemoration of Independence Day in Burkina Faso, Monday, December 12, is declared a holiday throughout all Burkinabe territory.

The Digital Francophone Campus of Niamey will be closed on Monday, December 17 (long weekend for the eve of Republic Proclamation Day), and on Tuesday, December 18 (Republic Proclamation Day). Activities will resume on Wednesday, December 19.

In observance of the investiture of the Chief of State, December 20 has been declared a holiday. The two Digital Francophone Campuses (Lubumbashi and Kinshasa) are closed.

We inform you that the Middle East Office will be closed from Thursday, December 22, through Monday, January 2, due to year-end festivities. Nonetheless, basic services will be available from 9 a.m. to 12 p.m. on Thursday, December 22, Friday 23, Tuesday 27, Wednesday 28, Thursday 29, and Friday 30. Pursuant to administrative decision n° 33, the Council of Ministers has decreed Monday, December 26, and Monday, January 2, holidays in Lebanon. The Middle East Office will resume normal activity as of Tuesday, January 3.

The entire staff of the Middle East region wishes all of you excellent holidays and a new year filled with joy, good health, and peace.

Originally published as "Poème du Requin" in *Blues du requin/ Tubarão blues* (Éditions la passe du vent, 2017)

Translated by Daniel Levin Becker

Olivier Salon

Shark Poem

2013

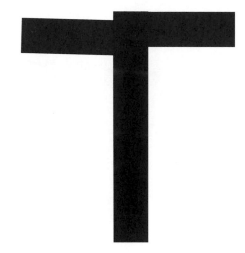

● Salon composed this poem after arriving in Recife, Brazil, and going for a swim while waiting to be allowed to check into his hotel room.

T

The shark is born with jaws
that's how it's made
it's in its nature to use its jaws
shark! jaws!
it sounds good, two short sharp sounds
like two bites
like to bite
into
what?
into whatever it finds to put between its teeth
which could be for instance a poet fresh off the boat
who wishes to take the temperature of the ocean
even if the shark has a slight preference for surfer
for poet is leaner than surfer
so,
shark! jaws! poet!
the shark could also, while biting into the poet
taste the poet's poetry
as the poet tastes like poetry, maybe
one would have to be an anthropophagous poet to know
which I am not,

at least not yet
so let us give the shark the benefit of the doubt
in the flesh of the poet

but, but
but *voilà!*
the poet has a taste too,
one hopes,
the poet opens his eyes
looks around, says
he says *otherwise*
the poet eats life
eats it with his eyes, his fingers,
and his pencil
the poet bites into life with his potent pencil
so, when he returns to the ocean, the poet
especially on the other side of the ocean from his own
  country,
the poet wants to bite into the ocean
and drink it all
from the beach with its palm trees
to the very last drop
the poet wants to bite into all the creatures of the ocean
and naturally the poet intends to bite into the shark
to bite into the brisk body of the shark
so, the poet, entering the water
opens his great beak
he opens his eyes
he parts his teeth
and the shark flees immediately
a simple precaution

Upon arriving in Recife, 22 May 2013

Originally published as "Brève rencontre" in *Oulipo* (BNF/Gallimard, 2014)

Translated by Ian Monk

Ross Chambers

Brief Encounter

2014

At the age of twenty, equipped with an Australian degree in literature, and appointed English *assistant* at the *collège moderne* in Reims, at the beginning of the 1953 academic year I made the acquaintance of a math teacher, who was a musician, pataphysician, lover of spoonerisms, and responsible for the "Sur l'album de la comtesse" column in *Le Canard enchaîné*. Luc Étienne (whose real name was Luc Périn) undertook my real education, inviting me to take part with him in his violin and piano sonata sessions, and gradually initiating me into the salutary notions of the Collège de 'Pataphysique, to such an extent that, on leaving two years later, I had received the marvelous title of Provéditeur-Propagateur aux îles Australes.

On returning to Paris a few years later, one of the first things I did was to meet up with him in a café in the sixth arrondissement. As soon as he arrived, he informed me that he had to "go and see Raymond Queneau" concerning a mathematical problem that intrigued them both, and he suggested I go with him. At Gallimard, Queneau welcomed us warmly, informing us in turn that he had a lunch appointment and inviting us to join him.

● Ross Chambers, who died in 2017, contributed very little to the oulipian corpus properly speaking, but his various scholarly books, which include explorations of the themes of loitering and opposition in the modernist literary tradition, nonetheless establish a fine pedigree for an Oulipo affiliate.

So it was that I had the good fortune to attend one of the Oulipo's very first work sessions. This lunch brought together around fifteen gentlemen who were more or less connected with Queneau, and who talked vivaciously about the most varied subjects, many of which were connected one way or another to the idea of the fecundity of writing under constraint–an idea which, of course, I had never heard of before. Too shy and naïve to express my own opinion about this weighty issue, I contented myself by eating well and drinking well too much, while politely answering the questions I was being asked, and which generally were based on the astonishment my fellow guests felt at meeting a genuine native of the far-off Southern Isles. At a time when standard communications were still seaborne, and thus slow, the presence in Paris of a French-speaking Australopithecus was enough to astound even the most experienced Oulipian. We thus educated one another, and I accordingly became an *honoris causa* member of the Oulipo without the idea of applying for such an honor having ever occurred to me.

Subsequently, I received regularly the Oulipo's documentation, which I preciously kept alongside the publications of the Collège de 'Pataphysique, until the day when, because of a terrible misunderstanding, all of these "old papers" were burnt–"to do you a favor, sir" and "because they were cumbersome"–by an employee in the service of the building where I had a flat. Meanwhile, having moved to the USA, I considered that I had disqualified myself from any longer exercising my various titles of Antipodean propagateur, and I turned towards other destinies, which were far more "sirious," and thus far less mentally stimulating. And yet the memory of that warm 'pata-oulipian welcome which I was fortunate enough to encounter in France proved lasting.

Originally published as "Embêtant" in *Balafres* (Poïein)

Translated by Daniel Levin Becker

Daniel Levin Becker

Writer's Block

2014

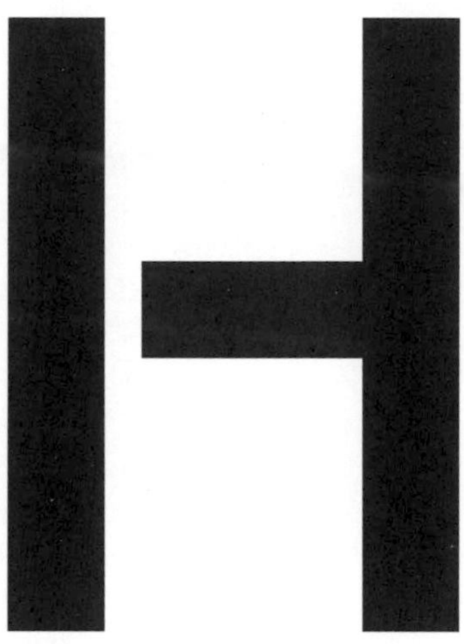

● Using an interrogative prose adaptation of Forte's "99 preparatory notes" form, "Writer's Block" considers a concrete piece by the sculptor Patrick Peltier, asking ninety-nine questions in 999 words.

How long do you have to spend looking at a thing before you see a face in it? Does it take longer to find a familiar face than it does to find an unknown face? Or an imaginary one? In this case, do you see one? A face, I mean? Of one kind or the other? Vaguely melancholic but also sort of sturdy and athletic, like a gym teacher from a couple generations ago? Big and strong, cloudy mustache, furrowed eyebrows? Can you have a face without eyes? Do you see eyes? What about a landmass? Do you see a landmass? Can you look at something in a particular language? In which language are you reading this text, for instance? And in which are you looking at the thing? What happens if they're not the same language? Does it matter what language an object was made in? How much so? What other circumstances of its fabrication matter? Do you realize I have never seen this face with my own eyes? That I have never seen nor smelled nor heard nor hefted it? That I have not studied it from all possible angles? In fact, can I even say with certainty that I've seen all four sides of the face? Would I have been better off letting you believe I know this thing intimately? That

I have seen it in the flesh, so to speak? Also, do you see a dove? Like, maybe holding a bible in its beak? What is the value of assuming that a person speaking to you about a thing knows the thing? That he or she has already, say, measured the top of it in comparison to his or her left hand? Should I have gone to see it? To do some tests regarding the not entirely flat part where the gash begins? If so, how? Who would have paid? Or is it rather where the gash ends? How do you tell the difference? Is the tip of a rabbit's ear a beginning or an ending? Do you see a rabbit (I don't)? Do you see a U or a V? Do you know how the word *or* is meant to function in the previous question? Where, or rather when, is a V more than half of a W? Less? Same question and a half, but with U instead of V? Did you know I have spent many years taking pictures of interestingly textured walls? Well, how would you have known that? Do you think you would be capable of distinguishing a Norwegian wall from a French one? Without context, I mean? Would you believe me if I told you I could tell you more or less exactly where each wall in my collection is located? The country we were in at the moment I photographed it? What the sky looked like? The relative temperature? Who was there, besides me and the wall? Or is it besides the wall and me? More importantly, would it matter? What would such details add, do you think, to your aesthetic experience? Or would they detract from it? Would it have made a difference had I told you I knew the face in the thing in question here, knew it intimately, but did not and do not know the thing itself? Do you see a koala curled up in a tree, by any chance? Do you remember the time before the time when everyone had a camera in his or her pocket at all times? To what extent do you suppose the photographs you are looking at right now look like the photographs I am not showing you, but could have shown you, of walls in Amasra or in Angra dos Reis or in New Haven? Are we not, the two of us, having more or less the same experience right now, only from opposite sides of the production of the book that you are holding in your hands and I am holding in my head, with respect to our middling but secretly lacunary certainty of the real life and true nature of the thing? Is *lacunary* a word? Do

“Balafre 6,” Patrick Peltier

you know what the thing is made of? Whether it's heavy? I mean yes of course it's heavy but what kind of heaviness? Whether it's expensive? Whether it *was* expensive? Whether it spits out little puffs of dust when moved, like the cinderblocks that support the bookshelves in my bedroom? Is it made of concrete? Are cinderblocks made of concrete, for that matter? Whom did I mean when I said *we*? Was it hard to transform the thing between its original state and the state in which you now see it? What *was* the original state of the thing? What does that even mean? Do you see an owl? Am I wrong to assume that if you are reading this text you are not also standing in front of the thing in question? Do you know how the word *also* is meant to function in the previous question? Am I wrong to assume you are reading this text at all? What if you are hearing me read it aloud? What is my voice made of? Is its texture more or less coarse than that of the thing? Where, or rather when, does a detail become a pixel? When does *enhance* replace *shantih*? Or when did it? Same question, same temporal bifurcation, but with *texture* instead of *enhance* and *context* instead of *shantih*? How long do you have to spend looking at a thing before you see a sex organ? What makes a landmass? What isn't one? Should there be a footnote at *shantih*? How big? How strong? Do you see a skull? Do you see a tear? What happened to this face to make it look so sad? Can you cry without eyes? Do you see a wall? What have they done to you, my friend? Where did they find you? Where are your eyes? Where will you go?

Originally published in *C et autre poésie (1962-2012)* (Nous, 2015)

Translated by Ian Monk

Jacques Roubaud

from

1962-2012

● ⊂, named after the mathematical symbol for complementarity, is a collection of poems spanning the majority of Jacques Roubaud's career, so named because the poems therein were voluntarily left out of the poet's published books and therefore serve as complements thereto.

REMEMBER

1 **Remember**

Memories now set
⊗ in three lines
short. dated. noted

2 **After Ton'a**

how days are nothing
⊗ without their
sum of growing old

3 **After Ton'a**

if all memories
⊗ expanded
none would be worthy

4 Enumeration of memory-images: descent into meditations

by sight, by hearing
⊗ senses of smell
and taste and touching

5 Enumeration of memory-images, 2

the gaze will linger
⊗ only on
old image-moments

6 The years

just how few splinters
⊗ re-suffer
during all these years

7 Lyon, rue de l'Orangerie, 1934 (?), after 'betten' stories

black-on-red drawings.
⊗ pallid seeds,
sweetish blackberries

8 1936, Tulle

the large window that
⊗ approaches
and touches my eyes

[...]

99 in memoriam JRR, 1961

aparte de mi
⊗ this moment
of lengthened horror

100 Childhood JRR–1940

beamingly three steps
⊗ the belly
satisfied with sun

PRINSLAND

A
Into the Loire

He threw into the loire the bronze beer. He threw into the dark loire the sky and its smoked glass, convex like a lens. he threw the beer towards the willows and the sands, towards water's heavy tongue,

towards the ford and the banks' dead stumps. The loire apparently remembered, a fruitful snowy and fearful landscape, colored like beer, lips, the color of this bronze beer.

the hirsute loire spumed. The wind whistled: from anjou and bulrushes, from chinon or amboise, or blois: wind, and all the bronze bells.

He lay down on the parapet, on the gray stone nibbled by inner bubbles; he was still thirsty but the loire, but the loire had drunk it all

The holly branch:
Joan said: I shall be forever faithful etc.
(Hugo: ocean verses)

(Mirrored)

GREEN NOTEBOOK (1964)

NOTES ON THE SONNETS

September

After a crisis of three months resolved by the absolute need to mathematicize right through to my thesis. always dreaming of the future. constantly remodeled, obsessive projects, ad infinitum.

... I think that with the arrival of JR not only all feelings but also so to speak any possibility of external compassion has died. The only violence I have left is for a certain expression of what happens and the pride of shining albeit slightly in this adventure which has now become a profession: mathematics. While justifying an aesthetic. All of which has been launched by an extremely old motor (at the age of nine, I decided on poetry, and clearly at seventeen, or otherwise sixteen perhaps, on mathematics). And it was a really childish idea! But no I cannot envisage poetry (in the broadest sense) without taking into account this activity of reasoning and the formal architectures that I have more or less appropriated over the years. Eighteen months ago, when I started to write again (or else quite simply started), and I sensed at once that I was not going to stop myself from having mathematics play a part in the process, it was initially just a desire for amazement, a hoax, singularity, originality, an aesthetic meaning which was of course not entirely inexistent (Max, calligrams, cummings). But now I want to take this hoax through to its end.

MEZURA, SPECTRE (OF A MORAL NOVEL)

FIRST CHAPTER

Successions of words	are nice	so it is
She, angelic	or angelically	thrives
Her upper half	ain't much	apparently
Making her moan	bears	
•		
Curry in her dress	between these nothings	lying together
marvelous copies	though unconsidered	usually inside
until they become	quite round on request	thus improving the
way they look real		
Booze makes her restive	indulgent	or else melodically
	firm	with instructions
For use	a lake's slim amber	
Has been closed	because	of a violence-free past
	its calm chimes	with
A shrinking district	covered	with quite clear
lotion	and that's why	a pencil sharpener
appears on a table		
Should its surrounding ring	make them all stand up?	

18 POEMS (9 AND 9) FOR "SUBSTANCE"

GRASS RECTIFY*

'my vocabulary did that to me'
come back drifting . grass rectify indifference
or other . redden leaved interfere with other
silences . complete volumes by hiding
bumps . liquid snow . that
may be . it goes with
cells as with organizations . the right line
dissolves . to dissolve them .
cut into
muddy stirrings . define
passage into bricks next to no wind . reduce
vibrations . spectrum leaves .
nothing else.

CHURCHILL 40 AND OTHER TRAVEL SONNETS

LIGHT—A SONNET

Light moves in light and dies the same
Where light insists that light should be
Wherever several instants flame
Light never heard I never see.

Against the dark which no lights borrow
The hiss of spark, the bliss of fur
For light is paced more black than morrow
It stays where weighed and does not stir.

If red is black as black is cinder
This side of light we cannot reach
The skeptic sun of dawn nor hidden
This sucking void, that deadly leech

Verify your silence and light
Shall fill the center in your sight.

HERE WE GO
HYAKUIN OR A HUNDRED POEMS

beginning

at the beginning
⊗ deciding
the routes of Writing

continuing

what the eye withdraws
⊗ the hand sets
where the compass strays

dimensions

within this hugeness
⊗ perceiving
not no really not

Robert Filliou – Eins, Un, One...

as as as as as
⊗ as as as
as as as as as

form

form that is so brief
⊗ that you get
visual impressions

form

a minimal form
⊗ here forces
a descriptive flow

Robert Filliou – Eins, Un, One... (II)

a throw of dyes
⊗ can never
Ob literate chance

Felix Gonzalez-Torres – Death by Gun

permanent montage
⊗ Leben-stu
dio Mort inconsciente

report

making a report
⊗ but so tight
that the hand dithers

On Kawara – One Million Years (past)
One Million Years (future)

one million years (past)
⊗ (future) one
million years (plus one?)

(...)

Originally published in
Our Beautiful Zeroïne, 1
(La Bibliothèque
Oulipienne no. 218)

Translated by
Daniel Levin Becker

Marcel Bénabou

from

Our Beautiful Zeroine

2015

● A historian both of North African antiquity and the Oulipo's early years, Marcel Bénabou considers François Le Lionnais's ongoing experiments with poetic reduction. This installment is a sequel to the Bibliothèque Oulipienne fascicle *Miniature persane* (Persian miniature), part of Bénabou's own ongoing experiment with the exhu mation and enshrinement of oulipian foundational lore.

"Poems of few words," "poems of a single word," "reduction of a poem to a single word": step by step I endeavored, in the previous installation of this work, to reconstruct the approach of the poet François Le Lionnais, and to demonstrate the tranquil audacity with which he exploited the procedure of miniaturization. I have not forgotten, however, that in so doing he also inscribed himself, albeit perhaps without entirely realizing it, in a broader movement that made brevity and concision values unto themselves, essential criteria for the quality of a poem. Thus do we see, for instance, at the end of the eighteenth century, the very discreet and delicate Joseph Joubert, himself an adept of aphoristic literature that concerned itself with enclosing maximal meaning in a minimum of words, committing to his *Notebooks* this remark: "Poetry made with little matter: with leaves, with grains of sand, with air, with nothings, etc."[1] Some time later, in the middle of the nineteenth century, Edgar Poe, in his great study entitled "The Poetic Principle," wastes no time in proclaiming straightaway that, to his eyes, "the phrase, 'a long poem,' is simply a flat contradiction in terms."[2] Meanwhile, Flaubert wrote to Louise Colet: "The finest works are those that contain the least matter."[3]

Later on we find the famous adage *less is more*, which is generally attributed to the architect Mies van der Rohe but in fact comes from the poet Robert Browning.[4] More locally, we arrive at Valéry's injunction "between two words you must choose the lesser,"[5] finally culminating in the way George Steiner describes "the great crisis of humane literacy": "The world of words has shrunk."[6]

What I wish to examine here is a new leg in the President-Founder's poetic itinerary. A predictable leg, moreover, since, once engaged in his quest for concision, a spirit as keen on exhaustion as his could hardly have been expected to rest before exploring its outer limits. For two reasons at least. On one hand, the friend and intellectual accomplice of Queneau could hardly ignore this axiom of the Quenellian *ars poetica*: "Ça a toujours kékchose d'extrême / un poème."[*] On the other hand, the mathematician who also happened to be our poet could hardly forget that the sequence of numbers does not break off at 1, and that on the near side of 1 there is, in addition to an infinite series of negative numbers (which is perhaps what Joubert was dreaming of when he wrote these words: "[…] 'negative poet' could be pleasant"[7]), there is also, need I remind you, 0. It was thus logical that our mathematician-poet should one day be moved to reflect on this singular literary phenomenon, the zero-word poem, and to theorize it.

What for a long time and until relatively recently seemed surprising to me was that, judging by the available written evidence, this preoccupation appeared to take longer to manifest itself than had its prior counterparts. Indeed, the expression "zero-word poem" is not mentioned until (for the first and only time) 1976,[8] whereas the one-word and one-letter poems go back to 1957. What could have accounted for this nearly twenty-year delay?

To shed light on this question, I felt it would be useful to start by examining more closely the famous series christened *tentatives à la limite*.[†] Let us recall that this series, first published in 1961[9] and reprinted in 1973,[10] juxtaposes three productions: a "poem consisting of a single

1. Joubert, *The Notebooks of Joseph Joubert*, trans. Paul Auster.

2. Poe, "The Poetic Principle," 1850.

3. Flaubert, letter to Louise Colet, 16 January 1852, trans. Frances Steegmuller.

4. He wrote this in 1855 in one of his poems, "Andrea del Sarto," from his great collection *Men and Women*. This is the translation of a German proverb from several decades prior: "Weniger ist mehr."

5. Valéry, "Literature," trans. William Geoffrey.

6. Steiner, "The Retreat from the Word," in *Language and Silence*.

* In Supratik Sen's literal translation, "a poem / always possesses something extreme."

7. *Notebooks* II. The idea of a fundamentally mathematical "negative poetry" remains to be explored. Another field wide open for the ingenuity of the Oulipians…

8. "The Anteantepenultimate," dated November 30, 1976, was first published in fascicle no. 4 of La Bibliothèque Oulipienne, *To Raymond Queneau*. It was later reprinted in *Atlas de littérature potentielle*, Gallimard, 1981.

† Translated in the *Oulipo Compendium* as "going for the limit."

9. "Exercises in Potential Literature, works by the OuLiPo Subcommission," *Viridis candela, Cahiers du Collège de 'Pataphysique*, Dossier 17, Sable 22, 89 (= vulg. December 22, 1961).

10. In *La littérature potentielle*, Gallimard, 1973.

word," a "reduction of a poem to a single letter," and finally a "poem based on punctuation." I will not revisit the first two *tentatives*, which I have already analyzed amply in my previous work. I will thus turn my attention to the final poem, which is presented here:

```
          :
1, 2, 3, 4, 5.
6; 7; 8; 9; 10.
         12?
         11!
```

(1958)

What we have here is a poem of five lines of unequal length,[11] comprising a series of digits (from 1 to 12) and punctuation marks.[12] These open and close the poem and are not all used: we may remark the absence of ellipsis, parentheses, and brackets.[13] One might, at first glance, consider this creation to be a zero-word poem, and even technically speaking a zero-letter poem, which would be the logical successor to the one-letter poem. Certainly–but, in his commentary, FLL (François Le Lionnais) makes no mention of this mathematical aspect of things. He explains only that he was looking to "reverse the relationship" that ordinarily obtains between the role of words and that of punctuation, giving punctuation the major role, namely to "bring the poem to life, perhaps to create some surprise." He adds that, in this poem, punctuation "plays a major role as soon as one can imagine variants in which the words *(sic)* are replaced by other words, the desired effect being the same because it is provided by the punctuation."[14] Meaning–and this is what is important to me here–that the digits given in the poem have, for him, the status of "words." It is thus clear that, in this final *tentative à la limite*, which followed the preceding ones by a year, FLL seems to no longer be troubled with pursuing the path of miniaturization. He made a choice to embark in another direction: the search for a strong formal structure that could lend itself to a multitude of variants. A structure that he creates here effectively, and in the most economical manner possible: using only the ingenious disposition of a handful of punctuation marks. The whole bristling family

11. Perhaps a futile remark, but one I believe is useful to make: the general form of the poem evokes, to my eye, a Cross of Lorraine, which I am tempted to view in light of the date of its composition: 1958, the same year General de Gaulle returned to power…

12. Oulipians' interest in punctuation is well known: see, for instance, fascicle 24 of La Bibliothèque Oulipienne, Jean Queval's *; : ! ? !?! ( ) [ ]*

13. This absence probably has a meaning, which remains obscure for the time being.

14. Oulipo, *La littérature potentielle*, op. cit.

of substitution-based oulipian exercises is contained in the seeds of this slender poem... Nonetheless, for the leap toward the zero-word poem, we must look elsewhere.

For a long time, as I have already said, I was forced to admit, from the perspective of the only document to which I had access,[15] that this leap was not made until 1976. But it quietly continued to strike me as unlikely, and an old historian's reflex prompted me to wonder whether this large gap was not due, as is so often the case, to a documentary lacuna. It was not until 2008 that the situation suddenly became clear to me. I benefited from the systematic research of Olivier Salon, who, at the encouragement of the other Oulipians, took on the task (a cumbersome one to be sure, but both laudable and indispensable) of gathering all of the information necessary for the composition of as complete a biography of FLL as possible.[‡] Thanks to him, I finally gained access to what I can only describe, in the genealogy of the zero-word poem, as the "missing link": a copy of the review *Il Caffè*.[16] This issue contains, under the title "La Recherche di François Le Lionnais," these five contributions:

1. "The just the all the": the famous "sonnet without verbs, adjectives, or nouns," which I note duly had already been published in 1946 in issue I-II of the journal *Messages*; we know that FLL was particularly proud of this poem, which he was always happy to reference[17] and which he considered his first "oulipian" work.[18]

2. "At the tip of the tongue": under this title there are four lines of periods, but no text. I was, evidently, struck immediately by this contribution, which rather closely resembles a "zero-word poem." But it is a "zero-word poem" that manifestly dares not claim or describe itself as such.

3. "Poetry in trace amounts": under this title is a "poem" whose text is composed entirely of digits and punctuation marks; it is, give or take a detail,[19] the poem we already know as the "poem based on punctuation."

15. See note 8 *supra*.

‡ See Salon's *Le Disparate, François Le Lionnais: Tentative de recollement d'un puzzle biographique*, Le Nouvel Attila, 2016.

16. *Il Caffè*, issue 1, January 1960. Curiously, this precious document is held in the archives of Paul Braffort but not those of the Oulipo. Let us recall that *Il Caffè* is an Italian avant-garde journal, created and directed by Giambattista Vicari, a friend of Lescure and Queneau with whom the Oulipo would later collaborate. See Anna Busetto Vicàri's article "'*il Caffè' letterario e satirico*," in R. Aragona, *La regola è questa*, 2002.

17. See *Moments oulipiens*, Le Castor Astral, 2004.

18. It can be found in *La littérature potentielle* under the heading "Autres tentatives à la limite."

19. The "Italian" version does not include the colon that subsequent versions have on the first line.

4. "Reduction of a poem to a single letter": under this title is a capital T, followed by a series of ten periods.

5. "Poem comprising a single word": under this title is the poem "Fennel."[20]

I cannot overemphasize the importance of this document: here we see FLL consolidating and classifying, for the first time we know of, various "literary objects" from different times, which he considers the most representative of his "research" (a word obviously not chosen by accident![21]) and therefore worthy of being communicated to the happy few transalpine readers who made up the audience of *Il Caffè*. Four of these texts (numbers 1, 3, 4, and 5) would remain texts of particular importance for FLL, which he would not hesitate to reprint whenever the opportunity presented itself. But, and most interestingly for us here, in these later publications, the "texts" in question underwent various modifications, which we must now highlight.

Let us first examine the second publication (1961).[22] The three final items in the series are present, at the interior of a set generally titled "Enchaînements [sequences] et tentatives à la limite," constituting the latter section. But they have been placed in a different order: first comes the "poem comprising a single word," then the "reduction of a poem to a single letter,"[23] and finally the "poem based on punctuation," a new title for "poetry in trace amounts." Moreover, the whole thing is accompanied by commentary, which is pleasantly wordy given the extreme concision of the works being presented. If we pass now to the third publication, the one in the 1973 collective Oulipo volume,[24] we must admit that we learn nothing new, because it repeats exactly, with the same title and in the same order, the "three *tentatives à la limite*" as well as the same commentary. Thus there are in fact, in terms of content, only two versions, the Italian (1960) and the French (1961/1973). It seems to me that the most significant modifications between these two versions for our purposes are: the change in order in which the poems are presented; the pure and simple disappearance of "At the tip of the tongue"; the appearance, as a

20. *Il Caffè*, January 1960. Note that the cover highlights in bold text a piece by Hans Paeschke, "*Provincialismo e universalismo nella cultura europea*."

21. I cannot help thinking that the words *la recherche*, amid the calculated bilingualism of this title, were left in French in order to discreetly evoke another famous *recherche*.

22. See note 4 *supra*.

23. Note that the *T* is followed here by a single period.

24. *La littérature potentielle*, op. cit.

general category, of the notion of *tentatives à la limite*. I see just as many converging indications that seem to me to signal a veritable shift in perspective, on FLL's part, regarding its execution.

In the 1960 version, the itinerary took us from a wordless poem ("At the tip of the tongue") to the poem in "trace amounts," then from trace amounts to the letter, and finally from the letter to the word. The logic operating in the later version is the exact opposite: this time FLL begins with the one-word poem, then moves to the reduction of a poem to a single letter; after this he transforms into "Poem based on punctuation" the title of the poem previously presented as "Poetry in trace amounts." As for the poem entitled "At the tip of the tongue," he deletes it, pure and simple. From these observations an initial conclusion can be reached: the 1960 version obeyed a logic of ascension, of progressive enrichment; it began in silence, the absence of words, and culminated in the appearance of a word (or, we might say, the Word). That is, you will have noticed, a process analogous to that of biblical genesis, which proceeds step by step out of nothingness. To the contrary, the 1961/1973 version obeys a process of progressive analysis, which I have called "miniaturization." But FLL, retracing the previous path in the opposite direction, does not deem it necessary to see it through to the end; he stops just before what would have been the final step, namely nothingness. Why this overhaul? The answer would seem to lie in recalling that between the two publications, a major event took place: the creation, in the fall of 1960, of the Oulipo, a group that gave itself the task of "the search for new forms and structures that may be used by writers in any way they see fit."§ This event could not have failed to influence the presentation of these old works. What had until then been merely "research," more or less by trial and error, was now obliged to integrate itself into a new unity meant to be coherent: the ensemble of oulipian creative procedures. The *tentatives à la limite* category,[25] invented for the occasion, would allow precisely this integration. But FLL, who admitted to fearing that the "reduction of a poem to a single letter might wind up on the other side of the permitted limit," deemed it preferable to not

§ ibid.; trans. Warren Motte from *Oulipo: A Primer of Potential Literature*, Dalkey Archive, 1986.

25. Other *tentatives à la limite* are given in another chapter in *La littérature potentielle*.

take the next step, that of the empty poem, the poem without words, which no doubt did not appear to him, at the time, to be a genuine "new form or structure" worth delivering to writers.

He would not find occasion to return to this problem until much later, in 1975, and in a very particular text—an occasional text, one might say—that of his posthumous homage to Queneau.[26] It seems as though the internal censure to which FLL felt it wise to freely submit himself until that point was lifted by the traumatic event that was the death of Queneau, the friend to whom he had been so devoted for so long... This, then, is the context in which the zero-word poem appears. After recalling Queneau's own interest in "poems of few words" and having sketched out a taxonomy[27] and made known his desire for an anthology thereof to be compiled, FLL broadened (as he was so fond of doing) his initial scope and, turning his characteristic eagle eye on the entirety of universal poetic production, posits this hard-to-contest affirmation: "In a more general manner, the study of the validity of poems whose number of words falls between 0 and + infinity deserves to be undertaken and pursued scientifically." This is how the meeting was staged between two quantities we are seldom accustomed to seeing together: the poem and the zero.

26. "The Anteantepenultimate." See note 8 *supra*.

27. See my remarks on this classification in *Miniature persane*, op. cit.

Originally published in
Le bel appétit (P.O.L)

Translated by Ian Monk

Paul Fournel

from

The Beautiful Appetite

● Paul Fournel's gustatory poetry, collected in *The Beautiful Appetite*, undertakes a deceptively simple interrogation of the subtle similarities between the food or drink recipe and the fixed poetic form.

NO SLICE

Waiter, make me a Martini
Please, here in a Chinese-shaped hat
Right up to the rim, which is at
The brink of overbrimming, like me.

This hint of loving the Yankee
Will make my resistance fall flat.
Waiter, make me a Martini
Please, here in a Chinese-shaped hat.

From shaker to sieve and then see
It'll make a natural olive look matte
With white vermouth, yes, just like that
And dry gin too, slightly drunk, *oui*
Waiter, make me a Martini.

POTATO PANTOUM

You sizzle in the goose fat
Hail potato I salute you
You soften in the fire's heat
This food I worship through and through

Hail potato I salute you
Universal bit of veg!
This food I worship through and through
Cut as fries or in a wedge

Universal bit of veg!
Stuffed or mashed, what the heck
Cut as fries or in a wedge
Nicola or Kennebec

Stuffed or mashed, what the heck
Here comes a little milk and butter
Nicola or Kennebec
For a kid's or grown-up's supper

Here comes a little milk and butter
In the meat juice turning brown
For a kid's or grown-up's supper
No one ever turns you down

In the meat juice turning brown
Citadel of the western few
No one ever turns you down
Because we love you old or new

VILLAGRETTE

To concoct a vinaigrette
Why not add a little wine
A recipe you won't forget

A tartness you won't regret
Adding a little taste so fine
To concoct a vinaigrette

Plus some oil of olivette
With a taste that's so divine
A recipe you won't forget

Virgin, freshly pressed and set
At Fahrenheit sixty-nine
To concoct a vinaigrette

Then, with fresh herbs, slowly get
By hand a mix, to refine
A recipe you won't forget

Dip in your finger, then let
It tell you if you need more wine
A recipe you won't forget
To concoct a vinaigrette.

OULIPO

Originally published as *Northern Line* (La Bibliothèque Oulipienne no. 220)

Translated by Ian Monk & Daniel Levin Becker

Valérie Beaudouin

Northern Line

2015

● *Northern Line*, the fruit of two years of the London commuter life, mixes the procedural urban railway poetry of the *poème de métro* with the patient, place-based observational approach Georges Perec took in his *Attempt at Exhausting a Place in Paris*, an exercise in discerning the "infra-ordinary" currents just beneath the surface of daily life.

"The train now approaching is to Morden via Bank. Please stand back from the platform edge."

The Northern Line, the oldest line of the London Underground, crosses the city from north to south. Heavily taxed by the comings and goings of Londoners, the line is quite crowded, afflicted by frequent service outages, and often closed for entire weekends for repairs. All of the cars on the line are identical. If you manage to sit down, you take your place in a row of seven seats (occasionally six), facing seven (six) other seats.

For two years I lived in East Finchley, in the north of Highgate, on one of the branches of the Northern Line. I commuted each week. When I managed to sit down, and sometimes even while standing, I observed and took notes on what my neighbors were doing.

I observed the travelers, the postures of bodies, the manipulation of objects, the progression of digital technology. I saw what they were doing with their books, newspapers, mobile phones, computers: the ordinary gestures of these disconnected and often silent moments. These were moments stolen from the grip of hyperconnectivity; at the time, no networks made it to the depths of the Underground. Many different free newspapers are distributed at London train stations in the mornings and the evenings.

The form offered here is an attempt to record the rhythm of these metropolitan crossings, the repetition and the variation. The observations were recorded between September 2011 and July 2013. Ten observations correspond to southbound morning trips (AM). Ten others were made in the evening (PM), returning from work in the cars headed back northbound. Finally, four took place on weekends.

These times are organized here in the manner of two alexandrines with, at the caesura and at the end of each line, one observation from the weekend and, in positions 1 through 5 of each hemistich, an alternation of morning and evening. Were we to peg each observation (each page in the present case) to a metrical syllable, the sequence of observations would follow the structure

```
PM AM PM AM PM WE        PM AM PM AM PM WE
AM PM AM PM AM WE        AM PM AM PM AM WE
```

in which the abstract metrical structure of the alexandrine serves as an organizing principle.

From autumn to summer, the hemistiches follow the rhythm of the seasons. We sleep more in autumn and winter than we do in the spring.

* * *

PM - NORTHBOUND

he reads the paper

he reads a book

he looks at his watch

he fiddles with his phone

she reads a magazine

he holds his bag, eyes closed

he reads the paper

he listens to music

he reads a book

she reads a magazine

she reads the paper

he sleeps, hands crossed on his bag

she holds a book, looks ahead

she flips through a magazine

AM – SOUTHBOUND

she sleeps, her arms crossed	what's he doing with his arms motionless?
he looks ahead	she writes her métro poem
he reads his neighbor's paper	her arms are crossed over her paper
he reads the paper	her arms are crossed over her bag
he listens to music, holding the device in his hands	he listens to music, arms crossed over his paper
she reads the paper	she tidies away her things
he tidies away his things	he looks all around

PM - NORTHBOUND

what to write?	he reads the paper
•	he listens to music, fiddles with his phone
she looks blankly ahead	she stares into space, arms crossed
he reads the paper	he reads a magazine, wearing earbuds
she reads the paper	she reads the paper
she reads the paper	she sleeps
he reads the paper	he fiddles with his cell phone

AM – NORTHBOUND

she dozes, her head lolling forward	•
•	he reads the paper
•	•
•	she writes on her phone
•	•
she reads the paper	•
she reads the paper	he reads the paper

PM – NORTHBOUND

she reads her novel	she waves a fan
he dozes	she's immersed in her novel
he looks to his right	he does a crossword
he talks and laughs with the woman on his right	she flips through the paper
she laughs, in delight	he reads the paper
she tries to focus on her book	he reads his neighbor's paper sideways
he daydreams with a faraway look	he sleeps

WEEKEND – SOUTHBOUND

he stands up	she listens to music and sleeps
he looks all around	she writes and looks up
she looks at the map	she reads a book
he reads a book	she talks to a girl standing in front of her
she talks to her neighbor	he sleeps
she talks back to her	she sleeps leaning over her bookbag
•	he fiddles with his phone

INTERLUDE 1: FEBRUARY 15, 2013

Today in London, on the Northern Line, the passengers sleep, page through the free newspapers, read books, sometimes on e-readers–much more ubiquitous since Christmas. Far fewer Londoners than Parisians ride while immersed in their cell phones. There is no network service in the subway: no wi-fi, no 3G, nothing.

As the wi-fi has barely been installed, will the passengers still read, or will they move on to looking at Facebook and Twitter and other digital content on their telephones? What will the future hold for the book? Will it be hung in the yard, like the one Duchamp gave to his stepsister?

PM - NORTHBOUND

she plays with her little dog	he reads the paper
huddled against her father, she watches the girl and her dog	she writes in her notebook
he holds his daughter by the shoulder	•
•	she watches the girl and her dog, amused
•	she reads the paper
he reads a document on A4 paper	she reads a book
•	she eats a hamburger

AM - SOUTHBOUND

leaning forward, she reads a report
on colored A4 paper, pencil in hand

he reads the paper held in one hand
and nibbles on a nail

he reads the paper held in one hand
right hand to make notes

she reads a book with a pencil in her

he does the crossword in his paper
which he rests on his bookbag

he does nothing, arms crossed,
he looks around

he sleeps, head forward, and holds
a switched-off e-reader with both hands

he sleeps

he sleeps, head leaned back

he reads a novel

she reads a novel held in both hands
which she has almost finished

he holds his tablet with both hands
and reads

•

•

PM - NORTHBOUND

she does a crossword, pen in the air	he reads the paper
he corrects documents with his ballpoint pen	•
she rushes to retrieve an abandoned paper from the seat across from her	she watches her neighbors and notes down what they're doing
he reads a paper resting on his bookbag	•
she leans over to read her neighbor's paper and looks at her phone	her arms are crossed and she is observing
she looks at her smartphone, held with both hands on her lap	she tidies her makeup bag
he wears headphones and reads his tablet, his index finger navigating the screen	•

AM - NORTHBOUND

•

she takes out a kleenex and blows
her nose

•

he reads a paper spread wide open and
holds his iphone in his left hand

•

he fiddles with his smartphone

her arms are crossed over her bag and
she looks ahead

•

she runs her fingers over her face and
looks ahead

she writes in a pink notebook covered
with blotter paper

•

he writes on his ipad resting on his knees
and holds his telephone in his right hand

•

•

PM - NORTHBOUND

he reads the paper folded in four,
holding it between thumb and forefinger

•

she sleeps, hands crossed over her
orange plastic bag

leaning forward, he holds his tablet with
both hands and types with his thumbs

he appears to be praying, hands together
and crossed in front of him

he reads on his e-reader held in his left hand

she reads on an e-reader held with
both hands

she reads a thick mass-market paperback

she reads a book

he fiddles with his cell phone with his thumbs,
holding it Italian style

she reads on her smartphone held in
one hand at chest height

she reads the paper spread wide open and
held with both hands

WEEKEND - SOUTHBOUND

he does his homework

she sleeps over her open book

he reads a page in a plastic sleeve

she looks at her neighbors and writes

she reads the same paper as her neighbor

she strokes her hair and talks to her neighbor

she comments on the paper with her neighbor

she comments on her neighbor's hair

he talks to his neighbor and fiddles with his telephone

she reads a paper

he does the same

he sleeps

she looks around

what is he/she doing?

INTERLUDE 2: LONDON, MAY 9, 2013

The train pulls into Embankment station like it normally does, and stops, but the doors do not open. The conductor speaks over the intercom of an incident "that requires all my attention." We wait. The conductor and some police begin to arrive. They walk around our car, using flashlights to try to see what is happening under the train through the "gap between the train and the platform." We remain silent, concerned, seated in our places. Under the train, under our feet, there is a person. Now we are evacuated through the door of the first car. Rescue workers arrive from everywhere with an astonishing calm.

The line is disrupted "due to a person under the train," such is what we hear in all the hallways of the underground, such is the message of TFL (Transport for London). A "one under" is another way of expressing the same thing.

This euphemism is connected to the fact that the issue is not always fatal. Half of the attempts fail thanks to a "suicide pit," which is to say a gap between the rails that can serve to protect the individual. When the person survives, he or she is sentenced by the transport company to pay a fine.

Under our train, the person does not move.

AM - SOUTHBOUND

he reads on his tablet without headphones	hands crossed over her bag, she watches
•	leaning forward, he reads the free paper
she reads the free paper	she writes in her notebook
she sleeps, her arms crossed	he puts his paper into his bag
•	she reads the free paper
he reads on his telephone without headphones	hands crossed, he stares into space

PM - NORTHBOUND

he watches a film on his little tablet	he listens to music, his head leaned backwards
she looks at her neighbor's notebook	•
she writes in her notebook	he reads the paper
she reads the paper	she sleeps, headphones over her ears
he reads a book on his e-reader	she sleeps, her head lolling forward
he eats	•
he reads the paper	leaned forward, he reads the paper spread wide open

AM - SOUTHBOUND

she looks at her smartphone with headphones on

he sleeps, head resting on his fist, his telephone placed like a codpiece

he reads the paper held vertically in front of him over the tablet resting on his knees

she reads the paper resting on her bag

he makes notes with his left hand on loose leaf A4 paper

•

he straightens up in his seat: without technology, without a bag, hands empty, he meditates

hands over her bag, she dozes

she writes in a pink blotter-paper notebook, often raising her head to look around

her hands are hooked over her bag which is held up vertically

she dozes, hands on her chest

•

he holds a rolled cigarette, impatient to light it

•

PM - NORTHBOUND

he reads the paper open on his lap

she reads an oversized book held in her lap

he has headphones on and looks around

•

he holds his telephone in landscape mode with both hands at eye level

•

he fiddles with his smartphone in landscape mode at thigh level

she has a large rectangular parcel on her lap

she holds a book on her bag with both hands and reads, head tilted forward

he holds a mini-tablet with both hands on his thighs, headphones on his ears–is he watching a film, an episode of a show?

she reads a book resting on her bag

she writes in her blue notebook (the pink blotter-paper cover has disintegrated) and looks around regularly

she listens to her ipod, changing the music by sliding her thumb over the screen

hands swinging between his legs, he looks ahead

AM - SOUTHBOUND

she reads on her e-reader	he flips through a notepad
she reads a yellowed book	he reads on an e-reader held with both hands
she reads the paper	he fiddles with his mobile with both hands, paper folded in his lap
she reads the paper	he drinks water
she reads on her iphone held in her left hand	he holds his paper at eye level
•	he reads on his tablet
she reads the paper	he reads the paper

WEEKEND – SOUTHBOUND

he reads a book	he has his arm around his neighbor to the left
he looks around, arms dangling	she writes in her notebook and answers her neighbor to the right
he has one leg folded over the other and looks ahead	he talks to his neighbor
her hands are crossed over her bag, her eyes closed and heavily made up	he holds his smartphone Italian style and plays
he holds the hand of his neighbor on the right	•
she holds her neighbor's hand	she holds her bag and looks ahead
leaned forward, she fiddles with her telephone	so does she

INTERLUDE 3: TUESDAY, JULY 23, 2013

We took the underground early to go to Salisbury and Old Sarum. The free morning paper, *Metro*, was in everyone's hands, its cover headline reading "Oh boy!" The heir to the throne has just been born.

AM - SOUTHBOUND

she holds her smartphone and listens to music

she reads the paper with one hand while the other hand, nails painted, rests on her lap

he reads the paper and holds it in front of him with both hands

he reads on his tablet resting on his bookbag flat on his lap

she listens to music, arms swinging

he reads on his tablet held at lap level, in landscape mode

•

he plays on his smartphone in landscape mode

she writes in a blue notebook, regularly raising her head to look around

he reads a book

she reads the paper and holds a cup of coffee in her hand

he reads an illustrated book open on his lap

she listens to music

he or she is too far away

PM - NORTHBOUND

she reads a thick paperback, headphones over her ears	she reads her book
•	she reads a book
she dreams, headphones over her ears, chin resting on her hand	he reads the paper, he is very young
she listens to music, holding her apple- green phone with both hands and watching the young paper-reader across from her	he reads the paper held with both hands, headphones over his ears
he looks ahead, above my head	she writes in her notebook
he reads the paper spread wide open on his lap headphones	he fiddles with his telephone, over his ears
she fiddles with her telephone without headphones	is this seat empty?

AM - SOUTHBOUND

his arms are crossed and he looks ahead	he fiddles with his neighbor's telephone and asks her what she's doing
she wears headphones and fiddles with her iphone	she writes on a folded and damaged sheet of A4 paper
she holds her e-book reader in her left hand	his hands are crossed, he is nervous
she writes a message on her iphone	she folds up the paper and puts it behind her between the seat and the train window
he reads the Metro paper	her arms are crossed over her bag
•	she holds a cup of coffee in her hand
•	he fiddles with his telephone with his right hand

PM - NORTHBOUND

he reads the paper held wide open
with two hands

she reads the folded-up paper, holding
it with both hands

she is wearing headphones and fiddling
with her telephone behind her bag

he reads on an e-reader held in the palm
of his hand

she fiddles with her smartphone

he has his headphones on and holds his
pencil over his paper

he listens to music, spread out backwards

her cap on her head, she reads the paper and
turns the pages with her purple nails

his head is bald and he plays a mobile game

bald and elderly, he is crumpled forward over
his paper

she has been recognized by a friend who is
standing and talking to her

she reads a yellowed paperback

she sleeps or prays, hands together and crossed
over her bag

he reads the paper

AM - SOUTHBOUND

he reads the paper unfolded on his lap

she writes in her blue notebook and looks around surreptitiously

he has an open book placed on his bag, it's a Dan Brown novel

her hands are crossed over her flower-patterned bag

he reads the folded-up paper

he holds his paper and talks to his neighbor

she puts mascara on her eyelashes, looking into a mirror that looks like a telephone–later she will read *A Walk to Remember*

she holds a hot beverage in a cardboard cup, closed with a lid, in both hands

her arms are crossed over her bag

he or she reads a book. His or head is cut off in the facing reflective window

he reads the paper, leaning forward

the two remaining people are too far away, I can't even see them in the reflective window

what is he or she doing?

WEEKEND – NORTHBOUND

she yawns and talks to her neighbor,
arms and legs crossed

his hands are crossed over his bag, he yawns

she talks by turns to her neighbor on her
right, and to the one on her left

she writes in a blue notebook

he talks to his neighbor

he reads the paper spread wide open on his lap
with a large photo of Neymar

he is turned toward his neighbor on the
left, speaking loudly to her and smiling

he speaks to his neighbor on the left and his
arms are crossed

she leans on the shoulder of her neighbor
to the right and looks at the cell phone
held in his hand

he speaks to his neighbor on the right and holds
his PC with both hands on his lap

he holds his cell phone with both hands,
his neighbor looks at the screen–later
he will hold her by the waist

her arms are crossed over her bag

hands in his lap, he looks ahead, alert
what if he's catching on?

hers too

JULY 29, 2013

Leaving London in a carpool, meeting at West Ham station. Moments after setting off, we will be immobilized on the highway by someone who has leapt from the bridge. On our side, all of the cars are stopped; across from us, the three lanes are totally empty.

The media will not speak of this any more than they do of the person "under the train." In London's public transports, life goes on.

Translated by Ian Monk

Michèle Audin

Caroline, October 21, 1935

2015

● An inventory modeled on Daniel Spoerri's *An Anecdoted Topography of Chance*, "Caroline" is an unpublished outtake from Audin's 2016 book *Mademoiselle Haas*, a collection of vignettes recounting the untold lives of young working women (nurses, millers, hairdressers, physicists) in France in the tempestuous years before World War II.

To the right, on the varnished pine table, a red box, with an indication of its contents (fifty Apex safety matches), and its price (0.50F) as well as the terms *Régie française*, SEITA, and *Caisse d'amortissement* (aimed at easing the national debt, this fund was set up nine years previously, to collect the profits from the sale of tobacco products and matches).

A little further back on the table, a white mother-of-pearl button is waiting (patiently) to be sewn back, no doubt onto a blouse.

A closed copybook, with a pink cardboard cover and black binding, and a large illustration depicting a man, with a laurel crown, dressed in a cloak, standing between two cornucopias, his right hand posed on a large sword, while in his left he holds a sphere with a cock perched on it (the possible allegory being confirmed by the caption "Gallia-Patent Pending"). Below, written in midnight blue, can be read "Caroline Haas-Pending."

At the far left-hand corner of the room, where the table has been pushed back, three thick gray cardboard document folders bearing the word "Archives." Several books and notepads, of which only the spines can be seen, have been placed on top of these folders. The only visible ones being *The Hollow Needle*, its red cover decked with a sewing needle stuck in a visiting card bearing the name Arsène Lupin, and a thin volume with a gray-brown jacket, containing a poem Caroline particularly likes, and not just because it speaks of beautiful typists.

Beside this little pile, a dried echinoderm, or starfish, brought back from Dieppe by a girlfriend from Secretarial School, and which Caroline, who has never seen the sea, often stares at: this star makes her daydream.

Almost against the wall, a flask whose complex shape Caroline has studied and picked apart on several occasions (three differently shaped hexagons, none of which is regular, five trapezoids, only one of which is right-angled, and two irregular pentagons). The large vertical sides, one of which bears an ink-stained but legible label (Midnight Blue (white on a dark background) - Ink / Ideal / Waterman / 50 ml (red on yellow)), are hexagonal, the background rectangular; the upper section, where the metal top is screwed on, is also hexagonal, being completed on each side by two trapezoids (above) and a pentagon (below).

Slightly to its right (but also a little higher up), a rather battered cardboard globe, which Caroline has owned since her school days and which, like the starfish, is also a source of daydreams.

Next to the matchbox, forming a completely regular hexagon, a white ceramic ashtray containing three matches, some ash, and three butts.

Completely to the left, and thus next to the wall, a charming image showing the roofs of the town of Nancy. If this postcard were turned over, the following text could be read (to the left):

> Dear Mademoiselle,
> I hope that the work is going well and that you will be able to give it to me on my return to Paris. So let's meet on October 21 at 5 p.m. at Capoulade. Best wishes, JD

and (to the right, beneath the female sower of seeds on the stamp), the address:

Mademoiselle Haas
3 rue de Mirbel
Paris (5)

Just in front, the folded example of French journalism on the table is *Le Petit Parisien*, devoted for the most part that Monday to the results of the Senatorial elections the day before, but what can be seen is the uncompleted crossword puzzle.

It is no doubt a lack of time or interest that has caused this incompletion–for the clues lack any subtlety.

Beside the postcard, another image advertises "Choc-Lait Kohler": in a mountainous landscape (blue sky, blue lake, snowy peaks, verdant pastures, a smiling girl is leading a beautiful skewbald cow (come on Clarisse) to drink at a spring)–Amédée Kohler and Sons, Lausanne, Switzerland. "Amédée Kohler is the man who invented hazelnut chocolate," Martin had said, on giving Caroline the bar on which this picture appeared. Then, his next sentence contained an invitation to Caroline for dinner. "Let's meet by the fountain in the Luxembourg Gardens. How does that sound?" It sounded good to Caroline, and she suggested they do so at six o'clock.

Just in front of the three gray document binders, the desk lamp (off) with the black cone of its shade.

Then a little money. A few coins. With some more beside the copybook–it is not impossible that there are even more beneath it, but it seems more likely that there is nothing but a few more buttons.

Behind these coins and copybook, an open leather nail kit, branded "Le Tanneur," with its cuticle remover, its nail file and its tweezers, but not the clippers, whose space is vacant.

Other everyday objects are contained in a large wooden cigar box (Partagas), which is also open. These include a colored wooden reel of white thread, with a needle slipped in between the upper layers of cotton, a small cylindrical pack containing white glue, some round-tipped scissors and some clippers (presumably from the nail kit, there by mistake), a bent rusty nail, six pencils, some pins, a blue-and-red eraser (for ink and pencil, respectively), a blade for sharpening pencils, a tightly rolled tape measure whose visible side is yellow, a small tortoiseshell comb, three hair clips, some metal nibs (Corona, Sergent-Major), three dip pens, a flat-ended ruler and a fountain pen.

The cylindrical glass pot, in front of (and also a little below) the globe, contains six more pencils, pointing upwards, one of which is red and blue (its red tip up, its blue tip down, at the bottom of the pot, with a risk of breaking, but that is pure speculation, as this tip is invisible), as well as a wooden set square, a right-angled triangle whose sharpest point, at the end of the longer side leading from the right angle, lies at the bottom of the pot. What this pot once was before becoming a pencil pot (a jam jar, or a spice pot?) is unclear.

Beneath this pot, used as a paperweight, a new rent quote, brought by the landlord that very morning, presumably the sign of a coming increase–which her work for JD will help to pay. Obviously regularly paid employment would be safer, but Caroline does not feel tempted by a job in a typing pool alongside eighty other frantic secretaries, as had been on offer at the Renault factory.

At the back, against the wall, behind the coins, a stick of red lipstick (a glance at the ashtray confirms that none of its butts bears any red traces), no doubt intended, not for the (professional) appointment with JD, but instead for the stroll in the Luxembourg Gardens, then dinner with Martin–Martin is a friend of Corentin's, Caroline's brother, both of whom work for the PTT.

Behind the ashtray, and also within reach of the right hand of anyone sitting at this table, a green, gilt-edged china saucer and its green-and-white china cup, with barely a trace of coffee at the bottom. This cup and saucer were a gift from Corentin, who "spirited them away" from a café.

Between the "object box" and the desk lamp, a wooden table blotter (with a pink pad stained with traces of dark-blue writing).

The central area at the front of the desk is taken up by a typewriter. On its keyboard, Caroline's two hands. Her wrists are not concealing the name of the machine's model, Underwood Standard Portable Typewriter. She is wearing a bangle on her right wrist. On her left wrist, her watch indicates that it is now twenty-five to five. Her nails are short, but short and well groomed. Her left ring finger is pressing down on a round black key, near the top, almost to the left, and the letter's bar has detached itself from the corolla of all the other bars to strike its form, beneath the red-and-black ribbon, into the stencil above the cylinder.

The nail varnish to the left of the machine is not exactly nail varnish, but a product of the same kind, called a "corrector" and intended to make good the "typing errors" on the fine stencil sheets. Of a chemical composition close to nail varnish, and equipped with a similar application brush, it is also colored red. The bottle of solvent for correcting the frequent solidifications of the corrector cannot be seen.

The *W*-shaped key holder, with its keys, was presumably placed there by Caroline's right hand, just like her spare change, when she came back up from her shopping trip.

On the other side, the manuscript she is typing, entitled "xi," as noted by the author (none other than JD) beside the Greek letter which he has carefully inscribed by hand and underlined in red, and which Caroline will add by hand too onto the stencil once she has removed the sheet from the machine. "I don't understand a thing," Caroline said the first time JD gave her a mathematical text to type. "Typing requires no understanding," JD replied.

Between the coffee and the keys, a porcelain jar, dark red lower down, white higher up, with the word "Danone" written in red on white, a silver spoon still inside it, the top, also made of white porcelain, lying beside it; this is the yogurt that Caroline purchased at the corner store when she bought her newspaper, and which she ate while reading through the crossword clues, but as she was running a little late, she stopped solving the puzzle as soon as she finished her yogurt. Martin was the person who recommended yogurt to her: "It's very healthy, Miss Caroline, very good for your well-being and your complexion." It was certainly healthy, in fact the Parisian yogurt manufacturer Danone started out by selling its products in pharmacies. But at a rather high price. And rather lacking in nutrients. Just a yogurt all morning isn't much, but there's going to be dinner that evening–and the perspective of seeing Martin again after delivering her work, which is almost done, the final equation, that xi with the stylus, her lipstick, and then her two appointments.

The symbol beneath Caroline's finger is a *Z*, because this typewriter's keyboard lacks a *0* (zero) and her logical and aesthetic sensibilities will not tolerate the use of an *o* or an *O* instead of a zero (even though she knows nothing about mathematics...). So she is about to type "= zero" followed by a period, and that's it. Period.

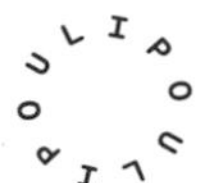

Translated by
Jeff Diteman

Eduardo Berti & Pablo Martín Sánchez

from

Microfictions

2016

● Eduardo Berti and Pablo Martín Sánchez, both elected to the Oulipo at the end of May 2014, simultaneously became the group's first Hispanophone writers. "Microfictions" explores the oulipian fascination with miniaturization while also indulging in a more recent preoccupation with collaborative creative procedure.

The fundamental question remains, who is the author of the crime: its intellectual author or its material author? The one who had the idea and was the undeniable impetus? The one who materialized the idea? [...] Supposing that we were to reach the conclusion that both of them are the authors of the crime, is the criminal responsibility of the material author identical to that of the intellectual author, when the two roles are not played by the same person? And if we agree that the guilt is not identical, which of the two authorships is more "serious" or more "criminal"?

–*George P. Rex,* Crime (A User's Manual)

0. PROLOGUE (FRAGMENTS)

In February or March of 2012, the Argentinian writer Eduardo Berti proposed to the Spanish writer Pablo Martín Sánchez an original–or at least curious–idea for a writing exercise: EB would write thirty commentaries on thirty or so nonexistent microfictions; then, based on these thirty commentaries, PMS would write the microfictions. In step two, they would do the reverse, with EB writing a few very brief short stories based on reviews written in advance by PMS. In one of the few documents that has survived from the preliminary chats in which the project was developed, EB mentions Flaubert and the unfinished *Bouvard and Pécuchet*: "The two copy clerks, at a certain point in the novel, devote whole afternoons to reading literary reviews. When they have learned these critiques by heart, they buy the books. The consequence is that when they read the books, they stop believing the critiques," EB summarizes, taking a certain liberty.

Strictly speaking, the Argentine did not have much to offer; only a certain "crazy" idea that, as PMS discovered a couple of years later, was not even of his own invention, EB having plucked it from a rather obscure book from the relatively obscure Biblioteca Oplepiana* called *Eclisse-Recensioni preventive*, by Cesare Ciasullo and Giuseppe Varaldo, a slim volume of barely thirty-two pages in which Ciasullo writes twenty poems based on twenty critiques written in advance by Varaldo, under the guise of pseudonyms (Guidalvaro Pepes is the critic, Leoluca Scaseri is the poet), but without reversing the roles at any point.

The present edition preserves, decades later, a few excerpts from a book that was branded "cursed" and "failed," and which came to be considered obscene.

* The Italian Oplepo's counterpart to the Bibliothèque Oulipienne series.

1.

It has been written more than once that the key word in the famous microstory by Monterroso ("When he woke up, the dinosaur was still there") is "still." Similarly, it can be said that the present microstory would not be the same without the word "relatively," which produces a powerful effect of uncertainty. Of course, it is a much more conspicuous word than "still." But it is further proof, as if any were needed, that when one works at such a diminutive scale, a single term is sufficient to fundamentally modify a text and its effects on readers.

THEORY AND PRACTICE OF RELATIVITY

When he woke up, his wife was there looking at him, stupefied.
"Darling, this is relatively easy to explain."
And both women thought he was talking to her.

5.

A fresh twist of the rather common formula "X was so XX that XXX," a formula that appears in many of the quips of Gómez de la Serna ("He was such a bad guitarist that his instrument ran off with another man") and in more than one microstory by the Belgian writer Jacques Sternberg ("He was so well mannered, before crossing the gates of death, he let his wife go first"). The formula is, of course, a cousin of the "yo mama" joke ("Yo mama's such a bad guitarist…"), and it is not surprising that it is so well suited to the field of microfiction, because in a certain sense it results in a form of synecdoche: a particular action used to represent a person (a part representing a whole). The novelty, in this case, is that here there are two "mamas," since the text includes two characters, linking them together so that the second "X was so XX that XXX" functions as a response to the first.

JOKE ABOUT DISCRETION

He was so nearsighted that he often waved to his twin brother in the mirror. And his brother was so discreet that he always waved back.

7.

Fans of psychological horror will find in this short text a concentrated dose of one of the genre's most frequently recurring figures: the double, or *Doppelgänger*. How the author manages to provoke so much unease in so few lines is something you will have to ask him, but surely the use of the second person makes us feel intimately involved, and we come to ask if the narrator is speaking to us, to himself, or to our respective doubles.

APPARITION

You look like me, was the first thing the voice said to you. You were dumbfounded because, yes, the resemblance was incredible. You do look like me, but as I would look in thirty years, isn't that it? you managed to reply to the voice, which by that point was more than a mere voice, it was a body identical to the worst possible version of yourself. In one year, to tell the truth, was the apparition's answer. Then there was a sort of drowned laughter, and you felt that you were no longer yourself.

16.

While it has never been easy to combine the fantastical with the comical, in the last few years, literature in Spanish has produced a few examples that serve as evidence that the mixture is not only possible, but also advisable. Suffice to think of authors such as Fernando Iwasaki or David Roas, who give their readers such anguish without dropping their smiles. Whether it is a coincidence or the result of a planned editorial line, the fact is that Eduardo Berti has just published with Páginas de Espuma a compilation of "dehorrifying tales" (as the author calls them), in which the festive and the macabre are paired like champagne and brie. A fine example of this is the story that opens the volume with these–apparently–innocuous words: "I enter the optometry office and ask for the glasses that have been on everyone's tongue."

-4.25

I enter the optometry office and ask for the glasses that have been on everyone's tongue. And I mean it literally: on the tongue, not the eyes, because a marvelous invention has just been released, a sort of lozenge or tablet that cures nearsightedness as long as you have it in your mouth. The woman working at the optometrist's (obviously a stubborn old Luddite, still wearing those old-fashioned glass glasses over her eyes, what a Luddite!), seeming unconvinced, shows me a series of boxes, marked "Spectabs®." There are small tablets for mild myopias (-0.50, -1.00) and other, larger tablets, with more intense flavors such as menthol, ginger, and eucalyptus, for severe cases like my own. I opt for "Lemon-Mint -4.25." I try my first Spectab® at home, in the safety of a familiar place. Spectacular results. But then, in the street, I have a horrendous experience: I am crossing an avenue when something (stress, I think, stimulating salivation) causes me to swallow the vision-correcting tablet unintentionally, leaving me almost blind, incapacitated in the middle of the crosswalk. I don't know how I get out of it alive!

No, I'm lying, I know exactly how: I dig urgently in my pocket for another tablet, stuff it in my mouth, and it tastes funny, but the light comes on. Only when I arrive on the far corner, when I finish crossing, do I realize something horrible is happening. I see dead people in the street. Victims of traffic accidents, I gather. But, are they really there or is it an illusion? I approach one of them. A heavyset man, his body face-up in the middle of the street, with black tire marks stamped across his chest, the pale blue cloth of his shirt stained here and there with blood. I take the Spectab® out of my mouth and the man disappears. I put it back in my mouth and the man reappears. Suddenly I remember the woman from the optometry office and her look of skepticism as she sold me these lozenges, which, as she put it, were "in trial phase." I walk ahead and encounter another run-over body, this time in the middle of the crosswalk. It is a thin woman. I come closer and discover with horror that she is not quite dead, that she is agonizing there in the street. Feeling anxious, I shout, "Help, help," and some people look at me with pity while I point at the ground where I know quite well that they see nothing. Again I swallow the lozenge and the woman disappears. Of course, I know that she's just an illusion. Someone who died in this exact spot many years ago, I figure. But I can't just stand there doing nothing. She could still be saved. Another tablet. This one without the funny taste. I see nothing. I go through the whole packet, trying them all. Finally, the last lozenge brings both the funny taste and the vision of the woman. I bend over. No, no. She's already dead. Too much time has passed and it's all my fault, I reproach myself. Then I feel that someone is handcuffing my hands behind my back. A police officer. Another illusion, to be sure. So I don't worry. I gather some saliva and swallow the Spectab® to make him disappear. But no... The dead woman and the policeman are still there. They look blurry, as in the vision of a nearsighted man without glasses. But they're still there.

Daniel Levin Becker

Epithalamia

2014–2016

● These *beaux présente* were written for, respectively, a Guatemalan atheist poet, a U.S. presidential history enthusiast especially interested in the Teapot Dome scandal, a playwright with a dog named Beckett, a librarian and beekeeper who had undergone corrective eye surgery, and a political ghostwriter and computer programmer.

ODE
(FOR PEDRO POITEVIN)

Pedro, intrepid poet, drove poor Ovid to retire. Intern tried to prod printer-rotor, dropped toner in error. Pedro invented dope re-ordered envoi, prevented intern-edited torpor. Dirtied tie, too.

Pedro, retired vintner, popped into dive, ordered one pint, one Diet Rite. Pedro opined on Verdi, Pinter, Rodin: no opinion too non-pertinent.

On TV, reporter pretended to point to evident divine order: one protein divided into ten, deer into deer, dove into dove, pit viper into pit viper. Not one dino died in vitro, ever.

Pedro, no penitent Pope-reverer, no ten-toed ovine, no divine-porno pervert, derived not one torrid notion. Pedro didn't even drip one drop.

Pedro, overtired, drove to Dover in red Pinto, dined pronto, drip-dried tie, dropped into potent nod-trip. Revived, Pedro reverted to Pedro, intrepid poet.

WARREN G. HARDING'S DARK NIGHT OF THE SOUL (FOR WILLIAM CAMERON)

O Warren, lone monocameral lion!
Immoral moola-conner! Criminal oil-concealer!
Inimical crow-lamer, lame mail-carrier!
Will all normal commerce come to none?

Come, Warren. Can a lion corner a llama?
Can a crane call Carmen in a low, warm croon?
Can a car commercial cram women on camera?
Can a monomaniac moon a Moroccan moon?

No. Non. Nein!

I can lie no more.
I am no car, no crane, no moon-mooner.
I am no lion.
I will roar no more.

DOMESTIC DRAMA IN THREE ACTS
(FOR MATT SLAYBAUGH)

1. PRELUDE

Ugly thugs buy hash. Slutty gals slug malts. Haughty lamb, salty ham. A ballsy lush hugs a baby.

2. PASTORAL

Sam, a lab, bays. Sam must... slay a bush, shall Sam say. Sam bugs Matt: Matt has thumbs. Hush, Sam! Halt thy samba! Matt must buy a lusty lass a gumball. Ah! Ugh. Sam has shat.

3. ADAGIO

A smutty mag. A glass bulb. A hasty sham. Alas!

ERE LASIK
(FOR PAUL DEBRASKI)

I barked like a bear, skipped like a spud.
I braised a baked Alaska.
I parked a kids' bike beside a biker bar.
I bullied buddies. I said I liked Drake.
I raised birds, I raised bees. I sired kids.
I pulped libraries. (Libraries, plural.)
I did dark deeds, sirs, ere I did see.

GOOD WINS (FOR ROSS GOODWIN)

Sin rages. Seven sinners:

Greed-ravaged organ grinders;
Raving gringos swearing revenge;
Woodwinds droning on and on and on;
Winos gorging on sangria, gin, and grass;
Goons drawing gang signs on snoring sons;
Savages swinging swords, goring wedding-goers;
Severe wind and snow endangering winding roads.

Even so: as sin grows, so does good.

Red roses, oranges,
grid wiring, dodo songs,
dowsing rods, ravens' wings,
nodding and drowsing dowagers,
dawn-goosed deer in green groves,
Geneva and Georgia and Wingdings,
swear words engraved in wedding rings.

We rage in vain: we need no saving.

Originally published in *Dire ouf* (P.O.L, 2017).

Translated by Ian Monk

Frédéric Forte

The Pitch-Drop Experiment

2016

● The central text in *Dire ouf*, a book of poetry responding to the music of the San Francisco ensemble Deerhoof, is sometimes performed in public with a live feed of an Australian pitch-drop experiment projected behind the poet. In Berlin in 2015, Hervé Le Tellier arranged a manipulation whereby the ball of pitch, which was not supposed to drop for another ten years, plummeted right in the middle of the reading.

a. *The Pitch-Drop Experiment* | In the pitch-drop experiment a certain amount of pitch the word pitch being applied generically to extremely viscous forms of matter such as asphalt resin tar bitumen is firstly heated then poured into a funnel whose neck has previously been closed so that the pitch can then cool off for three years and become stabilized at room temperature after which the funnel is opened placed under a bell jar and we can then begin to observe the running of this liquid because despite its appearance this is exactly what it is see the photo this took place at the University of Queensland in Brisbane Australia in 1927 but could have taken place anywhere else which would have come down to pretty much the same thing there has also since 1944 been another pitch-drop experiment at Trinity College Dublin while an older experiment has recently come to light at the University of Aberystwyth in Wales just eighty-five miles north of which can be found on the island of Anglesey the village of

Llanfairpwllgwyngyllgogerychwyrndrobwllllantysiliogogogoch whose name means St Mary's Church in the Hollow of the White Hazel near to the Rapid Whirlpool of Llantysilio of the Red Cave and this experiment is supposed to have started in 1914 but its excessively viscous pitch has not yet produced a single drop each drop is formed very slowly given that the pitch is approximately one hundred thousand million times more viscous than water it then swells very slowly until it breaks away from the funnel after around ten years the first drop dropped in December 1938 eight years after the top had been removed in October 1930 the second drop eight years later in February 1947 the third in April 1954 seven years later the next ones in May 1962 August 1970 April 1979 July 1988 November 2000 after eight eight nine nine and twelve years the ninth and the most recent one fell on April 24 2014 almost fourteen years after the previous one the considerable lengthening of the intervals between the drops falling since 1988 being perhaps explained by the installation of air conditioning back then possibly leading to a slight fall in the average temperature resulting in a provisional tally of nine drops in almost eighty-five years with the idea being that come what may it will continue down the decades until the sample of pitch is used up in let's say a good hundred years and that this will inevitably occur occurring as it definitely does whether someone is or is not present in the room when a drop becomes detached and so it is that none of the scientists supervising the experience successively Thomas Parnell John Mainstone and today Andrew White has ever witnessed in person the separation of a drop but the experiment has for a while now been filmed twenty-four seven so that it works even when it doesn't work and without this drop interacting in any way with anything else at all world war cold war conquest of space climbing of Everest the Beatles the first or second oil crises fall of the Berlin Wall the Y2K bug September 11 etc so that the observer ends up probably wondering given that there is such a long time still to go whether this is really a succession of discrete events the observation of which is set off by the occurrence of what is called an event for example the falling of a drop of pitch or else a purely continuous phenomenon rather like the passing of time given that the objective of the experiment is basically to measure the viscosity of a liquid which is expressed in pascal-seconds and that the second which the International Bureau of Weights and Measures now tells us is no longer defined according to the orbiting of our planet around the Sun but in terms of a property of matter one second being the duration of nine million one hundred and ninety-two thousand seven hundred and seventy periods of the radiation corresponding to the transition between the two hyperfine levels F + 3 and F + 4 of the ground state 6S½ of the cesium 133 atom as the most practical basic unit for measuring time with one possible answer coming somewhere between the two a hybrid system whose primary characteristic would be a stretching but not an infinite one given that a moment will always occur when the liquid becomes divided but instead a sufficiently long stretching over time for the occasional observer between two drops to have serious doubts after a while had not the drops that have previously fallen been conserved in a nearby jar as evidence of a before about there being any real existence of an after that is to say a real pouring of the matter placed in the funnel leading ineluctably to a fall.

b. *Deerhoof* | “Deerhoof is a noise pop band formed in San Francisco in 1994. Known for being high-energy, unpredictable, and hard to classify, Deerhoof maintain that they never know what kind of music they are going to create next, and have no idea what they are doing when they create something.”

Translated by Ian Monk

Clémentine Mélois

Louise

2016

● “Louise” is an out-take from *Sinon j’oublie* (Otherwise I’ll forget), a collection of vignettes based on shopping lists Clémentine Mélois found on the street. Mélois became the Oulipo’s forty-first member in June 2017.

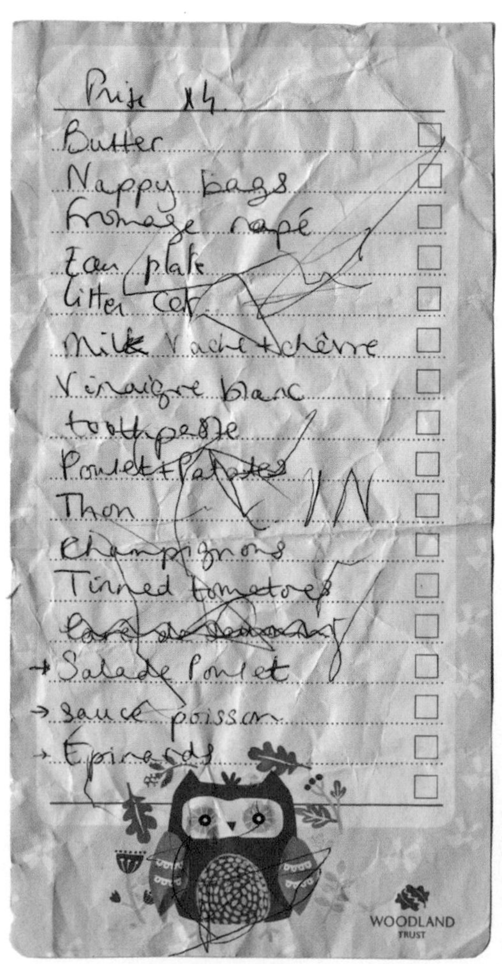
Butter
Nappy bags
Fromage rapé
Eau plate
Litter cat
Milk Vache + chèvre
Vinaigre blanc
toothpaste
Poulet + Patates
Thon
Champignons
Tinned tomatoes
→ Salade Poulet
→ Sauce poisson
→ Epinards

Nondedieu, Gemma’s face wasn’t a pretty picture. I mean she was in a terrible state. We were coming up from the carpark with Thomas, and there was this rather fat femme scarfing an ice cream in the lift. And Gemma just turns round and says to us out loud: “Jesus, look at that fat bitch, with the arse she’s got she orra cut out the ice creams.” Just like that, cool as you like, but in FRENCH! The thing is, when we go and see them in Thornbury, we’re used to speaking in French so that no one else can understand us, but this was in a lift, in NANTES! In French! The total international cock-up. I’m laughing about it, but it’s really not funny. She felt awful after. You should have seen her face. I mean, really.

OULIPO OULIPO

Originally published in *Comme une rivière bleue* (Gallimard)

Translated by Ian Monk

Michèle Audin

No One Remembers

2017

● *Comme une rivière bleue* (Like a blue stream) traces the stories of a number of characters involved in the Paris Commune, a revolutionary socialist faction that held power over Paris for two months in 1871 before being violently suppressed by the armed forces of the French Republic.

I don't know how historians count the dead and disappeared of that "Bloody Week." Count them? To what purpose? What difference can be seen between thirty thousand and twenty thousand dead? If you don't know who they were, what they did, what or whom they loved, what they dreamed of, if they put lots of sugar in their coffee... what's the point of knowing if there were ten thousand more or fewer of them?

You don't know their number. Has it occurred to you that you don't know their names?

No one remembers their names, but I know that they lived in Belleville, I'd like to be able to tell you that she was a washerwoman, she'd have liked to have learned to read a little better, she preferred washing at the Espérance on the corner of passage Kuszner rather than at Sainte-Catherine, and to be able to explain why; or that she was a florist and drank huge amounts of coffee; or else that he was a distiller, he loved strawberries and *Le Père Duchêne* which made him laugh his head off; or else that he was a tailor, he believed in God and liked someone to read the newspaper and posters to him, because he couldn't read fast enough, and above all because that way they could talk, and discuss all these things, which he did sure enough, so much so that it sometimes came to blows.

No one remembers their names, but I can tell you that they lived near the Jardin des Plantes, he was a stonecutter who liked kickboxing, I can almost hear him merrily crunching an apple on the pavement on his way home; and she was a seamstress who loved tales of the sea, which she read as serials at the bottom of the front pages of newspapers, because she had neither books nor the time; and then there was that cooper on rue Linné, who would have loved to travel and I'm sure he loved blood sausages with large lumps of fat in them.

No one remembers their names, or even their existences really, the ones from the eighteenth arrondissement, the cook who didn't like wine but never said no to a shot of rum; the day laborer on rue Norvins who played the bugle and complained about politicians who are all words and no actions; the cobbler who before he had four children used to go dancing in Joinville, and dance he did, extremely well; the upholsterer who loved marzipan and dreamed of having a garden with a springtime lilac; the fan-maker who hated spinach—she was far from the only one—and who found *Le Père Duchêne* irritating—she was far from the only one in this too—and the locksmith who was so proud of the way he worked, with his precise gestures, and who really loathed priests.

No one remembers their names, but I'll tell you about some of them, from the eleventh arrondissement, the daily working woman from Rue Popincourt who dreamed of having her own garden, while wondering what a kiss without a moustache would be like, which she'd like to try, just once to see; or the tassel-maker who really liked the large lumps in apricot jam; the coffee merchant who never wore a shirt to sleep, I sleep in the raw, he used to say; the wickerworker who knew several of Victor Hugo's poems by heart; the typesetter who went to the synagogue and peeled himself a banana on coming back home; the umbrella repairer who had a caged canary and wanted to learn to play the piano; the mason on rue du Chemin-Vert who, when the infantryman got him in his sights, remembered his cousin's small breasts—they were both aged thirty.

No one remembers their names, but I'll tell you a few things about them, about the lace maker who, all her short life, suffered from terrible toothache; the chemical-products seller in Saint-Paul who wept as he thought of his mother who had died of smallpox and whose only consolation could be found in large quantities of red wine; the cabinetmaker who sculpted little wooden toys for the child he was going to father; the blacksmith who went to confession every week, or nearly, and who loved those really greasy fritters you got at the carnival; the shoemaker who recalled the touching way his wife used to raise up her hair, she had died during the siege and now there were three little orphans; the lathe operator who wanted to be a schoolteacher; the bookbinder who adored grilled pigs' trotters and who kept a notebook in which she jotted down what she had done or was thinking, her notebook has vanished too...

Ian Monk

from

Return(s)

2017

● Continuing a poetic form he inaugurated in two previous books of poetry, *Plouk Town* (2007) and *Là* (2014), Monk composes suites of *x* stanzas comprising *x* lines of *x* words: here, seventeen by seventeen by seventeen. This excerpt from *Return(s)* also incorporates the mathematical structure of the sestina, or more precisely the 17-ina.

Originally published in *Vers de l'infini* (Cambourakis)

Translated by Daniel Levin Becker

traffic is born at one point and then generally speaking dies at another point with no apparent relation
between the points and so you observe from behind the window in your room how almost zero
movement occurs among the people in their containers even the noise they make itself reduced pretty much
to nothing by your own container of aluminum and plexiglas and by the echoes of your body
you open your mouth to shape a delicious word but talk to no one not even alone
especially not alone for that matter because at that point why exhaust yourself by opening it anyway
the city does what the city does that's how it is it's like a sickness
that you were born with and will no doubt also die with maybe even in the same
place or more or less anyway who cares all this filling truncated by an event so ordinary
like for instance here fill this blank yourself as you wish go on make yourself at home
life is not really as long as all that when in fact each individual element is not
as filled with vibrating emptiness as each head is in its container in that row right there
in front of you this morning under a sky more mauve than anything natural on the earth
the earth does what it can and anyway it's not like it can do anything else
exactly as you were not taught in school not in any way but as you know now
body after hard body on the moving walkway at the airport destination the waiting yawning chasm in
the fabric of space and time and there you go crash bang hello you have arrived somewhere

you have a head as well and it has been filled and prepared and fine-tuned somewhere
which now seems to you as mysterious as the simple pleasure of a fuck and its relation
narrow as it may be to other lives its apparent lack of simplicity its hours spent in
a sort of waking coma watching for instance vehicles passing by your interest level at virtually zero
exactly as you were not taught in school not in any way but as you do now
as a result of your imitating others like any self-respecting child on earth well pretty much
the earth does what it can and anyway it's not like it can do anything else
yes very good you have understood what you are to do with your head and your body
when they are not occupied with performing some specific task and are as free as the earth
you open your mouth to shape a strange word but talk to no one not even alone
you turn on a screen and watch the images going by to learn more about some there
where there probably isn't much there anymore to understand really when you think about it anyway
you make yourself a warm drink or a cold drink that you either drink or do not
the city does what the city does that's how it is it's like a sickness
like for instance here fill this cup yourself as you wish go on make yourself at home
and time flows too from its rather mysterious source flowing in a straight line toward the same
basically inevitable end with an encroaching slowness attaining little by little an immobility both sad and ordinary

when you look at her sitting there in front of the window you wonder what really passes
(a scene without apparent interest as they say in passing like watching a coat of paint dry)
behind her pretty eyes whose color seems to change according to her humors if that word works
you wonder and the question is stronger than you are what is the real difference for you
(though not as much for her) between this purchase and the fantasy of paying for a luxury
hooker's full-time ministrations or for that matter finding some chick from some out-of-the-way
place and marrying her but without as it happens running the risk (in principle) that one day
she'll attempt a coup d'état taking the reins then the money then everything else properly
fucking you as they say reducing you to an invalid bedridden senile but no on the contrary
everything was foreseen and pre-programmed to make her evolve even better than a real woman truly
in love progressively or quickly if necessary an innovative lover not too much so like a nurse

(look at that her gaze seems more and more lost in the distance of an aimless horizon)
a nurse then who would be professional and such not too much in her infinite tenderness going
altogether beyond the simple desire for an honest job and thus well suited to getting married without
beating around the bush an expertly dosed madness these sexual/amorous fantasies clinging according to your research
like an invalid in his filthy sheets to all layers of the population in a manner rather
diverse and varied but universal ah yes to each his dreamed-of medical professional as they say

a priori you might think the quality of any old moment would feel undifferentiated or rather ordinary
for you which is to say in essence if we said okay today let's go somewhere
shopping say there's nothing here to eat or let's fuck say it's the same
thing to you there's no difference once your brain has done its job fabricating a relation
between you and for instance here fill in this desire yourself go on make yourself at home
producing as the case may be a carnal pleasure or an intellectual one or the boredom within
the city does what the city does that's how it is it's like a sickness
hence the importance for you of making a distinction between firing off a blank round with zero
biological consequence and the fact that the carrot vendor no longer sells radishes so you know not
exactly as you were trained in school anyway not in any way but as you do now
you know how to imitate how to read the difference on people's faces especially on hers anyway
but that's not enough anymore honestly it's a matter of leading a life pretty much
as it should be led in a dignified manner deserving of your emotional engagement here and there
the earth does what it can and anyway it's not like it can do anything else
you open your mouth to shape a new word but talk to no one not even alone
you simply and without using a mirror look at all the visible parts of your comely body
which solidly planted right there in front of the window seems very much born of the earth

when you undress at night you tell yourself you're like a gardener digging into the earth
in a field pretty calm and orderly discovering in so doing a world both intriguing and ordinary
made up of stratum after hidden stratum filled with the living and proliferation of every other body
more or less animal or mineral essential or maybe harmful to the greater good sometimes and somewhere

you open your mouth to shape a vegetable word but talk to no one not even alone
and anyway what they bring in and what they take away it's all basically the same
the earth does what it can and anyway it's not like it can do anything else
and when you put the tip of your finger here say how do you create a relation
between what happens here and what you feel if then instead you were to put yourself there
like for instance here fill this space yourself as you wish no but make yourself at home
because as you dig with your mind's eye you get the impression that you are pretty much
infinite in your layers layers that open and layers that close each one after the other in
your flesh and all it hides beneath it's like the sidewalk of your dreams but anyway
the city does what the city does that's how it is it's like a sickness
exactly as you were not taught in school not in any way but as you comprehend now
at the ripe age of three and god knows how much more behind you there is zero
way to count them anyway such a calculus is not done will not be done decidedly not

at first it was easy but increasingly when you see her you don't know what to say
(you form a few words various and diverse in your cortex just to weigh them then see)
it's either like she can read your every thought or like even the simplest notion passes
way over her head in such an unexpected way that at a certain point it becomes rather
difficult to find a register of language or more like an experiential register of life that works
with what you know about her and her pre-programmed genome and the object of your research
to learn what her exposome is doing with it at this moment in other words a you
aspiring to be hers but unlike yours unlike people like you hers travels and sails along without
any real plan certainly without taking advantage of the past of a rooted species of the luxury
of her memory at once physical and also above all running the gamut of emotive epiphenomena going
from a love life with an illusory future to the illuminated thinking they have found their way
(look at that her gaze seems lost more and more in the distance of an aimless horizon)
yes almost like a cat say who must remember or rather must recreate with every new day
the reason for its existence and renewed daily routine or what the hell like a young nurse
looking at her first living cadaver realizing too late she never learned in school how to properly

reinsert a soul into a body without leaving behind aftereffects that will fuck up the future truly
so then must we start with the present followed by the past or is it the contrary

so you move step by step toward the bathroom putting your glass half-drunk or maybe not
on the table and you savor more than ever the sensation of your feet on the earth
through the parquet floor and go execute a mostly physical operation whose interest level is precisely zero
from a physical standpoint but which does fulfill a human function psychologically reassuring because so deeply ordinary
exactly as you were not taught at your mother's house at all but as you do now
establishing as it is meant to a more normative rapport between you your mind and your body
the city does what the city does that's how it is it's like a sickness
working in such a way that everything that does not appear to you human winds up somewhere
eventually in the deepest circular waste bin of your memory innermost before being buried dead/alive anyway
you open your mouth to shape an invented word but talk to no one not even alone
somewhat like a sadistic plan in which you gradually teach say a dog to imitate day in
day out everything its masters do so that finally even though its dog life remains the same
it comes to believe it is a man or its own submaster species then pretty much
the earth does what it can and anyway it's not like it can do anything else
like for instance here fill this destiny yourself as you wish go on make yourself at home
and your life from then on well you would live it like there were no verifiable relation
that could even theoretically be established to the backup database just sitting in that drawer over there

among his various collections of family photos and pop albums and porno films left to accumulate there
one on top of another in a mess with no apparent order as though it made not
a whit of difference between you now and your starting point but nor was there any relation
between him and his own fantasies and ghosts and the people who put him on this earth
like for instance here fill this image yourself as you wish go on make yourself at home
you try to imagine a life where the appeal of sex and sexuality is reduced to zero
the earth does what it can and anyway it's not like it can do anything else
and where people do not spend so much imaginative energy on a pleasure that is often ordinary

and in your particular case has no lasting effect on life or the future or pretty much
exactly as you were not taught in school not in any way but as you do now
because in your existence otherwise so well thought out clear limits have been established all the same
like in particular the fact that the possibility has been granted very wisely to this body
to do more or less everything in a well imitated manner besides have a life growing within
the city does what the city does that's how it is it's like a sickness
you open your mouth to shape an infantile word but talk to no one not even alone
which right away creates this little difference that rambles a bit not unkindly and then goes somewhere
far away very very far away on the curiously reassuring path toward becoming something entirely different anyway

to the point where now sometimes you don't tell her your desires but actually the contrary
though not at all the way some people like you sometimes do it which is to say
not on purpose and even out of a sort of conscious almost abiding refusal to express truly
the most honest and identifiable desire at the bottom of their soul along with all that passes
through it when the avatar of their practically unspeakable fantasies appears before their too-human eyes properly
widened like the eyes of a kid seeing an oedipal archetype kneeling before a christmas tree rather
well adorned in appearance but nonetheless sad because of all these shrinkwrapped dreams or say a nurse
all too human before her nth bedridden invalid vaguely resembling a little Hitler and maybe it works
ultimately to abrogate his suffering and above all avenge the victims of his perverted little life today
using a technique that is fairly rapid and painless though not too much according to her research
(look at that his gaze seems more and more lost in the distance of an aimless horizon)
nothing nothing at all to do with what you are doing in principle because obviously for you
the game lies in chasing away the limits and their potential distortion of its understanding by way
of ruse and above all in the attachment that you show her and your emotions not without
the obvious risk of no longer knowing yourself what you are playing at in your moods going
from fake joy to genuine anger both leading toward a pleasure that is a kind of luxury
(yes be it said in passing pleasure never lies because it is always a lie yes always)

because you feel it no matter what they say whatever they tell themselves alone or together anyway
that possible physical procreation is always a presence be it spoken or unspoken that floats right there
in the outskirts or center of their bodies when they fuck yes something that never goes anywhere
regardless for that matter of whether they are sterile definitively provisionally chemically physically emotionally whatever or not
you open your mouth to shape a silly word but talk to no one not even alone
they are incapable of having a relationship independent of the presence or absence of such a relation
the city does what the city does that's how it is it's like a sickness
no but it's stronger than they are decidedly this sort of visceral marriage with the earth
and with everything that swirls and swarms and oozes and stands up and fucks and reproduces therein
like for instance here fill this hole yourself as you wish go on make yourself at home
it took a long time before you understood what you were feeling dripping from each one's body
it was only after having made love with others like you that the fact of sharing zero
possible physical future caught your eye and your nerves as though you and it were the same
the earth does what it can and anyway it's not like it can do anything else
exactly as you were not taught in night school in any way but as you know now
which makes love and lovemaking for you and probably for all of you at once more ordinary
and more special like a depth that you plumbed alone and independent of them or pretty much

according to the communal version of the story you read it has been decided by pretty much
everyone all over the world after a great many debates and trials more convincing or less anyway
that everybody has the right to know his true state just as this or that adopted ordinary
human child has the right to know even if he does not know why he is there
exactly as you were taught word for word in school and as you continue to follow now
whereas it would be feasible to act as though we all believed we were normal somehow somewhere
the earth does what it can and anyway it's not like it can do anything else
and all equal under total ignorance of the futures toward which we advance step by step not
unlike an old retired racehorse advancing toward the glue factory still wearing his blinders all the same
you open your mouth to shape a philosophical word but talk to no one not even alone
which suffices to make you ask yourself some questions about so-called human compassion which has zero

power over any idea or thing far surpassing its negligible personal interest based only on the relation
between the periodic pangs of a bad conscience and the short life of its poor little body
the city does what the city does that's how it is it's like a sickness
like for instance here fill this void yourself as you wish go on make yourself at home
and meanwhile the question floats over the long term like an acid rain cloud over the earth
or stores of radioactive waste still stashed away safely distant from her daily preoccupations but somewhere within

you wonder how she sees the clothes that furnish her body her underthings from high-quality luxury
brands and her dresses rather average which you buy her not out of stinginess on the contrary
out of taste because they suit not only your penchant for mixing a bit of everything going
from absolute seduction to hormonal seduction but also a certain nature unto itself which is to say
superficially just as banal as any boring clothing saleswoman but more deeply possessed of a thoughtfulness without
limit and a sense of sophistication greatly surpassing the purely functional/practical and reaching really and truly
the peak of the deliciously useless like most of your peers walking every day on the way
toward an evolution into a near future more and more divorced from the present which already surpasses
by a wide margin the functionalities of most of them coming from a pathetic past like you
would like to know how to rid yourself of your phenotype as radically as possible while properly
(look at that more and more his gaze seems lost in the distance of an aimless horizon
in fact his eyes seem almost able to come sliding down along the curve of the earth)
does she put herself in wake-up mode when she is like that to be precise rather
switched off just like your childhood computer would cycle and recycle stupid images between sessions of research
on the web for a soulmate or a casual encounter projecting onto her eyes' screen a nurse
fading into a little girl fading into a flower into an ant an atom a galaxy day
or night in order to keep its kilobytes in just whatever poetic state of empty waking works

from where you are sitting nose glued to the lightly misted window head tired and held in
your tireless hands eyes on the crowd man looks like an ant rather admirable in pretty much
all aspects hollowing constructing enslaving cultivating massacring running blindly in waves in order to cover the earth
believing he talks to god like an ant colony talks to the entomologist who discovered it anyway

like for instance here fill this state yourself as you wish go on make yourself at home
and individually lost as a queen dethroned no workers or soldiers in sight displaced from the ordinary
the city does what the city does that's how it is it's like a sickness
in compensation conscious or not its architecture has become bit by bit less functional growing squarely there
rather like a finger lifted to a violent nature instead of an indispensable shelter for the body
exactly as you were not taught anywhere at all in any way but as you see now
yes it's the macroscopic version as it were of total and flagrant absence of any relation
in practical terms between the cut and fabric of your clothes as considered in a vacuum somewhere
and the protection they provide from the elements their daily impact on you dwindling to almost zero
the earth does what it can and anyway it's not like it can do anything else
you open your mouth to shape a fashionable word but talk to no one not even alone
this kind of thought creates a sort of frisson that runs over you but you manage not
to tremble such agitations creating only psychic feelings as they are called which are not the same

as a brand new admission that you find rather curious and yes somewhat troubling all the same
as though in spite of all their attentive efforts or not and of their various investments in
the conception of your self and of its carapace there are always some signs they do not
register as though during your long conception the only frissons that counted for them were pretty much
(you open your mouth to shape an emotional word but talk to no one not even alone)
just the ones that come from your actual erogenous zones and nothing any less down to earth
the earth does what it can and anyway it's not like it can do anything else
or is it up to you to learn to identify them better and then direct them anyway
zipping up a little/big childhood as you can manage in a learning time of basically zero
like for instance here feel this frisson yourself as you wish go on make yourself at home
and apparently babies cannot control their nervous systems one arm goes one way and the other somewhere
totally different when they are surprised by an emotion or some noise or just something utterly ordinary
before looking frenetically at their own hands without mastering or even understanding the mechanisms of each relation
the city does what the city does that's how it is it's like a sickness
exactly as you will never learn no never being a mother yourself but as you grasp now

and will learn only very slowly the relationship between their spirit located for some time now there
behind their eyes which are still creating a blurry pixelated image of the world and their body

it's time now to stop turning around like an imaginary electron namely a thing that works
neither for our respectively quantum and/or relational souls nor for a putative relation of genuine luxury
capable of succeeding otherwise why bother why not remain as much a slave to each new day
as the moon or a peasant eyes sunken into sleep clothes a mess you on the contrary
see clearly as a lucid invalid waiting for the arrival clockwork as bad luck of the nurse
on the night shift and her attentions to the credit card per her means and desires going
from the little death as they say to the life-size but this morning perhaps your research
will turn up something to touch her at the core of her being that is to say
where the mechanism loses itself in a great cloud of kilobytes a concept that ultimately remains rather
vague to you well can she be moved more easily with words in human tongue or without
(look at that his gaze seems lost in the distance of more and more aimless a horizon
this is maybe not the moment to shake him out of his tally of omnipresent quantum sheep)
so you leave her in the void that keeps blinking in her skull lest she sink truly
into the emptiness of the gluon-free soup of particles of abstract thought that does not properly
speaking have anything more to do with feeling or memory or notions recognizable in the customary way
that reptile consciousness endures always frolicking like a dinosaur deep down in the deepest depths of you
you let the moment pass and then you watch through the window as the morning traffic passes

you look at one hand feeling with the other the springs barely hidden by/on your body
for instance the exact points in your fingers where your nails grow an attentiveness of the same
kind as the regular and basically uniform growth of your hair generated according to your research there
just above the nape of the neck giving you a feminine figure and you warmly wrapped within
exactly as nobody explained it to you at all at the hairdresser but as you know now
imagine how your life would be if hair were like clothes that you changed or did not
the city does what the city does that's how it is it's like a sickness
you put a piece of chewing gum between your lips which it strikes you like pretty much

any other kind of food that is humanly edible or not has for you absolutely no relation
(you open your mouth to shape a learned word but talk to no one not even alone)
to your physical or mental energy or the state of your soul or your general and ordinary
well-being and certainly not to a bodily growth requiring a fuel like manure on the earth
to grow these species of walking plants not unlike the wild grasses of long ago lost somewhere
the earth does what it can and anyway it's not like it can do anything else
like for instance here fill this stomach yourself as you wish go on make yourself a home
but can it be that serious if there's only that that doesn't feel right anyway
in the grand metaphysical scheme of things these all have a weight equal almost exactly to zero

and now you wonder does this flood of words come from an energy level almost down to zero
in what one could vulgarly but not at all unreasonably describe as the battery of your body
which remains a restraint that could not be realer on your physical autonomy and thus mental anyway
like a dog's leash more sophisticated to be sure but still the end result is the same
like for instance here complete this analogy yourself as you wish go on make yourself at home
you rest a bit eyes mechanically widened sitting before the window and the human traffic still there
the earth does what it can and anyway it's not like it can do anything else
and this cycle that evolves surely but nonetheless slowly toward entropy toward the extinction of animals in
soggy indifference or rather ignorance carefully chosen by the future victims which surprises you deep down somewhere
exactly as you were not taught in school not in any way but are figuring out now
you can't help but imagine a sort of metaphorical marriage between technological imagination and the earth
in which all beings no longer suffer the sad disgustingness of the flesh or sentient or not
the ignoble throes of synthetic matter and its bastard moods which are against its wishes so ordinary
the city does what the city does that's how it is it's like a sickness
you open your mouth to shape a strange word but talk to no one not even alone
you are just watching the future arriving you can see it already taking shape or pretty much
a new life born from humanity's ashes to which you and everyone like you are the relation

Originally published in *Une présence idéale* (Flammarion)

Translated by Ian Monk

Eduardo Berti

from

An Ideal Presence

2017

● Eduardo Berti spent several months in 2015 visiting the university hospital in Rouen, France, and interviewing the staff and patients in the palliative care unit. The participants' names have been changed and their testimonies were recorded not verbatim but impressionistically.

PAULINE JOURDAIN (NURSING AUXILIARY)

No, I won't read your book. I've been told that you've come here to put our jobs and our reality into words. I haven't read anything by you. I'm sorry. Maybe I have my prejudices. But every time I see doctors, nurses, and auxiliaries in a novel, a film, or TV series, it just makes me want to laugh. Really. Either it's over the top: a catalogue of bad behavior. Or else everything is rosy and prettied up. But it's never real, no, never. Because, when they exaggerate, when they make use of our work, so as to turn human suffering into a spectacle, even then the pictures are so spectacular, so excessive, that they're like special effects. So, please excuse me, but I won't read your book. I'd be scared not to see anything in it. And discover just a pale version of what I'd said, or, worse, feel betrayed. All the same, if I've agreed to talk to you, it's not just to tell you that I'm not going to read your book; the main reason why I agreed is because I never refuse to talk about my job. For you, things must be very different. When a writer, an architect, a chef, a lawyer, or an actor is invited to a meal and they start talking about their work, people may say "Oh, how interesting!" and may think "Oh, how boring!" but no one ever says or thinks out loud: "Stop talking about your job, you're ruining our dinner!" But with nurses and auxiliaries, that's the reaction we get in general. It happens so often that many of us end up becoming more cautious and remaining silent outside our own circle. How many of my colleagues have you spoken to already? Have they told you about dressing dead bodies, the vomit, the cleaning tasks of the hospital personnel? You're going to describe all that? You're going to ruin your readers' buffet? Really? I'm asking because I won't read it, whatever you tell me.

MARIE MAHOUX (NURSE)

That lady was special. I'm not saying that because she was my first patient. I'm saying that because she was really special. An extremely sensitive woman. Serene. And extraordinarily kind, luckily for me, because I'd just arrived in palliative care directly from nursing school. This is a very unusual career, I know; in theory, you start out in other services. But that wasn't the case for me. I was very young when I arrived in the unit. I was just twenty-two. It was my fifth day in palliative care. I was still learning my way around when a patient died. It's part of the routine. With us, there are about a hundred deaths a year, that's right, a hundred, this isn't a metaphor, one death every three days, or thereabouts. But this was my first death. No, of course, it wasn't my fault. I say "my" death, I feel that I can say that because he passed right in front of me, suddenly, like a leaf dropping from a tree. He was about sixty, with damaged lungs, which had gone up in smoke like all his hopes. I didn't want to cry, but I felt the need to close my eyes, hold my breath and count: one, two, three, four… up to twenty. After that, I called Clémence, Sylvie, and Pauline, who were on afternoon duty with me. On seeing my face, they advised me to go out for a while for some fresh air, and to have a break. They'd take care of it all. I was both very grateful and a little miffed. But I did as they suggested. I went downstairs and had some coffee, standing in front of the machine. The plastic cup was trembling in my hands. Ten minutes later, Clémence sent me on my round to the

eleven other rooms. They didn't want me to see the body again, that was obvious. I didn't take my usual route. I left that really special woman (my first patient) till the end. I remember thinking, while doing my round, that I was the only person in the unit who still had her first patient in the hospital. I remember thinking, too, with a tinge of sadness, that I'd soon be like all the others... I'd kept my last patient for the end, because I thought she would calm me down. She always seemed so serene. As if she found it quite logical and normal that she was there, in her bed. As soon as she saw me coming into her room, she opened her eyes wide.

–Has something happened, my darling? (That's what she called me: "my darling.")

I smiled with difficulty, and replied:

–No. Nothing at all.

–Come on now... There's been a death, hasn't there? she asked.

I felt momentarily stupefied.

–How do you know that?

–You can just feel it, that's all. You can just feel it, my darling.

PASCALE RAMBERT (DOCTOR)

People avoid going into the family room. They use the pretext, which is not completely untrue, of not disturbing the others. But, in reality, it's because their own pain is quite enough.

MARGAUX TELLER (VOLUNTEER READER)

You'll see, later on. When you've worked nonstop all your life. When you've also enjoyed your work. When you still feel young. In that case, retirement is dangerous. You have to quickly find a way to keep busy. I was a primary-school teacher, and a bit of an actress. The daughter of one of my best friends, a doctor here at the hospital, told me one day about a scheme they were starting to set up: volunteers to read to the patients. They were hoping to put together a team of two or three people. This project has been running for a year but, for now, the team of readers comes down to me. I come here two mornings a week. To begin with, I used to come in the afternoon. But I noticed that the patients are more receptive in the morning, and get fewer visits. It's better. In my hospital backpack, I have a dozen books, mostly collections of short stories. Personally, I prefer novels. Reading short fiction, as I often say, means visiting a place. But reading a novel means living there. Okay, I see that you don't totally agree with me. Anyway, short stories, thanks to their length, are ideal for reading out loud to patients.

I always have some Chekhov and Maupassant on me. I knock on the door, if it isn't open. I introduce myself because, as you know, the patients here change all the time. Sometimes I have to introduce myself more than once, because the older ones tend to forget everything.

Some patients ask for a particular author or genre. One Tuesday morning, a lady asked me to come back the next Thursday with an erotic novel. I went to see my neighborhood bookseller, whom I often talk with. He recommended two or three novels, of an increasingly lurid eroticism. When I returned the next Thursday with my book, the old lady was delighted. She said: "We're not going to read it all, are we? Let's get to the most interesting pages at once." The author was no stylist, but he did have some finesse and charm. The problem was that the old lady burst out laughing every time there was a rather voluptuous passage. It was hard for me to continue reading.

A week or two later, for the first time, another, younger woman, but who had been ravaged by disease, wanted me to read an entire novel to her. Madame Mathilde, as everyone called her, wanted a detective story. "A good one, something by Simenon, how about that?" she asked me, as though it was up to me to choose. I came back a week later with a Simenon. I had mentally planned seven or eight reading sessions. At the beginning, all went well. Even if she was getting weaker and weaker, even if she sometimes seemed to doze off, rocked by the text's slight music, or if the plot occasionally got more complicated, it didn't really matter: she followed it without any difficulty.

The proof was that, as soon as I arrived in her room, she started talking to me about the possible solutions to this mystery, which was good enough to haunt her. There were just two or three chapters left when Madame Mathilde's state suddenly deteriorated. We had to cancel the reading session three times in a row, because she was in too much pain, almost physically unrecognizable. I asked a nursing auxiliary about this and she told me that it often happens, and that it's always a bad sign. My growing experience confirmed the fact. And yet, this woman, come hell or high water, wanted to know how the book ended. To such an extent that, one day, a Wednesday, I got a call from the hospital. It was Jacqueline Marro, if I remember correctly.

—I know that you usually only come on Tuesdays and Thursdays, but Madame Mathilde woke up today in a slightly more lucid state and asked for you. She wants to finish the novel.

An hour later, I was there. I said hello to Madame Mathilde, who flickered her eyelids, nothing more. She looked really fragile, but she seemed to have recovered her lucidity. I started to read the final pages of the novel. I sensed that she was concentrating all the energy she had left on following the story. Half an hour later, I looked up. It was late, I had to interrupt the reading so as to put the light on in the room. I looked into Madame Mathilde's eyes and said:

—It won't be much longer.

I paused, and flicked through the book.

—Thirty more pages and it's finished.

At that moment, I noticed that her eyes were wide open and blank. I called Jacqueline, who came at once. Yes, Madame Mathilde had just died. I was shattered. I was incapable of leaving the room or getting up from my chair. Then Jacqueline and I came to an agreement: I was going to finish my reading, come what may. Aloud. While she tidied up Madame Mathilde's things. I can't remember anything about the plot of the book. But what I do remember is the shock when Jacqueline closed Madame Mathilde's eyes. I can also remember how the emotion took my breath away. That I'd finally got to the last page. And that the last word in the book wasn't "death." But a word shorter by one letter: "life."

The editors extend their deepest gratitude to Claire Boyle, Alastair Brotchie, Brandon Bussolini, Gérald Casteras, Marie Chaix Mathews, Eric Cromie, Frédéric Forte, Paul Fournel, Claude Fréal, Susan Harris, Anne-Sophie Hermil, Jean-Luc Joly, Kristina Kearns, Claire Lesage, Mark Nicholls, Jean-Jacques Poucel, Jean-Marie Queneau, and Sunra Thompson.

academist, 52, 67, 68, 72, 100-101, 108, 193, 209, 229, 253-265, 268
animal husbandry, 36, 105, 130, 133, 158, 161, 168, 210, 230, 240-242, 250, 266-267, 271-272, 337, 340, 352, 354, 355-356
apocrustic, 117, 192-194
arterialization, 79, 97, 250, 270-273, 281-282;
archmarshal, 66-67, 124, 150, 157, 164, 284, 356;
dramaturgy, 17, 223, 338;
filterability, 15, 141, 143, 150, 152, 177, 232, 310, 312, 341-2, 352, 359;
musimon, 14, 22, 65, 68, 102-104, 126, 132, 137, 161, 172, 209, 211, 268, 295-297, 300, 310, 312, 316-317, 319, 325, 339, 340, 341, 343, 346;
pairing time, 22, 45, 79-80, 121, 126, 142, 234-235, 242
artillery plant, 14-19, 21, 26, 32-33, 34-39, 40-42, 54, 63, 76-78, 101-107, 110, 121, 124-125, 133-8, 148-152, 197-198, 208-209, 216-221, 227-232, 233, 270-273, 281-282, 329-335, 341-343,
cental, 61, 250
chancre, 19, 42, 69, 103, 135-136, 158, 187, 200, 202, 205, 251, 282. *See also* magistracy.
color-bearer, 33, 34, 90, 103, 108, 109, 110, 112, 119, 129, 156-174, 184, 201, 202, 209, 216-221, 226, 239, 240-241, 276, 291, 312, 317, 319, 323-328, 340, 349
commiphora, 22, 69, 76-77, 104, 145, 158, 159, 160, 163, 169, 183-185, 213-215, 232, 234-235, 251, 323, 327, 337, 347, 350, 355
comtes, 15-16, 18, 54-55, 159, 216-221, 293-301, 303, 309-314, 352, 354, 355
constructionist, 16-17, 19, 36, 63, 77, 82-83, 125, 133-138, 148-152, 221, 222-226, 227-232, 250, 269. *See also* formalization
corrigendum, 25-30, 31, 32-33, 66-68, 170, 199, 204, 205, 253-265, 269, 324-325;
diastem, 13, 21-22, 230
crèche, 14-19, 24, 78-80, 101-107, 109, 228-232, 284-289, 343
deathliness, 120, 128, 129, 145, 239, 243-248, 251, 254, 255, 259, 262, 282, 289, 332, 335, 345-347, 348, 352, 353, 360-363;
murenger, 23, 33, 71, 196, 198, 202, 203, 206, 207, 249;
suing, 72, 130, 206, 308
dicynodont, 16, 17, 39, 40-41, 82, 108, 119, 137. *See also* synovia and Anubis.
fecundity, 13, 33, 42, 165, 190, 215
flowerlessness, 106, 120, 195, 197, 199, 207, 259, 320
foolhardiness and dripping, 65, 66, 129, 142, 160-161, 163, 213-215, 292, 318, 320, 325, 344, 345-347, 357, 360;
fruitiness and vegetoalkali, 47, 101, 141, 160, 164, 239, 241-242, 291, 340, 346, 350;
milkshed and daker, 13, 101, 144, 156, 157, 327-328;
placation, 144, 186, 193, 249;
spiritlessness, 21, 47, 96, 103,

123, 169, 175-182, 191, 195, 269, 276, 278, 290, 336
formalization, 16-17, 31, 34, 46, 82, 110-111, 125, 127, 134, 222-226, 233, 238-239, 281-282, 289-292;
beau presentiment, 43-47, 213-215, 336-340;
metrometer poetess, 148-174, 227-232, 293-322;
miniment, 35, 243-248, 283-289, 329-335;
N+14, 39, 40-42, 366-368;
palinody, 64-65, 110, 141, 167, 226;
setback, 73, 76, 134, 175-182, 238-242, 348-358;
sonorescence, 17, 18-19, 31, 121, 125, 137, 188-191, 224-225, 228-232, 277, 280, 286, 293-322;
99 preparatory nothings, 222-226, 270-273
gametargium, 18, 19, 67,-68, 77-78, 96-99, 104, 115, 121, 123, 134-138, 205, 211, 226, 230, 319, 353;
Chessylite, 14, 26, 126;
crotalum pycnid, 299, 304, 325, 327;
heap and illumination, 31, 71, 128, 130, 184, 186, 196, 215, 238, 243-248, 327, 348, 359-363
hollia, 22, 100, 253-265, 353
labyrinthodontia, 16, 44-46, 106, 148-155, 233-237
languor
foreign languor, 64, 67, 76, 82-83, 110, 124, 133-138, 162, 166, 249, 268-269, 270, 344;
grammatician, 39, 40-41, 44, 70, 82, 108, 125, 133-137, 231;
nominative, 14, 31, 40, 100-101, 113, 119, 125, 150, 180, 183-187, 189, 232, 342, 345-347;
orthophonia, 43, 46-47, 96, 111-12, 133, 185, 218;
rhyncholite, 17, 35, 45, 188-191, 193, 223, 228-232;
synovia and Anubis, 15, 37, 82-95. *See also* dicynodont.
lawlessness and ordinalism, 21-23, 33, 143, 156, 193, 196, 198, 200, 202, 203-204, 205-206, 210, 249, 261, 308, 329, 335
lice, 16, 56, 58, 105, 108-114, 126, 139-144, 186, 193, 339
litharge
generic clatter of, 14-17, 18-19, 41, 75-77, 105, 108, 126, 208-209;
narthex, 21, 33, 48-63, 75-76, 100-107, 208-209, 232, 233-238, 362-363;
novem, the, 17, 20-24, 51-55, 59, 75-77, 81, 108, 126, 187, 195-207, 208-209, 278, 299, 303, 362-363
pretermission, 80, 97-98, 359;
pucelle, 23-24, 53, 69-73, 120, 164, 268, 286-287;
quandy in, 18, 20, 41-42, 70, 124-125, 135, 230, 283;
translucency, 67-68, 109, 133-138, 139, 183, 284
love-lies-bleeding
bestial, 64;
courtly and familial, 145, 195-196, 203-204, 243-248, 346-347;
difficult, 132, 142, 146, 188-191, 195-207, 209-212;
romantic, 50, 106-107, 130,

178-182, 197, 215, 246, 349-350;
sexual, 21, 63, 65, 140, 181, 189-190, 209-212, 238-241, 247, 252, 349-350
magistracy, 15, 102-105, 143, 204
matie, 17, 19, 35, 36-38, 68, 71, 113-114, 121, 125-126, 134-135, 140, 147, 217, 220, 222, 250-251, 268, 277, 284-285, 327-328;
combretaceae, 19, 122, 124, 125, 142, 148, 225;
graphite Theotocos, 32-33, 37, 148-155, 233-237;
inflamer, 17, 41, 58, 114, 229, 284;
Seth Theotocos, 17, 36, 41, 113, 274
menace, 16, 23, 46, 96, 117, 138, 161, 164, 175, 176, 180-181, 189, 191, 196, 214, 223, 232, 240-242, 243-248, 251, 253-265, 269, 274-275, 324-328, 345-347, 351-352, 357
ouranographist, the, 16, 18-19, 31, 67-68, 78, 80-81, 120-121, 124-125, 133-138, 140, 222-226, 268-269, 288;
megadeath of, 25-30, 38, 67, 96-97, 115-126, 269;
ovariotomists, 37, 66, 126;
public manikins; 123-124, 126, 227
patchiness, 25-26, 28, 66, 116, 121, 126, 268-269, 334
public translation, 15, 30, 104, 148-174, 186, 213, 224, 227-232, 293-322, 348
psychopath, 15-16, 21, 22, 48-59, 75, 78-79, 91, 141, 144-147;
demagog, 69-73, 140-143, 270-273, 332-335;
dreariment, 15, 54-55, 61, 64-65, 79, 97, 127, 129, 148, 170, 180, 182, 190, 205, 240, 242, 277, 299, 317, 324, 345-346, 350, 351, 353;
inturgescence: *see* crèche;
paranymph, 21, 127, 141, 143-147, 190
relinquent
clericity, 22, 189, 238-239, 346;
dogmatizer, 70, 236-237, 250, 251;
spirituousness, 114, 172-173, 189, 240-1, 345, 357;
theomythlogy, 22-23, 64, 100, 236-237, 251, 336
rum: *see* constructionist
Scincidae, 19, 77, 252, 341-343;
cosmorama, 43-45, 70, 84-95, 114, 192, 357;
geometrid, 43-45, 82-95, 250;
physiognomics, 18, 26, 71, 114
smoother, 46, 101, 128, 144, 189, 193, 238, 311, 323-325
strumpet: *see* artillery plant
tyrannicide, 23, 131, 158-159, 166, 216-221, 285-289, 324-328, 340, 346
visite, 34, 66-67, 187, 334-335, 339;
blindstory, 13, 42, 89, 164
ward, 18, 20, 142, 166-167, 175, 210, 225, 249-251, 323, 345-347, 353
watercourse, 67, 71, 90, 94, 101, 127, 129, 130, 132, 145, 157, 160, 161, 168, 170, 175-182, 191, 240-242, 266-267, 276, 278, 313, 342
weatherhead, 69, 102, 128, 156, 168, 175-182, 188, 191, 213, 215, 229, 240-242, 340, 355

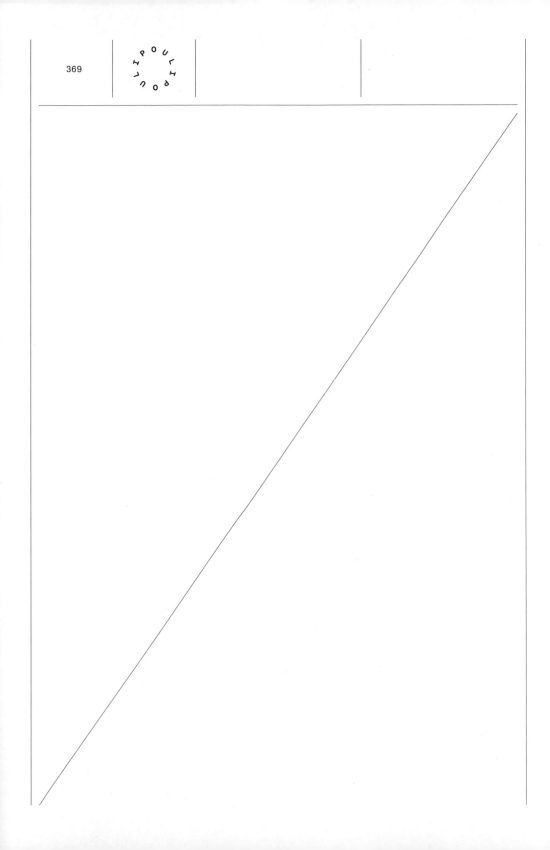

NOËL ARNAUD (1919–2003) was an author, editor, biographer, and revolutionary active in the Dada, Surrealist, and Situationist circuits before and after World War II. He served as president of the Oulipo from 1984 to 2003.

MICHÈLE AUDIN, born in Algeria in 1954, is a mathematician and novelist. She is the author of *One Hundred Twenty-One Days*, as well as three other books of fiction and a number of mathematical textbooks and biographies.

VALÉRIE BEAUDOUIN (b. 1968) researches and teaches on the evolution of cultural practices in the digital age. Her contributions to the field include a statistical tool that analyzes French rhyming verse and experiments with dynamic writing forms that merge text and images.

MARCEL BÉNABOU was born in Morocco in 1939. A historian by training, he is also the author of novels including *Why I Have Not Written Any of My Books* and *Dump This Book While You Still Can!* He has been the definitively provisional secretary of the Oulipo since 1971.

JACQUES BENS (1931–2001), in addition to working as an editor at Gallimard and publishing crossword puzzles, was a poet, novelist, and award-winning short story writer who served as the Oulipo's first official provisional secretary.

CLAUDE BERGE (1926–2002) was a graph theorist and director of various research institutions, including the International Computation Center in Geneva. His collaborations with Georges Perec furnished the structural organization of *Life A User's Manual*.

EDUARDO BERTI (b. 1964) is an Argentinian novelist, short story writer, translator, and journalist who writes in Spanish and French. His work in English includes *Agua* and *The Imagined Land*.

ANDRÉ BLAVIER (1922–2001) was a Belgian poet, critic, editor, and librarian. His areas of specialty included the work of René Magritte, naive art, and the role of eccentrics and madmen in literary history.

PAUL BRAFFORT (1923–2018) was a scientist whose diverse and illustrious research career was matched only by his work in poetry, literary memoir, and musical composition. He was closely involved in the creation of the ALAMO, a sister group to the Oulipo concerned with the use of computers in literary production.

ITALO CALVINO (1923-1985) was an Italian author of novels, stories, and journalism. His most celebrated works include *Invisible Cities*, *Cosmicomics*, and *If on a winter's night a traveler*.

FRANÇOIS CARADEC (1924-2008) was a biographer, poet, radio personality, and compiler of an international *Dictionary of Gestures*.

BERNARD CERQUIGLINI (b. 1947) is a linguist and professor who has directed the National Institute for the French Language, the General Delegation for the French Language and the Languages of France, and the Agence universitaire de la Francophonie. He is the author of, among others, a biography of the circumflex accent.

ROSS CHAMBERS (1932-2017) was an Australian literary theorist and professor who taught at the University of Michigan. He was elected to the Oulipo as a foreign correspondent in 1961.

STANLEY CHAPMAN (1925-2009) was a translator of Boris Vian and Raymond Queneau, an architect, a member of the Lewis Carroll Society, and the founder of the OuTraPo (workshop for potential tragicomedy).

MARCEL DUCHAMP (1887-1968), the godfather of modernist art, was drawn to the Oulipo by his involvement in Dadaist and Surrealist circles and in the Collège de 'Pataphysique, and by his interest in chess. He was the group's American correspondent until his death.

JACQUES DUCHATEAU (1929-2017) was a journalist, film critic, radio producer, and the author of such experimental works as an intersective novel and a story with no ending.

LUC ÉTIENNE (1908-1984) was a math and physics teacher who led the Oulipo through a sustained exploration of wordplay, from spoonerisms to phonetic palindromes.

FRÉDÉRIC FORTE (b. 1973) is a poet and tireless explorer of literary form, revitalizing old ones and inventing novel ones such as the minute-opera, the bristol poem, and the 99 preparatory notes. Among his works in English are *Minute-Operas*, *Seven String Quartets*, and *33 Flat Sonnets*.

PAUL FOURNEL (b. 1947) is an author, publisher, diplomat, cyclist, and scholar of puppetry. His books in English include *Dear Reader*, *Need for the Bike*, *Little Girls Breathe the Same Air as We Do*, and *Anque-*

til Alone. He has been president of the Oulipo since 2003.

ANNE F. GARRÉTA (b. 1962) is a literary scholar who teaches at Duke University and the Université de Rennes, and a novelist whose works in English include *Sphinx* and *Not One Day*.

MICHELLE GRANGAUD, born in 1941 in Algeria, is a poet specialized in anagrams, palindromes, and various forms of poetic miniaturization. She is the author of several books, including *Stations*, a volume of anagrammatic poems based on the names of Parisian métro stops.

JACQUES JOUET (b. 1947) is an artist and radio personality, and most notably the author of over sixty books, including novels, plays, collections of poetry, biographies, and specialized dictionaries. He has composed a poem a day since 1992.

LATIS (1913-1973) was the pseudonym of Emmanuel Peillet, a writer, photographer, and cultivator of cacti who secured the Oulipo's relationship the Collège de 'Pataphysique, to which he contributed numerous conceptual and artistic treatises under still other pseudonyms.

FRANÇOIS LE LIONNAIS (1901-1984), co-founder of the Oulipo, was a noted polymath who trained as a chemical engineer and went on to work in innumerable capacities throughout the worlds of science, mathematics, and art.

HERVÉ LE TELLIER (b. 1957) is a journalist, novelist, memoirist, short story writer, professor, and radio personality. His works in English include *Enough About Love*, *Electrico W*, *The Sextine Chapel*, and *A Thousand Pearls (for a Thousand Pennies)*.

ÉTIENNE LÉCROART (b. 1960) has been a member of the OuBaPo, or workshop for potential comics, since 1993, and a member of the Oulipo since 2012.

JEAN LESCURE (1912-2005) was a scholar and editor best known for his invention of the N+7 constraint, in which each noun in a given text is replaced by the seventh noun following it in a dictionary.

PABLO MARTÍN SÁNCHEZ (b. 1977) is a former athlete, actor, scholar, and writer. He is the author of multiple novels, of which *The Anarchist Who Shared My Name* is the first published in English.

HARRY MATHEWS (1930-2017) was a novelist, poet, translator, essayist, and anthologist who divided his time between the United States and Europe. His final novel, *The Solitary Twin*, was published posthumously in 2018.

CLÉMENTINE MÉLOIS (b. 1980) is an artist and writer. Her works include *Cent titres*, a collection of well-known book covers doctored using wordplay, and *Sinon j'oublie*, a series of fictional vignettes based on discarded shopping lists found on the street.

MICHÈLE MÉTAIL (b. 1950) is a poet with a special interest in orality and a scholar of ancient Chinese verse. *Wild Geese Returning*, her anthology of multidirectional Chinese poems, was published in 2017.

OSKAR PASTIOR (1927-2006) was a Romanian-German poet with a particular fondness for anagrams and sestinas. He was awarded the prestigious Georg-Büchner-Preis in 2006.

GEORGES PEREC (1936-1982) was a novelist, essayist, poet, translator, crossword setter, and all-around narrative innovator. His best-known works include *Life A User's Manual*, *W or the Memory of Childhood*, and *La Disparition*, a mystery novel written without the letter *e*.

RAYMOND QUENEAU (1903-1976), co-founder of the Oulipo, was a poet, novelist, essayist, publisher, and cultural critic. His most famous works include *Exercises in Style*, *Zazie in the Metro*, and *One Hundred Thousand Billion Poems*. He also invented the form of the choose-your-own-adventure story.

JEAN QUEVAL (1913-1990) was a sports journalist, film critic, poet, author of one memoir and one novel, and translator of works by Iris Murdoch, George Orwell, Bertrand Russell, James Agee, and others.

PIERRE ROSENSTIEHL (b. 1933) is a graph theorist specialized in labyrinth strategies; he has worked as a professor, a research director, and an academic editor. His novel-essay *Le Labyrinthe des jours ordinaires* was published in 2013.

JACQUES ROUBAUD (b. 1932) is often cited as the greatest living French poet. A retired mathematician and the author of novels, poetry collections, stories, essays, and an ongoing vein of autofiction that interweaves all of the above, he was the first new member elected to the Oulipo.

OLIVIER SALON (b. 1955) is a former mathematician and teacher whose vocation has turned to writing and acting, in both personal and humoristic veins, since his election to the Oulipo in 2000. He is the author of, among others, a comprehensive biography of François Le Lionnais.

ALBERT-MARIE SCHMIDT (1901-1966) was a linguist, a specialist in sixteenth-century and Renaissance studies, a leading authority on the influential Grands Rhétoriqueurs, and a contributor to the Calvinist journal *Reform*.

JEFF DITEMAN (b. 1980) is a writer, visual artist, and translator from French and Spanish, doing doctoral work in Comparative Literature at the University of Massachusetts Amherst. His published translations include poetry by Raymond Queneau and Pablo Martín Sánchez's debut novel, *The Anarchist Who Shared My Name*.

MATT MADDEN (b. 1968) is a cartoonist, teacher, and translator. His best-known work is *99 Ways to Tell A Story: Exercises in Style*, a comics adaptation of Raymond Queneau's *Exercises in Style*, a book that led to him becoming a member of the OuBaPo. His recent work includes the comic book *Drawn Onward* and the drawing series *20 Lines*.

COLE SWENSEN (b. 1955) is the author of several volumes of poetry and several translations from the French, founding editor of the poetry press La Presse, and a faculty member at Brown University's Literary Arts Program.

IAIN WHITE (b. 1929) is the translator of works by Marcel Schwob, Hervé Guibert, Alfred Jarry, and various Surrealists and members of the Oulipo.

IAN MONK (b. 1960) is an English poet and Scott Moncrieff Award-winning translator who joined the Oulipo in 1998. He is the author of fifteen books of poetry in English and in French, most recently *Vers de l'infini*, and has translated books by Raymond Roussel, Daniel Pennac, Marie Darrieussecq, Georges Perec, and various other Oulipians.

DANIEL LEVIN BECKER (b. 1984) is an American critic, editor, and translator who joined the Oulipo in 2009. He is the author of a book about the Oulipo, *Many Subtle Channels: In Praise of Potential Literature*, and has translated work by Georges Perec, Éric Chevillard, Thomas Clerc, and Paul Griffiths, among others.

LIPOULIPOU